I0665823

Hellsong Series

BOOK II

KNIGHT OF GEHENNA

SHAUN O. MCCOY

SISYPHEAN PUBLISHING

NOTE: If you purchased this book without a cover you should be aware that this book is stolen property. It was reported as "unsold and destroyed" to the publisher, and neither the author nor publisher has received any payment for this "stripped book."

This is a work of fiction. The damnation portrayed in this novel is fictitious, and similarities between it and any actual damnation are strictly coincidental.

KNIGHT OF GEHENNA

Copyright 2013 © by Shaun McCoy

All rights reserved.

Editor-in-Chief: Gabrielle Olexa
Associate Editors: Matt Michaelis, Justin Williams, Jody Mobley
Consulting Editors: Jason Thrower, Nicole Breton, James Mobley, Clay Mcleveen.

Title art: Thomas the Younger
Title Layout: Kirill Simin

A Sisyphean Publishing Book

Http://hellsongseries.com

ISBN: 978-0615889184

First Edition September 2013

Printed in the United States of America

0 9 8 7 6 5

PRAISE FOR SHAUN O. McCOY AND THE HELLSONG SERIES

"McCoy is a talented and bright young writer. Knight of Gehenna is a new kind of novel—a page turner in the truest sense—wrought from equal parts brawn and brain."
—*B. Butler, Author of Murder in Cairo*

"McCoy is a brilliant writer; insightful, intelligent, articulate, imaginative, and funny."
—*McKendree Long, Author of No Good Like it is*

"In Knight of Gehenna, McCoy masterfully creates characters, scenarios and the Hell where they live. He writes with a passion, layering emotion on fantasy and science fiction, drawing in readers from beyond his genre."
—Ginny Padgett, President of SCWW

"If Hemmingway was a Boxer, McCoy is a Cagefighter."
—*Monet Jones, Author of Rehoboth*

"Shaun is the real McCoy."
—*Laura Valtorte, Filmaker, Author of Family Meal*

"Exceptionally well written. I felt the pain of these characters physically and emotionally."
—*Fred Fields, Author*

"With the visionary aptitude of such writers as C.S. Lewis and J.R.R. Tolkein, McCoy further illustrates his unique underworld that has produced the spiritual vagabond Arturus in this sequel to Even Hell Has Knights. Arturus' quest for purpose in Hell is not unlike man's quest for purpose on Earth."
—*Len Lawson, Author of City of David*

"Reading Knight of Gehenna is like being privy to an argument between Camus and Aquinas—only in this book they've got shotguns."
—*Thomas the Younger, Author of These Windows*

OTHER WORKS BY SHAUN O. MCCOY

HELLSONG SERIES
Even Hell Has Knights
Knight of Gehenna
March till Death

HELLSONG SERIES INFIDELS
Affliction (Coming Soon!)
Soulfall (Coming Soon!)
The Eden of a Lesser God (Coming Soon!)

NOVELLAS
Electric Blues
Binary Jazz
Digital Muse (Coming Soon!)

For Gabrielle Olexa

Editor, friend, traveler, and Trenton Phoenix

ACKNOWLEDGEMENTS

First and foremost, I'd like to thank everyone who supported *Even Hell Has Knights*. Without your help, this sequel would have never happened.

I'd like to thank Matt Michaelis, Adriane Fry, and Helen Regan for keeping me pumped full of ideas.

The gun expertise of Scott and Jeremy Mason, whose advice for *Even Hell Has Knights* has carried over nicely into this book, was much appreciated.

Dr. Butterworth, I truly appreciate the insights you gave me on the ending of Joyce's *Dubliners*.

One of the things I enjoyed the most about writing *Knight of Gehenna* was the opportunity to create an apologetic for a religion that doesn't exist. To do so I studied the apologetics of several extant religions. Inspirational to me in that vein were the lunchtime conversations I've had with Eric Wolf, as fine a friend as I have ever known.

And lastly I'd like to thank all of the wonderful people at Sisyphean Publications. Gabe, Matt, Justin, Jason, Nichole, Jody, James, Clay. Also, I'd be remiss not to mention media mogul Kirill Simin and artist extraordinaire Thomas the Younger.

Oh, and one more. I'd like to thank Cae, my godson, for being so damn adorable.

CAVEAT

The philosophical views expressed by the characters in this book, particularly the villains, are not necessarily the views of the author.

KNIGHT OF GEHENNA

From Neostoicism: Philosophia

What use is flight if you cannot feel the cool spray of the brine or bask in the warmth of the sun?
Let them say, then, that I am he who flies on molten wings.
—Kent

Be wary of Heaven and Hell. They are extremes and therefore evil by Aristotelian standards.
—Endymion

Part IV
Pilgrim of the Carrion

From Gehennic Law: The King and the River

For the People so loved their King that they enclosed him in a steel cage; and thus the demons could not maul him. Then they found a horn of plenty and set it with him; and thus the hunger could not take him. Then they placed him on a barge and sent him down the river Janus; and thus the Devil could not catch him.

But soon they were assaulted by dyitzu and knew not how to save themselves. So they sent men down the river to beg advice from their King, and he told them to make weapons of stones and defend themselves. They did so, and they survived.

But then they were given women and knew not how to control them. So again they sent men down the river, and the King taught them how to clothe the women from head to toe; that their wives might forget they were human. They did so, and they survived.

And finally they were struck with famine and could not feed their people. So again they sent men down the river, but this time their King and his wisdom had floated too far away. They did nothing and wasted until death.

Many wish to meet this King, and many have tried. They say that if you travel far enough down this river you can still find him, drifting eternally through Hell. But they also say that since Damnation is infinite, then the river's end is also its beginning; its head is also its mouth.

If one waits here long enough, he may come again.

 — 1 —

I will never see Alice again.

Arturus lay in the cold, dark stone chamber with the five remaining Harpsborough hunters, separated from his home by countless miles of impenetrable devil-filled labyrinth, waiting for Galen to return. Waiting for execution or absolution.

Arturus' fingernails had grown long, and though he had bathed since his climb through Giant's Tunnel, there were half-moons of dirt beneath them. He pulled back the left sleeve of his black t-shirt so he could see the symbol that had been so artfully carved into his shoulder. Some of the long thin scabs peeled off, sticking to the cotton cloth. The pain was a distant thing, like the echo of a man's shout from a far off chamber.

He stretched out his arm so he might better see the symbol the priestess Kayla had cut into his person. It was a man, arms held straight over his head, palms touching and fingers pointing as if he were diving upwards. The man was only free from the waist up—below that, he was encased in stone. Hell heals all wounds, so the saying went, but it wouldn't heal this one unless Arturus was willing to cut off his arm and wait for it to regrow—a dangerous proposition under normal circumstances and probable suicide in the Carrion.

That meant the symbol stayed. That meant that, in some way, he was still Maab's.

He remembered Maab. Remembered her soft, wet lips as they coaxed him through his first kiss.

His heart quickened against his will.

I don't love Maab. I love Alice. Or maybe even Ellen . . . but I don't love Maab.

He looked to the five remaining hunters. They were a sorry sight.

We weren't ready for the Carrion.

They had failed to rescue Julian, who was now a slave of Maab's dark cult. They had failed to secure the devilwheat Harpsborough needed to survive. They had failed to even return home before Harpsborough sealed them in.

And four of them were dead.

Wistan, Mabe, Fitch and Patrick.

Aaron, the Lead Hunter of Harpsborough, seemed the healthiest. The muscular hunter caught Arturus' eye and stood slowly. He walked with a limp, having not fully recovered from the long needles the silverleg spiders had left in his feet.

Those spiders are still out there, waiting for us to try and go home.

Aaron squatted down next to him, nodding across the room. Arturus followed his gaze to Kyle, the hunter who'd suffered the worst wounds from the spiders. Even now, after nearly a week of rest, Kyle could easily be mistaken for dead. The spiders had flayed his legs, removing so much of the man's thigh and calf muscles that they'd only been able to take off his tourniquets yesterday. The healing had begun, but just barely. Loose clumps of scabs and congealed fluids leaked out between the masses of bandages which covered his legs. His face was gaunt, pale as a corpse's. Even his black hair seemed unnaturally thin.

He looks worse than he did before we took off the tourniquets.

Arturus glanced back towards Aaron.

The worried hunter leaned forward and whispered into his ear, "He won't be ready when we try for home."

Arturus bit his lip for a second. "We'll have to carry him."

"We should have never removed his tourniquets, Turi. Moving him might kill him now."

"But we can't stay," Arturus whispered back.

Aaron nodded.

Galen had done well in finding them a safe place to rest in a little traveled nook of the Carrion, but their week of safe rest was now pushing the boundary between good luck and miracle—and there were no miracles in Hell. Arturus wasn't even sure if they could make it another day without being sniffed out by a hellhound, and Kyle would probably need months to recover.

All we have left to do is die.

He imagined Kyle sitting there, abandoned in this Carrion room—waiting alone for the devils to find him. Arturus wasn't familiar enough with the man to know if he had a lover back in Harpsborough. He didn't know whose name Kyle might call if the dyitzu were to find him.

Arturus ran his fingers over the smooth peach fuzz that was collecting on his cheeks. "We'll have to get a stretcher. A woodstone door or something to carry him on, like we did with the Infidel Friend."

Galen can still walk well. He could carry one end of the stretcher.

But that wasn't a good idea either. Galen was the only one of them who was healthy enough to fight. It would be better if Aaron and he were to bear the burden—if they even could. Neither of them was able to walk very well. Arturus looked to the other hunters.

Johnny Huang, Avery, and Duncan were in bad shape, but there was also their captured priestess.

Maybe she can help.

She could hardly stand up straight, however. Aaron had told him that Galen broke her ribs. On top of that, Arturus had no good reason to assume that she would even be willing to help. She was just as likely to drop her end of the stretcher and run as she was to carry it.

Maybe Aaron and I could manage for an hour or so before we give out. Then Duncan and Johnny could fill in, maybe for half as long. And then . . .

Then nothing. There would be days of travel left after that. Galen would be forced to carry Kyle on his own, there was just no other way around it. He and the hunters would have to try and be ready to fight—except this was a terrible idea. Even if they were all healthy, fed, and weren't running low on ammunition, they would still be no match for the huge packs of dyitzu that roamed the Carrion.

We can't leave him. There's got to be a better way. Think,

Turi.

Arturus felt Aaron's hand on his shoulder. For as long as Arturus had known him, Aaron had been a very compassionate man, but he did not look so now. His expression was stern, even callous.

"Harden your heart, Turi." Aaron said, getting up to his feet.

"What? Why?"

Aaron did not answer. He looked as cruel as Arturus had ever seen him. Slowly, the hunter walked away.

What's going on?

Arturus looked back between Aaron's limping figure and Kyle. Kyle's eyes were open, staring up at the ceiling. His chest was rising and falling slowly. He looked so helpless.

Oh, no. Please no. We can't.

Aaron leaned his shoulder against the far wall and slid down it into a crouch. His jaw was set. Arturus looked back towards Kyle, and by some horrible coincidence, Kyle chose that moment to lower his head. Their eyes met. Kyle managed a wan smile.

I'm sorry, Kyle. I'm sorry.

— 2 —

Ellen sat at the kitchen table watching steam rise up off of Rick's hotplates. The table was a makeshift thing, an old door propped up by a few stone blocks at its corners. The wood was a lighter color where the hinges had been. She remembered that Arturus had often run his fingers over those slight depressions while he was thinking. Idly, she did the same.

Rick began to cut up a knowledge fruit. "You were out last night, and you snuck in this morning."

She felt immediately guilty. "I did."

"You need to announce yourself when you come in. I might shoot you on accident."

"I didn't realize you knew. I will, from now on. I promise."

Rick's gaze was unblinking. He was obviously studying her, trying to figure out if she was being sincere.

"I will!" she said.

"And when you go out, you should leave a block by the entrance that tells me where you've gone."

She shook her head. "But I'm just exploring. I wouldn't know what to write on the block."

Rick pointed his knife at her, a bit of red knowledge fruit innards hanging down from the end of it. "'Exploring' would be just fine. Okay?"

"Okay."

She looked back down at the table and began fiddling again with one of the door hinge depressions.

I'm going to give myself a splinter.

"This isn't quite ripe," Rick said, holding up a small section of the knowledge fruit he'd been dicing.

"I know," Ellen responded. "I like it better that way. More tangy."

"Sour you mean. What have you been doing with the ripe ones?"

"I was trading them to the Harpsborough hunters that would come and visit me. Now that I'm staying here, I don't know what I'll do."

Rick tossed the diced fruit onto the hotplate, turning the pieces quickly with his knife so as to only sear their edges. Then he gave her a pointed look. "You could trade them to me."

Ellen laughed. "You don't like these?"

"I'd rather eat like a villager," Rick flippantly replied.

"Well, I suppose I could get them for you, but there's hardly any left now. How long until they regrow?"

He picked up the pieces of fruit in between two knives and dropped them into the nearly boiling pot of devilwheat meal. "Perhaps a month, maybe a little longer."

That's longer than I've even been in Hell.

Rick wandered over to the supply closet and began fishing around in it.

"Well, there's got to be something I can do to help out in the meantime," Ellen suggested.

"Certainly," Rick called back over his shoulder. "I'll take you on some rounds this morning. As long as you feel comfortable with where things are, you can start gathering devilwheat and hungerleaf and such. At some point, I'll have to teach you how to hunt. Would have been better if Galen could, but . . ."

He didn't finish his sentence, and his rummaging stopped.

I'm sorry, Rick. I wish he could have, too.

After a moment, he continued searching through the supply closet.

He came out with a few sticks of dyitzu jerky. "Fresh meat is getting a bit scarce."

Ellen got up and walked over to stand next to him. She picked out her favorite plate, the one with a chip on its edge. It had been Arturus' favorite, too. The rock it was made out of had a dark spot in the center. She held it out to Rick. He shoveled some of the devilwheat meal onto it and added a piece of jerky.

"Yum," she said as she took the plate back to the table.

Rick joined her after a minute, passing her a spoon.

"Oh, yeah!" She smiled as she accepted the utensil. "Thanks."

She started on the devilwheat meal. The seared and sour knowledge fruit was the only thing that made eating it worthwhile. She ate all the fruit first and then looked dismally at the remainder. With a sigh, she began the serious work of finishing her food.

Rick stood up and moved around the table, holding his plate over hers. "Here you go, dear." He had eaten everything but the knowledge fruit. She laughed as he added that to her devilwheat meal. Rick's chair, fashioned out of an old barrel, creaked when he sat back down upon it.

There was a pattern in the grain of the stone plate. She imagined the dark swirl was Arturus, sitting on a ledge over Harpsborough. Her every bite revealed more of the city, and she pretended that one pattern was Kylie's Kiln, and that a dark spot was the Fore. Arturus would never walk her to the city again. She would never become a Citizen, or a villager, or whatever it was he had wanted her to be.

I think I'm going to cry.

She picked up the jerky while she stared at the plate. "We should go in there and get them."

Rick looked up at her. "To the Carrion?"

"We should."

He shook his head.

"Please," she whispered.

"We'll die."

"I don't care."

"There's no way we could find them, and you're not a good enough fighter. The Carrion would kill us both."

"I don't care," she repeated.

Rick's normally straight posture dissolved. He sat, back hunched, staring at his own plate. "Were death oblivion, I might not care either, but it's not. We go to a worse place."

Ellen's heart suddenly leapt. "Turi would go there too, then, right?"

She thought about this.

He could be there now, waiting for me. He'll keep a place for me where we can finally suffer together again.

Rick looked at her, his eyes wide. "Don't you dare."

"All I want is to see him."

"You aren't allowed to die."

She ground her teeth, staring at him for a moment. "What choice do I have? You won't take me to save him. I have to see him again."

Rick looked hurt. "Is it really so terrible, living here with me?"

"I don't want to live with you! I want to live with Turi."

Rick bowed his head. "I'm sorry, Ellen."

"Take me to him," she whispered. "Please take me."

"No."

"Why not? Don't you love your son enough to risk your life?"

Rick grimaced. "It's not about that, Ellen. We can't save him."

"Take me!"

"No."

Ellen stood up quickly, knocking over her chair. She ran for the exit.

Molly's eyes struck Michael as odd when she sat down in the front pew. For some reason he had forgotten they were blue. Her skin was of a darker complexion, and her hair was brown as well, so he had just thought of her eyes as brown—as if he hadn't spent so many nights staring into them while he'd made love to her. That was back when sleeping with Molly was something special. These days she was just a whore.

The shadow of one of the church's crosses darkened her right eye, but the left, shining and blue, was fully in the light. It glistened, and Michael guessed she was probably close to tears. She seemed calm, but her lips were giving her away. Inside, she was pouting.

He remembered kissing those lips, and her shoulders, and her breasts. God, how he missed those breasts. Kylie's were just as big, but they hung down like teats from a cow udder. Still, those udders weren't attached to a psychopathic bitch, so Michael supposed he'd better be happy about where things stood.

The church door opened on squeaky hinges and Mancini, Harpsborough's brewer, made his way in. It closed with a thud.

Michael had insisted Mancini join himself and Father Klein because the slick bastard made Molly feel uneasy.

Hell, Mancini made everyone feel uneasy.

Michael, Father Klein, and now Mancini, stood in front of her. Molly didn't even acknowledge them.

"We're worried about you, Molly," Michael said.

Molly continued to stare off to one side, not making eye contact with any of them.

"Do you hear me?" Michael asked.

She nodded, taking a deep breath.

"We've seen you going far out into the wilds," Father Klein said, his tone soft and comforting. "It's dangerous out there. You could get killed. You're not to go out there anymore."

She shook her head no.

Mancini snorted. "We're not worried about her dying, and she knows it."

"That's not true!" Father Klein shot back. "Her safety is my first concern."

Mancini ignored him. "We know what you've been doing out there, Molly."

"Nothing," Molly cleared her throat. "I haven't been doing anything."

Mancini did not relent. "You've been looking for the Infidel Friend."

Molly was suddenly shaken. She looked quickly towards Mancini, the movement letting loose a tear. "I have not! I've been looking for food. For a stash like Julian's. We all need it."

For a second, Michael almost believed Molly. Sure, she wasn't the most moral person in Harpsborough, but trying to save an Infidel Friend was a little beyond the Pale, even for her. Michael had dated this woman, however. He knew how easy it was for her to lie.

"Yes, you have been," Mancini said. "Graham's followed you. He's seen you trace the wall next to the Golden Door. We know who you're looking for. We can't let you keep doing it."

Molly shook her head again and wiped away her tears.

"We can't let you do this," Father Klein said softly, putting a staying hand on Mancini. "We can't let you keep going out."

Michael reached across and touched her shoulder. "It's for your own good."

"What?" she sat up straight.

"You'll get yourself killed," Father Klein said.

"My own good?" Molly leapt up to her feet, shoving her finger into Michael's chest hard enough to push him backward. "My own good? You must want me to be a whore!"

"That's ridiculous, Molly—"

"Is it? If I can't gather, then I have nothing to eat and nothing to trade for. I'll starve to death. You'll make me a whore. You've already made everyone think I'm one. Everyone says they've slept with me, and instead of agreeing with me when I say they haven't, you just call me a liar. I'm not a whore. I'm not. But fuck you, if you make me stay in Harpsborough, I'll have nothing left to do but that!"

"I understand you're upset, Miss," Father Klein said, "but this is God's house—"

"Fuck God's house! Fuck God. God damn all of you."

"*Molly!*" Father Klein stepped back in shock.

"You think I give a shit? Do you? You want me to fuck people for food, Father? Why don't I *fuck* you? Maybe you'll let me have some of those eggs you've stashed away—"

Michael stood up and slapped her. She quieted for a moment, but only that.

"Are you going to feed me?" Molly asked quietly.

The three men shared a glance. Without Julian's devilwheat, things were going to be bad enough. Without Aaron, they couldn't even count on a steady supply of dyitzu meat. Food was going to be tight.

We probably can't even afford to have Graham follow her around anymore.

"No," Michael answered.

"Then let me go out. I'll stay away from the Golden Door, I promise. I'll only go upstream along the Kingsriver. I won't go down it. I promise. I won't go anywhere near the door."

"No."

"How am I going to eat?"

Michael didn't answer. He didn't know what to say.

"How? God damn it, how?"

"For the last time, woman," Father Klein boomed, "don't blaspheme in this house. Or we'll have you thrown through the Golden Door."

Molly smiled.

Damn. That's where she wants to go.

"God damn God damn God damn God damn."

Well, we asked for that.

Michael slapped her again. The emotional effect seemed minimal, but at least she shut up.

"Molly, if you make us do this the hard way, we'll find a way. We'll chain you up next to Benson if we have to. But if you keep your head on straight, you can stay in the village. You can go through Harpsborough as you will. The hunters already know not to let you out. In a few days, maybe you'll have an attack of conscience, if you've even got one of those. Assuming you do, Klein will be here, waiting for your confession. If you tell him everything the Infidel Friend told you, and he believes you are truly repentant, and I mean *truly* repentant, then we'll see about letting you out into the wilds again."

The angry look on Molly's face didn't go away. Her nostrils flared and her head bobbed.

"You understand me?" Michael asked.

Molly kept on nodding, her eyes as wide as an animal's.

"I asked if you understand me."

"I do," she snapped. "I got you, Mike."

"Good," Michael told her, "then feel free to leave."

"And while you are welcome in the church," Father Klein said, "your language is not. See that you clean that up before you come back."

"Fuck you." Molly turned and stormed out of the church. She slammed one of the double doors as hard as she could causing some of the cross shadows on the far end of the church to vibrate.

"Jesus," Michael said, letting out a sigh. "Well, now she'll have no choice but to confess to you, Father."

Klein shook his head. "She doesn't have to."

"What? Is she going to starve?" Mike asked.

Mancini smiled. "No, she really can become a whore."

Ellen's hand rested against the Carrion barrier. She felt the thrum of the stone beneath her fingertips—slow and rhythmic. Her fingers walked her hand across the rock until they left the bricks that had been laid by Rick and the people of

Harpsborough, and then rested themselves instead upon the stones that had been laid by the Devil.

Somewhere beyond this wall in the vast expanse of the labyrinth called the Carrion, was Turi—or more likely, Turi's corpse.

Devil, you've taken my love. Would you ever consider giving him back?

Such a silly thing, to pray to the Devil. Perhaps even more silly than praying to God, because if the Devil were to listen, then she certainly wouldn't get her wish.

Best to keep my heart silent.

But Ellen's heart was not a thing that could be kept silent. She was reminded suddenly of a poem she had read once, in middle school, about a sailor's wife.

Ye are dead they say, but ye swore, ye swore.

She couldn't remember much more of the poem's words, only the image that those words had left her with: a woman standing by the sea each night, staring out into the darkness, waiting for her husband's ship to come home. Waiting long after the time that she must have known her husband would never return.

But, Ellen realized, Arturus had never married her. They'd not even kissed, not really, not in the way that lovers did— though he'd kissed her on the forehead once, while she cried.

O lover of mine, ye swore.

But had Turi promised to return?

Not that she could remember. In fact, it had been she, one day while they had been walking back from Harpsborough, who had promised not to die.

We're fools, Turi. I'm sorry. We made the promise the wrong way round.

That poor sailor's wife. Why didn't she just move on? Why didn't she just stop staring at the sea? But at least that woman could have some comfort in her memories. The woman in the poem had shared her husband's bed and received his promise of undying affection. Ellen had neither of these things. Even if Arturus did return, it would be foolish of her to expect that her vigil would be rewarded in any way. He would probably just go right on pining for Alice. At least the sailor's wife wouldn't have to worry about her lover returning just so he could fall into the arms of some hussy.

She balled her fingers up into a fist, but instead of beating the stone, she let her body slide down it until she was resting in a ball.

Don't cry, Ellen. Galen wouldn't like it if you cried. Turi would think you were weak.

He had to be alive, somewhere out there, on the other side of that stone wall. He would have to return. And when he did, he would come to his senses and love her. On Earth, she could have hoped that God would make such a thing happen—or Fate. Here, in the labyrinth, there were no such assurances. No one, no thing, was going to bring Turi to her. Despair welled up inside her, and she wondered suddenly how people on Earth could have survived without believing in gods. They must have been very sad people, if they ever had to face hurt like this.

"Ellen?" Rick's voice called to her.

She imagined that his sudden entrance should have scared her. Galen would have wanted her to jump suddenly and turn around. Maybe her hand should have reached quickly for her pistol. Instead, she stared at the stone wall.

She heard him approach, his boots crunching in the dust and gravel left over from their repair of the Carrion barrier. She checked her eyes to make sure she hadn't been crying.

"Is this where you've been?" he asked.

She nodded and looked back up at him from where she lay. "Yes."

"It's not safe here."

"I know."

"You're waiting for them to come home?" Rick's voice wavered a bit.

He was probably dealing with his own grief.

"If they come back," she said, "maybe they'd make some noise. I could get you, and we could tear it down."

"Maybe," Rick said. "Maybe you're right. But Galen will probably find another way. The Carrion barrier isn't complete, you know. Galen always warned us about that."

"But waiting could help," she insisted.

"It could."

"Then I'll wait."

Ellen turned back and faced the wall. She could hear Rick

shifting behind her. He started to walk away.

"Rick," she said. "Rick, I'm sorry."

"It's okay, Ellen."

"I understand why. I know why we can't go get them."

"And you still want to wait?"

"Yes."

Rick's footsteps came back towards her.

She felt a blanket fall upon her. Rick's warm body lay down next to her. He smelled of leather and gun oil—and of the forge's smoke. It was a comforting smell.

"Then I'll wait with you," he said.

— 3 —

Arturus leaned back against the cold Carrion stone while he tried to listen to Aaron and Galen's conversation. It was no use. They were just whispering too softly. Aaron glanced over to Kyle for a moment after Galen spoke, though, so he could guess what they were talking about.

Please talk some sense into Aaron. We can't do this.

After a few more traded whispers, Galen began to nod in assent.

No.

Aaron began moving about the room, shoulders hunched under the low ceiling, pausing to speak to each of the hunters. He did not stop at Arturus, and he did not need to.

He warned me first.

Avery crossed his arms and nodded when he was told. Johnny and Duncan turned towards Kyle simultaneously, their faces full of sorrow. After a moment, Kyle noticed that everyone was looking at him. He pushed himself up, using his arms to slide his body back so that he might sit straighter against the wall. Arturus could see his Adam's apple bob as he swallowed.

"We're ready to move out," Aaron said to Kyle. "Galen says his friend is ready for us."

Kyle set his jaw and nodded.

"It's going to be dangerous," Aaron continued, "and we're going to need every gun we have. You know what it's like out there. If we run into another of those dyitzu packs, there's no way we'll make it. We can't afford to have . . . for anyone not to have their gun at the ready."

Kyle bowed his head. His hand slid over to rest on his M-24.

"I'll manage. If someone carries me then . . ."

"Kyle—" Aaron began.

"I should be able to shoot off of their backs. Or maybe I can walk a little, if someone helps support me. I'll keep my gun at the ready."

But there was no way, even with help, that Kyle's legs could support any of his weight.

"Kyle, it's—"

"Just give me a little more time. I'll be able to move soon. My legs are getting better."

"It's not our choice, Kyle." Aaron knelt beside him. "Believe me. If there were anything else . . ."

Kyle looked at them all, but Arturus couldn't force himself to meet his gaze. He noticed that the other hunters couldn't either. Only the priestess was staring at him intently.

"Then take the gun," Kyle said quickly.

"What?" Johnny asked.

"If you're going to leave me, I understand. Take my gun. It's a good gun."

Galen shook his head. "You deserve a better death than that."

Johnny and Duncan were nodding.

Aaron grimaced.

"He's got a right to that," Avery said. "We've got to leave him some bullets too. Enough to kill some devils."

Aaron let out a deep breath. "You're right."

Kyle's face hardened, his grip tightening on the barrel of his rifle.

"Yeah," Johnny said. "If the devils stay out like they have been, you might even be able to heal enough to walk. You'll probably be back in Harpsborough before we will."

"The devils haven't been coming because of Galen, Johnny." Kyle said. "He's been protecting us, patrolling the wilds like we did for Harpsborough."

Johnny Huang grimaced and looked towards Galen. "Well maybe, then . . ."

Aaron let the silence hang in the room for a moment before speaking to the group. "Get your gear. We're gone in five."

Arturus didn't have much to get ready. He had a single pistol, four bullets, a blanket and a pouch of bent silver spider legs—and the blanket wasn't even his. He held it for a moment, wondering whose it was. Avery answered his question by snatching it out of his hands.

Arturus allowed himself a smile. Avery seemed too harsh a man to be sharing blankets, but perhaps he had a soft heart after all.

However, Avery had also killed Patrick, slitting the man's throat so that his cries of pain would not draw the devils to them.

Suddenly the hunters were all standing together, and Kyle was sitting apart in the corner.

Galen knelt beside him, handing over three bullets. "My guns don't use 'em."

But the rest of the hunters were using 700 Remingtons, and their ammunition was the same type as Kyle's M-24 used. Each of them passed by him, making an offering.

"Don't waste this shit," Avery said as he walked towards the wounded hunter. Then he knelt, grabbed Kyle by the head, touching their foreheads together. "You hear me? You put this shit in a dyitzu. Right in its heart."

Avery let go and leaned back. He held out a handful of bullets.

Kyle accepted the ammunition with both hands. He closed his eyes, his lips moving as if in prayer.

"Alright," Aaron said. "Move out."

Galen led them out of the room. Arturus tarried, unable to make himself leave. Kyle started loading some of his bullets into an empty clip. He slapped it into his rifle and looked up.

This was exactly what had happened to Patrick. Surely leaving Kyle alone in the Carrion was no different than taking a knife to his throat.

Galen ordered me not to make that mistake again.

"I'm sorry," Arturus mouthed.

Kyle nodded. "Happy hunting," he said aloud.

"Happy hunting," Arturus answered.

Arturus stood there for a long moment more before turning away.

Galen led while Arturus and Aaron carried the door they were going to use as a raft. The rest of the hunters filed after them as best they could. Arturus could tell from their ginger steps that their feet were tender, but everyone managed. They had to, after what they'd just done to Kyle. No one wanted to be left behind.

We should go back and get him. Then we could put him on the raft, maybe give him to one of Maab's people. Being a slave might be better than being dead.

The priestess' gorgeous face broke into a grotesque mask of pain while she followed them. She seemed unable to either bend over all the way or keep her posture completely straight. Her breathing was quick and shallow, as if she dared not inhale too deeply. Arturus couldn't help but respect her stoicism because she did not complain or whimper.

The river chamber they entered was dark, and the water was lit only by a distant illuminated cubbyhole. They lowered their newfound raft into the black river. Aaron sat on the bank, putting his feet, boots and all, into the water. He reached out and held the raft still.

Arturus looked longingly at the depressions the hinges had left in the wood. They reminded him of Rick's table back home. The door itself was about four feet wide and seven feet tall. It had been bound together with thin strips of iron.

"Our provisions are still going to get wet," Johnny noted.

"Provisions?" Avery asked as he tossed his pack onto the floating wooden door. "Shit, Johnny, we've got a handful of bullets and some blankets. What could you be worried about?"

"It'll be drier than with no raft at all," Aaron said. "Now stay quiet, people."

Galen set his pack and his MP5 Heckler and Koch down by the bank before lowering himself into the river. It was deep enough to make him tread water.

"Pass me your packs," Galen said, "and I'll tie them down."

"Make sure you have rounds in your chambers," Aaron ordered. "Rivers are busy places, and even busier here. We may need to shoot fast."

Johnny Huang complied, chambering a round in his rifle as he entered the water.

Arturus drew his pistol and joined them, putting a hand on the raft in order to keep himself steady.

Galen came out of the water in one swift motion. "You

ready, Turi?"

"No," Arturus said. "We should go back and get Kyle."

"It's too late for that," Aaron answered.

Galen nodded. "Aaron, Turi, push the raft to the edge."

"It's *not* too late," Arturus insisted. "We can go back and get him. We can give him to Maab's people. Maybe he'd be better as a slave."

"Turi," Aaron's voice didn't hide his agitation. "Kyle wouldn't want to be a slave."

"But he wouldn't want to be dead either."

Aaron looked about the chamber, perhaps searching for enemies. "We don't know what he'd want."

"Then we should ask him!"

"Turi," Galen said, "drop the issue."

Arturus imagined Kyle, sitting alone, waiting for death. "But you're the one who told me not to make the mistake again! This is the same as what we did to Patrick. We're killing him."

Aaron grabbed hold of the raft and shoved it towards Arturus, sending river water splashing up on the bank as he did so. "We're all going to die, Turi! All of us." Aaron swam up to him. "It's not just Kyle. None of us are going to make it home. We're still trying because we have to keep trying, because we've got nothing left to do. But we're dead men already. Dead men walking."

For a moment there was only the sound of the river. The priestess shifted uncomfortably from one leg to the other, her arms cradling her hurt ribs. Arturus furiously tread water.

Johnny reached out and touched his shoulder. "He's right, man. Your dad said that the guide is just as likely to betray us as help us, you know that. And the path that guide is going to take us down includes an offshoot of the Lethe. The Lethe, Turi. I wasn't with Michael and Klein and the Harpsborough people who fled the Carrion, but even I've heard of that river."

Arturus thought he heard the sound of a dyitzu claw.

"Aaron, Turi," Galen said softly, "gentleman, will you please push the raft to the edge."

Aaron and Arturus did so. The door rocked back and forth, causing the black water to slide across the wood and splash over their packs.

"God damn," Avery muttered. "I hope our shit will still fire.

I've got a clip in there."

"Now you worry." Johnny shook his head.

"It's the best we can do right now," Galen said.

"I cannot swim," the priestess told them, "not with my ribs."

"On the raft," Galen suggested.

She nodded, dropping to all fours.

Galen gave her a hand from where he stood, still dripping, on the bank. "Quickly, milady. Quickly."

The priestess grabbed his hand and crawled backwards onto the door. It shifted under her weight, causing more water to run back over the boards.

The sounds of the devils kept coming. Turi could pick out the call of a distant hound and the hisses of nearby dyitzu.

Galen returned to the water and stayed at the front of the raft, guiding it away from the bank. Duncan and Turi took the right while Aaron and Avery took the left. They each held on to the raft with one hand while trying to keep their guns in the air with the other.

The priestess sputtered a bit, coughing up some water. Her face reddened with pain.

"Ready?" Aaron asked.

Arturus nodded.

"Yes," Avery whispered.

"Let's go." Aaron let go of the river bank. "Galen, this guide of yours better be good."

The raft began to drift down the river.

"Just an hour or so," Galen told them. "Then we'll find out."

Rick was fond of saying that a river keeps its own house, and as far as Arturus could tell, this river was no exception. The arching brick structures and vaulted ceilings reminded him of the Thames chambers—indeed, Galen had pointed out to him earlier that much of the water here had actually flowed through the Thames river—however, the dark nature of the Carrion had warped that familiar and comforting architecture into something more foreboding. The red bricks of his home were replaced by dark grey ones, the color of ash, and their shape was periodically elongated so that every third one resembled a human skull. Out of the corner of his eyes, he saw the mass of those skull stones, all grinning teeth and hollow eye sockets, but when he turned to look at them directly, he saw only pitted grey bricks.

As always in the Carrion, the lighting was minimal. Distant yellow or white cubbyholes only illuminated them dimly and, even though he was neck deep in the water, Arturus could barely see his own body beneath the surface. Anything could be swimming below him.

The chambers were equally ominous—their floors uneven and covered in darkness. Who knew what demons could be lying in wait behind each jut of stone or in each pool of blackness?

Johnny inhaled some water and began to cough. His cough echoed throughout the chamber. Arturus strained his eyes, waving his pistol about, but nothing out there appeared to be moving.

Thank you.

"Tunnel ahead," Galen warned.

The river flowed out of their current room through an arched passageway. The dim light reflected off the water, undulating across the arch and into the darkness beyond. More of those dark skull-like stones lined the tunnel. The river filled the passage from wall to wall so that in there, at least, they wouldn't have to worry about dyitzu on the banks.

They entered the tunnel.

"Ain't no demons in the water," Arturus heard Avery whisper, who was presumably answering someone else's whispered question.

"You lie," the priestess said. "There are sirens and devils made betwixt an alligator and a man. They frequent the deep."

"Bullshit. You're the one with the damn fish stories," Avery whispered back.

"She's right," Galen said, "but we'd not see them in this water."

"They don't travel here?" Avery asked.

"No, I meant that you wouldn't see them, since the water is so dark."

Arturus caught a glance of Avery's horrified face from across the raft.

"Fuck me," Avery looked down at the water, his voice echoing oddly in tight confines.

The ceiling might get lower until there is no room to breathe. We'd be forced to try and swim back to survive.

As dark as the Carrion was, the tunnel was even darker. At first the skulls seemed to be grinning at him from the edges of his vision, but eventually even they faded away into the blackness. Arturus looked behind him, seeing only a receding grey blot.

"Fuck," Avery's echoed whisper reached Arturus' ears.

"Turn ahead," Galen warned.

Arturus had no idea how his father had seen the turn, but the man was right. The raft bumped into a stone wall, the impact echoing down the corridor, and then it bobbed a bit as its momentum shifted. Soon they were floating again. Arturus wasn't sure, but it seemed like they were picking up speed.

He cast another glance behind him. This time he could see nothing at all.

Damn.

"Are we going faster?" Johnny's nasal voice asked.

"A little," Galen responded.

"How can you tell?" That was Avery. "I can't see shit."

"I can't either," Galen said. "I'm trying to listen."

"Trying?"

"Harder to do when you're talking."

"Oh, sorry."

Arturus stopped attempting to use his eyes and let the sounds around him fill his ears. He heard the ripples of the water where they touched his raft. He knew the shape of the thing, but for a moment he imagined that he didn't and tried to guess its form with his ears alone.

I would not have guessed it was square, but I would have guessed its size.

He could tell just how wide the tunnel was from the water's ripples as they lapped against the stones. He could hear the echoes of those waves as they filled the empty air beneath the ceiling. Suddenly he felt as if he knew where everyone was in the darkness. In his mind's eye, he could imagine the shape of the stone ceiling as it descended on either side of him.

This is why Galen isn't afraid of devils in the water. He listens for them.

It struck him as important that this auditory information

was always around him, all the time. He just usually ignored it while he concentrated on his vision. Surely this was some great lesson to have learned.

Another grey blot appeared, this time ahead of them. It grew in size with their approach, until the skulls returned, and then the walls opened up into a huge chamber. A long shadow crossed over the water in this room. Arturus looked towards its source.

A dyitzu.

"Stay quiet," Galen whispered. "Don't shoot, it may not notice us."

The dyitzu leaned down to the water to drink. Its pupil-less black eyes looked directly at them. It stood quickly, forming a fireball. By that dancing firelight, Arturus could see the chamber. It was crawling with devils.

 — 4 —

Aaron's bullet struck the dyitzu in the side of its face, sending it spinning to the floor. The fireball it had been forming floated lazily away from the river, heading towards one edge of the corridor. The room lit up with flames as the dyitzu came alive en masse, hurling their fire, not at the river, but all around the chamber.

They haven't seen us.

The priestess shifted slightly, coming into contact with Arturus' hand. He could feel her shaking. She turned her head, and Arturus saw her face.

She was in agony.

The shivering, it must be hurting her ribs.

The raft drifted farther. The dyitzu had stopped throwing fire and were looking towards the room's exits. One gave out a long hiss as it spotted them. Aaron chambered another round and fired, cutting the hiss short—but its warning was enough. The chamber lit up again with fireballs.

"Let loose!" Galen shouted.

Galen wielded his Heckler and Koch one handed, firing with horrid form but surprising accuracy. The rest of the hunters followed suit, treading water to reload. Few of those bullets found their targets, but they did force the dyitzu to take cover and helped to disturb their aim. A fireball shot into the water beside Arturus, turning to steam as it did so. More followed. Arturus ducked his head beneath the surface to dodge under one, his pistol getting wet for a moment.

Please still work.

But he dared not shoot. He only had four bullets left and

did not know when he might need them most.

"Tunnel ahead!" Avery shouted.

Galen let off a few more bullets as the current dragged them closer to the next tunnel. One fireball impacted with the stone above the tunnel's arch, its fiery liquid dripping down, raining on the priestess as they entered. The priestess, driven beyond her limit, finally let out a scream of pain. Arturus pushed down on one side of the raft, covering her with water and quickly dousing the part of her robe that had caught fire. As the raft evened back out, the river washed the flammable liquid of the fireball away.

"This tunnel's not as long as the last one," Galen warned.

"I saw them running towards the exit," Aaron shouted. "If there's another way around, I think they'll be waiting for us on the other side."

"Everyone still got bullets?" Avery asked.

"Yes."

"Yes, sir."

"You got it."

"I'm good," Arturus responded.

"Everyone reloaded?" Aaron asked.

There was a similar round of affirmatives.

"How much farther to your friend, Galen?" the priestess asked.

"I'm sorry, milady. But we have some ways yet."

She nodded grimly. "Do you have a gun for me?"

"Oh fuck no!" Avery said.

"We have very few bullets, milady," Galen answered.

"I understand."

The grey blot at the end of their tunnel gave way to another room. There was no sign of dyitzu.

"Thank God!" Johnny exclaimed.

"Not many entrances here," Galen said, "but stay on guard. They can show up at any time."

The next chamber was much larger than the last. Its ceiling arched upwards, appearing to be over one hundred feet tall in the center. Near the middle of the room was a giant stone protrusion, reaching up from the ground until it nearly touched the ceiling. It looked more like a stalagmite than a tower. Near its base was a series of thinner stalagmite-like structures, though many reached just as high. Some were as thick as several men standing side by side, others as thin as a hungerleaf tree.

In the river, there was a sharp left bend near the base of that tower. At that point the grade increased and the speed of the water became fast enough for some of it to wash over its banks. A vein of skystone ran through the river, filling the room with an oscillating muted blue light.

Arturus peered into the chamber, looking for the enemy.

A shadow passed over them quickly.

"The hell was that?" Avery whispered harshly.

"I saw it," the priestess said. "Wings. Above us."

"You're not even looking up."

"Its shadow."

Arturus spotted it. The thing flitted from one stalagmite to another, staying near the edge of a wall.

"Icanitzu," Arturus said suddenly, "I think."

"The dyitzu, they got in front of us!" Aaron shouted.

The dyitzu came pouring into the chamber, appearing from beyond the tower ahead of them. Galen's MP5 came alive, firing round after round. Aaron also let loose, but the rest held their fire, trying to conserve bullets which otherwise would have almost certainly missed their targets. The dyitzu fireballs came rolling in, some of them impacting with the stalagmites, splattering flames in waves across the room. Galen kicked off of one wall, tipping the raft upwards so that several of the fireballs impacted with its underside. The priestess shouted, holding onto the raft. It came down, squelching the fire and making the water uncomfortably warm.

The dyitzu by the river bend were calling to each other. They began jumping into the water.

"We can't make it!" Aaron shouted.

The wavy blue light which was cast up onto the room's ceiling from the river was suddenly filled with darting dyitzu shadows.

"They're coming," Johnny warned.

Arturus caught sight of the devils, not more than a hundred feet away, as they swam around the river bend.

We're going to die.

"Out of the water!" Galen shouted, shoving the raft to their left.

Arturus and Duncan helped, kicking mightily, driving the raft—and the priestess with it—onto the shore. Galen was out of the river in an instant, water droplets flying all around him. He reached back in, pulling Turi and Aaron up. Duncan and Avery dragged themselves onto the bank.

"Avery, AK clip into the water!" Aaron ordered.

"That way!" Galen shouted, pointing diagonally across the chamber, past the tower, to where the river flowed out of the room.

Arturus picked up the back of the door with his free hand while Aaron grabbed the front. Duncan helped the priestess to her feet. The AK-47 reports drowned out all other sounds as they made a break for the exit. The field of stalagmites became denser as they neared the central tower, so Arturus and Aaron had to be careful not to bang the raft against the jutting stones. Arturus caught a glimpse of the priestess, running through a thick set of stalagmites. He saw a nearby dyitzu and loosed a shot, hitting the thing in the shoulder and sending it spinning backwards. Its fireball flew up towards the ceiling.

They were rounding the tower when Aaron halted suddenly, causing Arturus to run shoulder first into the door. As Arturus recovered, he saw what had stopped the hunter.

The Icanitzu was descending. It landed before them, dropping into a kneeling position as its backward jointed legs absorbed the impact of its descent. It spread its wings out wide and low, balancing itself before folding them back behind its shoulders. It stood majestically.

Arturus remembered how long their previous battle with the Icanitzu had taken. There was no time for a conflict like that now. Arturus looked behind him, the dyitzu had come out of the water and were headed towards them.

"No time to stop!" Galen's voice called from behind them, but having not made it around the tower, he hadn't seen the Icanitzu yet.

"Go go go!" Galen was shouting as he came around the stalagmite.

He did not stop as he caught sight of the Icanitzu but kept running right at it.

The Icanitzu flared its wings and let out a long howl, its

rows of incisor teeth showing as it did so. It advanced.

"Fuck!" Aaron shouted.

Galen, only ten feet away from the Icanitzu, pulled his flare gun and fired, hitting it full in the face. The thing shrieked in pain, dropping into a crouch, covering its body with its wings and its blinded eyes with its arms. Galen gave it a push kick with all the momentum of his run, sending it rolling across the floor.

"Move!" he ordered as he ran by.

They did, sprinting the rest of the way across the chamber. Galen stopped at the bank, raised his MP5 to his shoulder, and started firing behind them. Arturus and Aaron passed him, leaping, door and all, into the water. Avery slung his AK over his shoulder and came in after them. The priestess made a grab for the raft as she jumped, catching onto one of the ropes Galen had used to tie their packs on. Galen dove in, swimming behind the door and pushing it forward. Arturus and Aaron managed together to help the screaming priestess out of the water and onto the raft.

The river was moving faster now, dragging them forward with terrific speed. It pulled them first through one tunnel, and then another, and then another. Fireballs glided over their heads, illuminating each new room as the dyitzu dashed after them.

Aaron and Arturus had found themselves on a side together, and they began kicking. Duncan and Avery followed suit, propelling the raft even faster through the turbulent water. Aaron stopped for a moment, drawing his pistol with one hand, and fired behind them. Arturus watched a dyitzu collapse to the ground, twitching and clawing at the blood covered stones beneath it.

"Careful," Galen warned. "Keep count of your bullets."

Aaron fired twice more in the next room before the river began to outrun the dyitzu.

"That Icanitzu will be after us," Aaron warned.

Arturus looked to his stoic father. Galen's face betrayed no emotion.

"Will it, father?" Arturus asked.

Aaron let loose another shot before Galen answered. "I don't know, son. I don't know."

5

Just as long as nobody sees me.

In general Alice did her best not to steal, but after not eating for a couple days, she was willing to make some small compromises with herself. This was actually old hat, in a way. She'd been picked up twice as a teenager for shoplifting. Technically, she hadn't been allowed in any Wal-Mart in the country—not that they'd noticed when she'd broken the ban a few years later. She'd mention it to her friends as a bit of trivia while they shopped there. It had been her misspent youth, she'd told them.

This time is different. This time I'm starving, and somebody's going to have to feed Molly.

But this time she wasn't stealing from a faceless corporate entity. This time she was stealing from Rick.

It's not like I'm the first person to do this to him.

Rick should actually be thankful for her level of self-control. The Hungerleaf Grove was his worst kept secret. In fact, the grove was so well known that if one were to have an appointment with Galen or Rick, or even Arturus, it was common to meet them here.

When times were tough, many villagers would pinch a few leaves to trade. They'd tried to keep it unnoticeable before the famine, but now the grove looked almost wholly picked over. Thin, spidery branches reached out from their slimy, grey scaled trunks, almost totally devoid of foliage. Only the highest branches still had leaves, and most of those were out of her reach. She could even see where a few branches had been broken, presumably while someone had been bending them down so that they could reach the hungerleaves. One of those broken branches was on the ground and still had a few leaves on it.

She looked out across the mile long chamber as she squatted by the branch. On the day she'd met Turi here, there had been a corpse across the river. The Hungerleaf Grove was set in the middle of an island in a small lake that the Kingsriver flowed through. Arturus had a name for the type of lake it was. Foxbow, or something similar. On that day, the chamber had been filled with mists. Today, ironically, it was as clear as an old world spring.

Satisfied there were no devils—or a Rick—in the chamber, she turned her attention back to the branch.

These should be enough.

She began plucking the leaves. They came off easily, but they had not been separated from their tree for so long as to have dried out. Not that they would rot—unless, of course, a corpse had been through here. She stuffed them into her Hello Kitty satchel.

"Ellen," a girl's voice declared.

Alice froze.

Fuck.

If the Fore found out she'd broken a claim, she'd be up for punishment, and Michael Baker wasn't exactly very pleased with her at the moment. They might even take her hand. Alice turned and regarded the little brown haired girl which Arturus had taken a liking to.

Ellen was crossing the stepping stones onto the island. Her balance was good, at least. Still, Ellen was new to Hell, and it showed. She was too damn happy, for one thing. Her clothes were pretty clean as well. She wore some old world faded blue jeans which flared out towards her ankles along with a thin, white cotton long sleeve shirt. Her hair was brushed back into a pony tail.

Ellen had been a good friend to Turi, and rumor had it that she'd moved in with Rick after he and the villagers had fixed the Carrion barrier. The Hungerleaf Grove could well be considered her property by the Fore.

Well, I'm caught now.

It was best not to be apologetic about these things, and

Alice didn't feel like having to explain herself to a girl who'd probably just started using tampons.

"You're looking chipper," Alice said, trying to keep any guilt out of her voice.

Ellen looked stunned. "Really?"

"Yeah."

"I feel wretched," Ellen looked away.

Maybe she didn't notice me stashing the leaves.

"Oh no! Poor girl! Why?" Alice said in her sweetest voice, coming closer to her. "You've got it made here. Rick's taking care of you."

Ellen shook her head.

Alice could smell aroma of the hungerleaves coming up from her Hello Kitty satchel. Her stomach gave an audible growl. She hoped the odor wasn't too noticeable. Ellen, for her part, seemed oblivious.

God, is this chick really so dumb? Maybe she doesn't even know that I'm stealing.

Ellen looked back up at her. "Why won't the Fore send someone out to the Carrion to get them back?"

"I wish they would, girl," Alice said. "Everyone's afraid of the big bad Carrion. They tell stories of it, of how horrible it was. Michael doesn't want to lose any more hunters."

"Everyone's hungry, aren't they?" Ellen asked.

Alice nodded at first but then shook her head. "Not everyone. Not the people in the Fore."

"Aaron was a member, wasn't he?"

Alice felt pressure building up behind her eyes. "Yes."

Don't cry in front of her. Keep cool.

"If you two had gotten married," Ellen was saying, "would you be made a Fore member too?"

Alice frowned. "He was trying to get me to be a Citizen, yes."

Ellen stopped questioning suddenly, her brown eyes growing wide. "Oh, I'm sorry. I didn't mean to . . ."

"Ellen, it's okay."

". . . if anyone should understand your grief . . . I have these nightmares where they all come back, except for Turi. Except for Turi."

Alice took the girl's hand and tried to give her a soft smile.

Way to go Alice. Way to steal from a grief stricken twit of a teenager.

Ellen had a question, Alice could tell, but the girl didn't want to ask it.

"Rick," Turi's father announced himself as he entered the chamber.

Oh, now I'm fucked for real. The Fore will have my hand for sure.

"Rick!" Ellen shouted.

"Not that loud!" he replied with a smile. "No need to let every demon know my name. How are you girls doing?"

Alice was about to speak, but Ellen cut her off.

"I gave Alice some of our hungerleaves because things are so bad in the village. I hope that's okay."

Alice tried to hide her shock.

Thank God. I love this little girl.

Rick nodded. "It's okay for Alice, but don't go making a habit of it."

Ellen smiled and ran up to a tree. She climbed it and began to gather some of the leaves left on the top branches.

Rick walked up beside Alice.

Does he know?

"I think I approve of you two being friends," he said.

"You weren't fond of me and Turi spending time together."

"That was mostly his fault. He liked you too much."

Ellen slipped a little on the grey bark but caught her balance.

Rick's eyes narrowed as he watched her. He leaned in closer to Alice and lowered his voice. "How bad is it in the village?"

"Bad."

"How long until fighting breaks out?"

Alice pondered this for a moment. Ellen was pulling her hands along the branches in order to get the leaves off.

"Hopefully it won't," she said finally.

Rick nodded. "That's answer enough." He put his hand up to his mouth and called to Ellen. "Come on down, dear, that's plenty."

With an agility which surprised Alice, Ellen slipped through the branches and slid down the tree's trunk.

Alice left the grove with the pair of them and then started her trek home. Ellen had known she was stealing. Ellen had covered for her. She owed the girl something.

But I have nothing to give her.

She tried to swallow her guilt, but it wouldn't go down.

I'll find her something.

Her stomach growled. She took out one of the leaves and sucked on it. The sour taste made her stomach even angrier. She looked down into the satchel at the handful of leaves. It wasn't much, but she could trade it for something, maybe devilwheat or a share of spider eggs if someone had any left.

Something.

Huxley had a good eye, maybe the best eye of all the Harpsborough hunters, but he was new—damn new—and that made Graham a little suspicious when he claimed to have found anything important.

"This had better not be like that healed over hound burrow you thought was a worm's hole," Graham warned.

"No, Graham, this is serious. Come on!"

If it's serious, then how come you're so bloody cheerful?

Graham shrugged his shoulders and motioned for his two other hunters to follow. They jogged after Huxley as the man made his way down a series of grey hellstone corridors. The rock's color deepened into a darker grey with a blue undertone while they ran.

After about ten more minutes, Huxley stopped. "Here."

"Where?" one of Graham's hunters asked.

Graham didn't know why the stone in front of him looked fishy, he just knew that it did. He'd learned to trust his instincts on such things. Huxley pushed on the stone wall, and it slid to the side like an old world screen door. Behind it was a small cubbyhole, maybe three feet high and three feet deep. A pile of string and the remains of some devilwheat lay there.

"Great, Huxley," Graham said, shaking his head. "Real great. Way to find someone's hideaway."

"I know, right!" Huxley said smiling. "I thought it wasn't anything special either, but if you get down in there, you'll see there's a slit by the floor. I think they were trying to slide food down it."

Graham shrugged. "Not interested, Huxley."

"And I wondered how they were going to get it out if they

were storing the food in there. So I tried to get around to see. Couldn't find a way though, so I thought I'd ask for your help."

"I'm not interested in busting someone's stash. That's their property unless they cede it to the Fore."

One of the other hunters frowned. "They might have been pulling up the devilwheat, instead of dropping it down." The hunter bent down into the cubbyhole. "Goes down at about a fifteen degree angle. Be pretty tough to get anything up, but it's possible. Might go down about ten feet. You know the Fore's about to change the tax rules. We might be able to catch somebody skimping on taxes. Could be a reward in it."

"Could be!" Huxley agreed.

"And would you blame someone for skimping on the new taxes?" Graham asked, looking each hunter in the eye. "With times like they are, and with how they're going to be getting, we've got a lot more important things to do than bust someone trying to get some food. This isn't the time for the Fore to be increasing taxes."

"But we're hungry too, sir—"

Graham raised his hand suddenly. "Wait."

His hunters quieted.

"Huxley, where are we?"

"Downstream from town, about a half mile from the Kingsriver."

Graham started shaking his head.

"What's up, boss?" Huxley asked.

"It couldn't be." Graham started jogging back towards Harpsborough.

The hunters fell in line. They jogged for about ten minutes before Graham recognized the area.

"Shit!" he shouted.

Huxley's eyes widened. "What, sir?"

Graham grimaced.

That little bitch.

"This is the passage that comes down from the Golden Door," he said.

The hunters looked amongst each other, bemused.

Huxley's face lit up with understanding. "You mean someone's been sending food to where the exiles go. To . . . to the Infidel Friend?"

"Huxley, you lead," Graham ordered. "Take us back to town, now. We've got to let Michael know this right away."

"But she's stuck in Harpsborough! She can't do no more harm!"

"No more than she already has," Graham said, "and God help us if that includes letting Cris back out of the Golden Door."

6

Arturus was shivering from the water's cold when Galen finally stopped them.

I hate this place.

Arturus peered down the tunnel where the river continued, but it was too dark for him to make anything out. He could hear the sound of rushing water, however, and it seemed like the river's speed picked up dramatically somewhere in there. Arturus and Aaron clung to the stone bank, keeping the raft still as they pulled themselves out of the water. The stone walls here were made of two foot wide bricks. Typical of the Carrion, the rock which made up those bricks was black and purple. Running through these stones were veins of ruby, however, which Arturus had never seen before. The ruby veins were slightly transparent and appeared to have flecks of other types of stone caught up in them. Galen stayed in the river the longest, helping the priestess up on the bank before getting out himself. They untied the ropes from the floating door and shouldered their packs.

Arturus watched as the door drifted away. It sped up as it neared the tunnel, drawn on by a quickening current.

"Just in time," Aaron mentioned, "rapids down that way."

Galen dropped some rope as he knelt to take stock of his Heckler and Koch. "Tie the priestess up."

The priestess spit out some water as Avery and Duncan took a hold of her.

Avery was particularly rough. "Sorry about tying up your ribs." He didn't sound very sorry.

I wish they'd take it easy on her. They might make her scream.

Arturus moved about, stretching his legs. Water poured out of the sewn up seams Galen had previously cut into the insteps of his boots.

"The meeting place for our guide is just ahead," Galen said. "We'll talk to him, see what he thinks about the priestess. Girl, it's best you stay behind right now."

"I say we kill her." Avery tied off another knot with malicious intent. "She's too big a liability."

"All I want is to live." Her voice was strained from the pain.

Avery shrugged, unmoved.

"We may not be able to take her," Galen said. "The guide has a hatred of her order."

Arturus checked his gun. It had gotten wet, certainly, but he thought it would probably fire.

"We'll be right back." Arturus told her.

She did not respond.

Galen led them away from the river and through an arch marked with an overlarge purple keystone.

Beyond it was a long passageway made of the same black and purple stones that were in the river chamber. The passageway wound haphazardly through the Carrion, turning blood red in color where it met with the ruby vein.

It opened up into a room so dark that Arturus couldn't see more than fifteen feet ahead. It was full of the gravel funeral mounds he had noticed elsewhere in the Carrion, but these were so old that each pile had nearly coalesced into a single boulder. Some had even melted halfway into the floor.

A shadow covered man stood in the middle of the room. The figure raised his hand.

Galen turned around, looking at Aaron. "Stay back."

Arturus couldn't help but agree with his order. This room may have been a meeting place, but it was also a hell of a place for an ambush.

Finally, we get to go home.

Galen entered the room. "We're here."

"Sir, I'm sorry," their guide's voice seemed shaky. "I didn't know."

"Know what?" Galen asked, sniffing the air. His shoulders tensed. "La'Ferve."

Galen turned quickly, dropping down into a ball. A muzzle

flash went off in the far corner of the room. The first bullet dropped their guide. More bullets followed. Arturus' father dove for cover, lead skipping all around him, some of it hitting him. Galen landed face first on the floor, then stayed there, motionless on the ground.

Arturus screamed and darted behind a funeral mound. Avery leapt down beside him while the other hunters ran back into the passageway. The room was filled with gunfire as Carrion soldiers popped up from behind the half coalesced rock piles. One was on the other side of the mound Arturus and Avery were using for cover. Arturus' bullet took him in the face. Arturus popped his head up to look for Galen. His father lay motionless on the stones. It seemed unlikely that, even considering the man's fine body armor, he could still be alive.

Arturus was filled with the sudden need to rush to his father's side. He began to stand up, but Avery grabbed his collar and forced him back down. Bullets cut through the air over their heads and waves of buckshot ricocheted around the chamber.

"Now's not the time to have a soul," Avery shouted over the gunfire.

The hunter fired a couple of rounds and then hunkered back down. He was bleeding from the shoulder and neck where some buckshot had hit him. Those wounds didn't seem bad, however. More bullets flew back over their heads as Aaron and the others responded.

The man who had shot his father did not bother to take cover. The bullets did nothing to hurt him.

La'Ferve. He has Icanitzu skin armor.

Arturus thought to shoot him in the head, but a grey, skin tight hood covered the man's face. The figure reloaded a Ruger pistol with a clip as he approached, stepping over Galen's fallen body. Galen was back up in a heartbeat, grabbing the arm with the Ruger.

Father!

Arturus wasn't sure how many bullets had struck Galen's protective armor, or if any had made their way through it. Even assuming the best, however, Galen had to be hurting badly.

La'Ferve spun quickly, throwing punches with his free hand. Galen wrapped up the man's gun arm completely and used it to generate a throw, dragging them both to the ground. La'Ferve rolled with it, coming back to his feet and bringing Galen, who still had the man's arm trapped, up with him. The Ruger pistol had come loose in the fall and it skittered across the room's stone floor.

The Carrion men came up from behind their mounds, firing buckshot. La'Ferve wouldn't be hurt by it, but Galen could be.

"Fire!" Arturus ordered.

He fired his last two bullets at the Carrion soldiers. Avery and Aaron were firing as well. The Carrion men dropped for cover.

La'Ferve was one of the few men Arturus had ever seen who was larger than his father, and the man used his extra weight to good effect. He powered Galen over to the side of the room, pressing him against the stone wall. Then the man reached up to try and gouge out Galen's eyes. Galen got a hand up, stopping La'Ferve's limb at the elbow.

"Galen!" Aaron shouted. "Bullets!"

I'm not the only one out of ammo.

"Avery!" Galen ordered, his voice strained. "Ready the AK."

"Last clip," Avery whispered as he shouldered his automatic rifle.

La'Ferve was throwing knees towards Galen's midsection even while his fingers reached for Galen's eyes. Galen let his blocking arm go slack for a second as he opened his mouth. He took a bite out of La'Ferve's pointer and middle fingers.

That's my dad!

La'Ferve shouted, and as he pulled his hand back, Galen pushed off of the wall, spinning away from his opponent before hurdling over the funeral mound towards the exit. Avery let loose, but La'Ferve did not care. Still firing, Avery retreated. Arturus and Galen ran quickly after him.

"This way," Arturus heard La'Ferve's order.

Arturus pulled out his pouch of silverlegs and scattered them behind him. They might not slow La'Ferve, but they'd slow his Carrion men.

Arturus chased after the hunters, sprinting down the winding passageway so quickly that he found himself running into the walls as he made the turns. He heard the yells of the Carrion soldiers echoing down the tunnel.

"Go around," La'Ferve's voice boomed.

Aaron and Duncan were running with noticeable limps. Arturus looked back and saw that La'Ferve was gaining ground.

Galen turned to face him. "Stay with me. He's outnumbered."

Arturus and the rest of the hunters gathered together.

La'Ferve's hulking figure slowed to a walk and then stopped, unwilling to face them all.

"Quickly," Galen said, eying the still La'Ferve, "it will not take long for his soldiers to get around."

"But where are we going?" Johnny asked.

Galen did not answer, but he and Aaron took the lead, running back into the chamber with the river. Arturus' father pulled them all into a huddle when they'd made it to the bank.

"Into the water," Galen ordered. "Hold your breath for a sixty count. Do it for six different intervals. Then stop and we'll try to gather back together."

Galen pulled out a knife and sawed at the priestess's bonds. She was free in a moment, and as soon as she was, Galen dragged her into the river. The hunters jumped in after, showering Arturus with water. Arturus was about to follow, but he stopped when he saw La'Ferve approaching through the corridor. The man was walking towards him without any sense of urgency.

I want to kill him.

La'Ferve had ruined his chance to get home. Ruined his chance to see Alice. Ruined how happy Rick would have been to see him and Galen again.

I am too weak to hurt that man.

"La'Ferve!" Arturus called.

"Yes, boy?"

Arturus pulled up his sleeve and showed La'Ferve the symbol carved into his shoulder. La'Ferve's eyes narrowed. Arturus winked and dove into the water. The current pulled him madly along as he began his first count.

One. Two. Three. Oh hell, I have to make it to sixty? Five. Six.

7

Dust covered Julian, sticking to his sweat. His young muscles were close to giving out, but that didn't matter. He swung his pick at the stone anyway. Anything less would draw attention. Attention meant pain.

I'd die fighting this, in the old world.

But this wasn't the old world, and there were things so much worse than slavery. They could shackle him back up to the granite slab. He didn't think he could survive another round of that. He'd probably die inside and get the stilling. They had ways of taking things here, ways that defied even the fundamental rules of Hell. Hell heals all wounds, the saying went, but Maab's women could make sure that didn't happen. When her priestesses took a finger or a hand or something even more important to a man, those things didn't grow back. Julian wasn't surprised by this power. His mother had talked about magic from time to time. He thought she'd been dumb, then. He thought it was stupid for anyone believe in something so mystical.

Obeah. Voodoo.

They had other magic as well. One among Maab's men could command corpses. They would do his bidding, carrying stones wherever the High Priestess Selena wished. And the hounds, the man called Gilgamesh could control them. At first Julian thought this had been done simply through training, but then he had seen them using potions to keep the things under control.

At least the hounds required potions. They could make Julian do things without any magic at all.

They called him a serf, but that was a lie.

They said he was not a slave because if he worked hard, he could become baptized. Julian knew better. Some were going to be baptized and others weren't. Some were going to spend their damnation doing this menial labor. He had heard about a false promise like this one in his sixth grade social studies class, right before he'd died in the old world.

Work hard for freedom, the Nazis had told their Jews.

Julian wasn't working hard because he wanted to be baptized. He was working hard because he didn't want to be hurt anymore.

Enough rubble had collected at his feet to justify him bending down to gather it. On certain days there were enough slaves to warrant the formation of separate crews whose sole purpose was to fill and carry off the wicker baskets. On those days he never had an excuse for a break, but on days like this he could catch a breather. He began shoveling the loose rubble into the wicker basket they'd assigned him. Around him, and along the dark, candlelit tunnel, the others kept picking. A priestess and her two soldiers walked by. She looked at him, and he feared her retribution. He had done nothing wrong, and gathering the rubble was certainly part of his job, but even so, he was relieved to see her move on without any comment.

Thank you, Lord.

He worked a bit slower now that she was gone but made plenty of noise so it sounded like he was being busy. The man next to him stopped to gather rubble as well. Julian made eye contact with him, but the other serf wouldn't keep it.

Julian looked to his left. This serf was called Bailey. Bailey also avoided his gaze. Julian felt the hair rise on the back of his neck. Something was wrong. He finished filling the wicker basket and lugged it back down the tunnel.

On the busier days, someone would take it all the way out of the mine, but right now he was expected just clear it from the work area. They might all be forced to move the rubble at the end of the day if he wasn't lucky. As he walked back down the corridor, a different priestess entered. She was about eleven years old, a Little Lady, and she had two soldiers flanking her.

Julian made sure not to look directly at her. He had learned from hard experience not to think of the Little Ladies as children, even if, like this one, they appeared to be three or four years younger than himself. Quickly so as to seem like a hard worker, he grabbed an empty wicker basket, hefted his pick, and walked back down the corridor. He got the uneasy feeling that she and her soldiers were following him. He knew he was just being paranoid. There was only one path down the tunnel. It wasn't like they were meaning to follow him.

They *were* matching his pace, however.

When he stopped, so did they. They watched him work for a while. Julian became increasingly nervous. He made sure to work harder than he usually did, and the rubble began to build up around his feet. Even so, he felt clumsy. Not all of his strikes were as measured as they normally were. His muscles began to burn in pain. Finally he'd knocked enough debris loose to justify filling another wicker basket.

"Stop," the Little Lady ordered as he bent down.

Julian began to straighten.

"No," she said, "you may remain low."

Julian's shaking legs gave out beneath him, and he fell to his knees.

"Do you pray?" she asked.

Every day. And you can't take that from me.

"No," Julian answered.

He looked around him. Someone must have heard him during the night. Someone must have snitched.

"Never?" she asked pleasantly.

Julian kept his eyes down at her feet, which he couldn't even see because of her black satin robe. "Never. Not anymore. Sometimes I talk to myself at night—"

Her tone didn't shift as she spoke, "I didn't ask you if you talked to yourself."

"Sorry, my lady."

Her robe shifted slightly. "I've felt a dark presence here. Felt the vile stench of that devil, Yahweh. You haven't been praying to him, have you?"

"No, my lady."

"You haven't?"

"Of course not, my lady."

The workers around him had all stopped. When Julian saw the expression on Bailey's face, he knew he was in some serious trouble.

"Deny Jesus," the Little Lady demanded.

Never!

"I deny him." Julian choked over the words.

"Say 'fuck Jesus Christ.'"

Julian set his jaw.

You've got to do this. You won't survive another three days on the slab. You've got to say this.

Tears formed in his eyes.

"Fuck . . ." Julian struggled to say the next words, but they wouldn't come. ". . . you."

He stared defiantly into the Little Lady's eyes. "Fuck you."

One of her soldiers slammed a shotgun into his face. Julian crumpled to the stones below. The soldiers dragged him to his feet.

Fuck you. You can't take this away from me. I won't let you.

Graham burst into Harpsborough with a purpose. His hunters fanned out around him. The villagers were settling down for the night, and a few of them had to hurry to get out of his way. Others followed after him, curious to see what was going on.

"Huxley," Graham ordered, "report to Michael. Don't let him ignore you or send you away. Tell him what you saw."

"Where are you going, sir?" Huxley asked.

"To find Molly."

Huxley left them and trotted towards the Fore, dodging through the villagers as he did so.

Graham turned to face the growing crowd. "Anyone seen Molly?"

"She's been in the river room, Graham," a helpful man said. "Been there well near an hour."

Graham nodded his thanks and hurried towards the river room passage, his two hunters in tow.

"Stay here," he ordered them. "Don't let anyone come down this way unless it's Mike. I don't care if they have to shit their pants, you got me?"

"Yes, sir."

Graham jogged down the corridor and stopped when he made it to the river room. He saw Molly sitting there, her feet dangling in the water.

"Molly," Graham said.

The girl took her feet out of the river and stood. Graham admired her form, watching intently as her breasts moved beneath her shirt.

No time for that Graham. This girl's been bad.

He approached her, coming within a couple of feet. He was close enough to hear her breathing over the rush of the water. She smelled of something.

Hungerleaf?

"We found your hiding spot in the wilds," Graham said.

Molly's blue eyes looked dead. She shrugged.

"We know you were funneling Cris food. We need to know what else you've done."

"Oh, Graham," Molly said, her face suddenly filled with sorrow. "I've always kind of liked you."

Graham felt his pulse increase. "Me?"

"You."

"Why?"

"You're sexy in your own way, particularly now that you're large and in charge. You never said you slept with me, either. All the other hunters said they did."

Said?

Graham thought they all pretty much had, but maybe he'd gotten her all wrong. He'd seen her cry very sincerely when he'd followed her before. Maybe she wasn't such a slut. Maybe she'd only been around a little bit before rumor did the rest. He surely hoped this was the case. Molly was a lot of woman, and she was a lot of woman in all the right places.

Wait a minute, this girl's been cavorting with an—

She cut his thoughts short when she stepped forward, her hands finding his shoulders.

Don't you do this, Graham. Don't kiss this hussy.

Her lips were slightly parted. He could tell her skin was flushed. Her blue eyes were nearly hidden by fully dilated pupils.

Maybe for a second. Then you can stop her, and promise you'll be with her only if she straightens up.

He thought of how jealous all the other hunters would be. He'd be the man who reformed the whore.

He tilted his head, closed his eyes, and waited.

Graham had never been kneed in the balls so hard in his entire life. Stars filled his vision. He didn't even remember dropping to the ground. His stomach began retching on its own, causing fresh waves of absolute agony to come crashing down around him. He sputtered for breath as he looked out across the stone floor through water blurred eyes. Molly was reaching for his weapon. He tried to straighten up, to get out of the fetal position he had found himself in, but that was impossible. Molly took his shotgun. She searched around in his pack, taking other things as well.

Her face suddenly filled his vision.

Fucking bitch!

"I really have always kind of liked you Graham," Molly's voice was sweet. "No lie. It's just unfortunate that you would be the one to have caught on to me."

He tried again to straighten and reached up to grab her. She overpowered him easily in his weakened state, batting his hands away. The pain quickly became too much for him, and he curled back up into a ball.

"Don't worry sweetie," Molly's voice came down on him from above. "Hell heals all wounds. They'll grow back."

He heard a splash of water, and just like that, Molly was gone.

Graham still couldn't stand by the time Michael arrived with Father Klein and Chelsea. He'd managed to crawl into a corner, however.

"What happened?" Michael demanded. "Where's she gone?"

"We found her hiding place," Graham managed, trying to focus his eyes. "We think she was in contact with Cris. We think she was feeding him."

"I know that," Michael sounded exasperated. "Where is she now?"

"In the river, wherever that goes."

Michael stepped back suddenly. "God damn. What the hell were you doing? Interrogating her without the Fore's permission?"

"Michael—" Klein began.

"I know. Sorry, Father."

Graham managed to sit up and lean back against the wall. "I'll be good in a minute. I'll lead a party to search for her. Where's this branch of the river go?"

"Nowhere," Michael said.

"What?"

"The ceiling is too low, Graham," Father Klein explained. "We've spent days going down it with ropes, holding our breath. There's no air in that tunnel."

"What?" Graham couldn't believe what he was hearing.

"She's dead Graham," Michael said. "The river goes nowhere. You let her die."

Fuck. I was just getting to like her too.

 — 8 —

Arturus understood why Galen ordered everyone to hold their breath for sixty second intervals. They were less likely to be spotted underwater, making it less likely for them to pick up any pursuit—whether from La'Ferve or the devils. It made sense, but the task simply wasn't possible.

The water pulled him along at terrific speeds, slamming him against stone banks and occasionally against the river's floor. Arturus did his best to keep his count going.

Thirty-one. Thirty-two. Thirty-three.

He struggled upward, fighting the pull, searching for air. He broke through to the surface and took a breath. That breath was interrupted as the current suddenly pulled him down. Water caught in his lungs. He was coughing beneath the river's surface and had to ignore his instinct to inhale. He worked his way upward again.

A rock wall hit him, knocking away what little breath he had left. Dazed, he could not figure out which direction was up. He hit another stone wall.

Not the wall, the floor.

He re-oriented himself and swam towards his new up. Wrong again. His chest was convulsing on its own. There were only a few directions left. He tried another, kicking off of the wall he'd just hit. His face broke the surface, and he was suddenly able to feel the air, but that was no relief. His lungs were on fire. He wanted to breathe more but all he could do was cough water out of his lungs.

Desperately, he tried to remember what count he was on.

Forty-five? Forty-six? Forty-seven. Forty-eight.
The river took him again.

Fifty-eight. Fifty-nine. Sixty.
The river had smoothed out after a small waterfall. Arturus' heart was pounding in his chest, and his vision was shaky. He wanted to take in deep breaths, but the pain was so severe, his need to cough so strong, that he could only manage to inhale shallowly. He struggled towards the bank, surprised at how heavy his limbs were. The room was huge, over a mile across, and it reminded him somewhat of the chamber that housed the Hungerleaf Grove back home. Further down along the river he saw Johnny.

Galen was near him in the beginning. Where's Galen?
His father had taken more than a few bullets. He could well be dead. The body armor could not have protected him against an entire clip.

Arturus grabbed hold of the bank and was about to cough when his eyes focused on Johnny. The man had a finger held up to his lips. Arturus let go of the bank and allowed himself drift towards the hunter, winning an internal battle between his need to cough and his need to stay silent. The chamber's ceiling was mostly natural, giving way in only a few places to brickwork laid out by Hell's architect. Huge veins of ruby ran along the ceiling, shining down onto the river with their red light. This had the unsettling effect of making the river look like it was a river of blood.

He caught onto the ledge beside Johnny. The hunter was terrified. He pointed at his own eyes, and then out across the chamber. Arturus looked, trying to see what had frightened Johnny so badly. He was expecting to see a pack of dyitzu, maybe some hounds, or even a group of Carrion soldiers. At worst, he feared there would be an Icanitzu. He wasn't prepared to see a Nephilim.

The urge to cough was now so bad that he could feel blood rushing to his face. His chest convulsed, but naked fear kept him quiet.

At such a distance it was difficult to judge how big the thing was. Certainly it was larger than a human. Arturus' best guess was that it was about fifteen feet tall. It was masculine in nature, with terrifically broad shoulders and long locks of dirty grey hair which obscured its face from view. The hair was the same color as its wings, which were folded behind its back. The dark grey wings gave it an air of authority, as if they were a cape. It walked as a man might, except with softer and more balanced steps.

Has anyone in Harpsborough ever seen one before? Maybe Klein?

Arturus helped Johnny slide into the water. Together they let the river take them into the next chamber.

Aaron, Avery and the priestess lay in the next room. Avery had no weapons on him at all, and Aaron, though he had his rifle, was missing his pack.

I have no pack or weapon either.

"Did you see that?" Avery whispered harshly.

Avery's eyes were wide with fear. His nostrils flared with his breathing. Arturus nodded as he helped Johnny to the bank. Aaron helped pull Johnny out of the water and then offered a hand to Arturus. Arturus let himself be dragged out of the river before finally being overcome by a fit of coughing. He coughed so hard and for so long that he almost blacked out. When he recovered, he noticed that he was sitting unnaturally close to the priestess, but he didn't have the energy to care.

Looking at her, she seemed unable to hurt anyone. She was curled into a ball, shivering with cold and in horrific agony. Arturus could tell that only fear kept her from screaming out.

Is she even on our side?

"Where's everybody?" Arturus asked.

"Galen's gone further down to see if we missed anyone," Aaron answered.

"Is he okay?" Arturus asked.

Avery nodded.

"I think his body armor took most of it," Aaron said. "He was bleeding a little, but he said a bullet didn't get him. He said some of his vest was ceramic, and that a few of the pieces got forced into his body."

Arturus swallowed deeply.

"Don't worry," Aaron said, "he'll be fine." Then he looked upstream towards the room where they'd seen the Nephilim. "As fine as any of us."

Arturus nearly leapt to his feet when he heard the water ripple at the far end of the room. Galen surfaced, coming out of the water with surprising energy. He still had his MP5 and his pack, though both had been thoroughly soaked.

Galen walked briskly up the stone bank. "No sign of Duncan."

"Jesus," Aaron whispered harshly.

"It could have been a lot worse," Galen said.

Arturus' father stopped next to the priestess. He knelt down beside her and put her head in his lap. He reached into his pack and pulled out a flask.

"What's that?" Avery asked.

Galen smiled. "Bloodwater."

He fed some of it to the priestess, who drank it gratefully. It made her cough, though, which made tears stream from her eyes and snot pour from her nose. Galen, being thoughtful, tossed the rest of the flask to Avery. He promptly drained it.

"Don't worry," Galen told the priestess, "the pain will recede quickly."

The priestess looked up at him, grimacing.

"Now, we just saw that Nephilim back there," Galen said to her softly while running a hand through her hair, "and for us to live, I need to know what's going on. What's happening to the Carrion, milady?"

Arturus was struck by how exquisitely beautiful she was. He found himself entranced by the sharp angles of her face. In Galen's arms, she seemed like only a little girl. Harmless. Completely incapable of the horrors he knew she must have inflicted upon her own people.

"I'm barely more than a Little Lady," she said, her voice shaky. "Maab doesn't tell me much. I do know that our western tribes have been coming back, seeking Maab's protection and asking for places to hide. We're not able to harvest a lot of the food caches that are farther out in that direction either. Maab's had some of her best architects come by to advise us. She's given some us and some of our neighbors serf labor to help shore up their defenses and better camouflage their hiding holes."

Avery snorted. "I don't know that we should trust a damn

thing this whore says."

"She speaks the truth," Galen said.

"When she says west, what way does she mean?" Aaron asked.

Galen frowned and looked up at the stone ceiling. "Assuming that this river is indeed running with the vein, downstream along this river is west. Upstream would be east. Harpsborough is to the east."

"Curse the Devil," Avery sputtered.

"We could consider ourselves lucky," Galen said, laying the priestess's head down gently upon the stone. "If whatever is building up out here gets too bad, Maab may be forced into action. She may try to migrate her people to the other side of the barrier."

"Let her," Avery said, "for all I care."

"How is that lucky?" Aaron asked.

"Lucky that Harpsborough may get a warning. It's doubtful Maab will want to find her own resources," Galen said. "More likely, she'll want to take yours. The Pole, Macon's Bend, Harpsborough, Kingsport, Tucumcari, they're all in danger. None of those settlements have enough men or firepower to resist her, but now you all may at least have warning."

Aaron nodded. "We've got to make it home."

"Are you up for a swim, priestess?" Galen asked.

"Yes. Can I tell you my name, sir?"

"You may."

"Kelly."

"Nice to meet you." Arturus said.

Avery gave him an angry glance.

"Sir, may I ask for a weapon?" Kelly sat up. "I will use it only as you direct."

Galen shook his head. "I have not even enough weapons for my own people, Kelly. You may ask again, though, when we get more rifles."

"The hell she'll get one!" Avery shouted.

"Shhh," Aaron warned.

Arturus tore his eyes away from the beautiful girl. "What about Duncan?"

No one answered.

 — 9 —

Rick stared thoughtlessly at his half-empty water cup until he was interrupted by the sound of heavy boots on the woodstone bridge outside his home.

Well that's certainly not Ellen.

Rick's right hand dropped to his holstered pistol as he stood. The gravel crunched under his soft footsteps as he made his way to the entrance of his home.

"Rick, you in there?" a deep scratchy voice called.

The voice was familiar.

Rick stepped out of his home, right hand ready at his hip.

A tall man, lanky, yet full of muscle, stood on the bridge. The man's posture was stooped, but not badly enough to be hunchbacked. His hair was dark brown, long and pulled into dreadlocks. Some of the dreadlocks were adorned with beads, others with what looked to be—or at least Rick hoped them to be—the bones of devils. The shirt he wore was so covered in the caked remains of dirt and sweat that Rick could not guess what its original color was. The sleeves had been torn off. The man's long arms were a mess of scarifications. Odd symbols, perhaps artistic, or maybe in the form of some superstitious totems of protection, were raised on his flesh. A bow, short and recurved, along with a quiver of arrows, was set across his back. At his belt was a tomahawk, made out of hellstone and tied together with what was probably devilgut.

The fellow smiled, an expression perhaps meant for reassurance, but the sight of the man's teeth, which were filed into sharp points, brought bile up into the back of Rick's throat. The man's pants were made of devil-hide which had been poorly scraped and probably improperly cured. Rick could smell the pants from here. Almost everything the man wore seemed to have been made from Hell itself, except for his shoes. Those shoes were black with red trim and were adorned with a Nike swoosh and a logo meant to represent Michael Jordan in flight.

"Hidalgo," Rick said. "I don't see much of you these days."

The man picked a huge flake of dried skin off of his scalp and looked at it. For a second, Rick was horrified by the thought that Hidalgo might eat it, but the man mercifully flicked it over the side of the bridge. The huge piece of dandruff fluttered like a snowflake into the Thames.

"Yes," the man's scratchy voice replied. "Since the Fore, they be claiming my portion of the Kingsriver for their peoples, I be hunting on the far side, way downriver of where you be."

"It wasn't right of them to move you," Rick said, sympathetically.

Hidalgo shrugged. "Me, I be not caring which way the wind be blowing. I be not liking to see them starving ladies. I like them fatter, no? So the Fore, they be getting my hunting grounds, and I be getting fatter ladies."

Rick laughed. "I see your point."

"I not be coming to banter, or even to be talking about thick-thighed women . . . though I be liking banter and thick-thighed women. I come to show you something. But if you want to see it, you must follow your friend, Hidalgo. Do you have the time?"

"Lead on, my friend."

Even if Rick had been blind, he was pretty sure he could have followed Hidalgo by smell alone. Why Hidalgo would wear such rank pants bothered him, though.

Oh. He wants to be found. There's so little to hunt, he's been using himself as bait.

Hidalgo stopped in a corridor, looking at the bricks, getting his bearings. Rick walked up next to him and got a solid whiff of the man's pants.

Well, no dyitzu is going to be able to miss him, that's for sure.

Rick was grateful when Hidalgo continued on. The man brought them across the Kingsriver at Michael's Crossing, which was about a half mile south of the Bordonelles. They continued on at a fast trot, occasionally coming close to some Carrion barriers. Then they met back up with the Kingsriver in a large chamber which Rick hadn't been in for about a decade. There was a small room off to the side of this one, and he remembered it having a waterfall. He could hear that waterfall now.

Hidalgo led him towards the sound of the rushing water.

It was as if that room had once been a single, perfectly smooth and cylindrical tunnel which had then been partially filled with earth. The ceiling itself, the top half of the cylinder, was supported by what appeared to be a series of arches running diagonally along the tunnel. As Rick studied it further, he guessed that the arches were actually a single support structure, and that if the floor were removed, he would be able to see it running in a spiral all the way down the tunnel. For a moment, Rick felt as if he were inside a giant slinky.

A small branch of the Kingsriver ran down the middle of the slinky tunnel for about a hundred feet or so. Hidalgo led him to where the waterfall began. The ceiling continued on, but the floor fell away. Here Rick could see that his guess about the arches actually being a single continuously spiraling stone buttress was correct. The river fell, perhaps fifty feet, as a thin waterfall to the ground below. The impact of the water had carved out a small pool into the rock before continuing on as a trickle that ran down the center of the tunnel. Lying there by that pool at the base of the cliff was a slain corpse.

Hidalgo began climbing down the cliff. "This way!" he shouted over the water.

Rick considered trying to slide down that supporting buttress, but thought better of it, and followed Hidalgo down the cliff.

Hidalgo leapt the last few feet, landing in a crouch next to the fallen body. Rick jumped as well, stumbling slightly as he landed. He checked to make sure he hadn't sprained his ankle, and when confident that it would support his weight, he turned his attention to the body.

Intuitively, he could tell that something was wrong. He tried to analyze the corpse to find out what that something might be.

It had been hit with two arrows. One of those wounds must have come earlier than the other. The first arrow was still imbedded in the body, but its back half had been broken off. The woodstone it was made out of had become badly rotten, probably from corpsedust. The second arrow seemed fresher, and it had not been broken. Not even the odd fletching—made out of toothpick-like wood slivers—was disturbed.

But there were more wounds than just these. The body's skull had been cracked open, probably after it had become a corpse, because otherwise, while the head was misshapen, some hematomas should have formed and remained, frozen by the thing's undeath.

He saw another wound, the exit wound of a bullet, which had come out through his chest. The bullet was probably what killed him originally. Also, the man's right foot, shinbone, and tibia were bare, completely devoid of flesh. The corpse must have been walking on a foot almost purely made of bone.

"Me, I be seeing the corpse, he worry you," Hidalgo said. "Rick, you be wiser than Graham and his hunters, they be not listening to my warning."

"You shot it twice?" Rick asked.

"Yes."

Rick suddenly inhaled. The face looked familiar. "Is this one of the Harpsborough people?"

Hidalgo cackled. "Good eye. Two of them, they found dead by Graham and his men. Them hunters, they be claiming those bodies shot each other, fighting for some stash. Them hunters, they be saying this why the Fore wants all caches official. It stop murder. Me, I think they be wrong. Me, I think that the Fore, it be filled with fat greedy bastards and skinny uptight bitches. But me, I be thinking them fools, too, because those two men did not kill each other."

Rick's eyes had not left the body. "Why do you say that?"

Hidalgo laughed loud enough to send echoes down the chamber. "You not able to tell, but before this body, it got up and started walking, both men be together. And both men, they be shot in the back."

That is unlikely.

"Murder is not so odd," Rick said. "Maybe the Fore suspected murder, but just didn't want to dig too deep."

"I be thinking this too . . . at first. And me, I be thinking that maybe Graham or one of his hunters be doing it. They hungry too, yes? But I don't think that anymore."

Rick shifted his focus to the corpse's foot.

Or maybe that's what killed him. A hound got his leg.

But there were no teeth marks on the bone like he would expect to see from a hound bite. There were some lines there, though, almost as if a knife had been used.

Hidalgo's voice became very serious. "I shot him twice, Rick. Once when I be hunting, and I be having no time to make sure he be dead. He been falling off of this cliff here."

"That's when he busted his head?"

"Yes. The man, he be distracting me from a dyitzu hunt, so I didn't be checking for him. When I be coming home, when I finish with the hunting, I be stopping back by. Sometimes a corpse, he be living after falling like that, you know. The corpse, he be living, because his body be not down here. Him, he be wandering somewhere down that tunnel. Today I thought I be double checking, and the corpse, he be wandering his way back here. I be shooting him again."

Rick pointed to the new arrow.

Hidalgo nodded, the beads and bones in his hair rattling together. "That's right."

"And?"

"When I be shooting him the first time, he be having two perfectly normal legs."

It took Rick a moment to understand what Hidalgo was getting at. Shocked, he looked up at the tall man.

Hidalgo's head was half obscured by the light of the tunnel around him. That great mane of dirty dreadlocks rattled again as the hermit shook his head. "That's right. Someone, they be cutting and eating off that leg meat *after* he be turning into a corpse."

 — 10 —

Copperfield moved quickly through Harpsborough, past the cold Kylie's Kiln and over to the side of the village that was the farthest from Father Klein's church. The Still was the only underground room in Harpsborough, save for Ben Staunten's Storeroom under the Fore.

The village was sleeping. Only the two guards by the entryway would be awake at this hour. He heard a nearby villager coughing in their sleep. Copperfield looked towards their hovel, but no one stirred.

Smoke seeped up through the cracks in the nearby hatchway, and he could feel the heat emanating from the stones here. It had been this smoke which let Copperfield know Davel Mancini was awake. Bending down, he rapped on the woodstone hatchway three times before waiting for an answer. He inspected his knuckle where he saw his knocking had torn loose a bit of skin. He bit it off and sucked the blood away. The taste reminded him of poorly distilled bloodwater.

"Who is it?" Mancini's distant voice echoed up from deep in the pit.

"Copperfield."

"Come on in."

The heat blasted him as he opened the hatchway. He was already sweating a little from his walk across the village, but the perspiration came pouring out of him as he descended the first few steps. After he closed the hatchway behind him, he found himself in complete darkness. He made his way down by touch alone.

The stone stairway was tight, even for a man of normal build, and in places Copperfield had to turn his padded frame sideways in order to squeeze through. As he approached the bottom, a light from the room beyond illuminated the stairway. The smoke swirled up to the ceiling, traveling over his head and back towards the village.

He suppressed a cough and entered the still. Inside, Mancini was feeding woodstone blocks—not unlike the kind that Copperfield himself made torches from—into the furnace. Above the furnace, Copperfield could see the reflected glow of the hot copper vats. The vats' tubing rose up to the top of the chamber before descending over Mancini's lowered head to a set of sealed receptacle barrels. Kylie's pottery vessels lined the walls, some filled with Mancini's brew and corked with woodstone, others open and empty.

"You're up late," Copperfield said.

"Early. I went to bed right after Michael did. Couldn't sleep, so I thought I'd get working on the bloodwater."

"You haven't been buying as much woodstone lately," Copperfield said, watching the man as he removed some more blocks from a chest.

"It's this new kind of brew I'm making. Doesn't require as much heat."

"No one's buying much woodstone these days. This may make me poor, Davel, but I love this new brew's taste. What's different about it anyway?"

Mancini bent over and fed the rest of the woodstone into the furnace. "Oh no. Trade secret, my friend."

"No doubt, no doubt. And I'll be damned if I let anything happen to you. Can't let a devil get between me and my booze."

"Nah, you'd just order a villager to save me."

Copperfield laughed. "True enough." Copperfield's eyes rose up to the jars of corpsedust that lined the uppermost shelves. "Hard to believe that when I drink your juice, I'm drinking little bits of those corpses."

"You're not," Mancini said. "If it makes you feel better, I have to clean the corpsedust out of the vats every now and again."

"Can you re-use it?"

"No."

"Then we're drinking some part of it, my friend. It's sinfruit, isn't it? You've added it to the bloodwater."

Mancini shook his head. "I've always done that. Sometimes, whenever we get a trader from the Pole, I'll add honey. But that's not the secret."

"You're a devious man, Mancini."

Copperfield looked for a place to sit down, but there were no chairs in the still. The heat and the smoke were making him lightheaded. "Did Mike take much of your brew, last night?"

"No, he only had a glass. Took Kylie to bed, though. Hard to sleep with a woman next to you, I always say."

Mancini closed the door to the furnace and stood up. The smoke around his head swirled with the motion.

"Kylie's a nice girl," Copperfield said. "Good head on her shoulders. Ugly though. Surprised he sleeps with her."

"Why shouldn't he?" Mancini asked. "He's slept with all the pretty ones. He's got to pick between ugly and a villager."

"I'd go villager. Aaron had the right idea, trying to chase down Alice."

"Michael likes powerful women."

"Bitches, you mean."

"Them too," Mancini nodded, staring at the flames through the furnace's grate. "Now did you really come here to talk about women and wine?"

"The villagers are starving. My own miners have started doing underhanded deals. There's rumors of caches being found by hunters, far out caches, that nobody is reporting. Before Michael . . ." Copperfield stopped to cough up some of the smoke he'd been breathing. "The villagers want change, Davel. And what do we tell them? The same old shit everyone else has been spilling about how everyone needs to have a goal. I couldn't give a rat's ass. I'll shovel those lies myself if someone asks me, but I'm not giving up what I have. I spent three years of my damnation running around the wilds. Now I've got villagers to mine my woodstone for me. I'm not going back there. The villagers are going to rise up, Davel. They are. They're going to come knocking on the Fore's door curtain and ask us for some food. And you know what? Michael's going to give it to them. Think about it. Under Charlie, opening the stores wouldn't have even been an option."

"Those are dangerous words," Mancini said, a smile on his lips.

"You're a cat, Davel. Always landing on your feet. You're the guy who whispers into the ears of the First Citizen, no matter who he is. The bloodwater you make doesn't do anything useful, but people will starve to get it. No matter what happens, Davel, you'll be okay . . . even if you were the one to make the revolution happen."

"And you too, Copperfield. You'd be fine if the Fore fell. With your woodstone miners and torch makers," Mancini smiled harder. "Or would you, now that you've taught others how to make them for you? What if they get greedy, and want more than the devilwheat you pay them? Why, without the hunters backing your claim, they could just make the torches all on their own."

Copperfield gave him a dismal look.

"You should be careful who you trust with your secrets," Mancini went on. "I mean, look at me. I haven't shown anybody the first thing about how to do what I do. You should make sure that whoever you give information to is a trusted ally. Someone you can stick with through thick and thin. Someone who will support you, even if the First Citizen happens to change. But it would be a dangerous thing to go against Mike. Anyone doing it would likely be killed."

Copperfield nodded. "I imagine they'd need some powerful motivation, if they were a Citizen.

"They would indeed."

"Of course, Staunten would almost certainly die in a revolution." Copperfield said.

Mancini turned towards him and raised an eyebrow. "Why would you say that?"

"Oh, he's the keeper of the stores. The key is in his room. I'm sure the villagers would storm it first. Break down his door. It'd be a shame. But then some of the things that were Staunten's storeroom would have to be redistributed. Even what's in those black barrels."

Mancini walked across the chamber, displacing the smoke on the ceiling as he did so. He stopped at the end of a condensing tube. "Could you check that quicksilver over there by the furnace? Can you tell me what mark it's on?"

Copperfield eyed him warily, but walked over to the quicksilver. It was a thermometer, and the liquid metal had risen past two hash marks.

"As I got better at the brewing," Mancini continued, "I realized that one of my marks was wrong. For the brew to be just right, the heat should run between the second two."

"That's the secret then?"

"I suppose I better be careful now. If I keep telling you things like that, you'd be able to brew your own."

"Yeah," Copperfield said, "if I wanted, I could steal away your business. I guess you'll just have to trust me."

"Through thick and thin."

Copperfield smiled. "No matter *who* happens to be the First Citizen."

— 11 —

"We do need to rest," Aaron said. "Galen, I know you want to figure out what's happening to the Carrion, but we may want to go ahead and try to get home. As hopeless as that journey might be, we're not going to last long out here."

"You'll not make it back like this," the priestess said.

Kelly's her name.

"Sadly she's right," Galen said. "We need rest and munitions."

"There's no place in the Carrion that will afford you that," Kelly said.

"Well, look who's all Miss-Doom-and-Gloom." Johnny Huang said.

The priestess raised her delicate jaw at him. "*Unless* you were to find the favor of one of Maab's priestesses. I could take you to such a place and negotiate on your behalf."

"Fuck," Aaron said, and dropped into a squat.

Absentmindedly, the Lead Hunter began to rub the back of his head. River water flicked off of his hair as he did so.

"Is it worth it?" asked Avery. "Would it be better to join them than die? Even after everything Arturus said about what they do to the slaves?"

"You would be made slaves." The priestess began to wring out her hair, angling her body and neck oddly in a way that kept her midsection from moving much as she did so. "You'd be forced to renounce either your religion or you genitals. But it's not hopeless. If you work hard, you can become baptized. Become a soldier. If a priestess takes a liking to you, you can even become her consort."

Aaron swallowed and looked at Galen. "Tell me there's another way."

Galen frowned. "There is. One other way."

Kelly's eyes narrowed.

"Will we like it?" Aaron asked.

"It isn't without its own risks. We can beg succor from Calimay."

Kelly sucked air in through her teeth. She must have done it hard enough to hurt her ribs because she bent over slightly, wincing.

Aaron stood back up. "Calimay?"

"One of Maab's former priestesses." Galen opened his pack and held it at an angle, letting it drain. "Just because she's turned against Maab doesn't mean that she'll be sympathetic to us. We're also toting a lot of baggage. She may or may not take kindly to us carrying around a priestess. She may or may not be happy with Turi's marked up shoulder."

Aaron looked towards the single exit. "Better than being a slave, right?"

"If we're lucky," Galen said. "She may still carry on the institution. But she's not one of Maab's, so that gives her some room to have changed for the better."

"That seems to be the best solution. Do you know where she is, Galen?"

Galen shook his head and looked towards Kelly.

She pursed her lips for second, thinking. "I don't know exactly where she is. But I know about where. As a Little Lady, I visited the place they say she's taken up hiding."

"Where?" Galen asked.

"Near the Asphodel Fields. East of Nephysis and his corpse eaters."

Galen grimaced. "Aaron, you may wish to reconsider."

"Why?" Johnny asked. "Who's Nephysis?"

Kelly tied her hair up into itself, wincing in pain as she pulled it out into a ponytail. "Maab's Necromancer."

"You believe in magic, huh?" Aaron asked sarcastically.

Kelly nodded.

"There is no need for magic to affect a corpse," Galen said. "And where they are thickest, the dyitzu may be lightest. I know a quick way to get there. Hopefully we can be discovered by one of Calimay's soldiers without shedding any blood."

"Can you get us there safely?" Aaron asked.

"Yes," Galen said. "I think so, though I've never seen any place as thick with devils as the Carrion is now."

Aaron stood. "Then let's try it."

Arturus' father walked towards the exit. They followed.

Galen took the lead, his Heckler and Koch held at the ready. Johnny Huang came next, Galen's pistol held before him. Arturus and Avery took up the center. They had no weapons. Arturus had lost everything except his clothes and his razor. He kept the razor in his right hand, not because he thought he could use it to save himself from the devils, but because it was all he had.

Aaron took up the back, carrying his rifle. "Just so you know, I've only got two bullets left."

This is bad.

They left the ruby veined area and started down another path. The arches here had white marble keystones as opposed to the Carrion's more typical violet ones. Unlike the portions of the Carrion Arturus had seen earlier, the rock varied dramatically—changing from granite, to sandstone, to black and purple hellstone—but the architecture remained consistent.

The hunters were moving as quietly as they could, but everyone was walking with a limp—except for Galen. Even so, Arturus was able to make out echoes of dyitzu claws, clicking against the stone.

He thought seriously about their chances of making it home . . . and about what would happen if they got into a fight while he was armed with only a razor. He could hold them off for a while, until they backed him into a corner. His friends would be dying around him. Eventually, the devils would tear him down, too.

We're not going to make it. Father, why did you bring me here?

 — 12 —

Julian had no way to measure how long he'd been lying there because no one had come to feed him. Anticipation of the insidious things they'd do to his soul, mind and body was driving him mad. He almost wanted them to come—almost.

The door opened.

Light shined into his prison. He tried to stand up, but hunger had taken his strength. Three Carrion soldiers entered. They ripped off his clothes, tearing them like dry paper. Two held him down while the third pulled on his masculinity and tied a string around it. His cock was a black wrinkled worm, struggling to make itself as small as possible. He could feel his testicles trying to withdraw, but they couldn't because of the knot the soldier had made. The pain hit him so hard he vomited. The retching contracted his stomach muscles, pulling his testicles back into the string, which only caused more pain.

His manhood hadn't had time to fully heal from the mutilation it had received during his time on the slab. In the old world, he knew, the damage would have been so severe that he would never have been able to heal. He would've had useless sacks of pulped flesh between his legs. In Hell, they had the chance take that from him all over again.

They dragged him to his feet. He wretched once more, feeling the pull again on his testicles. Julian's world went dark.

Rick got an uneasy feeling as he approached the Harpsborough guards. They seemed a little too nervous. Even when Rick was standing before them, they didn't pay him much attention. They kept looking over their shoulders as if they expected something to be happening back in town.

"Everything alright?" Rick asked them warily.

"Yeah," one said.

"I'm just here to trade."

"Sure, sure," said the other, "of course you are. Come on through."

Rick entered. He was surprised by how many people were in the village. Since their rations of spider eggs had run out, the town had been mostly empty. With Julian's food supply gone, and with the hunters unable to find any devils, the villagers had been forced to wander the wilds in hopes of finding food. But now there were almost as many people lying amidst the stone hovels as there were just after Michael had brought back the giant spider.

Except this time things were different. This time there was no vibrant hum of conversation or feeling of vitality amongst the Harpsborough people.

About a dozen were sitting on the church steps. A few dozen more were lined up along one of the Fore's walls—one that didn't have the still man. Martin, the hunter, was the only one on that side.

They all seemed dejected, morose . . . or something a little different—as if they had the stilling themselves.

God, these people are starving.

Rick realized that he was the only person standing in the village. He could see the Fore's second story balcony. Two Citizens sat there, laughing and eating. Their joyous conversation seemed callous when compared to what was happening on the village floor. The villagers wouldn't take that forever.

The villagers began to rise, one after another. They started heading for Rick.

Rick felt the hair standing up on the back of his neck. They moved slowly, almost like corpses.

One held out his hand. "Can you trade me some food?" he asked.

Rick couldn't remember his name.

"I'll give you anything," the man continued. "I don't have anything now. But the next thing I find. I promise. No matter what it is—"

He was cut off by someone else. "I'll give you my shoes."

"Do you have anything to spare?" Another asked.

They were upon him now. Some were grabbing him fiercely.

"What right have you to refuse us?" One blond headed man shouted. "Can't you see we're hungry?"

Rick tried to shake himself loose, but they clung to him, their voices a chorus in his ears. He struggled more violently, his shoulder colliding with someone as he pushed them away. As soon as he was free, he retreated, putting his back against the uneven Harpsborough cave wall. Slowly, so that all could see, he let his hand drop down to the pistol he kept at his side. Then he let his pack slide down off of his left shoulder until it fell to his feet.

The laughter in the Fore had stopped. The Citizens were standing. More were gathering with them on the balcony.

"You shouldn't have done that, Rick," the blond haired man said.

"Tell him, Constance."

Constance. I remember him. Helped me rebuild the Carrion wall.

"I didn't mean to hurt anyone," Rick said, "but you've got to give a man his space. Especially a hermit like me."

"If you want space then you should ask for it," Constance replied.

He's desperate. I wish I could feed him.

"I behaved badly," Rick said. "Forgive me. Let me have my space now."

"You punched Aleck here in the face!" Constance pointed to his friend whose nose was indeed a little red. "You should give him something for what you did to him."

The crowd murmured its agreement.

"I had not realized it had gotten so bad here so quickly," Rick said. "Just the other day I mourned with you as we buried our friends behind a wall of stone. Buried them in the Carrion."

A gunshot went off. For a second Rick thought he might have been shot, and dropped to one knee. He was about to return fire—but everyone else had frozen still.

"You don't think it's been hard for him too?" Martin's voice boomed. "He's lost two good hunters of his own, Galen and Turi, and taken in a new mouth to feed. And he's done that in these hard times."

Constance sneered. "But the Fore's allotted him too much. He's got the entire Hungerleaf Grove, plus some devilwheat and sinfruit. Each cache is more than anything we have."

"You say he's got the grove," Martin said, "but you know we've all picked through it. There's hardly a leaf left there at all. Those trees have been picked so clean they might up and die! Let the man breathe, for God's sake."

The two guards had moved to join Martin. Constance didn't look intimidated, but those around him did. Rick knew those hunters were outnumbered, but they were of a different breed than the villagers. The villagers might have to fight once in a while, when they couldn't run, but the hunters didn't go out into the wilds looking to run—they went out to kill. In a game of chicken, the hunters were bound to win.

"We've got you outgunned, Martin."

"Don't be silly, Constance," Aleck said, grabbing Constance by one shoulder. "He just hit me on accident. I deserved it, too. It was with his shoulder, not his fist. We don't want to fight just so we can touch the guy."

Constance shook him off but cooled down soon after. "Sorry."

When he left, the other villagers did as well. Except for Alice, who came running up to Rick.

I can't give you food, Alice. That'll bring them right back. Damn girl, I thought you had more sense than this.

"I'm not—" Rick began.

Alice held something out to him.

It was a Dreamcatcher, not unlike the one that hung over her own hovel's door. She'd smoothed off the top of one of Kylie's wider pots to form the ring. Yarn was strung inside it, forming a net that looked almost like a spider's web. Caught within those strands were stones—some jade and others tiger eye.

"Here," Alice said. "It's for Ellen. For the hungerleaves."

Rick nodded, and then wrapped her up in a hug.

I misjudged you, girl. I'm sorry I ever told Turi to stay away from you.

Julian awoke, his legs spread into a split. He wasn't that

flexible, they had just ripped his groin muscles. There was a stone block between his legs marked with a slight indention. His half ruined manhood rested in that indention. It looked like such a small and pathetic thing, tied up there on the cold stone.

A Little Lady stood before him. In her right hand she held a Bible. An honest-to-God Christian Bible. In her left she held a rock. The edge of the rock had been sharpened into a bladed edge. It looked like an axe, but rougher, and without a handle.

She placed both items down. He felt the vibrations of the sharp rock settling on the stone in his balls.

"You know what happens to lambs, don't you?" Her voice was soft, sweet.

It was a young girl's voice. He might have found it beautiful had she not been on the verge of gelding him.

"I asked you if you knew what happens to lambs." Her voice was still sweet. "Your participation is required."

Julian nodded.

"Now we don't want to take your penis away from you, Julian. We really don't. That's why I'm here. I'm showing you the error of your ways. Now it's okay to disagree with me, or question me on some points. You may even be stubborn, to an extent. But I warn you, don't let emotions take over. We find that many, after hearing arguments that are true, fail to see that truth. Normally, you'd get angry and keep to your side. Then you'd cool down after a few days, admit you were wrong, and move on. You don't have time for that here." She placed her hand on the rock and twirled it. "So you need to watch yourself and your feelings, or by the time you find out I'm right, you won't be a man."

He could lie. He could pretend. He could tell her he denied Jesus but still keep the Lord in his heart. That was all he had to do.

Remember, once you've accepted Jesus, you can't deny him, or he's gone forever.

"What was Satan's name?" she asked, holding up the Bible, "in this?"

"Satan's name. Satan?"

"His real name," she clarified.

"The Enemy? Lucifer?"

"Lucifer! Good. What does that name mean?"

I know this. Someone told me long ago.

But he couldn't remember it, so he shook his head.

"Lightbringer," she said.

That's right. That's what Lucifer means. That's what he was before he fell.

"Do you love Jesus?" she asked.

"No," Julian managed.

"Do you know what happens to liars?"

Julian shook his head.

The Little Lady reached out her hand. The black robe's sleeve pulled back a bit as she stretched out her arm, revealing her delicate white wrist. Her fingernails were carefully manicured, trimmed neatly. Her fist looked alabaster as it formed over his black genitals. She dropped that fist downward.

He lost consciousness.

Julian awakened to see vomit all over his stomach. Tears of pain were still in his eyes, but he couldn't move his bound hands to wipe them away. The Little Lady was smiling at him.

"You threw up some on the Bible," she said.

I'm sorry. Jesus, I'm sorry.

Her laugh echoed in the small chamber "Are you ready to begin?"

He nodded his head.

Don't give up too easily. Resist a little. Otherwise she won't believe that you've let go of Jesus.

She walked around the table, untied his wrists, and handed him the Bible. "Did Jesus die for you?"

"Yes."

She walked back to the far side of the stone table and sat down. "Oh? Then why are you in Hell?"

"I guess he didn't die for me. But he died for people I love."

You can't deny him. You'll lose him forever.

"I think you're wrong," the Little Lady said. "This may surprise you, but I think Jesus did, in some way, die for your sins. I think you probably followed him well, or at least his teachings about Yahweh. Did you know that your God's name is Yahweh?"

"Yes."

"Good. That shows some promise. He has another name, a

secret name, which I will teach you as we go. But he didn't like that name, Julian. Did you know that?"

"No."

"Why do you think Yahweh wouldn't want people to say his real name?"

"I don't know."

Julian looked at his ankles. They had been chained down. He wished they hadn't been so that he could stand up and kill the Little Lady. So he could bash her head against the wall.

She smiled. "You hate me, don't you?"

"No."

She sucked air in through her teeth. "Don't lie."

She formed her alabaster fist again. This time he wasn't lucky enough to lose consciousness. He began to sob in pain, cringing with each heave as it pulled on his testicles.

"I'm sorry," she said, "I truly am. And I understand that you hate me, but really, I'm doing you a favor. As painful as this is, forcing you to face the truth here will save your masculinity. Understand? I want to help you save your manhood. Maybe I'm doing it because I like you. Maybe I want you to be my lieutenant when I grow up. Or maybe it's just altruism. But in any case, you have to realize that I'm arguing to save you. Do you understand? You know when this stone cuts off your dick, it stays cut?"

Julian nodded, gasping for breath.

She pulled back the sleeves of her satin robe to her elbows as if she was getting ready to start working. Her blonde hair bunched up behind her as it flowed into the hood of her robe.

Best to say as little as possible.

"Now, do you hate me?"

"Yes," he answered.

"Good. You are forced to tell the truth, because I can tell if you're lying and will break your stones. And likewise, you should know that I am bound to tell the truth by Mithras, the holy representative of the great God of Light, Ahuramazda. Understand?"

He nodded again.

"What is the name of the God of Light?" she asked.

"Ahura . . ." he couldn't remember the rest of the name.

"Mazda," she finished for him. "Ahuramazda. Good," she

smiled. "And the God of Darkness, Deceit and Lies?"

"Ahriman." Julian remembered that one.

She smiled.

"How many of the Epistles of Paul were written by Paul?" she asked suddenly.

"I . . . I don't know. All of them?"

"How many are there?"

"I don't know."

"The New Testament has fourteen such letters," she answered. "Did you know that your contemporary scholars consider only seven of them to be truly Paul's? One is even left anonymous in the text. Three are outright forgeries, and three others are thought likely to be forgeries. Did you know that?"

She's lying.

"No."

"You went to church. You went to Sunday school. No one ever told you this? They just left it in the Bible, knowing them to be lies? Never thought to tell you?"

"No. That can't be true."

Of course she's lying.

But it didn't feel like a lie. It felt like she was telling the truth.

She pointed to the Bible. "Did you know this book claims you can be bitten by snakes and survive the venom?"

"That's a metaphor," he answered.

She shook her head. "Not even that. Another forgery. In the earliest versions of Mark, that text doesn't appear. It only shows up in versions written down almost a century after the text was first penned. That means Mark, whoever *he* was, didn't write it. Never told you about that one either, I'm guessing?"

She can't be telling the truth.

"'Let he who has not sinned cast the first stone.' Did Jesus say that?"

Of course he did!

"Another forgery. That one is really bad, showing up first in the 10th century. Of course, that one's kind of obvious. By the end of the scene it's just Jesus and a girl, so I'm not sure who was supposed to have been giving an unbiased account of the story."

"Someone would have told me about these things."

"I'd like to think they would have. But your God is a God of lies, and his priests are liars too. They knew, believe me, they knew that much of this book was a forgery. They were even taught that in seminary . . . but they didn't tell you. Even if you're questioning the text's validity, they won't bring up the forged nature of the Bible unless you do. In the old world, they'd actually give sermons on stories they knew were forgeries. They wouldn't bat a lash. Most of them didn't believe everything they preached, either. They'd have to make compromises because they were being paid by one denomination or another. I mean, can you believe it? They all knew! And none of them told you."

The pain in his groin muscles faded away. He felt heat on his cheeks. If he could just get his hands on her. He threw the Bible at her as hard as he could, but the motion brought so much pain to his manhood that he lost his vision for a moment. He didn't think he had even hit her.

"Careful," she said. "Remember I'm here to save your masculinity."

I have to listen. But I can't. I won't. I won't deny Christ.

"Of course, it is to be expected that the book is full of forgeries. Oh, and it gets much worse than that. The story of Jesus' birth? That's taken right out of the Avesta of Zoroastrianism. Of course the story is a rip off. I mean, can you imagine anyone running a census where you had to travel to your home town to be counted? No one's that inefficient, let alone the Romans. And the whole scene, it turns out it's entirely unnecessary. You don't need it to fulfill the Old Testament prophecies. You really don't. You don't even need the two contradictory versions of half-baked genealogies to uselessly prove that David was related to Joseph, who incidentally, is not thought to be the father of Jesus. You know why?"

Julian shook his head.

"Because the Hebrew word meaning young girl was translated into a Greek word meaning virgin. Now pay attention. Remember, your cock is on the line. But there is some truth to these testaments. Jesus was a person, and he serves Yahweh, a very real God. I want you to open this Bible in the place I've saved for you. I want to show you the truth." She handed him back the vomit splattered book. "Open it."

Julian obeyed.

"Now read."

Julian obeyed.

"Do you know who Cyrus the Great was?"

"No."

"He was a Persian. A conqueror of Judea. In this book, he speaks with the voice of God. A foreign man of the Persian Empire. The Jews said he spoke with the words of their God. *Their* God. Do you know why?"

That did seem odd. Julian knew the Persians weren't Jews. Why the hell would their King, or emperor or whatever, be Jewish? But he was reading this, right there in the texts.

"Cyrus was Zoroastrian, like me. At one time the Jews were too. They worshiped the same God. But Yahweh got his hands on your holy book. He corrupted it. And you can tell, too. Even older than the Jews were the Zoroastrians. They believed, we believe, in two Gods. One of good, one of evil. One of Light, one of Dark. What's the God of Light called?"

"Ahuramazda."

"And the God of Darkness?"

"Ahriman," Julian said, putting the Bible down and pointing to it. "Okay. I understand. It's all bullshit."

"Now listen!" she shouted. "And understand!"

She leaned forward, her light eyed gaze a torrent of fearless emotion. He tried to recoil, but there was no escaping her.

She smiled as she began to verbally devour him. "What states in old world America were the most Christian?"

"I don't know." Julian's balls hurt so badly he couldn't think.

"What states?"

"Maybe Alabama? Arkansas? Mississippi?"

"Good boy, those are some of them. Which states had the most poor? Which states had the most homicides? Which states had the most abortions? Which states had the lowest standard of living?"

Intuitively, he knew the answers.

No!

"What states?"

"The same ones." Julian answered.

"What countries are the most Christian?"

"I don't know!"

"Which?"

"The ones in Africa, and South America?"

"Close again. Which are the worst off?"

No. It can't be.

"Which ones?"

"The same ones," Julian said.

"Did Christians in the United States of America go to jail at higher rates or lower rates than non-Christians?"

"I don't know."

"Which?" she demanded. "You know the answer."

"Higher," Julian hoped this was a lie, but it felt like truth.

"Did Christians in the United States commit more murders or less than non-Christians?"

"More."

"Why, if that God is good, are all who follow him cursed? What is the name of the Devil?"

"Satan."

"WHAT IS THE DEVIL'S REAL NAME?"

"Lucifer."

"WHAT DOES LUCIFER MEAN?"

"Lightbringer."

"SAY IT AGAIN!"

"Lightbringer!"

"What is the name of the God of Light?"

"Ahuramazda."

"What is the name of the God of Darkness?"

"Ahriman."

"What is Yahweh's real name?"

"I don't know," Julian said, tears coming to his eyes, but he knew the answer.

She did not relent. "Why are there so many Christians in Hell, Julian?"

"I don't know."

"Why? All of us here were Christians, before Maab saved us. Everybody you knew in Harpsborough was a Christian, weren't they?"

"No. That's not true." Julian shook his head, trying to find some way to deny the words she was saying.

"What is Yahweh's real name?"

"No! You're lying to me."

"I can't lie, you know that. Everything I tell you I believe to be true. What's Yahweh's real name? He claimed it was a sin even to say it, to pronounce it. He did his best to keep it secret, but now you know what it is . . . *say it!*"

Don't make me say it. Don't make me say it.

"*What was it?*"

Julian felt the pressure of her will bearing down upon him. He tried to believe that she was lying to him, that all of her talk about the forgeries and the lies of his fellow Christians, past and present, was a deception. Surely his own priests would not have hid this information from him. If they were to have done this, to have so misled so many people about so many things that were so important, they *must* have been evil. They *must* be considered liars. Not priests. Or if they were priests, then they were dark priests. Priests of . . .

"*Say it!*"

"No!"

"*Say it now! What is Yahweh's real name?*"

"Ahriman." Tears were running down Julian's face. "Ahriman is Yahweh's name." Making the admission felt the same as receiving a blow. "I've been tricked by the Devil, the real Devil, by the God of Darkness. Ahuramazda is the God of Light. He is the Lightbringer."

The priestess was exultant, caught in the throes of religious ecstasy. Her voice reached a fever and power that the more reserved Klein could never have hoped to match. "That's why you're here Julian. That's why you're in Hell. Not because you did something wrong, but because you put your heart and faith in Jesus Christ, the messiah of Ahriman, God of all that is evil and wrong. That's why the countries which serve Jesus are the most stricken by poverty and crime. That's why his priests are so full of lies and deceit. That's why you're here. You did make it to the afterlife you prayed for, it just turns out you were following the wrong God."

Julian's eyes were wide. "I didn't know. How could I have known?"

"But it's not over yet. This place is bad, but if you follow Maab, Mithras will save you. He's being born of the rock even now. He's going to come and lead all of our mighty hosts out of Hell and into the Land of Light where we belong. It is NOT too late, child. It is not too late. Repent! Give up your sins. Give them away. Say it with me now. Say it. Say 'fuck Jesus Christ.'"

It all made so much sense. God was the devil. Julian wasn't in Hell because he had been a bad person. He had been tricked. They had fooled him, taken him in. And of course it was a trick. His own people, his enslaved ancestors, must have known the truth so long ago. His people, ripped as they were from their native land by the white devils who were worshiping the God of darkness, being told that an all merciful and loving God would somehow condone slavery and order them to serve their masters. And isn't that Bible the Bible one would expect it to be if it were written by an evil God? This God who ordered genocides and the stoning of children. Who would slay His own Son? Of course God was the Devil. They had all been tricked. All those hundreds of years, wasted.

He shouted his heart out. "Fuck Jesus Christ!"

But hadn't Dr. Martin Luther King Jr. been Christian? Hadn't he followed in the words of the Lord? Hadn't he led his people to freedom by quoting from that book: "Let my people go!" No. He had to think this through logically. He couldn't get blinded by emotion. She was going to cut off his dick. She could tell if he was lying. Even if he was lying to himself. He couldn't afford to not be clear headed. No white Priest ever preached for his people's freedom. And A. Phillip Randolph, he didn't believe in any God. He was the one who led the march on Washington.

Of course they would let his people free *after* they had accepted the dark messiah.

And it was no wonder the Anti-Christ never came. Christ was the Anti-Christ. Mithras was the true savior, and he had already come. It was Christ who was the copycat. Christ who was the servant of the Devil, the servant of Ahriman.

"Again!" the Little Lady screeched, her voice in pitched ecstasy, "Deny evil. Say it again.

"*Fuck Jesus Christ!*" he shouted it so hard that he hurt his own balls, but he didn't care anymore.

The priestess had her hands raised into the air. "Oh Mithras, take this child into your bosom. He has rejected Ahriman. He is coming home. Again! Again! Say it again!"

The words built up behind his throat. The burning in his balls and groin muscles disappeared. He could say it. He could deny Christ. Jesus had turned his back on him. He didn't deserve to be in Hell. He'd died young. That time he'd shoplifted from the neighborhood Seven Eleven didn't count. He was just a boy.

Tears welled up in his eyes as he tried to find his voice. He searched his memory for the devilish workings of the church. For the horrors they had committed upon his people. For all the HIV they had helped spread. The poverty. The genocides. The slavery. The crusades. If he could just feel those offences, he could deny Jesus again. He could shout those words again. He could. He knew he could.

He tried to think of these things, but he could not. Instead all he could think of was his mother's white hat. The one with the pearls and the lace net which reached down around her hair. The one she always wore to church. Of his sisters as they fought while they got into the car. Of the dirt and gravel parking lot they would walk across. Of how the dust would settle on his polished shoes. Of the soft feel of the silky white gloves his mother wore while she held his hand and walked with him towards the loving house of God. Of the sweat that beaded up on her forehead in the humid summer morning.

As they'd approached, the people inside were already singing. His family was late this time, the time he remembered best, and the music was pouring out, rising with the mirage of heat waves from the rocks of the parking lot and up, up, up, into the heavens.

All he could remember was its joy. All he could remember was the ecstasy of prayer as he raised his hands to the rafters, knowing that there, beyond that roof, was a Father that loved him in the way he deserved to be loved. Was a Father that was willing to give His life for him. A Father that would literally withstand torture and mutilation to make sure that he was okay. Who would make sure Julian would receive the love that was so badly missing in this world. The Father that reached down on that day, on that service he'd been late for, and sent waves of spiritual electricity down through Julian's outstretched arms and into his beating heart.

All the wrongs would be righted. Every tear would be dried. Every twinge of pain would be soothed. God loved him that much. God so loved the world—that much.

He could smell the food they'd eat soon, cooking in the kitchen. The platters of mashed potatoes and barbeque pork and fried chicken. The green beans and collard greens. His sisters would soon be laughing, chasing each other around the white tables—his mother would watch them—and one time she was crying as she did so.

But why was she crying? He'd tried to help her. To offer her a tissue.

No, honey. Not those kind of tears. It's the good kind. The thankful kind. The kind that come from God.

No.

He wouldn't do this. He couldn't do this. He wouldn't deny Christ again.

The Little Lady raised her sharp stone in a lightning quick motion that sent her blonde hair swirling about her. He could see a drop of liquid coming down from the bladed edge of the rock. It must be that liquid which would ensure that the permanence of his mutilation. His testicles tried to pull in again, struggling uselessly, weak as they were, against the ties that bound them. He looked down at the pathetic excuse for a shriveled dick that lay there, so vulnerable, in the depression of the stone.

"Again!" she shouted, her voice full of lust.

Jesus wouldn't want to hurt him. Jesus wouldn't want him to go through this.

"Fuck," Julian sputtered the word, and the rock paused in the air. He felt his soul break. *"Fuck Jesus Christ!"*

The priestess collapsed, sated, back into her seat. The rock fell from her hands. She wiped sweat from her flushed forehead.

The door opened and the Carrion soldiers came in. They unbound him, first the shackles at his ankles and then the string about his cock. He curled up into a ball, his ripped groin muscles sending waves of agony into his brain. He felt a hollow ache where his manhood still remained.

They dragged him back to his cell and left him there, all spit and snot and tears, lying on the cold stone.

That's why. That's why He sent me here. He died for me. He faced the cross. And I wouldn't do any of that back for him.

Sobs, so loud he feared they would call back his captors, escaped from him, but he could not keep them quiet. He couldn't stem the tide. It was too much.

I did the right thing. I did. I did.

He kept lying to himself as he clutched protectively at the wounded little lump of flesh between his legs.

"I'm sorry! I'm sorry Jesus. I'm so sorry. Take me back."

But the joy inside of him had died. He writhed on the floor, pounding his head into the stone.

Julian had never been so damned.

 — 13 —

This is the last time. I won't come here again. I promise.

Ellen knew she was lying to herself, but the lie eased her guilt a bit. Her fingers seemed so white against the stone. It had been a long time since her skin had seen the sun. She wondered idly if, maybe, in one of the other Hells that her soul could go to, there might be another sun.

The stones lain by Rick and the people of Harpsborough seemed so much less ordered than the ones lain by the Devil. Rick's bricks were not all exactly the same, and there were scattered chips in them. Hell's natural wall was so much more symmetrical. So much more perfect. She closed her eyes and let her senses dim. There was a thrumming in the stone, matching her heartbeat. She imagined her soul leaving her body, racing through the rock, seeking out Arturus.

Rick's care was the best that could be hoped for. She could wish for no more from that man. This was a life worth living . . . or it would have been, were Turi here.

Ye swore, ye swore.

Behind the thrumming, though, she began to think she could hear something. Something so far away and faint that she wasn't even sure she was really hearing it. It was as if someone was singing to her. She shook her head and tried to listen, but there was nothing. Nothing at all.

Her thoughts slowed and sobered.

I can't keep coming here. I have to move on.

She heard the crunch of a footfall in the detritus Rick and the Harpsborough hunters had left behind. Her hand immediately jumped to her gun. The motion brought a smile to her face. Galen would have been proud of her.

"I'm sorry, Rick," she said aloud, her voice echoing down the corridor. "I just hope, sometimes. I imagine that I'll hear their voices and . . ."

The footsteps continued, but Rick did not answer. She spun around.

Coming down the long corridor was a corpse. She started, and her finger clamped down on the trigger.

Her safety was on.

She flipped it off and leveled her muzzle at the corpse. She waited for it to get close so that she would not waste a bullet. It was moving particularly slowly.

The corpse continued forward, step after step. Blistering pustules of rot were sprinkled on the right side of its face. Dried, grey, peeling skin covered its throat and peeked out from behind the holes in its shirt. Its eyes were milky as if covered by cataracts.

This was a person, once.

"I wish you could hear me," she said, surprised at how strong her voice sounded. "I wish that your body could tell your soul, wherever it might be, what I'm saying. If you can hear me, if you can hear me at all, and you are in the Hell after this one, will you do something for me?"

The smell of it hit her hard, and she felt bile rise in the back of her throat. She did her best to ignore it.

"Can you deliver a message for me?"

Another step, and another.

"If you find someone named Turi, in that Hell of yours, tell him not to die again. Tell him to wait for me. Tell him that someday I'll find him, and that I love him, and that we'll be damned together. Like we were meant to be."

Step. Step.

She gritted her teeth.

"Sorry," she told the corpse.

The thing tripped and fell. Slowly, it pulled itself to its knees and raised both of its hands. "Please," it begged, "save me."

Ellen's breath left her in a rush. Her gun fell from her hand, clattering on the stones.

"Please," the thing repeated.

Dumbly, she nodded.

Rick stared at the corpse from across the table. He did not look happy. The corpse twitched suddenly, arms jerking. It hit the table, causing the woodstone to tilt off of its supporting blocks. Then the corpse stopped moving altogether.

Ellen felt guilty about the mess it was making.

Rick didn't react to the corpse's movements at all. He had a hard look in his eye that Ellen didn't like. It reminded her of Galen.

Rick addressed the corpse. "You're still hallucinating, aren't you?"

It nodded.

Rick put his hand on Ellen's shoulder. "We need to restrain him for as long as the hallucinations last. Go into the forge room and get some rope."

She ran, feet crunching on gravel, and grabbed the rope. She returned as quickly as she could, panting slightly.

Rick still hadn't moved. "How long since you last had corpsedust?"

It tried to answer. Its mouth opened. Ellen could see that its tongue was rotten inside its mouth. Parts of the mouth were pink, though. She looked away for a second to keep from vomiting.

"Two . . ." was all that it managed to say.

"You told me corpses weren't people," Ellen accused.

"They're not," Rick said. "He's a corpse eater, not a corpse. Corpsedust gives hallucinations. It also causes you to rot, from the inside out. Then you do become a corpse. This man's right on the edge."

Rick stood up and took the rope from her. He began to tie up the corpse eater, taking no pains to make the act a gentle one.

"He could die," Rick said, pausing to cinch a knot. "Or he could recover."

"What can we do to help him?" Ellen asked.

"We," Rick said firmly, "are going to do nothing. If Harpsborough wants to nurse him back to health, then so be it."

"But they won't want to!" Ellen said. "They don't have any food there. They'll just let him die. We have to help him."

Rick shook his head. "They have good reason."

"What reason?"

"He has friends," Rick finished the knots and then lowered his head to the level of the corpse eater, staring into his eyes. "Don't you?"

He nodded.

"And those friends killed some people, didn't they."

There was pause, and then, to Ellen's horror, another nod.

 — 14 —

The stone skulls returned to harry Arturus' peripheral vision. He tried to cock his head to one side to keep their dim shapes in better view—hoping that he could see clearly that they were only stones. At first it worked, but as they traveled farther, the light grew dimmer, and the task became impossible.

It was as if Hell was watching him through those empty eye sockets.

How long will we go on pretending that we can live? How long until we all admit aloud that we're going to die?

Galen stopped suddenly.

Arturus' hand shot down into his pocket and he drew his razor. It was such a pitiful defense. The other hunters froze around him. Johnny was so scared he was shaking.

Arturus was unsure as to what his father was worried about. Even the echoes of the dyitzu claws had faded away. Perhaps they'd been detected, and the dyitzu were just stalking them quietly. Arturus tried to empty his mind, and he closed his eyes—using again the trick he'd learned in the river. The ambient sounds of the other hunters filled the room. He tried to gauge the distance between himself and each of them. But beyond the hunters, he could hear nothing.

Not sound, smell.

The odor was faint, but it seemed to be feces. There was something else, too.

Shit and rotting bodies.

Galen motioned for them to follow him with a wave of his

hand.

Arturus' grip on his razor tightened.

They moved after Galen as quietly as they could. Aaron began to fall towards the back, his limp becoming more pronounced.

Arturus noticed the priestess getting close to him.

Oh yeah. Like I'm going to be able to protect you.

But her closeness changed something in him. He felt more aggressive, more willing to fight. Galen had told him long ago that everyone needed something to die for.

Maybe defending a helpless woman was something enough, never mind that she had probably been responsible for more pain than anyone Arturus had ever met before coming to the Carrion.

The smell became more noticeable. Avery motioned to Johnny Huang, and then pointed towards his nose. Johnny nodded. The ceiling began to arch higher above their heads, and the light began to come back. There were flecks of skystone in the ceiling, giving everything a blue cast.

We've moved far from the ruby vein.

The odor became intense, overpowering enough to cause Johnny to dry heave. Galen turned back and gave him a warning glance. Johnny tried to stay quiet. His eyes were watering badly.

The next room was filled with the bodies of dead men and dead demons. Arturus had never seen such slaughter.

Martin clenched his fingers to try and relieve their twitching. He had to be especially careful about the nails. He had torn one off when he'd fired his rifle in the air to save Rick, and he had a dull ache where the skin was exposed to the air. Still, he intended to return to hunting this very day. Since Julian had been missing, he'd not been able to store any more food, and he knew how hungry he could get after a long fruitless range. A couple of binges and he wouldn't have anything to show for all his disciplined savings.

Come back to us, Julian.

But they had walled the Carrion opening shut, leaving Julian and Aaron trapped on the other side—assuming they were even alive at all. That meant that there would be a new

Lead Hunter. Martin considered who that might be. With Aaron and the rest of the best hunters missing, the choice would be a hard one, and he couldn't imagine Michael Baker reclaiming the title.

Surely it'll be Graham.

Graham was a good hunter, but he was rash. And he wasn't *that* good. It might be hard as hell to catch a dyitzu these days, but he should have caught more than just one since Aaron left.

Aaron. We're lost without you. And starving.

They were stubborn, the Citizens. Worse than stubborn, they were heartless. They could watch the people of the village wander around starving while they stuffed their faces full of honeyed dyitzu meat on the Fore's balconies.

Graham would become one of them.

Martin had seen people accepted by the Fore. In the beginning they'd be the same. They were so kind, often helping their old friends out with gifts from the storehouse. But eventually they'd change. After a while, they'd make new friends in the Fore and forget their old ones. They'd start talking about how it was the promise of reward that kept the whole system going.

Not me. I'd remember where I came from.

There was no system of rewards, he knew. There were just the people who had to brave the wilds, and the people who didn't. The good guys, and the people who would live off of the hard work of others rather than putting in their fair share of effort. That wasn't a system. That was someone taking advantage of someone else.

I'd be like Aaron. I'd fight for fairness until the end. Until they kicked me out of the Fore.

Aaron hadn't wanted to cut off his hand. Aaron had been ordered to do it. He'd had no choice. It was just bad luck. Aaron had made up for it too. Martin had received a new life. He had gotten free food and a long needed rest.

He looked towards the entranceway.

Beyond it were the wilds he knew so well and the devils he searched for to earn food. The devils which, he'd always known, would somehow find a way to kill him.

But there was more out there in the wilds than just demons. There was the Pole and Macon's Bend—and other places and people he'd never heard of. Hell was big. Some people even said it was infinite.

But there are Infidel Friend out there too.

"Hey, Martin?" It was a woman's voice.

Martin turned about to see Katie. She was a black haired stocky girl, heavy set. Martin had called her a poor man's Molly.

Except that Katie's not a giant bitch.

The woman had breasts though, and even despite her extra weight, Martin had to give her that.

She's kind of shaped like my pot.

"Yeah, Kate, whatchya need?"

"You have any sinfruit?"

"Nah, sorry."

"Devilwheat? Anything other than spider eggs?"

Martin laughed. "Yes, princess, I do have devilwheat."

"Will you trade with me? Please? I've had so many of them. I want my last meal to be something else. I might die rather than eat them."

Martin considered it. Not many people in the village had anything to trade at all. This might be his last chance to swap out to a different kind of food.

You should be happy with the way things turned out. If you'd still had your hand when this famine hit hardest, you'd be worse off than anyone.

"Well, I think I'd rather die than watch you," he said.

Katie laughed.

She's got a cute laugh.

He took her over to his hovel and sat down by his pot. He pulled out a handful of devilwheat. She traded him a share of spider eggs.

He placed them into his pot, careful to make sure they were all bunched together in one corner. Their silky outsides stuck to some of the wheat. They stuck to his hand, too, so he had to flick a few of them off of his fingers. It was tough to do with his weak hand, so he ended up brushing them off with his sleeve. There was one last hanger on.

He ate it.

Katie laughed again.

"Man's got to eat," he told her.

"Yes he does."

She looked uncomfortable, as if unsure as to whether she should leave or not. He found that he didn't want her to go.

Say something.

But she spoke for him. "That was very brave, you standing up to Constance."

Martin shrugged, trying to act nonchalant, but he could feel the heat building in his cheeks.

She produced a blue cloth and laid it on Martin's floor. She dropped her devilwheat into the cloth. Martin watched her breasts move as she wrapped it. He was careful to make sure he looked away before she finished.

She smiled. "Most people won't stand up to Constance. Even Graham was afraid to."

Mouth's not as big as Kylie's.

Martin smiled back.

"What's right is right," he said.

She got up and exited his hovel. He stood up as well, leaving right after her. He wandered over to Benson as she walked away.

That's a lot of butt.

He sat down next to the still man.

"You think she's cute?" he asked Benson.

Benson's eyes were as empty as ever.

"I might hit it," Martin confessed. "Lot of woman to handle, but most of it is the good kind, you know."

Benson's mouth was open, probably from Mancini's treatments to rid the man of the corpsedust. His gums had receded so that his teeth looked very long. Massan's handcuffs still hung about the man's ankles.

"Lot of woman. Could hit it from behind, you know. Be like driving a Mack Truck."

Martin scratched his chin.

"I hear you, Bense. I hear you. Girlfriend? You always were a little bit crazy. My father said that, though. Said never to date a pretty woman. Everyone wants her, and she knows it. Now a woman who nobody wants, she's got to make up for it in the sack. That's what my old man said."

Martin sighed, finding he had another spider egg stuck to his sleeve.

"Want it?" he offered.

Benson made no response.

Martin shrugged and popped it into his mouth.

"Suit yourself," he said as he chewed.

Martin looked towards Katie's hovel.

"Nuh uh, buddy. Don't you be talking to her, Bense. Us hunters got to stick together now. You can't be taking my woman."

"Jesus fucking Christ," Aaron whispered as he took in the scene.

The ceiling of this room was that of a natural cavern, and its grey and black stalactites hung down—thrust as if spears into the rock below—displacing cracked bricks where they had buried themselves into the floor. The cavern was flecked with skystone, and though the light was still not the neon blue Arturus was used to from his homeland, it was easily bright enough to see the carnage.

Human bodies lay in heaps behind stalagmites that showed the blackened scars of dyitzu fire. Here one lay separate from the others, his leg mutilated. Both of his hands were outstretched, as if he had been trying to keep himself from being dragged away, and his body was riddled with bullet wounds.

Dyitzu corpses were more evenly spread out, many were shot down around stalactites, but others had been killed in random places throughout the chamber. Here and there, amidst the dyitzu bodies, were dead hounds. Some of them showed evidence of dyitzu fire. There must have been corpses amongst the fallen too, though it was a little hard to determine which bodies had started as undead, and which had risen before being felled again.

The priestess was shaking her head.

"How many?" Johnny whispered.

"Perhaps as many as a hundred humans." Galen crouched beside one particularly rotten body. "Maybe twice that in demons. Who knows how many corpses."

The priestess stopped beside a dyitzu, and knelt, slowly and carefully, keeping her torso erect as she did so. The dyitzu at her feet was missing a jawbone.

"La'Ferve," she said. "This is his doing."

"It doesn't seem like him," Galen said. "Maab's men tend to avoid fights with dyitzu packs."

"Maybe," she answered, "but it's him, nonetheless."

Galen nodded, the gesture sending Johnny towards one exit. The hunter slowly picked his way through the bodies, his pistol raised.

"We won't be here long," Galen warned. "Look here." Arturus' father was pointing at the side of one of the bodies' head.

Arturus, Aaron and Avery gathered around.

"What's that?" Avery asked.

"Stitching?" Aaron guessed.

It was stitching, and the skin had scarred up around the dark thread. It was as if someone had cut a headband into the person from temple to temple before sewing the skin back together. Black veins, spread out like tree roots, were caught up in the raised tissue around the wound. The body's hands had been mutilated too, with each fingertip removed at the first knuckle.

"And there's another one like that over here," the priestess advised them.

"The hell?" Avery said, his eyes narrowed and jaw open. "Why are they like that?"

Both of these bodies seemed more decayed than the others. Either they had died here prior to the battle, or they had entered this room as corpses.

"They're Nephysis' pack mules," the priestess said.

Aaron shook his head. "I don't understand what you mean."

Arturus felt like he was getting dizzy from the room's rank stench.

"It's one of the ways to keep corpses docile," Galen said, spitting onto the stone floor. "You lobotomize the person, kill them, and then raise them. It's not perfect, but that's probably why they took off the things fingers, and . . ." Galen reached out, leaning his head back and away from the body, and pulled down one of its lips. "and their teeth."

"Wouldn't they heal?" Avery asked.

"Rustrock," Kelly answered.

Arturus' father ripped off one of the corpse's sleeves, which was so rotted from the thing's own corpsedust that it tore like paper. Galen pointed to more of the incisions on and round the corpse's elbow.

"Smart," Galen said. "Nephysis is good, I'll give him that."

Kelly nodded. "He cuts the tendons, so if they do go wild, they can't do much to harm. Like I said, pack mules."

Avery had moved to one of the stalagmites the Carrion men had used for cover. He was inspecting some of the score marks buckshot had left in the stone. "It looks like people were fighting people. And like the demons were allies with one side."

Galen shook his head.

"But there are bullet marks here," Avery said, "where there are only people."

"Battles are fluid things," Galen answered. "Either some corpses were firing at them or this place must have been controlled at one point by devils."

"Well, it looks that way, anyway," Avery muttered.

Arturus started to look for differences in the clothing of the fallen, wondering if Avery could be right. They all wore the Carrion soldier black, and though there were many variations in their clothing and boots, the fallen soldiers didn't seem to divide up nicely into two camps.

Even if they did, they could just be two different clans fighting under La'Ferve.

"But then why are all these hounds hit by dyitzu fire?" Avery asked.

The priestess smiled grimly. "Check their toes. Gilgamesh, one of Maab's generals, keeps warhounds that still have their teeth. Even so, he cuts their claws for safety."

"Hey guys," Johnny called softly to them. They looked at him across the room, hands on their weapons. Avery had his Remington raised as a club.

He must be out of bullets, too.

Johnny had a pair of shotgun shells held up for them to see. "Some of these bodies still haven't been looted. Most have, but not all."

"They must have left in a hurry," Aaron surmised.

"If Kelly is right, and this is La'Ferve's doing, then he might have left early for his appointment with us," Galen said. "But we've tarried too long already. Gather what you can as fast as you can, and then let's split."

As the hunters began to loot, Arturus noticed Kelly approaching Galen. He found a couple of bodies to sack within earshot so that he could listen in.

"No, I didn't say that I didn't believe you," Galen was saying, "but Maab must be feeling the push pretty damn hard if she wants to strike out against groups this big. And the amount of people they lost, it can't be worth it."

Kelly's voice was soft, so Arturus stopped rummaging to make sure he heard her.

"All three of her generals were here, Galen," she said. "Gilgamesh, Nephysis, and La'Ferve. This is bigger than you think. She never lets them work in concert."

"That is odd."

Galen stood suddenly and walked quickly across to the far side of the chamber. Arturus jogged to keep up. The bodies there were different, he began to notice. Their clothes were also dark, but they had red upside down crosses patched into their shoulders. There was a hound among them, claws removed, with two deep wounds in its side. One of the wounds had a broken off Minotaur horn in it.

No wonder they left in a hurry.

But Galen did little more than glance at the hound. He crouched by two more fallen bodies, one a human with an upside down cross, the other a dyitzu. They both had been sprayed with buckshot. It was as if they had fallen while fighting side by side.

Galen cursed in some foreign language. "Avery," he said after a moment, "I think I owe you an apology."

 — 15 —

Michael stood alone—save for the sleeping John who lay curled up behind one of the Citizen dining tables—on the third floor balcony of the Fore, looking down on his sleeping city. They would be awake soon, he knew. He could already see the first signs of stirring through the patchwork hide and cloth roofs of the village's hovels.

It was not going to be a good day.

The still and Kylie's Kiln would be silent. No one had anything left to barter for bloodwater, and no one had anything to store in a pot. As if for support, he looked around the right corner of the Fore to see the tall, twin crucifix topped steeples of the church. He would be in that church later today, trying to pass some motions in the Citizen meeting. The most important motion was one designed to give the hunters another stipend. He had tried to pass a law which would guarantee them food from the stores every week, but the Citizens refused to support it. From now until the foreseeable future, he realized, he was going to have to fight, tooth and nail, every single week in order to grant that stipend.

And the deaths had continued. Two more murders. Mancini was going to try and convince everyone that the only way to stop the killings was to make people register all of their caches with the Fore—consequently ensuring that they would be taxed ten percent of whatever it was they gathered. If that passed, Michael had no doubt that there would be mass desertions at the very least, if not a descent into outright bloodshed.

He looked back towards the city and then started suddenly.

Rick was standing in the middle of Harpsborough, staring directly up at him.

How long has he been there?

Rick was nothing like the man he'd been when Michael had last seen him. His face was calm, serious and stoic. It was as if he'd become Galen. For a moment, the man reminded Michael of the Infidel Friend whom he'd sentenced to exile through the Golden Door. Rick had that same defiance, that same remorseless disdain for all that surrounded him. And Michael couldn't blame him. Rick was no enemy to this city, surely, but Constance and his new band of goons had tried to lynch and loot the man.

Michael saw a villager exit his hovel out of the corner of his eye, and after apparently noticing his and Rick's locked stare, the man hurried out to the river room.

Michael tapped John with his foot. The young boy stirred.

"Go down and let Rick into the Fore," Michael Baker ordered him.

John stood, groggily, and after gaining his balance, rushed downstairs. The boy's sandals sounded out against the stone as he ran, became muffled for a moment on the dyitzu skin carpets of the parlor room, and returned to being loud again, echoing down the stone stairwell.

Michael nodded at Rick, who returned the gesture and headed for the door curtain.

Galen broke into a sprint.

Oh hell.

There was nothing to do but chase after him. It was not an easy task for Arturus, even on healthy legs, to keep up. Avery, Aaron, and Johnny Huang were slow to start, falling behind Arturus immediately. Galen did not wait for them, and Arturus found himself torn as to whether he should try and keep up with his father, or lag behind to stay near the others. Soon the choice was made for him. Galen was so far ahead that if Arturus didn't fall back, the hunters wouldn't know which passageway to run through.

The chambers passed by in a blur as they ran. Galen ducked into a short, natural tunnel, which sloped downwards. It was nearly pitch black, but his father didn't slow down at all.

Arturus paused until he heard the other hunters entering the tunnel, then he ran on.

Galen wouldn't leave me behind.

Arturus didn't notice that the passage he was running in had a dead end until he was only a few feet away from a rock wall. He threw his hands up and rebounded off of the stone. He saw stars in his vision and lost his footing, falling backwards into a seated position. He heard the hunters coming.

"Stop," he whispered loudly.

Aaron and Avery managed to avoid running into him. Arturus rose as quickly as he could and caught Johnny before the short hunter could collide with the wall.

"Where's Galen?" Avery said.

"Up here," Galen's voice came down from above.

Arturus shook his head. Stretching out his fingers, he felt along the wall for handholds. The climb didn't seem like it would be too hard. He began his ascent. Behind him, Johnny cursed.

"What are you bitching about?" Arturus heard Avery ask the man.

"I hate climbing."

The wall led them into a tiny chute which spiraled upwards. Jagged rocks caught onto Arturus' clothes, but the tight confines made the climb easier. At times, when Arturus couldn't find a handhold, he would just kick out with his legs, wedging his body against the rocks before squirming his way upwards. The chute seemed to be over one hundred feet tall. He could hear the heavy breathing of the hunters behind him. The wheeze from Johnny Huang's broken nose was particularly loud, but that noise was soon drowned out by the sound of rushing water. The higher they climbed, the louder the water became.

As Arturus reached up to get his next handhold, he felt a familiar calloused hand grip his wrist. Galen hefted him up onto a landing.

"Stay quiet," Galen whispered just loudly enough to be heard over the water. "And stay low."

Galen helped the rest of the hunters up as well, repeating his commands to them. After he helped Johnny, Galen looked down the chute. "Where's Kelly?"

Aaron sat up and shrugged.

"I said stay low," Galen warned harshly, and then he practically dove into the chute.

Aaron lay back down.

Arturus pulled himself along the ledge, looking after his father. Then he turned to Aaron, Avery and Johnny. "Did you guys see her?"

"She was behind me in the tunnel," Johnny said.

Arturus crawled past Johnny, trying to take stock of where they were. The chute had set them on a landing that was fairly high up in a large natural chamber. He guessed they were at an intersection between the ruby vein and the skystone vein, because both kinds of stone lit up the chamber. In places the huge room was predominately blue, in others red, and where the two stones were close enough together, a brilliant purple. The lighting made it difficult to judge the distance of the terrain. A river, looking like sapphire in some places and like blood in others, rushed through the room with terrific speed. Arturus felt sure its noise would cover their whispers.

He looked for exits. If something other than his father came up that chute, Arturus guessed that he might be able to make the jump into the water. Then, if he survived the fifty foot fall and was somehow able to get out of the water, he would have a hundred foot dash before he made it to an exit.

He saw movement in the chamber out of his peripheral vision.

Dyitzu.

Four or five had entered so far, and Arturus had no idea how many more there might be. They seemed peculiarly dark in color, and more hunched than any dyitzu he'd seen before. Their stub wings appeared more pronounced too. Not full enough to fly, but oddly oversized. Their arms were longer, and hung down almost to their knees. One, the most misshapen of them all, actually used his arms as an extra set of legs to move across the chamber. That one stopped, crouching by the river in a place where its waters were purple. It cupped its hands together and raised some of the river to its lips.

Arturus slid slowly back onto the landing, flattening himself against the cold, hard stone.

"Dyitzu," Arturus warned.

Aaron, lying on his back, pushed his way to the edge before looking down and over his shoulder at the scene below. He moved away immediately.

"They're pouring in," he reported.

Johnny and Avery didn't even bother looking. They just froze.

Aaron dared another peek before scooting back, his eyes wide. He said nothing.

Arturus heard scraping coming from the chute. He drew his razor. Galen climbed up, the priestess clinging to him, her arms wrapped around his neck.

"Dyitzu," Arturus warned.

"I know," Galen replied.

Kelly's face was covered in snot and tears. The sprint and the climb could not have been easy on her ribs. Those tears were running down her face, though she was not sobbing. She looked lost. Arturus turned to the hunters.

Hell, we all look lost.

"Hundreds of them," Aaron whispered, pointing behind him. Galen nodded.

Kelly's mouth opened like she was going to scream.

Please stay quiet.

Arturus felt his heart beating quickly in his chest. He wanted to help her. He wanted to relieve her pain. He wanted to go home. Slowly, he reached out and touched her hand. Their eyes met as her mouth hinged opened and closed with her silent agony. She gripped his hand fiercely—so fiercely that Arturus thought his fingers might break—but he didn't care.

I hate you, Devil, that you let such suffering occur in your Hell.

After a few minutes, her breathing slowed, and her tears stopped coming. She let go of his hand and rolled over into a seated position. She cradled her ribs with her arms and rocked back and forth, snot still covering her face.

The Carrion is wearing us down. It won't be much longer before it takes us all.

Galen cast a glance over the ledge and then moved back.

"Hundreds," he reported. "How many shells did we pick up?"

"Ten," whispered Avery, "and they're all in my shotgun. I

gave all my .300 shells to Aaron."

"And I've got this." Johnny said, holding up the pistol Galen had given him.

I've got no ammo, and Galen and Aaron are the only ones who have their original rifles. Avery must have dropped his in the run.

Worse than that, Johnny Huang, Avery, and Aaron had all lost their packs and canteens in the river. For his part, Arturus had lost everything but his canteen and his razor. Only Galen had managed to keep his supplies intact.

Arturus heard a few echoed clicks of dyitzu claws over the sound of the rapids below. He tensed suddenly and held his breath. No one spoke for a long time.

"Are there any humans with those dyitzu down there?" Johnny asked.

Galen shook his head. "Can't say for sure, but I didn't see any."

"But the men and demons seemed like allies at the battlefield. Is Maab working with the devils?"

Galen pursed his lips as he thought about it. "No. Maab is an evil woman, perhaps the most evil woman I have ever met. She gives no thought to the happiness of anyone but herself, but even she would not cavort with devils."

Kelly nodded her agreement.

"So who are they, then?" Aaron asked.

"I don't know," Galen said, "but it looks like Maab's men got the upper hand on them, at least for that one battle. Let us hope that continues, because if it does not, Maab will not quietly go into her next damnation. More likely she'll flee and seek the resources of more peaceful lands."

"Lands like Harpsborough." Aaron said.

"Yes, like Harpsborough."

Galen's eyes suddenly narrowed, and his head perked up.

"What?" Arturus asked.

"I know where we are," Galen said. "Come, we've rested enough. Follow me."

Galen crawled back into the chute. Arturus stayed behind the hunters this time, determined to help Kelly. For a second, he thought she might not go, but her face became as expressionless as a statue, and then she climbed in.

At first they traveled back down, but not for long. Galen had them rising again shortly. This time the landing they came to was at an entrance to a spiral staircase. It was lit by a dull, grey ambient light and was only wide enough for one person to traverse. The center of the steps had been worn down as if the feet of many thousands of men had somehow compressed the stone. Arturus doubted this structure was made by Hell's architect. The stone walls were too irregular, the steps too uneven. But as to why someone would build a staircase in this place, Arturus had no idea. Perhaps there had been a complex here once, and the rest of it had fallen down.

After another few hundred feet, the stairway emptied out into a completely natural cave which was lit only by a few flecks of skystone.

Kelly collapsed, again in tears. She reached out, and Arturus grasped her hand again. Johnny noticed, shaking his head in disapproval. Galen grunted, though, so Arturus knew he was doing the right thing.

"That's as good a trail break as we're likely to find," Galen said. "No hound will be following us through there, and only a very determined dyitzu would complete such a climb. Finish off the water we have, and we'll sleep for two shifts."

Arturus took a sip from his canteen and then passed it to Johnny. Johnny drank from it deeply.

"Arturus, you take first watch," Galen said. "I'll take the second."

It seemed odd to Arturus that Galen would pick him over Aaron for the duty. Maybe Galen thought that since Aaron's feet were still hurting from the silverlegs, he would need more rest.

"Come on Turi," his father said, "follow me. I'll show you the chamber you have to watch over. It's an amazing thing."

Michael set himself down in his favorite chair before looking upon the chess board the boy Turi had fashioned. The water clock on the far wall kept time, ticking along with the beat of John's sandals as the boy ran up the stairs. He listened for Rick's footsteps, but didn't hear them. The man must have been caught up doing something below.

It was so dark in the parlor room that he was having difficulty making out the chess pieces. Mancini must have been the last one to bed the night before, leaving his customary amount of blankets on the light orbs.

Michael heard John approach him and saw the boy's shadow out of the corner of his eye.

John touched his arm. "First Citizen."

Michael looked up to see what the boy could want. "What?" Rick was standing in the parlor room doorway, a hulking shadow.

Jesus. I didn't even hear him come up the steps.

"Rick," Michael said, rubbing the back of his neck, "would you mind pulling off some of those blankets for me? It's bloody dark in here."

Rick gave no sign of hearing him. The man walked across the room, his boots making no noise as he passed over the dyitzu skin carpet. He sat down across from Michael.

John's head moved back and forth between the two.

Rick ignored me.

Rick and Galen didn't like to be ordered around, but the request had been a friendly one.

"I'm the First Citizen of Harpsborough," Michael reminded him.

Rick turned his head towards the boy for a second. John swallowed deeply.

Michael looked back down at the chess board before refocusing on Rick. "I'm sorry the villagers attacked you. I assure you, the Fore has nothing but admiration for you. Their actions should not be mistaken for the true feelings of Harpsborough."

Rick's gaze on him was unflinching.

"I'm not used to being accused of anything, Rick," Michael said. "I don't take it well, even when it is my fault. In this case, Constance's attack on you was not my fault."

Rick leaned forward. "You appear to be eating well."

"What do you mean by that?"

"Constance appears to be starving. Is that also not your fault?"

John ran, his thigh brushing against the chess board. Pieces shifted and toppled over. A bishop fell, bouncing across the floor before settling on the dyitzu skin carpet.

Michael bent down and picked up the piece.

Rick was still staring at him.

John's sandals were clopping down the stairs.

Michael wasn't about to back down. "You're too smart to pretend that this village's welfare is so simple. You have no idea what the consequences would be if we fed the people the Fore's food."

"I know what one of them would be."

"I live in the Fore, don't pretend you know it better than I. Why the hell are you here, anyway?"

"I'm here to help you," Rick said.

"Well it doesn't God damn sound like it to me."

Rick leaned back in his seat. "Have there been more murders?"

Michael bowed his head over the chess set. "Deaths. Not murders. We're not positive that they are murders."

"But there have been more."

Michael stood up from his chair. "Yes, there have been more." He began pacing. "Of course there's been more. People are so hungry, they think any shadow is a dyitzu."

"And the people who tend to mistakenly identify villagers as dyitzu, they all haunt the downstream halls of the Kingsriver, don't they?"

Michael paced over towards the light orbs. "Yes. Yes they do. I know what you're thinking. You think there's some resource there that they've found. You think because they attacked you, that they're willing to murder for food now. Well it's not true. Not true at all. Hidalgo showed us all the caches out there—"

"I found a corpse eater, Michael."

Michael had lifted a blanket off of one orb. He let it drop onto the floor before returning to his favorite chair and sitting down. "One of ours? Surely they haven't gotten so hungry that they'd . . ."

Rick shook his head. "Not yet. It wasn't one of yours."

Michael let out a sigh. "Good."

"But he has friends, Michael. Hidalgo and I have reason to think that there is a group of them camped somewhere down the Kingsriver. They've been killing your people."

"Thank you for your warning," Michael said. "They must be pretty far out, though, or Graham's hunters would have found them. I'll keep them posted, though."

Rick didn't respond.

Michael stood up again, motioning to the door. "I really appreciate it, but—"

"Sit down."

Michael felt his blood rise. No one spoke to him like that, no one but—

Galen. Rick has become Galen.

Michael nodded and retook his seat.

"They're closer than you think, I guarantee it. I've got one of their men. He's still too far gone to answer many questions, but I'm sure he'll be able to lead you there after you nurse him back to health."

"We're stretched for food as it is," Michael said. "You want me to feed a corpse eater out of the Fore's stores? You must want me dead. There's no way I'd get the Fore to approve such a thing."

"Then mandate it."

"I can't keep doing that Rick. It makes the Citizens mad."

Rick put his hand into his pack. For a second, Michael thought he was going to pull out a gun. Instead, the hermit held out two chess pieces. They were the missing Kings for his set. Rick placed them on the board.

"You owe us commission," Rick said.

"You picked a hell of a time to collect. I'll have to defer that until—"

"Use it to feed the corpse eater. When he's well, he can lead you to the others."

Michael gritted his teeth. Finally he smiled. "Hell. Okay, Rick. I can see you're just trying to get us to do the right thing."

Rick nodded.

"Besides, I'm just dying to kick Staunten out of his room again. Bring the corpse eater in."

"You have a couple of hunters you can spare to bring him back?"

"Can't he walk?"

"Walk? Yes. Just not in straight lines."

Michael laughed. "Very well. Two hunters it is."

Galen led Arturus through a short tunnel and then into

another natural cave.

"Stay back in the shadows," he warned. "There are devils below."

As Arturus stepped down into the cavern, he caught sight of what his father had spoken of earlier. This chamber was perhaps the largest he had ever seen in his life, dwarfing even some of the immense expanses that surrounded the Kingsriver. Dozens of complete Harpsborough chambers could fit in there. Forests of stalagmites covered the floor of the purple chamber, as impressive a set of natural structures as Arturus had ever seen, but that wasn't what took his breath away. In the center of that massive chamber was a city. Its walls were high and mostly still intact. At its base, the wall was made of huge grey granite blocks. From this distance it was difficult to judge their height, but Arturus would not have been surprised if each block was over twenty feet tall. Behind the wall, and eclipsing it in height, were a series of towers and wide buildings, forming together a skyline of dark shapes which stood in stark contrast to the purple flecks of mixed skystone and ruby which painted the chamber's ceiling. Perhaps thousands of people, maybe even hundreds of thousands, could have lived in that city.

There was one structure even more impressive than the wall or the tallest of the towers. An aqueduct spanned the chamber, supported at its tallest point by hundreds of arches, each set in at least a dozen layers on top of each other. Slowly the structure descended, sloping down at an almost imperceptible angle as it crossed the chamber and passed over and through the city until it was only one arch level high where it disappeared from view.

For a second, Arturus dared hope that there were people living behind those walls, but his hopes were crushed almost as soon as he'd formed them. Moving along the top of one of those tremendous edifices was a dyitzu. There were a few more traveling amongst the stalagmites.

"What is this place?" Arturus asked.

"It was called Londinium," Galen's deep voice answered, "but now it is infested by devils. Don't go near those walls, son. Inside an Archdevil has taken up residence."

"But people did live here?" Arturus asked.

"Yes. And they were happy for a time, before Hell reclaimed it."

"How? How did they lose? How could they let the devils take a place like this?"

Galen only shrugged. "Civilizations fall sometimes. Usually it happens from the inside first. Men care about silly rules that have nothing to do with surviving. They confuse the importance of those with the ones that really matter. Sometimes the devils are just finishing them off."

"Are there any places like this now, where men live?"

"No, son. The men of this day are no longer able to build and defend things like this."

Arturus could not help but wonder what it would be like if this city could again be settled by men. There would be no Fore, no starving masses. All would be fed. People would find some shelter from their damnation. They would never let it fall again. Never. Not to an Archdevil, not even to Satan himself should he come to call. Arturus no longer felt tired. The fire of the idea caught in his mind, and the breath in his lungs seemed charged with electricity.

"Remember," Galen said, "stay in the shadows. That way you can see them, and they can't see you. If they come, or do somehow manage to spot you, don't try and fight. Come get us. We may have to retreat back down the chute."

"We have to retake it," he told his father.

Galen grunted. "Someday, son. Maybe someday."

But that day might not ever come, Arturus realized, and if it did, it would be long after the Carrion had claimed all of their lives.

He tore his eyes away from the city. "We're going to die, aren't we?"

"We won't last much longer," Galen admitted. "Avery's ankle is swelling. Kelly's ribs can't heal. Aaron's feet are getting worse. But we don't have to last much longer. You see that ridge, along the edge of the chamber?"

Arturus looked to where his father was pointing. "Yes."

"We'll travel that, crawling if we have to, tomorrow. From there we will not be far from where Calimay stays. If we can heal, if we can find weapons, if we can find a guide, then we can find a way out."

Arturus nodded. "You could make it out without seeing Calimay, couldn't you, without us."

Galen shook his head. "Not an option."

"Could we, you and I?"

"Maybe, but that doesn't much matter, Turi. I cannot go back before I go deeper. Before I see this force that is pushing Maab. This force made of men and devils who work together."

"Why? Why do you have to learn about these forces? How can they possibly matter that much?"

Galen did not answer his questions. "Don't drift off to sleep," Galen said after a long moment. "Come get us at the first sign of trouble."

And without waiting for an answer, he disappeared back into the cave.

"It's me," Kelly said.

The priestess entered Arturus' cavern and sat down next to him. She gazed out onto the city.

"You should be sleeping," Arturus told her.

"Can't. The pain in my chest is too much."

Arturus nodded.

Her black eyes sparkled in the purple light of the chamber beyond. She drank in the sight of the city, but she wasn't surprised to see it. Arturus guessed that she must have been to this place before. He was struck by how beautiful she was. Her skin was so pale, and her hair so dark. If there were any imperfections on her face, they were hidden by the soft light. Her lips were thin, cruel, and just slightly parted. Her cheekbones were sharp, her face angular. She was beautiful in a way that Arturus had never seen in a woman from Harpsborough.

She met his eyes and then reached out, touching his arm. She leaned forward so that she was close to him. Memories of kissing Maab suddenly flashed through his mind.

"Calimay will have no reason to want to help us," she whispered, "and your father has nothing she wants. Galen is a fool if he thinks she no longer keeps males as slaves simply because she has distanced herself from Maab. It is very likely that I will be useful to her, and she may even accept me as her own. When that happens, Turi, try to be mine. You have been sweet to me where your friends have not. If you become my slave, I will take good care of you."

Arturus could not understand why, but his heart was beating quickly in his chest. Just the slightest bit of color was in her cheeks. Her pupils were so dilated that he could hardly see their irises. His own breathing became short.

"Thank you," he said. "I will try."

Her cruel lips formed a soft, warm smile. Then she stood and walked back into the caves.

He watched her go.

— 16 —

Ellen sat uncomfortably at the kitchen table, taking stock of her two surprise visitors. In her experience, Rick had never had a guest over—other than herself of course. What made it all the more awkward was that Rick wasn't here to entertain them. She would have felt somewhat guilty letting just Alice into their home, but Massan, the dark and hairy Middle Eastern man who sat across from her, seemed to be the leader of the pair.

That is one fierce unibrow.

His eyebrows, or eyebrow, might have actually been thicker where they met over the bridge of his nose.

For her part, Alice seemed calm and collected. She had her hair down, and was absently running her fingers through it, clearing it of tangles.

I should get them something. Not food. That would set a bad precedent. Rick would be mad.

"Water?" Ellen asked.

"Please," Alice answered.

"If you wouldn't mind," Massan's deep voice intoned.

She smiled, getting up from the table. The scoot of her chair against the stone seemed unnaturally loud for some reason. She walked over to their supply closet and got a trio of cups.

"Rick," Rick announced his presence from outside.

She heard the crunch of footsteps on gravel. Smiling, she grabbed a fourth cup.

"Ellen," she called back, and then—because Massan and Alice didn't seem too keen on announcing themselves—she added, "Alice and Massan are here too."

The pair stood as Rick entered. Rick smiled and shook their hands. Neither of them would meet his eyes, however.

Are they guilty? Are they here to beg for food?

"Alice," Rick said, smiling. "Good to see you. You should see what Ellen has done with the Dreamcatcher. She's posted it up right over her bed. And Massan, always a pleasure."

"Thank you for having me in your home," Massan said.

There was an odd silence. Ellen interrupted it by passing out the glasses of water. Alice's stomach grumbled as she took a sip.

"Sorry," she mumbled, looking down at the table.

"I'll get you some food," Rick said.

"No." Alice shook her head. "I'm not here to be a charity case."

Massan let out a little high pitched laugh which seemed almost feminine. "That she is not. But I am."

"You need food?" Ellen asked.

Massan gave the laugh again. "If only I was asking for something as simple as that."

Rick pulled out a chair and sat down at the table. "What do you need?"

"I haven't been the most helpful to you," Massan said, "that I admit. I have driven many a hard bargain, and at times when all has not been well, I've asked for a charity pound of dyitzu for a trade."

Rick stopped him by leaning forward. "Don't pretend you haven't been a friend to us. I've seen how carefully you let your scales slack until you feel you've paid us back the pound. You've kept secrets for us as well, and we've kept secrets for you."

Massan nodded. "Thank you. But don't let this obligate you. What I ask for, well, I will not be sorry one bit if you say no."

"What do you need?"

"Remember when I got lost, years ago, and found myself up near Macon's Bend?"

"Yes."

"I was actually even farther than that. I was at Tucumcari. You know the place?"

Rick's eyes narrowed. Ellen didn't know what was going on, or where this place was, but this was a very serious conversation.

"I know it."

"Do you know the way?"

Rick's eyes narrowed farther. He took a long drink from his cup and then looked at the ceiling. "It has been nearly a decade since I've traveled that far, when Arturus was still very young. But yes, I could get you there. Near there. In those days it wasn't called Tucumcari, but it was in about the same spot."

"Are you willing, then?" Alice asked, suddenly eager.

Ellen looked at Rick. One could usually tell almost exactly what he was thinking from his expression. Not so now. Now he might as well have been Galen.

"That depends. Why do you wish to go?"

Massan turned to Alice. "Go on."

"I'll be right back," the girl said.

She trotted out of the room, her footsteps spilling gravel out of the hallways.

"I'm going to have to sweep that up," Ellen muttered to herself.

"Karma," Rick joked, but she couldn't understand what he meant by it.

Massan didn't either.

"I find it difficult to guess why you would want to go so far out," Rick said. "I know things were bad in the village, but I didn't think they were *that* bad. Is Kara wanting to go, too?"

Massan shook his head. "No. She will stay. And I have every need to return. I am not fleeing Harpsborough."

"Why then?" Rick asked.

"You know, sometimes I joke about how bad it was to be lost. To be so far away from home. I even told your son once that I would have made a deal with an Infidel Friend to get back."

"Oh?" Rick asked.

"I wasn't joking. I did make a deal with an Infidel Friend. And now it's time for me to pay the Piper."

More footsteps crunched on the gravel.

Alice.

But the footsteps seemed too loud, for some reason.

She's brought someone.

Molly entered the kitchen. Alice came in after, standing at

the doorway, watching.

Molly moved to stand beside Rick. "Please." The girl seemed as sincere as Ellen had ever seen anyone be. "Take me to Tucumcari."

Whatever stoicism Rick had managed to gather about his person was gone now. His jaw was agape. He looked at Massan.

Massan nodded. "She wants to get infidels. Not to hurt Harpsborough, but to help rescue Cris. You know he could hardly walk when the Fore exiled him."

Alice stepped into the kitchen. "And they might be able to help find Aaron and Turi and Galen as well."

"She's right," Molly said. "I've followed the Golden Door's path. It leads into the Carrion. I love Cris. I can't let him die."

Ellen felt her chest swell suddenly. She looked at Rick, taking up his hand. "We have to! We have to help them!"

Rick looked again to Massan. "With the village the way it is, they won't want anyone leaving. Might cause a panic. They'll try and stop you. And an infidel—"

"I know you don't hate them like the Harpsborough people do," Massan broke in. "I know it. I know there's more love in your heart than that. And what does it matter if you make a deal with the devil when you're in Hell, when everything you love is out of reach? They're not like everyone thinks, Rick. They're not all evil. One took me home, for no reason. I didn't have to give him anything. He just took me."

"Pro bono," Rick said, "like what you're asking now."

"Yes. But I'll pay you back," Massan said. "You know I'm good for it."

Rick stood, finished his water, and put the cup back down on the table. Ellen watched him as he walked behind the cooking counter.

He rubbed at his stubble covered chin. "Leave Ellen and I for a moment, all of you."

Molly took Alice's hand, and the pair left the room. Massan followed them.

Rick waited until their gravel crunching footsteps faded away and moved to stand next to her. "I want to do this, but I don't like how it might affect you."

"Why?" Ellen asked, suddenly filled with desperation. "I'll be fine. The journey will do me some good. Get me experience. I'll have to—"

"It's as safe to travel as it has ever been, Ellen. That's not why I'm worried."

Ellen was confused. "Why then?"

"Because you think this might get you Turi back. But it won't. It won't. They won't be looking for Turi. They'll be looking for Cris. And they'll find him if they can, and they won't find him if they can't. And it doesn't matter anyway, because we have to face the fact that Turi's dead. We have to face it."

Tears streamed down Ellen's cheeks, but they weren't tears of sorrow. Not for her sorrow, at any rate.

Rick's not saying this to me. He's saying it to himself.

She stood quickly and hugged Rick. She hugged him as hard as she could.

Rick broke down in her arms.

"It's okay to have hope, sometimes," Ellen whispered into his ear. "Galen wouldn't be too mad. You don't have to keep it for long. You can give it up long before Hell has a chance to take it away from you. It'll be okay. You'll see. We'll promise together. We'll only hope for a little while. Just a little while."

Rick cried for a bit longer. Finally he straightened. "Get your things. Not everything, just what's useful. I'll get us some food. This will be a long journey."

Ellen grinned, doing her best not to run as she made her way to her room. The room that had been Turi's room. The room which she hoped would be his again.

Hope.

They would get the infidels.

Hope.

The infidels would go to find Cris.

Hope.

But they'd find Turi instead.

Drip drip. Drip drip. Drip drip.

Arturus peered into the haze. The mist hung so thickly in the halls of Hell that a dyitzu, even if it were only a few feet away, might be undetectable to his eyes. Hell's architect had worked over most of this area, but some natural features remained. Walls made of stone bricks melded into uneven natural rock. Here and there stalactites and stalagmites jumped out at them from the mists, breaking through the floors and ceilings, sometimes meeting each other. In other places, water dripped from the stones above them.

Drip drip. Drip drip. Drip drip.

"Damn this mist," Avery said.

"It comes from the Lethe," Galen explained. "We are below the level of that river. There is a great lake where it pools some miles before it meets the river Erebus. These mists flow down from there."

Galen led them up stairway after stairway. The mists lessened as they rose, but even after a few hours of travel, the haze covered the floor in opaque sheets. The half natural, half worked pattern of the stone stayed the same, though, so Arturus knew they were traveling within a vein. The intensity of the purple stone varied some as they moved. Galen seemed to be aiming for a bright purple, but not so bright as to be neon. The effect this purple illumination had as it coated the mists was beautiful, but frightening.

There is nothing like this back home.

Galen froze.

The rest of the hunters followed suit, but when Johnny went to draw his pistol, Galen stopped him with an upraised hand.

Aaron, who already had his rifle held at the ready, slung it behind his back.

"We seek Calimay," Galen said to the mists. "Would you be kind enough to take us to her?"

A trio of Carrion born entered the chamber from a dark passage. Arturus hadn't seen them or heard them at all. Two were soldiers, each armed as if Maab's—with shotguns and pistols—but they wore grey shirts with their black pants. The woman with them was dressed like a priestess, but her robe was a deep lavender rather than the black satin Maab's servants preferred. Her shoulders were far broader than those he'd seen on any of Maab's priestesses, and her cheekbones were wider too.

"Why should we trust you?" the priestess asked. "How do we know you are not Maab's spies?"

Galen shrugged. "I've no idea how you would make sure we're not spies, but I *can* tell you how you can trust us."

One of the soldiers raised his eyebrows.

"Oh?" asked Calimay's priestess.

Galen handed her his Heckler and Koch. He motioned for Aaron and Johnny to do the same. Aaron complied immediately. Johnny grumbled, but did so as well. They looked to Avery, but he had no weapon at all.

"I find it hard to argue with you there," the priestess said as she eyed Kelly. "Come. We'll take you to Calimay. She'll figure out if you're spies or not . . ." She grinned wide, the purple light of the chamber glinting off of her teeth. "And if we can't tell, we'll still kill you."

From Neostoicism: Philosophia

In my experience there is no emotion so potentially damaging to the human condition as hope. Hope is, like faith, a denial of reality.
—Endymion

Faith defends all positions equally and none of them sufficiently.
—Cris

Part V
The Lover of the Queen

From Gehennic Law: The Miser

Each day the Miser would gather what wheat he could and cover it up in a stone hole. He did so for several years, for many men around him were starving, and he wished never to be in such company.

Then one day the Miser despaired, for when he went to add to his cache, he found that his devilwheat had been stolen. Overcome with woe, he bemoaned of his fate to his famished friend.

"What am I to do?" the Miser lamented. "How am I to go on, when so many years' effort has been taken from me in but a single day?"

"Why cry?" his friend asked. "Place mere rocks in your cache, and pretend all is as it was. When tucked away, the wheat and the rock will feed you just the same."

"Where are you taking me?" Carlisle asked.

"Where is not important," answered the demon. "It is a *whom* to which I take you. It is a man who will complete your training. Who will teach you how to climb the ladder of a soul in order to make it back to Gehenna. Then you will find your angel's get."

Carlisle looked back. Behind him was an infinite trail of his own blood fed by the slow steady geyser in his side. The trail sat on top of the knee deep water, unable to mix with the substance.

"Why is it doing that?" Carlisle asked aloud.

The shadow that was the devil Mephistopheles turned around. Carlisle saw the reality of the scene melting away as it succumbed to the will of the thing beside him.

"You have two beliefs that affect your blood so." In the beginning, the devil had only been able to speak in whispers within his own head, but as time wore on, Carlisle was getting better and better at hearing the devil's voice. "One is that your blood is pure, like holy water, and for that reason cannot mix with the lake of Hell. The other is that your blood is polluted by your sins, like oil, and that the lake of Hell is somehow too pure for it."

"Very well. I'm ready," Carlisle said.

"Good, now imagine a hallway, as long as the distance from the Earth to the sun. At the end of that hallway is Jealousy. At its beginning is ourselves. The hallway is grey, made of old wallpaper like the one in your father's house. At its top is blue trim, formed like vines, but with yellow flowers hanging down from them. Every ten feet, on both the right and the left, is a wash basin. Within those basins is all the piss made from all the blood that men ever drank or ate from living things."

"Why? Why the basins?"

"The blood is the essence of life, it is for Elohim alone. After it filters through the body of man, polluted as men are, it becomes impure—rotten. It is for this reason that men were to pour out the blood of an animal before they ate it. Do you have the image in your mind?"

"I do."

"Close your eyes."

Carlisle did so. He felt the blood from his side coming down his body, streaming between his thigh and his groin before rushing along the back of his leg. The blood filled his boot.

"Walk with me," said the devil.

Carlisle did so, his eyes still shut.

"I'm taking you into the tunnel, now."

Carlisle nodded.

"Can you smell the urine?"

The rank odor of piss suddenly filled his nostrils.

"I can."

"Then open your eyes."

It was exactly as he imagined it. The wallpaper just as he had once seen in his father's house. Blue painted vines were hanging as trim along the top of the hallway. Yellow flowers, sometimes painted and sometimes real, bloomed there.

"Good enough," the devil said. "Now walk with me."

Of course it was just as he imagined. It was Mephistopheles who had taught him how to control his thoughts, and by doing so, control the nature of the Hell around him. Carlisle wondered idly if this skill would have helped at all on the previous level of Hell . . . or if perhaps it would even work in the old world.

"Now the piss will change just ahead," Mephistopheles coached him. "The piss men make of the blood of animals ends here. Beyond it is the piss men make of their own blood."

The smell was even worse. The bowls were full, some of them overflowing with orange urine.

"Good," Mephistopheles said. "Very close. Very close indeed. You need imagine no more. The place you are heading toward is far too real for your mind to alter it. Just continue walking."

It looked as if there was a door at the end of the tunnel, but that made no sense. He had imagined this passage to be as long as the distance from the Earth to the sun. He looked to Mephistopheles to see what he would do about the mistake, but the devil didn't seem to care.

The door, I'm meant to see it.

It was a golden door, almost like one of the old Infidel Friend passages—but not quite. Whereas the Infidel's golden doors would have been adorned with the iconography of pagan gods, the relief on this door was of a much holier sort. A pair of fig trees stood, one on each door, and at their feet were nets which were full of fish. The trees were obviously crosses, and the leaves and branches added to them did little to hide their true nature.

Carlisle ran his fingers over the gold relief. He could feel the individual strands of the net which held the fish. As for the fish themselves, he swore he could feel their scales. The nets were so full they were almost bursting.

"So many fish!" he cried.

"One hundred and fifty three," Mephistopheles said.

The devil often made odd observances, but Carlisle had learned to ignore them.

"Open the door," Mephistopheles ordered.

Carlisle placed his hand on the door and struggled to open it. He could not, either because it was locked, or because the door was too heavy.

"Not that way," the devil told him. "Look at the right cross, below that branch of the fig tree, to the distant hill."

Carlisle did so, and was amazed to see such astonishing detail. The metal worker must have spent some great length of time with a very fine tool. He could see a few hills there, and nestled between them a lake. In that lake was a small wooden boat. In the boat was a fisherwoman, and she was looking towards the shore. He tried to follow her gaze, and moved up right next to the door—close enough that his nose touched it— so that the door was all he could see. She was looking at something. Somehow, the artist had managed to get a village there. The fisherwoman was looking at the village. There were two men by the front gate, each standing, almost like guards. They had no weapons but had ploughshares instead. Past them was the main road that led into the city. He could just see, just barely, behind those two men, that there were a couple of shops on the street. To the right was a person selling bread. To the left was someone selling fruit. There was a child at the fruit stand, trying to buy some of the fruit, but the pouch at her belt was empty. There was a rip at the bottom of the pouch, and a single coin lay at her feet. Beyond that, and farther down the street, was another coin, and another, and another, until the trail stopped at the last house at the end of the road. Its windows were not the kind that Carlisle was used to seeing, and they had no glass. Rather, the shutters which might seal those windows were wide open. He tried to see through the windows, but he could not. Between the windows, was a door, however, and through the door he saw a woman, perhaps sick, laying on a pallet. Beyond that, was another Golden Door. It seemed to be the same as the one he was looking at now. A perfect replica, with the two fig trees and the nets full of fishes. Seventy-five on the left side. Seventy eight on the right. And in the upper right hand corner there were two hills—and between the hills a lake with a fisherwoman who was looking past the shore to the village where two men stood with ploughshares before the two shops with the little girl who had the ripped purse at the end of the trail of coins which led to the house with the windows and the open door with the sick woman on the mat by another golden door . . . a replica of this one. It seemed almost exactly the same. He tried to remember the original two doors, but it was hard because they were so far back from where he was now. There were seventy-five on the right side, and seventy-eight on the left. Was that different? How many had there been on each side before? He felt a cool, black tide welling up within him, quenching the fires which he had not even known were torturing his soul—setting his mad mind at ease with its smooth bubbling waters. He was borne forward, up into the corner door, over to the hills. The tide poured down into the water, mixing with the lake in a way that his blood had not been able to do, foaming and frothing until it engulfed the little fishing boat with the woman. It dragged him forward to the village, and past the men, and down the trail of coins and through the doorway. It stopped by the sick woman. Carlisle stepped over her, leaving a trail of his polluted blood across her body. She was sick, he could tell. Her forehead was moist and her cheeks were red with fever. She was shivering too, beneath a coat that was being used as a blanket. The dirt floor crunched beneath his boots. The blood poured out from over the lip of his right boot with each step, mixing there with earth, foaming when it touched the ground into a red froth in just the same way that the black tide had mixed with the lake. He reached forward and touched the golden door. He felt its energy traveling through him.

"This door," Mephistopheles' voice came flowing up from within him. "This is the door I want you to open. The key is on the table to the right."

Carlisle looked behind him. The black tide had receded. He could see the long trail of his blood which led back through the village. The little girl was running back, collecting her coins. She was wiping the blood off of one. A little boy had stolen a coin that she hadn't been able to retrieve fast enough. He bit it to see if it was gold. Of course it was gold. Everything here was gold. Even the streets.

Carlisle moved over to the table and picked up the long golden key which sat there and then walked over to the door. The key fit, and the door unlocked. He heard the song of angels blaring in his ears, except it was not beautiful or joyous, but sad, melancholy and bitter. Deep where the angelsong was high, slow where the angels were staccato, death where the angels were life. He opened the door. Behind him he heard the girl shouting, demanding that the boy give her the coin back.

"I have to buy the fruit!" she said.

The boy taunted her with words Carlisle couldn't understand.

"Go on," Mephistopheles bade him.

He stepped into the midnight black room. Light came in from over his shoulder, so he shut the door behind him. Its hinges squealed out a high pitched whine, like a woman's issuance after being beaten by someone she loved. It closed with a sudden thud.

Like a coffin.

The room was midnight black and lit with red. He could not see the walls, but he could guess where they were. Hooded monks, carved out of obsidian, stood to either side of him. In their raised hands were bowls of blood. The blood of men who had been cannibalized, and whose killers had died while that blood was still in their bellies. The red light was coming from that blood. He saw an ear floating in one of those bowls, but the rest were empty. As the ear moved about in the blood, its shadow moved across the ceiling. In the center of the room was a carpet made of red human hair. It was soft as he stepped upon it.

I'm not bleeding any longer.

The carpet led him away from the red light. There, in the darkness, a man sat.

Slowly, he stood.

He was tall, and broad of shoulder. His beard was all black, and trimmed short. His robes, like those of the obsidian monks, flowed down about him, rippling like water as he moved. His expression was calm, almost emotionless, but slightly combative in a way that made Carlisle think that he must be ready to do great violence. A silver chain hung around his neck, and resting on his rippling robes. At the chain's end was a silver cross, except it was upside down.

The man was real. Too real. More real than anyone Carlisle had met since after his first death. Usually Carlisle could feel his mind working on the other souls of this damnation, feel his subconscious expectations compromising the reality of the soul before him. Not so with this one. This man was immune to his subconscious conjectures.

Carlisle felt a shadowy presence to his right, and turned to see Mephistopheles. Carlisle's blood ran cold. The devil was kneeling.

He swallowed and knelt himself.

Mephistopheles spoke, "I have brought him, milord."

The man nodded and stepped forward.

"I'm sorry," Carlisle said. "I can't. I can't learn from you. You're not a man of God."

The man crouched down beside him, his robes whisking around him with the sound of rustling paper—or skin. "You—who walk with a demon—choose an odd time to wax moral, but you are mistaken. I am more a man of God than any in Hell. Know that this is no boast, but a curse in this foul place. I say it humbly."

Carlisle shook his head. He was so scared he felt his heart beating in his chest—as if he really had a heart. He felt the testicles Maab had once taken from him receding into his body. "Your cross is upside down."

The man's cruel lips formed the semblance of a mirthful smile. "You mistake that for a mark of Satan. What you fail to consider is that not all saints were crucified right side up."

Carlisle nodded. The hellsong was loud in his ears, drowning out even the beating of his own illusory heart. "I accept. I understand."

"Good."

"I'm Carlisle."

"I don't care."

"Can I have your name?"

The dark eyes narrowed, and then opened again. "Yes, brother. You can call me Simeon. My understanding is that you seek the Boy of Heaven?"

"I do."

"Good. Then let's teach you how to climb souls. I take it you know a soul who straddles both these Hells?"

"Yes, Simeon. His name is Benson."

— 18 —

Rick called it a gondola, but Ellen knew better. This was a canoe. Ellen had thought they wouldn't be able to carry it without more help, but the thing was surprisingly light for its size, and they were able to move it. Rick's back was to her, and he had the canoe resting on one of his shoulders. The weight didn't seem to bother him at all, but Ellen felt herself tiring quickly. She'd tried carrying the thing on both shoulders, over her head, on her head, and to one side, but none of these positions were especially easy.

"Can we rest?" she asked.

She could only see the back of him as he shook his head no.

"I'm tired, Rick."

"I know, Ellen, but Molly's at the Kingsriver. We can't leave her there long. What if a hunter stops by?"

I must keep going.

For some reason, the idea that Molly was out there, vulnerable, made the job easier. It wasn't that she was any less tired, it was just that she understood why the task had to be done quickly.

Maybe that's why Galen was so strong. He always knew why things had to be done.

They finally entered into the Kingsriver chamber where the Hungerleaf Grove was. A light mist hung over the trees, but it wasn't thick enough to blot out the far walls. Alice and Massan stood together by the bank. Molly was crouching down, ready to hide, perhaps, in case the wrong person entered the chamber.

Ellen's arms were on fire, but Rick obviously intended to

put the canoe right next to the river. She held on for the last few moments. Rick set his end down, but hers slipped out of her hands a little too early, and the canoe hit the stone with a thud.

"Sorry," she said, but Rick didn't seem to care.

Molly stood. "Thank you, Rick. You're a good man."

Massan grasped his shoulder and Alice hugged him. Ellen felt an odd twinge of jealousy. It was as if, at that moment, Alice were hugging Arturus. She tried to stomp out that emotion quickly.

If you are going to start being jealous of Rick, this is going to be a long trip.

Rick set his pack down in the canoe. "I've brought some tarps. Best to give me your supplies now. I don't intend for us to capsize, but if we do, we need to have everything wrapped up."

Massan's unibrow became more pronounced as he went through his mountain climber style backpack. He loaded a few shells into his shotgun and then tied the pack's flap shut.

Alice packed unusually light, perhaps because she was just that thrifty, or perhaps because she owned very little. Molly had absolutely nothing other than her shotgun.

"I'll take the back of the canoe," Rick said. "Massan, you take point."

Massan raised his hand.

"What?" Rick asked.

"I thought this might be a good point in time to let you know that I can't swim."

Rick's jaw slackened for a second. "Yeah, good thinking. Alice, you take point. Massan, you're in the back with me."

Alice shrugged. "I'm a better shot than he is anyway."

"Truly?" Rick asked.

Molly smiled. "Fucking Annie Oakley, that one."

Rick picked up one end of the canoe, and Ellen got the other. Together they lowered it into the water.

"Alright then," Rick said. "Everybody in."

The Kingsriver was wide, and its current was slow, pulling them gently along through tremendous chambers. Usually the ceilings were natural, but occasionally they were domed and made of millions of small red bricks. Islands emerged from the light mist, some natural, and others formed from raised stone blocks. On both kinds, trees grew from patches of earth. Some of the trees were hungerleaf, which she recognized from their grey, scaly bark. None of them had any leaves remaining. Others she didn't recognize, which had black, single pointed leaves that hung from their branches in clumps of five. Their bark was more brown, though it was just as scaly.

The light in these chambers was usually a soft yellow, and it was often unevenly spread about the room so that, in certain corners, it was hard to see through the golden mists. It gave Ellen the impression that they were canoeing down a river at sunrise.

Rick worked the paddle in the back while Ellen rowed from her bench near the front. Alice knelt where there was no seat, seemingly intent on looking ahead of them. Ellen couldn't see her face, just the back of her blonde head. Alice had tied up her hair with a blue bit of cloth. Blue seemed to be her favorite color, which annoyed Ellen for some reason.

Blue is everybody's favorite color.

"I hear something," Alice said.

Ellen turned back to Rick. The man cocked his head to one side.

"Best to get down, Molly, just in case."

The river pulled them out of one chamber, dragging them slowly along. Rick had stopped paddling, letting the current do the work, and Ellen followed his lead. All was quiet. Then she heard voices. They seemed very distant. The next chamber they entered was particularly gigantic, with a long, even bank made of worked red bricks. This chamber was so deep that the light mist was able to block out the far wall, but she could see silhouettes of men moving. There must have been a dozen of them.

Rick shouted, "Don't shoot, it's Rick."

The silhouettes stopped and looked their way. As the canoe was moved forward by the slight current, Ellen began to make out the figures and faces of the Harpsborough hunters.

"Massan," Rick said softly, "I want you to lean down like you're fixing something in the boat. Then I want you to cover Molly with that blanket. Make sure it never rises above the edge of the canoe."

Ellen readjusted her grip on her woodstone paddle, realizing how sweaty her palms had become. There wasn't much room in the bottom of the canoe, and the blankets that covered Molly were going to look extremely suspicious.

"Fuck," Alice said, "it's Graham."

"Let me up." Molly's voice was muffled by the blanket she was edging over herself. "I'll take him out again."

"Quiet, Molly," Rick said.

"Ahoy," one hunter's distant voice called.

"What's that guy's name again?" Rick asked.

"Huxley," Massan answered. "He's Graham's right hand man these days."

They drifted closer.

"Come on over to this bank if you don't mind," Graham called, motioning to them with his gun in a gesture which could either be considered as completely natural, or horribly threatening.

"Be happy to," Rick yelled back. "Any danger ahead of us?"

Ellen started paddling again, keeping all of her effort on the right side. Rick let her turn the canoe until they were facing the hunters, and then he evened them out with long strokes on the left.

"If only!" Huxley replied. "Then we wouldn't be so hungry."

The hunters laughed in unison. The laughter didn't sound genuine. It made them sound like predators.

"Try and act normal," Rick said. "Try and look calm."

How in the hell am I supposed to do that?

Ellen looked towards Molly. She was completely covered, but the shape of the blankets around her didn't seem natural. Massan moved some packs on top of her, which helped.

"Don't look," Rick warned.

These hunters wouldn't really shoot us, would they?

Ellen tried to gauge their mood. Graham seemed particularly malicious, and the rest of the hunters were studying them a little too intently.

Could they know?

Ellen looked at Massan and then back to Alice. Was it possible that one of them had ratted them out? Who else knew that they were leaving?

Turi, I may be coming for you soon. I'm sorry, I know I promised. But this I can't help.

"Any chance we'd win?" Massan asked, his voice as soft as the river.

Rick snorted. "There's eleven of them. Not a chance."

As the canoe pulled up to the bank, Rick reached out and put his hand on the stone, slowing them until they halted. Ellen put her hand out as well to help hold them in place. The hunters had a perfect view into the bottom of their boat.

"So you're headed out, huh?" Graham asked.

"That we are," Rick said. "Headed all the way to Macon's Bend."

Graham nodded. "Hear there's good trading out that way." He put his foot up on a rock by the river and leaned down. "Hear there's a good bit of food."

"I'm afraid not," Rick said. "Galen scouted out that way before the . . . well before the failed expedition. He said the dyitzu had left there too."

Graham nodded.

Huxley put his own foot up on the rock as well, mimicking his leader's position. "Have to admit though, it is interesting timing."

"That it sure is," Graham said, putting his fist under his chin as if he was pondering something. "This wouldn't have anything to do with that recent incident in town, would it?"

The man's gaze settled on Rick.

"It does," Rick said.

Both Graham and Huxley straightened, the rest of the hunters nearly took a step back.

"Martin and a few of your men did an admirable job of keeping the peace," Rick said quickly. "I was truly impressed by your fearlessness. By how you stood up to a group of villagers who had you outnumbered, and by how you all reached a peaceful resolution. It renewed my faith in your city. That's why I'm willing to take a trip where I'm protecting your villagers."

Graham's face darkened, but the mood of the some of the other hunters seemed to change.

Rick's so smart. He's driving a wedge between them. Graham will notice it soon.

One of the hunters stepped forward. Ellen didn't know his name, but the man had traded her some bullets once.

"It's the least we could do," the hunter said. "I can't believe

Constance acted that way. I'm sorry, Rick. You've been with us a long time. We haven't forgotten that."

Graham looked back at his hunter. Ellen couldn't see the expression on his face, so she didn't know if he was surprised or angry. Slowly, Graham returned his gaze to the canoe. For a moment, his unreadable eyes rested directly on Ellen. She shivered.

Then he looked back to Rick. "You all look tense."

"It's their first time in a gondola," Rick said.

"And I can't even fucking swim," Massan added, eliciting some laughter from the hunters.

Graham didn't laugh, but he seemed slightly amused. "So what all are you intending to trade?"

There was silence for a second. The amusement left Graham's face, and he switched his rifle to his right hand.

"Okay," Massan said finally, "but you have to promise not to tell anyone. And I mean anyone at all."

What is he going to say?

Ellen looked back at Massan. Maybe he had a plan. Maybe he was just stalling for time.

"Secrets ain't safe in Hell," Huxley said. "Liable to get people killed."

"It's not that kind of secret," Massan answered, giving out some surprisingly genuine laughter. "I'm getting Kara a ring. I'm going to have Father Klein give us a union ceremony."

Despite how good he sounded, Ellen was beginning to notice his body odor. The man was sweating fiercely.

Some of the hunters laughed a bit, and they seemed more at ease, but Graham was still suspicious. He leaned forward. "Ahh, you see that's good news. Rumor around Harpsborough was that you were abandoning us. Maybe that explains why you have so much in your canoe. I wouldn't have listened to them, except that you were taking Alice with you. People talk, you know. They've been saying that Alice didn't forgive Mike for not trying to rescue Aaron. They've been saying you blame Mike for Molly's death."

The mention of Molly hit Ellen so hard that she made a small sound. She turned and looked at Rick, but the man was a better actor than she would have given him credit for. He always seemed so honest, but now he wore a poker face.

"Look," Massan said. "Do you really think I'd leave Kara behind if I went somewhere?"

"Of course you wouldn't—" one of the hunters began, but he was cut short by a glance from Graham.

"We didn't say that everyone in this boat was skipping town," Graham said. "Did we?"

Ellen looked back towards Rick, hoping he would have some answers. What she saw, though, was Molly's ankle, poking out from under the blanket. A backpack must have shifted, and there she was, exposed for all to see. They probably only had seconds left before someone noticed her.

Rick caught her gaze, and his poker face gave way for a second when their eyes met.

She saw his fear.

Oh please, God, help us.

But she was in Hell, she realized, and no prayer was going to save them.

Rick cocked his head to the side for a second and stared out across the lake. Some of the hunters, even Graham and Huxley, also looked that way. Then, calmly, Rick put his paddle down with his free arm into the canoe and leaned forward. The motion pulled the blanket over Molly's ankle. Even as he did so, he looked back at the hunters, as if he had thought he'd heard something and ignored it. His acting was so perfect, the action so natural, that the hunters didn't seem to think anything of it.

I love that man.

Ellen's sweaty hands were shaking badly enough that her grip was slipping on her own paddle. She put the paddle into the boat and then stuck her freed hand behind her back so no one would notice. Her hand on the bank was shaking too, but she hoped they'd think that was from the strain.

"So, Alice, why are you going along?" Graham asked. "Never heard of you leaving the village before."

"I just need . . ." she began, but obviously didn't want to finish what had popped into her head. "I just need to be helpful."

Massan began to stand up, grabbing onto the bank as the boat began to rock. He pulled himself halfway up onto the rocky shore. The blanket that covered Molly caught on his heel. He shook it off and then stood up. He pulled Graham aside, whispering into his ear, but the whispers were loud enough for Ellen to eavesdrop.

"What are you trying to do man?" Massan accused suddenly.

Graham was like a rock. "We don't take kindly to people abandoning us when the chips are down. It's not right to stay through the thick and leave in the thin."

Massan completely ignored the man's intimidation and continued on. "You know damn well Alice hasn't been able to get food lately," Massan pointed at her and then put his arm around Graham's shoulder, pulling him in tight. "Damn well. And you probably know that the only reason she offered to come and help us is because we'd have to feed her on the way. I sure as hell knew that. Rick sure as hell knows it. Fuck, even Ellen probably knows it. But that doesn't mean you have to run around and make her admit it! Why do you want to shame a girl like that? You know she doesn't sew like Chelsea. You know without Aaron she doesn't have a way to feed herself. Why do you have to be like this, man?"

"Oh," Graham said, doubt appearing on his face.

"'Oh' is right. It's not like she hasn't had it rough. Her lover's dead, her best friend turned out to be a fucking psychopathic Infidel lover . . . and you know she feels guilty about that. Why are you trying to make her feel worse? That's just sick, man."

"I didn't know, I wasn't thinking . . ."

"Sure. Sure you weren't," Massan said, rolling up his sleeves. "You know, Aaron would have never done something like this, and not just because it's Alice, either. You get one little bit of power, and you just want to lord it over everybody."

"Look, I'm serious," Graham insisted. "I didn't mean it like that."

Massan stood back for a second. Ellen could see the sweat stains around his armpits. She wasn't sure how the smell wasn't bothering Graham, but in her experience men didn't care as much about such odors.

"You sure?"

"I'm serious. I'll apologize," Graham offered.

Even from the boat, Ellen could see Massan's eyes grow wide. "Oh no. You shouldn't!"

"Shit! You're right," Graham admitted. "That would just make it worse. Okay, go on. Just get out of here, okay? I'll handle the guys."

Massan gave him a quick glance and then climbed back into the boat. Ellen realized as he sat down that she was holding her breath. His smell hit her hard, but she gritted her teeth and made sure not to breathe through her nose. She saw that Rick's hand, the one holding the paddle, was shaking. He was pressing it down to make sure the blanket didn't move.

"Well, I know things ain't as dangerous as usual," Graham said, clearing his throat, "but keep a careful eye out. Dyitzu might be rarer, but they haven't gotten any nicer."

"Will do," Rick said.

Ellen waved at the hunters and let go of the bank.

"Oh, Rick," Graham said suddenly.

Ellen caught her breath.

"Yeah?"

"We hadn't seen one, but a couple of days ago we heard some hound calls down that river. Be careful now. You know some of them devil dogs can swim."

Ellen let the breath go.

"Thanks for the warning," Rick said. "We'll be back soon."

He pushed off from the bank. Ellen's arms were so shaky that she bumped Alice with her paddle while she was getting it back into the water. She mumbled an apology, but Alice hadn't even noticed. Ellen's arms felt like jelly, and she barely hit water with her first attempt at paddling.

Rick's powerful strokes set the canoe moving, however, and he alternated sides to make up for her.

They passed through a tunnel and then into another chamber.

Alice began laughing and crying at the same time. Rick gathered up the blankets and Molly emerged, breathing hard. Ellen caught Alice up in a hug.

Molly leaned forward, grabbed Massan's head with both hands, and planted a loud kiss on his forehead. "Mwa! You beautiful man!" She was laughing while she spoke. "You beautiful, beautiful man. I can't believe how lucky Kara is to have you. You know, you really are going to have to get her that ring now."

Ellen felt her grin split her face. She looked over and saw Rick. She couldn't believe how well he had handled the situation. Molly may not have noticed his smooth misdirection, or even that her foot was exposed, but Ellen knew. Rick met her gaze and nodded.

"And to think," Rick said, "that was the easy part."

19

Calimay's lavender robed priestess knelt, almost disappearing into the mists. Her shoulders moved as she felt around the stone floor. After having found what she was looking for, she raised one arm and motioned to her two soldiers. They bent down beside her, thrust their arms into the mist, and grunted as they grabbed something on the ground. The priestess stood aside as they hefted up a piece of stone and set it aside.

"Ingenious," Galen congratulated them. "Yours would be a hard place to find."

Kelly's eyes narrowed and she stepped forward to challenge Calimay's priestess. "By showing us this, you just sentenced us to death. Why did you not blindfold us?"

The smile on the lavender clad woman's lips was no less cruel than the smirk Arturus remembered seeing on Maab. "Dakota will lead you. Myself and my other soldier will follow you."

Kelly grabbed her arm. "You will answer me."

Calimay's priestess, though shorter than even Johnny, dwarfed Kelly. She closed the distance between them, looming threateningly over the slighter woman.

Galen was suddenly by Kelly's side, and almost as quickly, the two soldiers stood up and leveled their shotguns at him.

"Go ahead, Dakota," Calimay's priestess ordered without taking her eyes off of Kelly.

Reluctantly, the soldier she'd called Dakota holstered his shotgun behind his back. He dropped down, disappeared into the mists, crawling into whatever passage had just been uncovered.

"And you, you Little Lady," the lavender clad priestess said with a derisive sneer, "you can follow Dakota."

Slipping into the passage will bother her ribs.

Kelly's face showed neither emotion nor pain as she bent down to enter the secret passage, though Arturus heard a small grunt as she did so. She too disappeared.

Galen searched through the mists with his foot until he had verified where the entrance was. Then he followed Kelly down.

Arturus lowered himself in after Johnny.

He hadn't expected the tunnel to be so small. In some places it was tighter than others, and he heard Galen's armor scraping against it as they moved. The walls were uneven, giving Arturus the impression that they had been carved out of Hell unnaturally.

If Kelly's right, then we're all about to be put to death. Or at least she will, we might get to be slaves. Her dreams of becoming a priestess, of having me as her slave, they won't come true. And all because that other priestess showed us their secret entrance without a blindfold.

The stone was beginning to heal back together in places, making the crawlway extremely tight. He felt liquid on some of the stones. He sniffed it.

Blood. Someone's injured.

He heard Avery cursing behind him.

"Everything okay?" Arturus whispered back over his shoulder.

"Quiet," one of Calimay's soldiers ordered.

The passageway reminded Arturus very much of the one he and Galen had used to infiltrate Maab's ceremony, except that this one hadn't been lined with rustrock. It might have been his imagination, but even accounting for the roughness of the walls, the previous crawlway seemed to have been better constructed.

They climbed up and out of the passage after traveling for what Arturus guessed to be thirty yards, emerging into a place so dark he couldn't even tell if it was a room.

Arturus searched about himself with his hands until he found a wall. He heard grunting as the last of their group exited the crawlway. Stone ground on stone, and Arturus could feel the vibrations of the passage closing in the floor beneath him.

He felt a hand touch him.

"Sorry," Avery said.

Arturus guided him to the wall.

"Thanks," Avery whispered.

"Wait here," Calimay's priestess ordered. "I'll be back for you."

Arturus listened to her and her warriors' footsteps as they left. He breathed out a sigh of relief.

"Are they gone?" Aaron asked.

"For the moment," Galen answered.

There was still some noise in the chamber, however. It sounded like someone was breathing rather hard, but perhaps was trying to keep it quiet. Arturus cocked his head to one side and focused on the sound.

Kelly was crying.

Arturus had hoped that this room was not cloaked in total darkness, and that his eyes might begin to adjust after a few minutes—but it had been a few minutes, and the blackness remained.

Avery was sitting so close to him that he could feel the hunter's shoulder against his own. For some reason this gave Arturus a certain amount of comfort.

"This ain't good, Turi," Avery whispered.

"I know."

"I think they probably still have slaves, is what I'm saying."

Slavery was a terrifying proposition in and of itself, but Arturus knew that if Calimay were anything like Maab, Avery's life was about to be far worse than he was imagining. For some reason, he thought of Kyle.

We shouldn't have let you die.

Kelly's show of weakness had shaken him deeply.

This is what Hell is. It keeps you alive until it's broken you. Only then does it take you.

"I want to tell you something," Arturus whispered back, "something that Julian told me when I spoke to him."

"What?"

"Even if they don't kill us outright, bad things are going to happen to us. Very bad things. Things you haven't even imagined yet. Punishments that the Fore would never think of doing, not even to a murderer. Not even to an infidel. When it gets bad enough, the stilling will take you. You have to fight that, no matter what. Don't give in to it. When it gets that bad, when all of your dignity has been taken from you and you are left broken in ways I don't even want to tell you about, just try to remember. Remember something. Anything. From your life. From Harpsborough. Something you've imagined. Think of that one thing that makes you happy, and don't let go because if you do, the darkness will take you. The stilling will take you."

He heard Avery swallow. "I'll try. I'll try to fight the stilling."

"But there's something worse than the stilling, Avery. Something that Julian was so afraid of he could barely even talk to me about it."

"Worse than the stilling?"

"Yes. They can hurt you so bad that you'll start to like it. Then it'll be worse than the stilling."

"Why? Why would that be worse?"

"Because then you'll be one of them."

20

Michael had hoped that the addition of the actual king pieces, previously represented by wine glasses, would make it more obvious when Davel Mancini was about to check him. It hadn't. He felt like Mancini had him good and trapped. He didn't see how he could move a piece without inviting disaster. He moved a pawn instead, almost out of frustration.

Mancini leaned forward and took a long look at the board, pursing his lips as he did so. It was an expression that Michael knew well. Mancini only made that face when he had many good moves available but couldn't figure out which one was the absolute best. As Michael's eyes roved the board, he began to see what moves Mancini might be considering. This was a lost game, he figured, and it wasn't going to last much longer.

Michael felt his frustration boil over. "I'm going to feed the people, Davel."

Mancini's gaze snapped up at him.

That had gotten his attention. The dimness of the parlor room wasn't very flattering to Mancini's face, adding depth to the dark circles under his eyes and to the ridges on his brow. The man's brown eyes looked even more beady this way—but dim what Mancini preferred, so dim it was.

"You aren't serious," Mancini tried.

Michael massaged the bridge of his nose with his thumb and forefinger. "I am."

"It won't work how you think it will," Mancini warned. "There are almost five hundred of them. It may seem like we have a lot of food here, but it won't look that way after you start trying to be noble. Particularly now that we're feeding the hunters."

"How long has it been since you started a brew?" Michael asked.

Mancini's jaw clamped shut.

"How long?"

"It's been a while."

Michael stood up and walked across the plush dyitzu carpet. He stopped before a glass decanter that was half-filled with bloodwater. "See, I'm helping you out," he joked as he poured himself a glass. He sipped the red concoction, feeling the burn in his mouth. "If we feed the village, you may have customers again."

Mancini's beady eyes returned to the board. "How long would we last? A month? Then what would the villagers do? Would they even believe us when we told them we'd run out? Would they not come looting?"

Michael let his eyes wander to the dimmed light orbs. "We wouldn't have run out, then, would we?"

"Of course we would have."

"If they looted the Fore, they'd find all our personal stashes."

"Those are our property," Mancini said, "not the Fore's and not the village's. Ours. We earned it. You can't suggest that anyone, even you, has the right to take that away from us."

Michael slammed his glass down a little harder than he'd meant to, causing a bit of bloodwater to splash onto his fingers. "I don't have the right. I don't even have a way I could make you all do that. But just because I can't make you do it," Michael walked back across the carpets and pointed his finger towards one of the drawn window curtains, "doesn't mean that they can't. Open that curtain, Davel. Open it and look. They're out there, sitting in the village. Not hunting, not doing anything. They're just looking for an excuse."

Mancini's eyes left the chess game for a second time.

"You know they will come, Davel. They almost mugged Rick. People have been leaving."

"Let them leave."

"But they don't really leave, do they? They just haunt the same wilds and stop paying taxes. They compete with our hunters. We've got to adapt to this new Hell, or they're going to come in here and make us adapt."

Mancini leaned back and closed his eyes.

"I need you, Davel. You think I've gone soft, that I've lost my loyalty to the Fore, but you've got it wrong this time, and you know it. I've just been seeing what was coming all along, and you're just now getting it. I need you, Davel. I need that brain of yours. You've got to whip something up. You've got to start some tap dancing. You figure it out, and I'll support you when it comes to the votes."

Mancini kept his eyes closed as he leaned forward. He put his elbows on the table that supported the chess board and rested his head in his hands. Michael knew what this gesticulation meant as well because he had seen it many times while playing the man in chess. Sometimes even the crafty Mancini would suddenly find himself in a dangerous position. Most men might give up and admit a loss. Not Mancini. He'd rest his head in his hands, just like this, and think his way out.

Sure, the Fore seemed doomed. Michael certainly couldn't think of a way to save it. But with Mancini, there was hope. He'd played the man dozens of times over the course of the last few weeks, and Mancini had never lost.

Ellen awoke gently from her sleep. The canoe rocked, ever so slightly, back and forth. Rick, who sat high on the back of the canoe, propelled and steered the craft all at the same time with his strong, even strokes. The rest were asleep, Massan the most noticeably so. His snoring was as even and as peaceful as the canoe's movement.

Rick noticed she was awake and gave her a smile. His smile filled her with warmth.

Mist clung to the river. Islands came out from the fog like shadows, coalescing into stone as they passed before returning into the mists to become shadows again. Her thoughts did the same.

"Where does the river go?" she asked Rick softly.

Rick smiled, his eyes narrowing on something in the river that he carefully maneuvered them around. "To Macon's Bend."

"No, I mean, where does it go, really? Where does it end?"

Rick paddled a few more times, not answering. Ellen didn't mind. She let her head rest on the side of the boat and looked up towards the ceiling. She couldn't see it at all in most places, but here and there the brick stonework was visible through the haze. She had almost forgotten that she'd asked a question when Rick responded.

"I don't know. Some say that Hell is infinite and that the river flows forever. Others say that the end of Hell is also its beginning and that the rivers are like this too. They say that they flow into themselves, feeding themselves, like serpents eating their own tails. Others say that they begin and end like any river might on earth."

The branches of a tree she did not recognize passed over her. Its bark was white in places, and grey where the top layer bark had peeled away. Its branches were full of leaves so small they looked almost like needles.

She wondered if it was her imagination, or if the mist was getting thicker.

"Which do you believe?" she asked.

"I believe none, until I have reason to. There could be many other ways, as well, which rivers run."

"Surely you must believe one. It'd be silly not to!"

Rick chuckled. "Galen would set you straight on that one, dear. He'd tell you it was silly to believe something with no reason. He'd tell you that the default position is to believe no claim until it has evidence, and then to give it only a provisional acceptance."

"Do you think he's right?"

"Well, that method certainly does cut out a lot of bullshit, doesn't it?"

Ellen laughed. "But the river running into itself, it's such a beautiful idea. I wish it were true."

"Then I'll wish that with you—"

There was a loud thud and the boat shifted suddenly. Ellen sat up straight. The others were startled awake.

"What was that?" Molly asked.

A black substance was trailing out from behind their canoe.

"Is that blood?" Alice asked.

"Too dark," Massan said.

"A corpse's blood," Rick warned.

Ellen turned and looked at the river before them. Hands, bloated grey and rotten, were rising up from the misty waters.

She screamed.

21

The lavender robed priestess returned carrying a single flickering candle. Its burning produced the smell of dyitzu fat, reminding Arturus of Maab's bathing chambers. He stood slowly.

"I have spoken with Calimay." The candle wavered in her hands. "You are to be imprisoned. She will sentence you at her convenience."

Avery rose to stand beside Arturus. He looked like he was about to speak but Aaron got there first.

"We understand. We look forward to bartering with her."

The woman laughed. "You have nothing we want."

"We represent a city, Harpsborough." Aaron said. "You'd be a fool to refuse our extended hand of friendship."

"There can be no friendship between wolves and lambs."

Galen stood. "That, most honored priestess, is something that Calimay must decide herself. Unless, of course, you presume to speak for her?"

"I speak for myself. Now follow me."

She led them through dark purple corridors that spiraled inward towards some central point. They were built in much the same way as the tunnels Arturus remembered surrounding Maab's ritual chamber. Still, the area must not have been completely safe because the Carrion born that flanked her kept their shotguns at the ready.

Men, not Hell's Architect, had laid the bricks of these walls—though they'd done so in a cunning way in order to make them blend in with the surroundings. Two hints let Arturus know of the corridors' human origins. For one, the smaller and elongated grey stones, evenly spaced, did not look like skulls when they were on the edges of his vision. Secondly, in many places the stones were trying to heal, some dripping down across the rocks as if they were melting, others growing odd, almost crystalline structures.

As the priestess led them farther in, Arturus began to see places where the pretense of camouflage had been abandoned altogether, and sandbags had been used to bolster some of the construction.

They need rustrock to make their illusions last. They must not have enough.

Arturus felt a small hand enter his. He looked down to see Kelly. She gave him a reassuring smile. He gripped her hand tightly.

They were led to a wall that showed no signs of healing. Arturus turned to one side to see if the illusions of skulls appeared. They did not. Calimay's priestess walked up to the wall and rapped on it twelve times. The wall rose, and a blue undulating light poured out from behind it, washing over them all. The chamber beyond was more beautiful than the parlor room of the Fore. It was more beautiful than even Maab's bathing chamber.

Its ceiling was twenty feet tall and made of some sort of clear glass. Or perhaps there was no glass at all, and the people who fashioned this chamber had simply managed to make a lake float in the air. The wavy water above them was illuminated with that blue light, oscillating smoothly as Arturus watched. The chamber beneath the water was fifty feet wide, over a hundred feet long, and its masonry took full advantage of the space. Stone statues, carved out of a white marble that shone sky blue in this environment, marked off a walkway in the center of the chamber. The statues themselves were the size of fully grown persons, men and women frozen in varying poses. Here a man was bent back to throw a javelin, and there another was poised to hurl a discus. There was a woman with a jug in one arm, pouring crystal water into the open mouths of the knee high children clinging to her legs.

A single carpet made of some cloth that Arturus couldn't recognize traveled between those statues, leading towards an arched exit that was closed off by a drawn, red curtain.

Embroidered on the curtain with gold thread was the likeness of a supine Minotaur, its head pulled back by an angry hero, its belly slit open and spouting golden blood. To the right and left of the carpet and the statues were long wading pools, each about ten feet wide and nearly eighty feet long. Each pool was only a foot or so deep, but they were filled with waters so smooth that they appeared to be solid glass.

Two fountains stood out in each wading pool. The fountains' bases were carved to look like groups of men, each wearing the armor of a bygone age, each carrying a body shield in one hand and a short sword on the other. On the shoulders of these men were women whose toga draped bodies wound together into each other until their outstretched hands became one with a jar. Arturus expected that water would issue forth from those jars if the fountains were turned on.

He looked back towards the lavender robed priestess. There was a smirk on her face, and she was staring intently at Galen.

"Not bad," his father said.

Arturus felt drawn towards the carpet, towards the curtain with the bull, but Calimay's priestess had different plans. Her men pushed them with leveled shotguns to the right side of the chamber and out of the small exit there.

The room they entered was lit by brilliant spherical lightstones. They were exactly like the ones the Citizen's kept in the Fore's parlor room. There were more of Calimay's Carrion born waiting there. A gate closed behind them, sliding down from the ceiling. The iron slammed into the stone with a thud. They'd been locked in with the lavender robed priestess and five of her men.

There was another exit from this room, Arturus noticed, but it was gated as well.

"Now strip," Calimay's priestess ordered. "We're to make sure you have no weapons on you."

Arturus did as he was told, taking off his sewn-together boots first. The lavender robed priestess smiled at the modesty of the Harpsborough hunters who were covering their nakedness with their hands. Galen would give her no such pleasure. He stripped without shame. Arturus didn't care what any of the others thought of him, except for Kelly. He looked to her. She, like Galen, had no fear of her own nudity. Her body was slender and much better muscled than Arturus had imagined. Her breasts were nothing like Maab's. They were spare where Maab's were over proportioned.

He looked up into her eyes. She was staring back at him and only him. Abashed, he looked away.

The other hunters had just finished getting their boots off. Calimay's priestess was admiring Galen's form. Arturus pulled off his black t-shirt, which obstructed his view for a second. When he could see again, he saw the lavender clad woman had moved to stand in front of his father.

"You," she was saying, "you I'm going to enjoy tonight."

If the threat meant anything to Galen, he wasn't showing it.

Her robes swirled around her as she turned towards the Harpsborough hunters.

They had all been stripped now. Johnny and Aaron were still covering themselves with their hands. Avery was doing his best to pretend he didn't care. The soldiers searched them thoroughly, inspecting every orifice. Arturus did his best to remain as stoic as his father while they checked him.

The soldier next to Arturus gasped and grabbed his arm. "You'd better take a look at this, milady."

Oh shit.

Calimay's priestess turned towards him suddenly. "What is it?"

"He's been marked. He's one of Maab's chosen."

The lavender robed woman's lips parted. She rushed forward, grabbing his arm and inspecting the tattoo. "And you, my little duckling," she whispered into his ear, "you are a long way from home. You're the stranger boy who escaped Pyle."

She knocked twice against the iron bars in front of them. They opened, revealing a dark hallway.

"Lock them up," the lavender priestess ordered. "And send someone to Calimay. Tell her we have one of Maab's. Tell her we have the angel's get."

The bloated hand grabbed the lip of the canoe only inches away from where Ellen sat. Swollen black veins stood out from its puffy blue grey skin. The force of its grip caused pus to spew out from lesions along its knuckles. More leaked out from under its fingernails. The canoe began to tip with the corpse's weight.

Its head rose up out of the river, water pouring down over its face. Its rotten, waterlogged stench hit Ellen like a blow. One of its eyes was nearly bloated shut, the other only an empty socket.

The blast of Alice's gun so close to Ellen's head nearly deafened her. The corpse fell back, but its hand still clung to the craft, its body trailing along with them. Massan used the butt of his paddle to lever the hand off of the canoe. Frenzied strokes from Molly kept them moving.

"Keep the corpses from grabbing hold!" She heard Rick yell over the ringing in her right ear.

Ellen saw another hand emerging from the water and she batted at it with her paddle. It managed to touch the canoe, but her blow made it fall just short of being able to get a grip. It tried anyway, its fingernails digging into the woodstone lip of their craft. The fingernails gave way, ripping off of the hand as the canoe was sped forward.

Ellen gritted her teeth, swinging out even harder, keeping the next offending limb clear from the craft altogether. Alice fell into her suddenly, and Ellen saw a corpse's hand rise out of the river just a little ahead. She struggled past Alice to try and bat the thing's hands away, but she wasn't going to make it.

The canoe rushed forward and turned just slightly from one of Rick's paddle strokes. The front of the craft met the corpse head on. Black blood and water fountained up from the impact.

"Row, Massan!" Rick ordered. "I need more speed so we can beach her. Molly, take the right side."

Ellen swung her paddle back and forth, never able to guess quite where the next limb would rise.

"Wrong way!" Massan shouted. "Wrong way!"

The boat turned suddenly and Ellen looked up from the water. The banks of the river were packed with the undead, massing together, knocking each other into the river in places.

"Where are we going?" Molly shouted.

"Keep swinging, Ellen!" Rick ordered.

Ellen saw another hand rise from the river and swatted it down, surprised at her own strength.

"Where are we going?" Molly shouted again.

"I don't know," Rick answered.

"You have to fucking know!"

The hands kept coming. Ellen continued, swinging with abandon. Swollen limbs broke at times before her blows, filling the air with the sound of cracking bones. Elbows popped out of joint, and fingers were splayed by her crushing downward strikes.

She missed a hand, which clutched firmly onto the canoe. Alice fired again, and this time the corpse let go with the blast.

Rick steered them down a fork. The river here was only ten or so feet wide. The mist was so thick that Ellen couldn't see the walls of the chamber. Here and there she saw silhouettes of the corpses walking through the fog. The river current was dying away. Massan was sweating badly and breathing hard.

Arms had stopped coming up from the deep, but Ellen kept a close eye on the water and kept her paddle at the ready.

"Stop for a sec, Massan," Rick ordered.

Massan did so. His dark face flushed with the effort. She couldn't smell him through the stench of the waterlogged undead.

Ellen looked to Rick, who had his head cocked to one side.

He's listening.

The canoe was still moving slightly, but most of that was their momentum. The water here was almost still. She could hear the wake of their canoe splashing against the sides of the river and echoing down this chamber. There were other sounds in the mists, though. Scuffs of shoes, and dried skin rubbing against rotten cloth. The corpses were all around them.

"Massan, take a break," Rick said. "Molly, your turn at the oars."

The canoe rocked a bit as they switched places. Molly grunted as she sat down. From the center of the canoe she could place her paddles between sets of notches and use two at once.

"Nice and easy, Molly," Rick said. "Nice and easy."

The air seemed unnaturally warm. Water began to condense on Ellen's skin, and she started to feel almost like she was breathing water.

Molly's even strokes pushed them forward.

The stone banks were uneven, seeming natural in places. She saw what she thought was a hand, maybe thirty feet downstream, rising up from the water. But it wasn't moving, and as they drew closer, she could tell that the limb had no digits. There was a tree just beyond it.

Ellen thought it must not have been a corpse's limb at all. "What's that?"

"It's a root, a cypress knee," Rick answered. "I think I know where this fork goes."

"Is that to a good place or a bad place?" Massan asked.

"That I don't know."

Ellen wished Rick would just lie.

"I can't see the bank," Molly said aloud, "or the walls."

It was true. Trees, cypress trees if Rick was correct, were all that Ellen could see, and most of those appeared only as shadows in the thick air. The branches which hung directly over their heads drooped low over their canoe. Their leaves, arranged almost like a fern's, dragged across her face.

There was the sound of wood scraping on wood, and their boat vibrated.

"What was that?" Ellen asked.

"It's nothing," Rick assured her.

The cypress knees were thicker now, some almost five feet high, and Rick had to work to avoid them. They were taller and more numerous near their tree trunks, thinning and shortening as they radiated out in circles.

It must have been a knee that scraped the bottom of our boat.

Alice inhaled quickly and aimed her pistol. A corpse was standing between two trees. It wasn't moving towards them. Some of the knees had grown up about it, spiraling around its legs and torso.

The corpse was trying to come towards them, but it couldn't move.

"Oh God," Molly breathed.

"Slow and steady," Rick said.

He steered them closer to the corpse in order to get around a root cluster. Here some of the knees had grown back down into the water, making a series of small arches. A few of those arches were large enough for their canoe to fit under.

The trapped corpse extended its arms and leaned forward, struggling to escape its wooden prison. Its head was oddly misshapen, its skull caved in on the right side. That eye socket was empty. As it struggled, water poured out of its missing eye.

It receded into the fog as Molly rowed.

Ellen could hear the waters rippling around them. It was far too much noise to just be the wake of their canoe. The forest must be full of corpses. She looked up, but there was no sign of any ceiling through the mist.

"Does this end, Rick?" Massan asked.

"I'm not sure," Rick answered.

Jesus, can you please lie?

Their boat bumped into a cypress arch.

"Back up, Molly." Rick whispered. "Then move ahead slower."

Ellen didn't want to go slower. She wanted to go faster. There was more scraping as they negotiated their way through the roots. The trees were much thicker now.

But the mist is thinning.

She still couldn't see an end to the chamber they were in, either left or right, or even up. All she could see was the lake and the trees.

"Hold your fire," Rick said.

Ellen turned to Alice, who was looking out across the water. There was corpse picking its way towards them.

"Only shoot when they get close."

The canoe vibrated again as it scraped its way through more knees.

"It's getting tough to row," Molly said.

She was right, the roots kept getting in her way as she swung the oars. The canoe stopped after only a few more strokes.

Rick jumped into the lake. The water came up to his mid-thigh. "Everyone out. Quickly."

There were more corpses, maybe five or six, in various places at the edge of the mist. Frightened, Ellen crawled out of the boat. The water came up to her waist.

Rick hooked his rifle strap around the horn at the head of the canoe and then put the strap around his shoulder.

"Surround me," he ordered. "Keep pace. Massan, lift up the back of the canoe if I need it, okay?"

"Okay," Massan answered.

Just three feet away from Ellen, immersed completely in water, was the torso of a corpse. It was waving its hands at her.

Like the previous corpse, it seemed stuck—locked in by cypress roots.

They can be anywhere in the water.

Rick began tugging the canoe over the knees. The sound of the wood scraping on wood was horrendously loud, echoing throughout the forest. Ellen did her best to stay focused on the horizon, trying to see if there were a pack of corpses headed their way, but it was no use. To step through the knees without tripping, she had to keep her eyes on her feet—particularly in case there were any more submerged corpses.

"Stay with me, Ellen." Rick's voice hit her ears. "Don't fall behind."

She didn't dare fall behind.

The mist continued to thin. Massan began cursing, stopped, and beat at the water with the butt of his rifle. Black blood welled up around him. He rushed to catch up.

"They're caught in the roots," he said. "Some of them are completely below the surface."

"Why don't they float?" Molly asked, panic in her voice.

"Undead don't float." Rick looked up. "Straight ahead," he warned.

"I've got him," Alice's voice was high pitched, but calm.

Her pistol cried out amongst the trees. There was a splash of water. Ellen didn't want to see, so she kept her eyes on her feet.

"Good shootin'," Massan congratulated her.

The roots almost seemed to be trying to grab her. She was stepping on them in places where they grew into the floor of the lake. Her jeans clung to her legs, rubbing her skin raw. Her thigh muscles were burning from the effort.

Massan was also struggling badly, wheezing as he breathed.

She saw another arm, reaching out at her . . . but it was just a root.

Even her shoulders felt tired now. She looked at Rick. The weight of the canoe was wearing him down, badly. His chest was heaving with deep, gasping breaths.

"How much farther?" Massan managed between his own gulps for air.

"I don't know," Rick admitted.

Just fucking lie.

The mist had cleared greatly, but she could still only see trees around them. Ellen craned her neck backwards, hoping again to see the ceiling. She lost her balance and fell. One root hitting her in the stomach while another caught on her pants leg.

She saw stars.

A slender hand cupped her elbow and helped drag her to her feet. She looked up to see Alice's tired smile. Ellen tried to breathe, but she couldn't. She couldn't even stand up straight, and when she tried to step forward her left ankle buckled. She dropped again.

"Are you okay," Alice asked.

No.

Ellen fought for breath as she struggled back to her feet. "My ankle."

"Can you walk?" Rick asked.

Ellen didn't know.

"Ellen, I need you to walk right now, okay. I need you to do that for me. I don't care how much it hurts."

Ellen tried again. Her ankle stung badly as she put her weight on it, but it held her. She was starting to get her breath back, too. Another step, and another. Then her foot landed on a root, bending her ankle. Ellen almost shouted out in pain and tears formed behind her eyes.

The others were moving, so she had to keep up. Massan was lifting the back of the canoe, helping Rick make his way forward.

There was still no end in sight. She looked to the right and the left, feeling like a trapped animal. With the mists gone, she could see farther into the woods behind her.

The corpses were there, a wall of them, shoulder to shoulder, advancing slowly through the woods.

"Rick!" Ellen called, hearing her tears in her own voice.

Rick spun around and looked. They all did.

"Keep our pace the same," Rick ordered. "You're going to want to speed up, but you can't."

Ellen put her hands on a cypress knee to ease some of her weight off of her left ankle. The next few steps were torture. She heard someone sloshing forward quickly. It was Massan.

"Keep your pace!" Rick yelled.

"They're behind us, Rick!" Alice warned.

"You can't go much faster." Molly was saying. "You'll leave Ellen behind."

"I can keep up," Ellen lied.

"It doesn't matter, Rick answered. "Massan, stay steady."

"Why?" Massan was shouting, his eyes wild, his wheezy breathing erratic.

"Listen to me," Rick grunted as he pulled the canoe over more roots.

Massan did not appear to be listening. "I'm going to run."

"Slow down." Alice's voice was soft, but desperate.

Molly grabbed Massan by one shoulder as he tried to pass her. "Listen to him!"

"Why?" Massan asked again.

"Because we get tired," Rick said.

Ellen's vision was blurred, but she didn't dare stop walking. The pain was getting intolerable. She could see her ankle swelling through the water when she lifted her left foot.

"And they don't," Alice finished.

Behind Ellen, the woods creaked and the waters rippled with the passage of the legion of corpses.

22

A second of Calimay's priestesses arrived, her robe adorned with golden trim. She seemed similar to Calimay's other priestess in her broad build and square face, but her hair and eyes were a much lighter color.

She was followed by nearly a score of guards.

"Tamara, see Calimay," she said, dismissing the first priestess. "Calimay wants them imprisoned in pairs. The angel's get is to not to be placed with Maab's priestess."

She looked at the nude men, her gaze stopping on Galen. "Put the angel child with the big one. And this one," she said, pointing at Avery. "Put him with the priestess. The other two go with each other. Double shifts on guard duty. No breaks."

She turned on her heel and left the chamber. The soldiers hastened to obey. Avery managed to stay next to Arturus as the iron gate was rising slowly. Arturus guessed they were using a counterweight system similar to their battery back home.

Arturus' heart was in his throat.

"You can put your clothes back on," A guard told them.

Gratefully, Arturus obeyed. For some reason his clothes made him feel more human.

"Guess I get the room with the lady," Avery joked as he pulled on his pants.

Arturus nodded.

"I can't wait to spend some quality time with that bitch."

Arturus felt stunned and looked over at Avery past the guards which held him. "You don't mean you'll . . ."

Avery grinned. "No one's going to stop me. Nobody here

gives a damn about Maab's people." Avery turned to one of the guards who held him. "Do ya?"

Calimay's guard grinned back and shook his head.

Arturus was struck with the memory of Maab breaking the bullman. "Don't!"

Avery seemed surprised by the emotion in his voice.

"Promise me you won't," Arturus demanded.

"Okay, okay," Avery said. "You've got my word."

After the gate had receded into the ceiling, they were dragged into a dark corridor. The doors on the right and left were rusted somewhat, so they must have been exposed to corpsedust after they were installed. Still, they were thick, and iron, and would probably be strong enough to hold a Minotaur. Some of the doors had barred openings in them. Through the bars, Arturus could tell that the cells were occupied, often with half a dozen or more people crammed into the tiny rooms.

"Jesus," Aaron muttered. "They've got a lot of prisoners."

"Not prisoners," Galen said. "This is how they treat their own people. This is where the serfs stay."

Two soldiers tossed Arturus into the first open cell. They tried to push Galen in too, but the man's massive frame remained still while the guard shoved at him. Calimay's man only managed to push himself away. Galen strolled into the chamber.

Arturus set his jaw, trying to feel a bit of pride for his father's dignity.

The door closed behind Galen, its echo filling the chamber. After a moment, the sound died away. It was almost completely black. Arturus could only make out the barest shadow of Galen while his father moved to explore the room.

Kelly promised she'd keep me safe, but she'll probably be killed first.

"I guess Rick was right, huh?" Arturus asked. "I shouldn't have come."

"I'm sorry, Turi." Galen's shadow moved along the edge of the chamber, searching for weaknesses in the rock.

Arturus knew he would find none.

This is my life now. No Alice. No Rick. Just slavery. My only hope is that Kelly gets power, and that my slavery is bearable. Galen can't protect me against this. He's not strong enough. He's failed me.

"If you find a weakness in the rock, where would we escape to, father?"

Galen grunted noncommittally, but did not stop his search.

"I'm tired of fighting."

"I raised you better than that, son. You won't be tired for long."

You're wrong. I'm tired. I'm dead tired. I've found out that I'm ten times as strong as I thought I was. But I also found out the Carrion is ten times stronger than that. We've lost.

Arturus moved so that Galen could search the wall where he'd been sitting. "What did they mean when they called me an angel's get?"

"For some reason they appear to think that your mother is an angel."

"Is she?"

Galen didn't answer.

"Is that 'some reason' a good reason?"

His father began working at the door. "They say that about a decade and a half ago, an angel was captured by Maab. The angel was pregnant. Maab was going to raise the child, but a man came and took the babe away. They were unable to find him afterwards."

"Are you that man, father?"

Galen did not respond.

"Is my mother an angel?"

"Arturus, you have to know that we have good—"

Arturus stood up. "Who's my mother?"

"That's not a fair question."

"Did you steal me?" Arturus shouted. "Did you take me from my mother?"

Galen's shadow stopped moving.

"Did you?"

"Son . . ."

Arturus felt tears forming in the corners of his eyes. His heart was beating so hard that he felt his blood pounding in his ears. "Did you steal me from my mother?" Arturus' voice echoed in the chamber.

"Maab wanted you, son. She was going to raise you."

"Where's my mother?"

Galen was still silent.

Arturus felt his rage boiling over. He stepped forward towards his father, his hands raised. "Where's my mother?"

"Turi—"

"Why didn't she raise me? Galen! I want to know her. Isn't that fair since you took me from her? Where is she? Is she still out there, longing for me? Is she still alone, captured by Maab?"

"Son the less you know, the less they can take from you."

"Let them take it! Let them! We're lost. There's nothing we can do. This is the rest of our lives, Galen. We're going to be slaves or we're going to be dead. Can't you see that? You keep on trying, searching the walls like we've still got a chance. Like there's some place to escape to. But there's not. For once, just once, why can't you just feel something? Why can't you quit pretending you're some kind of machine? You can't keep fighting. We've lost." Arturus felt his legs quivering. "We've lost."

"Son, it's been a long time since you've slept."

"Where's my mother?"

Galen's hands touched Arturus' shoulders. "Sit down, son, and—"

"Where is she?"

"I said sit down!" Galen ordered.

Arturus felt his legs give out beneath him.

"And now you'll listen, boy," Galen knelt beside him and whispered harsh words into his ear. "It was all I could do to keep you safe, son. All I could do. It was your mother's wish that you be free from Maab. I loved your mother. I loved her with my whole heart. I loved her like Paris loved Helen, except that in Hell, lovers can't get very far. I made an oath to her, son. I made it, and I intend to keep it. Now you may think all is lost, you may think that things look bad for you, but trust me— compared to the hell you would have grown up in, this isn't shit. Maab's not the only person who's looking for you. There are other far more powerful forces that want you. Maybe it's better that Maab gets you than they. Maybe you should have been left behind, but I don't believe it. I think you love the life that I and Rick and Harpsborough tried to give you. I think you love those first years, and I'm sorry that they had to end. I'm sorry that you're here facing Hell as it was intended to be, but you've got to grow up sometime, don't you?"

Arturus' anger had fled. "My mother, she was really an angel?"

Galen's tears dropped onto Arturus' shoulders. "She was. The most perfect girl I'd ever seen. She'd fallen because of that perfection. Because the things that made her beautiful to me made her ugly in the eyes of Heaven. But they got her, son. Maab got her, and I could not retrieve her."

"She's still Maab's?"

"I can't tell you these things. If they break you, you'll give up your own mother."

Arturus swallowed. "Is she safe?"

"No, son, no she is not."

"Am I your son? By blood?"

"Yes, Turi. Yes you are."

Arturus let out a sigh.

I'd always thought so.

"Can we just stop fighting, Father?" Arturus felt weak. His father's tears ran down his chest, soaking into his shirt.

I don't have anything left in me.

"Your mother's eyes were blue, son. Her hair was so blonde that her eyelashes looked spectacularly dark. It brought out those eyes—if they watched you now, would you want to give up in front of them?"

Arturus reached up and put his hand on his father's shoulder. "We've lost, father. It's okay to give up after it's over."

"In games, sure. But this is no game. It is not acceptable that you lose. That's the way it is when you have children, Turi. In almost any other enterprise, it's okay to fail when things are beyond your control. With children, it's not. In Hell, with our lives and souls, it's not. Now the people, the universe, the gods and devils who are responsible for torturing your mother and trying to enslave her offspring are still alive. Some of those we never had a chance to defeat. Surely you must have some anger in your heart for them. Surely these things make you unbreakable."

Arturus felt his father's warmth. "Am I?"

"You remember the rocks as we entered?"

"Yes, sir."

"Do you remember anything about them?"

"Some of the walls were artificial. Some needed repair.

Other's didn't."

Galen leaned back away from him. "Which means they need what to repair the walls?"

"Rustrock."

"That's right, son. Rustrock is rare. Maab's got control of the mines where Calimay used to get it from. Now that Calimay's split, she no longer has access to them . . . and I know where some is."

Arturus' own tears rolled down his face, falling onto his own chest, and mixing there with the tears of his fathers. Even so, he smiled. "You do?"

"I do. And as long as I have something she needs, and she has something I need, then . . ."

"Then we can't be slaves, because if she tries it, she'll never get the rustrock."

"Now she may torture me. She may mutilate me and take all my limbs, but she'll eventually have to undo it all, or her kingdom will crumble around her, and the devils will find her."

Arturus felt exhausted but peaceful. He very much wanted to go to sleep. "I'm sorry I gave up on you, father. I'm sorry. Even if the rustrock thing doesn't work. Even if we have nothing Calimay needs. I know you. I love you. I should have known better."

"Evariel."

"What?" Arturus was confused.

"The name your mother chose, after she had fallen from Heaven. Evariel."

"Why did she fall?"

"Not even the devils know why for certain. She thought she knew, and I had some ideas. But it was Rick who probably had the best theory."

"What was that?"

"I'm sorry to say it, Turi, but your mother was clumsy."

Arturus tried, for a moment, to figure out what his father had meant. Then he laughed. He laughed until his chest hurt. He laughed until he cried. And when his father joined him, he laughed some more.

23

"They're gaining on us," Massan warned.

Ellen's foot exploded in agony each time she put it down, and she dared not glance behind her for fear of falling again. She thought she could feel the corpses' breath on the back of her neck, and her shoulders tightened involuntarily.

"I'm here for you, honey," Alice said, pulling Ellen's left arm over her shoulder.

Suddenly it was so much easier. They moved together as if they were some strange, three legged beast. Ellen tried to keep her wounded foot back behind her. It felt weak, and tingled in pain each time they took a step, but it was much less painful now with Alice's help.

She felt like they were picking up speed. Feeling more stable, she dared a look behind her.

Massan was right. The corpses were getting much closer. The pack was less than a hundred feet back. A single corpse had broken away from the main group and was struggling mightily through the roots. It was getting very close.

"Alice," Ellen said, "One's right behind us."

"I'm on it," Molly turned around, leveling her shotgun.

The blast brought the ringing back in Ellen's ear.

"Got him!" Molly reported.

Massan grunted audibly as he helped push up the back of the canoe. Rick pulled it farther forward over another series of tall cypress knees.

"I think the trees are thinning out," Rick said.

"Doesn't seem like it to me," Massan shot back.

But Rick was right. The patches of empty water were getting larger and the roots seemed, for the most part, to be getting smaller.

"We're going to have to pick up . . . speed here in a minute," Rick warned around his heavy breathing. "As the trees thin out, the corpses will get faster. We'll need to stay ahead . . . until it's clear enough . . . to get in the gondola."

Ellen had no idea how she could go any faster.

"It's okay, hun," Alice told her. "You and I are going to do this."

Alice began to quicken her pace, almost dragging Ellen along with her. Ellen began to let more and more of her weight rest on her. Alice's face was beet red, and her chest was heaving, but she kept going.

Massan grunted as he powered the canoe over another obstacle.

"That's it!" Rick shouted back to him. "Keep it moving."

Molly dropped behind, not because she was tired, but to protect them. She fired another shell from her shotgun.

"All clear," Molly called back. "We're making it. We're going to make it!"

"Almost there, Ellen," Rick called to her. "We're almost there."

Ellen felt a surge of adrenaline. Her heart came alive in her chest and her ankle didn't seem to hurt so badly now. She plowed ahead, even lowering her hurt foot into the water to help her balance once every few steps. Alice seemed to gain strength, too, as if they really were one being.

"Almost there," Alice repeated.

The forest continued to thin out. Molly's shotgun boomed again.

"Now!" Rick shouted. "Get Ellen in the boat."

Alice lifted her up. Ellen raised her leg as Massan's hands grabbed her from the far side, easing her down. Rick returned to pulling the canoe, so Ellen picked up a paddle and tried to help.

Rick drew his pistol and fired next to his feet. There must have been a corpse down there. The water seemed to be deepening and was up to Alice's waist. A cypress branch hit Ellen in the face, but she didn't care.

"Everyone in the gondola," Rick ordered.

Massan came in first, rocking the boat almost to the tipping point. Alice and Molly came next. Rick let the canoe pass him before jumping in towards the back.

"Molly, Massan, get me some speed," Rick said. "Alice, shoot anything that comes at us."

The canoe began to move forward. The trees disappeared altogether, and they found themselves free in the middle of a lake. Finally, Ellen was able to make out the far away ceiling and distant walls.

"There," Alice said, pointing across the lake. "That's where the water flows out."

"Good," Rick said. "Stop everybody. Catch your breath. We'll try to make a run of it in about fifteen minutes."

Ellen looked towards where Alice was pointing. There was indeed a place where a river left the lake. Some corpses were wandering there along the bank. She watched one walk up to the river. Then it took a step in. She expected it to sink, but it didn't. It was almost like it was walking on water. It took a few more steps forward, so that it was standing in the middle of the river.

"Oh God," Ellen said aloud.

"Are they walking on the water?" Molly asked.

Rick shook his head. "There's some kind of barrier at the mouth of the river. It looks like they're standing on it. Maybe that's what's keeping all the corpses from leaving this room."

"There's more headed that way," Massan pointed out.

He was right. For some reason, maybe because it was the closest point to the canoe, or perhaps because the undead had enough intelligence to guard the only visible exit, packs of corpses were converging there.

"Move," Rick said. "Get us going. Now."

Massan and Molly got back to paddling. Ellen did too. The canoe was rocketing through the water.

Ellen could see the river more clearly now as they got closer. The river left this main chamber, running through into a smaller tunnel.

"They're only able to stand in a single file line," Rick said. "That barrier can't be very thick."

"What do you want to do?" Molly asked.

"Ram it. We should be able to bounce over to the other side. Alice, see if you can't kill all the corpses standing in our way."

Alice nodded. "Got it."

The canoe picked up even more speed from the power of Massan and Molly's paddle strokes. Ellen felt the wind in her hair. Alice was crouched down near the front of the boat.

She raised her pistol.

"Not yet," Rick warned. "We're too far out."

Alice fired anyway. And after she'd hit, she fired again, and again, and again, and again.

She'd dropped all five of the corpses that were in their way.

Massan looked up from his rowing for a second. "Damn."

Alice grinned back over her shoulder before returning to her task. She kept firing, and kept hitting, knocking down the corpses that were trying to replace the ones she'd felled already.

"Almost there!" Rick said.

Ellen could see now what the corpses on the river were standing upon. There was a metal grate, just below the surface, keeping the corpses from being drawn downriver. The current had pulled many corpses into the grate. They were five or six deep, just under the surface, their hands reaching up towards them.

"Shoot into the water!" Rick shouted.

Alice loaded another clip into her pistol. "I see them."

She began firing into the water, sending little spurts of water and black blood flying into the air. The canoe was suddenly over the reaching hands of the submerged corpses—and then they hit the grate.

Ellen was forced forward, her head hitting the seat in front of her. She heard a crunch. She was aware of Rick jumping over her, moving with the momentum of the crashed canoe. Her eyes would not focus, and she tried to sit back up. The world was spinning around her. The pain coming from her nose was excruciating.

She reached out to both sides, trying to regain her sense of balance—but the world kept spinning. The canoe was caught halfway over the grate. It toppled. Bullets were ripping through the water, shooting past Ellen. The hands reached up to get her. Some grasped her legs, clawing at her jeans. She felt teeth sinking into her calf.

Her scream was cut short by water. Instinctively, she fought to get up to the surface. More hands came from that direction, grabbing hold of her. She fought those too. They dragged her back, getting her most of the way over the grate and pulling the corpse on her leg up with her. Ellen tried to kick it loose. It opened its mouth, spitting out her blood, broken teeth and ripped pieces of her blue jeans. A shotgun boomed, and its head snapped backwards. Ellen's big and middle toes disappeared, turning into a mist of blood.

Water was in her lungs, but her body went on trying to scream anyway. She couldn't breathe.

"Ellen!" Rick was screaming. He yelled something else at her too, but it was lost as her head fell back into the water. She felt metal beneath her, scraping against her back. Suddenly the hands that were on her torso won out and she was dragged upwards. There was more gunfire.

Molly pulled her onto the bank. Ellen saw Rick standing on the grate, swinging his paddle left and right. He turned back and shouted something to Molly. Alice was yelling too. The world was still spinning. She tried to breathe through her nose, but it was full of blood. She tried to breathe through her mouth, but her lungs were full of water. She collapsed into a coughing fit so severe that she couldn't see. Water poured up out of her throat.

New hands were grabbing her, stronger than the ones before.

She tried to fight them off.

Rick was shouting again. The same thing over and over.

Ellen looked past the hands to her foot. Her toes were gone. Other hands, holding cloth, were grabbing at them. She tried to fight her way free of them.

"Ellen!" Rick was shouting at someone, "Ellen! Ellen!"

She couldn't get enough air. It came and went, and she was breathing as hard as she could, but the air was empty. Her vision was blurred.

She tried to scream for help, but she couldn't get the words out.

"Ellen!" Rick said. "Look at me, dear. Look at me."

His face filled her vision.

"Listen!" Rick was shouting. "Hell heals all wounds, Ellen.

You're going to be fine."

The hands were Rick's hands, Alice's hands, and Molly's hands. She was safe. Hell healed all wounds.

"I've got you," Alice said. "Don't worry, girl. I've got you."

 — 24 —

Michael looked down the long single aisle of Father Klein's church. Light streamed in from the Harpsborough chamber, shining down through the open arches near the church's ceiling and illuminating the pews. The crucifixes in those windows left evenly spaced cross shaped shadows along the sides of the aisle. At the far end of the church was a giant woodstone cross, hanging down from the fifty-foot ceiling. It was at that far wall that the villagers would pray. There was a line of grime where they would put their hands.

When the church was filled with all fifty Citizens, as it was now, it smelled different than when it was filled with villagers. Molly had called the villagers' odor desperation, when she was still alive. They reeked of sweat and grime and blood. The Citizens were a far cleaner bunch, and they had access to deodorants, or at the least, to perfumes which could mask their scent—but maybe Molly was right. Maybe a person could actually smell desperation.

There was a hum that filled these holy walls, created by the amalgam of worried Citizen voices. The church may have smelled better, but it *sounded* as if it were filled with villagers.

The voices did not die away as Michael walked down the aisle. Nor did they quiet as he stepped up and stood in front of the pulpit. Mancini was the only one not talking. Whatever webs he'd weaved must have been completed already.

Kylie walked up beside Michael and took his hand. Normally she stayed quiet and distant during such meetings, but she must have known that this one was going to be different.

Michael took a deep breath.

Alright, Mancini. Let's see what you've got in store for us.

"It's become clear now that we have problems," Michael said loudly, his voice echoing throughout the church.

He was pleased to hear the hum drop away. For the first time since he'd sentenced the Infidel Friend, Michael found that he had the Citizen's undivided attention. "Many have accused me of being soft hearted when it comes to the villagers, but I think we can all see now that this is not the case. Harpsborough's villagers are misbehaving. Some have begun to murder each other. Others have begun to sleep in the wilds. They are still gathering their food, but they are not paying their fair share to the Fore. Others speak quietly, or not so quietly, about how much food is in our storeroom. We thought before that we could simply help the hunters, and that their guns could help secure us. It was a good idea at the time. After all, who would stand up to a hunter? But now people will, and we have to do something. I am, of course, open to suggestions."

Copperfield led the sudden rush of voices, leaping to his feet. "I know what you mean to suggest." His baritone was deep and loud enough to enforce silence around him. The Citizens directed their attention to him. "And I'm telling you, we can't feed them from the Fore! It is better that we kick them all out—"

"But we may not be able to kick them out!" Chelsea broke in.

"Then it is better that we gun them all down," Copperfield shot back. "Better than letting them have our stores."

"Peace, Copperfield." Mancini gave a laugh, which seemed so out of place that it quieted the Citizens. "No one has suggested that we open the Fore's stores to the people. There are other ways."

"Fool," Staunten spoke up next, "that's all they want. How could you assuage them without giving them what they want?"

"Have some imagination," Mancini said. "There are many solutions."

Michael tried to gauge Mancini's expression. The man's face gave nothing away.

What have you cooked up for me, Davel?

"We should redesign everything," Kylie said suddenly. "We

should find out how many people we can feed with the resources we have. We should find out how long we can last if we give each person an equal share. It's time to be fair."

For a moment there was dead silence, then the church exploded with voices of derision.

"Please, please!" Mancini managed finally to get the crowd quiet again. "Please! I hear you all. Like you, I worked hard to get this position, and it isn't fair to just take all that work away, but what Kylie mentioned is *a* solution. We need to look at them all, even the ones we're not comfortable with."

Kylie squeezed Michael's hand, and for the first time that he could remember, Kylie gave Mancini a warm smile.

"Surely you can't be suggesting . . ." Copperfield seemed to almost be in shock.

"We could look at a few less drastic solutions, first," Herod the Gunsmith broke in. "Maybe some small changes which would make the villagers feel better."

Chelsea stood up and walked down the aisle, as if leaving the church, before turning on one heel. Her braid of red hair swung around after her. "We could start by not eating on the balconies."

"It's our food," Copperfield insisted. "We can eat it wherever we want."

"It would just be until the famine was over," Chelsea responded.

"But the famine might never be over."

Michael felt his heart suddenly in his throat. "Listen to her."

Is it not enough to rob them? Must you flaunt it in their faces as well?

"She's right," Staunten said. "By eating on the balconies, we're just asking them to come and kill us."

From the sounds of their voices, Staunten seemed to have a good amount of support.

"See," Mancini said, "all kinds of solutions. These are the kinds of sacrifices that we are going to have to make if we wish to keep the current system running. If you vote against these types of measures, then it's a vote towards Kylie's plan of reapportionment."

Kylie's grip tightened even further, and she glared at Mancini.

"Alright," Michael said. "Let's get a couple of votes knocked out. First, all who are for continuing aid towards the hunters."

Almost everyone raised their hands, surprising Michael more than just a little.

"All against?"

The naysayers didn't even bother to vote.

"The rest I'll count as abstentions." Michael felt as if there was electricity in the air, prickling across his skin. Things were changing. "All for Chelsea's vote to keep us eating in private until the famine ends?"

This time the support was a little less overwhelming, but it was still a clear win.

"All opposed? Abstentions?"

Wow, we did something.

"I have another proposal," Mancini said.

Here it comes.

"What is it, Davel?" Michael asked.

"I think we need to replace Graham with a different temporary Lead Hunter."

Michael stepped back, running into the pulpit and shaking his hand free of Kylie's grip.

Surely this can't be his plan. What's going on?

"What on earth for?" Michael asked.

There were similar murmurs of concern from amongst the Citizens. They all looked towards Mancini.

"He's failed in his two main tasks. He failed to keep Molly safe, and he failed to get any dyitzu. His men haven't caught a single one yet. Even while Aaron was Lead Hunter, he wouldn't have gone more than a day without catching one."

"That's a bit unfair," Chelsea said. "The dyitzu might still be decreasing in number, and we couldn't expect him to be as good a hunter as Aaron. Particularly not right at the beginning."

"The villagers have reported several kills," Mancini answered. "There are still just as many dyitzu in the halls as when Aaron left. If the villagers are out-hunting the hunters, then I think either we need new hunters, or a new Lead Hunter."

As the Citizens made their agreement with Mancini's suggestion known, Michael began to figure out why Mancini might have bothered to make the suggestion in the first place. If the Lead Hunter changed and things got better, the villagers might be inclined to blame Graham for their lean times rather than the Fore—even if there were no rational basis for doing so. A villager could even think that if Aaron returned, things might be just as they were before he left. In a way, this made sense. Not much had changed in Hell since the expedition to rescue Julian, but they'd be missing the broader point. It was attrition that was wearing them down. Aaron's return would do nothing to stop that.

"But who would replace him?" Copperfield was asking.

"Martin," Michael and Chelsea said simultaneously.

There really isn't another choice. We lost some of our best on that stupid Carrion expedition. I was right about that, too.

A buzz of support began to grow in the church. Martin was an old hunter, and a familiar one. He could be a bit over the top at times—and there was that odd habit he had of talking to Benson—but he was a man that could be trusted.

"These things are not enough to fix all our problems, though." Mancini stood up and ascended onto the stage to stand next to Michael. "Are they, Mike?"

Here it comes.

"No," Michael answered. "They are not."

Mancini turned to the crowd. "Michael's been telling us that we need to give to the villagers, and we've been ignoring him. We thought our ability to refuse Mike showed how well our system was working. It showed us that Michael was no tyrant. That if we disagreed with him, he would not arbitrarily overrule us—and for that knowledge we are grateful. But we underestimated you, my good friend. You were right. We are going to have to give."

Mancini paused, and Michael took the opportunity to check the Citizens' reactions. Most seemed ready, finally, to hear the news. A few, like Copperfield and Staunten looked even more stubborn than ever. Copperfield's face was actually red, his fingers clenched into angry fists. Chelsea had a smirk on her face.

It's Mancini. She knows real change won't be coming from him.

"They've got our backs to the wall," Mancini went on. "By leaving the city and not paying taxes, they've forced our hand.

Our hunters still protect them, yet they do not pay us taxes. Are we willing to gun them down? I think not. It would anger their fellows left in town too much. This we cannot do. And we cannot let them keep leaving. We must have something to draw them back in."

"Mancini!" Copperfield erupted.

"Have you not learned to trust me yet?" Mancini shouted back.

Copperfield's nostrils flared while his fists opened and closed again and again. Finally something in Mancini's gaze broke through to him, and he sat down.

"Like I said, we need to give to them, but they need to give to us, too," Mancini said. "Isn't that, after all, the essence of compromise?"

Copperfield began to nod.

Mancini had them all spellbound now, hooked by his intellect. "We've long wanted all caches that exist to be subject to the Fore's taxes. I propose a new legislation. Once, every three weeks, we provide a feast day. That's when all people in the town are treated to a free meal from the Fore. If someone hasn't paid taxes, and has been living in the wilds, then they don't get to participate. In exchange, all caches, even new ones, are taxable by the Fore. It's the price of living under our protection."

Michael felt something break deep inside him.

Had I really hoped for anything more?

This new legislation might even make the Fore richer, particularly in the long haul. It would make it more difficult for any villager to hoard, and in so doing, might allow the Fore to continue hoarding a bit longer.

"How are you going to enforce this?" Chelsea asked. "As things are, I can't imagine the villagers volunteering to us knowledge of their secret caches."

"Most are common knowledge," Mancini said, "but you're very right. We need someone to collect the taxes. A scapegoat of sorts. We could elevate a second hunter to a high status. He would be in charge of domestic things, like investigating these new murders, collecting the taxes and finding new caches. He'd need some new men, too, who would be easy to hire since everyone is looking for a meal. And that would put another couple of guns on our side."

"But who would we get to lead the crew?" Herod asked.

Mancini's smile split his face. "Why Graham, of course."

When the light came to Julian, it was as a stranger. It filled his vision even through his closed eyes. Opening them was a difficult task. The blood from his forehead had clotted in his lashes, so he had to rub them until they were clear. He had not remembered the light being so bright.

Two silhouettes stood in that brightness.

"It's okay, Julian," a male voice descended upon him. "It's okay. It's time for you to go home."

"Home?" Julian croaked around his dry tongue.

"Yes. Selena has approved your conversion. You're not a lamb. You're free to return to work."

"Home."

Harpsborough. Turi. Aaron. Kylie.

But he was never going to see those people again. It was as far away from him as the old world. He might as well have died again. The soldiers helped him to his feet. They were gentler this time because they thought he was not a criminal. Julian didn't know if they were right. He didn't know what he believed.

You better believe you're not a Christian. You abandoned Jesus already. Ahuramazda is your only hope.

He tried to get adjusted to this new light, this light that was the blessing of Ahuramazda, but it was too bright for him. It stung his eyes.

"Mother," Julian called.

"He's delusional," one voice said.

"He needs water," said another. "And a bath."

Force welled up beneath him, supporting him, keeping him warm. It helped him down the corridor. He kept his eyes shut, but even through his eyelids he could tell there was light. It was easier to take with his eyes closed, however. It was softer. Redder. Familiar, like the red bricks around the Thames river.

Water poured down over him. It washed away the blood from his face and the sweat away from his clumped hair. The smell of his own sweat and blood was enough to make him swoon. He tried drinking. It hurt his stomach, but he couldn't help himself.

His stomach began cramping uncontrollably. He curled up into a ball. When the pain finally passed, the light didn't hurt his eyes as much. The two men half carried him down familiar tunnels and then stopped at an unfamiliar cell.

God, are you there? I'm sorry. I didn't mean to abandon you. I was weak. I love you still. You can damn me as many times as you like, it won't change me. I love you. I love you.

He tried to feel God's warmth in his heart, but nothing was there.

Please don't let me be lying.

The door closed behind him, and he was finally free from that strange light. He collapsed to the floor. The floor was dirty, covered in dust, human hair and other filth. He crawled over it until he made it to a corner. He could hear that there were other people in the cell, but not many.

All I want is to eat some honey.

The idea of the sweet syrupy substance filled his mouth with saliva. Honey had never been merely a food to Julian, not even when he was in the old world. It meant things to him which were far more important. Things like comfort, safety, and love.

He was reluctant to open his eyes. When he did, he could see a little, perhaps four or five feet in front of him. A man emerged from the darkness. His hair was long and blond, his beard just slightly darker. His skin was as pale as a ghost. He wore the grey robes of a slave. The same robes that Julian wore.

"Home," Julian said.

The man drew closer, looking as determined as anyone Julian had ever seen, as if he were at a point beyond reason. He had a cup in his left hand. It was shaking.

"You," the man began, and he reached out, grabbing one of Julian's wrists earnestly. "They just converted you."

You can't withstand that again. You must love Ahuramazda. You must remember to hate God.

"They did," Julian said, unsure of his words.

Did they? Am I lying?

"They did that to me, too," the man said.

Even in the darkness, the man's white hands stood out against Julian's black skin. Two of his fingernails were broken to the quick. The black bruising below those missing nails looked painful.

Julian didn't know what to say to him.

Just leave me alone.

"I . . ." he began. "I know. I know what it's like."

Julian nodded.

"I . . . it's good right? Feels good. Being converted."

Julian nodded.

I'm sorry, mother. I didn't mean to. I didn't. They took it from me. I didn't mean to give it up. I'm sorry. I love you, mother. If you can see me from Heaven, forgive me. I know I'm a sinner. I tried, mother. I tried.

The man let go of Julian's arm. He dipped one of his fingers into the cup. Slowly, with a trembling hand, the man used the water to dampen the dirty stones. His finger traced a shape. Then he looked at Julian intently, so nervous that his entire body was shaking.

I know I should have kept the faith. I know it. I knew better. I know I disappointed you. Just try to understand. I didn't mean to fail you.

Julian looked at the shape. He couldn't make out what it was. Not a shape, really. Just a single curved line. It looked like a check mark, except it was round where there was usually a ninety degree angle. Maybe it was supposed to be a bent ladle.

I failed you, Ma. You raised me right. Don't you feel guilty for this. This shit is from my own failings.

Maybe it was half of a teardrop. Maybe it was fishing hook, lying on one side. Maybe the man was mad. The man seemed like he thought this line was the most important thing he'd ever drawn. Like what he was drawing could mean the end of his life.

Julian jerked forward, looking closer at the line.

An Ichthys.

Julian reached out with his own hand, holding it up before his fellow slave. The man held forth his cup and Julian dipped one finger into the warm water.

Julian finished drawing the fish. The man's white hand wiped the symbol away. They lay down next to each other, grasping each other's arms. Their faces were so close they were touching. The man leaned forward even closer, so that their mouths were by each other's ears.

They whispered together so softly that sometimes Julian wasn't even sure that the words were always leaving his mouth, but his heart had never said any words so loudly. Every once and awhile, he could hear the other man over his own whispering. Somehow, they managed to stay in sync.

"Our Father who art in Heaven, hallowed be thy name . . ."

25

Arturus awoke from torchlight flickering through the crack beneath the iron door. The light was licking at his boots, illuminating for brief instances the makeshift laces which were holding them together. Arturus sat up.

Galen, who was already standing, offered him a hand. Arturus took it, and his father helped him to his feet. Metal clinked in the lock as the key turned, but the rust must have made the process difficult, because the noise went on for some time before the door opened.

Torchlight filled the room. Four shadows of armed guards stood awaiting them.

"Calimay will see you now." Arturus recognized the man as Dakota.

The guards moved past Dakota, eager to grab them. Arturus let himself be dragged out of his cell with his father and into a hallway full of Calimay's guards. One group of Carrion soldiers was working on the next door. A Carrion born grunted as the other lock gave way with a metallic thud. The door opened on shrieking hinges.

The soldiers marched in and then came out pulling Aaron and Johnny with them. The pair were pushed towards Arturus and Galen.

"Did you hear the screaming last night?" Aaron asked.

Galen nodded. "Turi slept through it."

"Is Avery okay?" Johnny asked.

Galen's eyes gauged the guards around them. "He was angry with Kelly."

Johnny looked down to the ground. "She must have done something bad to him. He sounded like she'd stabbed him. I heard the guards that came in say he was bleeding badly."

Johnny pointed to the stone floor.

A bloody trail streaked across the floor which Arturus doubted was there the night before.

"He might be dead," Aaron said.

"The priestesses of Maab are trained to break a male's member during intercourse," Galen told them. "If something tears, there can be a lot of blood."

Aaron's jaw dropped. "You don't think . . ."

Galen nodded.

Johnny let out a deep breath.

"I thought this would go without saying," Galen told them, "but I'll say it anyway. No raping the priestess."

The Carrion soldiers were working in the third chamber. When that door opened, none of them dared go in. Kelly walked out, a sneer and a smirk somehow sharing her lips. Her robe had been returned to her at some point during the night. It was covered in dried blood which stood out in the torchlight. She walked forward, like Maab might, with no switch to her hips. Johnny avoided her gaze.

Her sneer faded into a smile for a second as she met Arturus' eyes.

Arturus felt his heart beat faster.

"Alright!" Dakota shouted. "Tamara, we're ready."

From this side, Arturus could see the giant pair of square stones lower as the gate rose. Tamara, flanked by two other priestesses, a Little Lady and another score of soldiers, awaited them on the far side.

Tamara motioned to the Little Lady, who walked forward with four sets of clothes.

Arturus tried to swallow his horror.

"Put these on," the Little Lady said.

The clothes she offered them were the grey robes, pants and shirts of slaves.

"Sorry I had to boil that water," Rick said. "It's just that the river is chock full of corpsedust. I wouldn't want to get any in your blood."

Ellen lay back across the cool stone of the chamber, her head resting upon her pack, her wounded left ankle on Rick's lap.

Rick readied the still steaming water. "This is going to hurt."

"I don't care," Ellen said. "I'm too tired to care."

He began to clean her wounds, starting with the teeth marks in her calf.

She was wrong—she did care. Gritting her teeth, Ellen managed to hold in the scream which welled up in her throat, but a small whimper escaped.

Rick wrapped her calf quickly and tightly. "Hush girl. Here, bite down on this." Rick handed her an unused bandage.

The cloth barely fit in her mouth and tasted salty when she bit into it. Rick then moved down to inspect her missing toes.

Ellen noticed that Molly was watching.

"I'm really sorry about your toes, babe," Molly said.

Ellen smiled, taking the cloth out of her mouth for a second. "It's better that way. The corpse could have killed me."

Molly nodded and left to help Alice with something.

"Here it comes again." Rick warned.

For some reason the toes didn't hurt as badly as the bite on her calf had. Again, Rick bandaged her wound with great skill.

"You doing good, dear?" he asked.

Ellen nodded as best she could, her head rising and falling back onto the pack. She tried to hand him back the bandage in her mouth, but he stopped her.

"Not yet." Rick inspected her ankle critically. "I'm going to work your ankle around, okay. Feel free to let me know if it hurts."

He touched her foot.

"It hurts," Ellen said suddenly around the cloth.

He moved it around anyway. Bending it forward, back, to the left, and most painfully, to the right.

Her voice was muffled by the bandage. "I said it hurt!"

"I don't think anything is broken," Rick said. "Sprain, I bet. We're going to try and keep your foot elevated to minimize the swelling. I'm going to wrap your ankle in a bit, too. Should help support you in case we need to run again. We didn't make it any better, dragging you through that cypress grove and shooting off two of your toes, but we'll see what we can do."

Massan leaned over her. She could see up his nose, or rather, she could see the mass of hairs which stopped her from seeing up his nose. He passed her an oar which had cloth wrapped around the top.

"Should work as a crutch," Massan said.

Ellen took the cloth out of her mouth.

"Thank you, Massan." Ellen responded, smiling.

"No," Massan said. "Thank you."

Ellen felt confused. "Why would you thank me?"

"Rick can't make me row now, that was my paddle!"

Ellen laughed.

"Rest for a minute," Rick said, taking the bandage out of her hand. "We'll get the gondola ready for you."

Rick stood up to walk away, but Massan put a hand on his shoulder.

"What's up?" Rick asked.

Massan whispered to him, perhaps hoping for privacy, but Ellen could hear him anyway. "I'm sorry about my behavior back there."

"You did fine," Rick whispered back.

"No, I didn't. You asked me to help you with the canoe, and I was trying to run. I was thinking only about myself."

Ellen could see the back of Rick's head from where she lay as he shook it from side to side. "No, Massan. I guarantee you, you weren't."

"I put my survival over yours."

"Don't be foolish, Massan, you were thinking of Kara. Of how, if you died, she would be left all alone in Harpsborough. Of whatever promise you made her before you left."

Massan was quiet for a second. "It was still wrong of me." Ellen was surprised by how much emotion was in the man's voice.

He must really love her.

"Trust needs to be built. You just didn't understand the strategy, is all."

"I'm going to say something to you," Massan warned, "and it's going to hurt you. But it is something that needs to be said."

"What?"

"When we were there, and the corpses were all after us . . .

well, you were just like Galen, my friend. Just like Galen."

Ellen could see Rick's posture slump, but only for a moment—then the man straightened again.

"Don't give up hope, Rick," Massan begged him. "I was missing for nearly a year. No one believed I was alive. No one. Not even Kara. But I came back."

"Galen doesn't get lost, Massan. Not even in the Carrion. He had Turi with him. It's time I mourned my friend and my son."

"Turi was special, wasn't he?"

"He was. Very special. He was supposed to do something very important. Something that only he could do."

Massan's whisper got even softer, but Ellen could still hear him. "Well, you've got someone else now, Rick. And I think she's special, too. As special as Turi."

Rick nodded and turned back to look at her. Ellen closed her eyes and did her best to pretend she hadn't heard them.

Strangely, with her eyes closed and her head tilted back, she thought she heard something. A whistle? No, a voice. A distant singing voice. It seemed so far away, so faint, that even the whispers of Massan and Rick were drowning it out. She tried her best to ignore them and the rush of the river. She began to succeed.

There was a voice and it was singing.

It is I that ye hear in the calling wind
I have stared through the dark till my soul is blind
O lover of mine, ye swore,
Lover of mine, ye swore.

"Rick!" Ellen said suddenly, sitting up. "I hear someone. Someone singing."

Rick cocked his head to one side. So did Massan.

"That's hellsong, Ellen," Massan said.

"No, it's a person singing. She's singing the words of a poem I know."

Massan knelt beside her. He scratched his unibrow with one finger. "It's not what you think. Hellsong, it sings to you the words that are in your heart. It sings to you your hopes and dreams."

"But why?" Ellen asked. "Why would Hell sing you your hopes and dreams?"

"Because," Rick said, "it knows you'll never get them."

Arturus was led with Galen, Johnny and Aaron down the long red carpet which lay between Calimay's two huge fountains. It was difficult to shake the idea that the water above their heads was somehow defying gravity. Arturus looked up, trying to see what might be above the oscillating blue lake which hung over him, but he could see nothing.

He froze when he heard Avery's screams.

Dakota walked ahead and held open the red curtain. "Don't worry about your man, he's getting stitches. He'll be returned to you.'

Beyond the curtain was a well lit hallway made out of a black marble stones with purple veins running through them.

Damn, if only I had been able to make my chess set out of that.

The three lavender robed priestesses and their Little Lady walked through first. Tamara wasn't the most important, Arturus noted, but he didn't know the name of the one who seemed to be in charge.

The hallway had many corridors leading off of it, some ending in rooms, and others turning off into the darkness. This portion of the complex showed none of the dilapidation that was so obvious around the exterior. The construction seemed impeccable too, as if these corridors had been laid out and designed by some people who'd possessed greater skill than even Hell's architect.

Calimay's people can't be this good.

The more he thought about it, the more Arturus became convinced that the builders of this complex were a different group than those who had designed the false walls that hid it. If they'd had enough rustrock to do all this work, then surely they would have used it on the outer walls, too.

The corridor ended in Calimay's throne room. Its walls and ceiling were made of the same black and purple marble. Ceremonial columns, four to the left and four to the right, flanked them, rising up towards the ceiling without touching it. A set of eight guards, dressed the same as the others but with purple trim on their black pants and grey shirts, stood at attention, one to a pillar. In between each pillar was a raised light orb, suspended nearly eight feet high in the air.

The floor was covered in hound hide carpets, which were more worn down in the center of the room, their hair stripped away, revealing the skin beneath. It was to the worn spot that they were dragged.

In front of them was Calimay's throne. It was made of the same marble as the rest of the inner complex, and was placed on a four foot raised stage. Two more thrones, raised only three feet high, flanked her.

Calimay herself was an imposing figure. Her hair, long and black, hung down around her face in a mass of shiny curls, spilling over her shoulders. The purple robe she wore was decorated from hood to hem with golden runes. It was open in the center, revealing an enticing patch of pale cleavage. Her fingernails, long and red, rapped slowly and repetitively on the stone arm of her throne.

Her lips, also crimson, broke into a smile. Her face was broad, reminding Arturus of the other priestesses here, but her square features suited her particularly well. Arturus dared to look her in the eye, for she was staring at him intently. Those eyes caught him off guard. They were pale green, shining with the reflected light of the orbs.

Vanity. She placed those orbs there so they'd make her eyes more beautiful.

Perhaps that vanity explained why her priestesses were so different than Maab's. It was entirely possible that Calimay killed the ones she felt outshone her own beauty. Then again, because of the similarity of all the girls' features, they could all be related.

Arturus looked away from Calimay as the purple robed priestesses moved to stand together in a line near the front of the room.

The throne to Calimay's right was empty, but a man was seated to her left. At first Arturus thought that he must be Calimay's favored mate, but the man's body language seemed somewhat antagonistic towards the priestess. His curiosity piqued, Arturus let his gaze linger on the man. He had short cropped black hair and blue eyes. His shoulders were more slender than Aaron's, but Arturus would not be surprised if the man's strength were more similar to Galen's. The man's fingernails were trimmed and his face clean shaven. He was well armed, a double-barreled coach gun, sawed off, sheathed at his calf, and an M-16 slung across his back. There was a sword slung across his back as well, next to the assault rifle. Its gilded hilt had a decorated crosspiece. Arturus focused on it to see if he could guess the design.

A hound and a bird of some sort. A vulture.

That's the symbol of Ares. This man is an Infidel Friend.

The Infidel Friend's gaze met Arturus' before roving amongst the rest of them. When he saw Galen, the Infidel Friend shot up into a standing position.

Arturus stepped back into one of the guards that still held him. Calimay herself started, leaning to one side. The infidel came down the steps from his throne and walked up to Galen, standing only inches away from Arturus' father, his expression almost unreadable.

A cruel smile formed on the Infidel Friend's lips. "You."

Galen's chin rose and his nostrils flared.

"Calimay," the Infidel Friend addressed her in an even voice, his eyes never straying from Galen, "you should not have such vermin in your court."

Galen's gaze did not waver either.

"I," Calimay's husky voice responded, "don't give a fuck who you think should have my audience. Malkravyan, you should sit down now."

Malkravyan, his eyes staying with Galen, ascended the steps to his throne.

Calimay grinned, her white teeth glaring out from behind her blood red lips. "I'd been told that I'd been brought a couple of horses and a filly." She paused as her assembled priestesses laughed. "But I know you, warrior." She leaned forward, looking straight at Galen. "I know you *very* well." More laughter. "Carlisle, Benson, Charlie, Klein, Pyle. They were all sent out to look for the angel's get . . . but you, apparently you were the one who got him. The one who stole him out from the Infidel's arms. Maab's scouts never knew it either. They reported you had failed. That you had joined Charlie's rebellion, childless. How did you do it? How did you trick so many?"

Galen stood silently.

"No matter. You have delivered, in looking for my help, little red riding hood to the big bad wolf. I shall enjoy mixing my bloodline with the angels'."

Kelly took a step forward, perhaps about to protest, but stopped when Calimay looked her way. Kelly lowered her head demurely, stepping back, but from this angle Arturus could see the anger on her face.

She won't be able to fulfill her promise. I'm helpless. I'm Calimay's.

But then he looked at his father. He had seen Galen horrified once, while Maab's men were dragging him away in her vile ritual. Judging from Galen's expression, things weren't quite that bad.

"And you, thief of children," Calimay said, turning back to Galen, "and the men who travel with you . . . what should I do with you?"

Aaron stepped forward. "Calimay—"

"Speak not my name!" Calimay's husky voice turned into a roar. "I am a Queen."

"Queen," Aaron continued, slightly shaken. "I represent the village of Harpsborough. Resisting both Hell and Maab can't be easy. The resources of Harpsborough could help you greatly—"

Calimay's laughter interrupted him. "You think I don't know of your little village? Many years ago, Maab's spies, under my direction, took stock of your Harpsborough. And Macon's Bend and the Landing. We in the Carrion need nothing from your pathetic village. I'm surprised you've even survived this dark time."

She doesn't know. Maab may not know. They may not realize that the devils are only thickening in the Carrion.

Calimay's fingers tapped a few more times against the stone of the armchair. "Take them to the pits. You'll make good slaves. Leave the angel's get and the priestess."

The soldiers moved towards them again, but Galen's voice stopped them. "How long till your outer wall collapses?"

Calimay frowned, ordering her soldiers to move again with a flick of her wrist. "Don't stop, take them away."

Rough hands grabbed Arturus' arms, pulling at him, trying to separate him from his father.

"That's right," Malkravyan agreed. "Take him away."

The corners of Calimay's lips curved downward for a second.

Doesn't he know she doesn't want to agree with him?

Arturus was surprised the Infidel Friend could be so ignorant of just how much the Queen despised him.

"Would certainly be nice if you had some rustrock," Galen said loudly.

Calimay stood up. "Stop," she ordered her soldiers.

The hands released Arturus' arms.

"What are you saying, Galen, stealer of children? I also know where rustrock can be found."

Galen folded his arms. "If you're talking about where Maab's mines are, yes. I am familiar with them as well. But that is not the only place in the Carrion where it can be found."

"You're lying," Calimay said. "If there were, my men would have found it."

"I do not lie. I can tell you of the silver mines in the high caverns of the Lethe. I can tell you of the rustrock veins that shoot north of Silverstream. I can tell you of the gold that can be found beneath the asphodel fields of the Deadlands—and I can tell you of another place the ancients used to mine—and in that mine, is rustrock."

The Infidel Friend's face darkened.

"How could you know of such things?" Calimay asked, an amused grin on her face.

Galen smiled. "Queen Calimay, I knew the Carrion's secrets long before Lucreas met Maab."

"You need not deal with such a fool," Malkravyan said. "You can get the rustrock from Maab. Surely she'd trade you in order to get her hands back on the angel's get—particularly since she now knows he was in her oblivious grasp."

They have contacts with Maab.

Of course they did. Arturus wasn't sure how Maab had figured out who he was, but for that information to make it to Calimay, Maab almost certainly would have had to send someone here with the message. That meant Maab was still looking for him.

That's why she risked La'Ferve in a battle against those who wore upside down crosses. It's me she's after.

"She might," Galen said, "but I don't think this Infidel Friend has your best interests at heart. Sooner or later, you'll need rustrock again. And in the meantime, you'd be down one angel's get."

Calimay nodded. "Very well. Take the rest to the pits. Leave Galen here. Galen, once you've shown us to the rustrock, I'll let you free."

Galen's lack of reaction kept the soldiers from moving. After a moment of silence he spoke, "No."

Calimay pursed her lips, and her fingers again began drumming again against the stone. "I assume you have conditions."

"I do."

She shrugged. "Go ahead. State them."

"I and my friends, including Kelly, remain free. In exchange, I'll lead your people to the rustrock."

"Acceptable."

"I'm not done."

"Careful, I can still have you killed," Calimay said, bringing some chuckles from the soldiers.

Galen smiled. "You might after my next request."

More laughter.

"Go on," Calimay said grinning, "test me."

"I want my boy, too."

The smile disappeared from Calimay's blood colored lips. "Impossible."

"Either I'll have him, or Maab will. Maybe you'd rather spite Maab than me."

"Fool. You should've taken your freedom while you could—"

"I have more on offer," Galen broke in, "if you'd pardon my interruption."

"What else could I possibly want?"

Galen walked forward. The soldiers followed him but they dared not touch him. He put one foot on the first of the three stairs that led up to Calimay's throne.

"Maab will fall," Galen said. "Maybe not tomorrow, maybe not the next day, but even she won't be able to resist this kind of Hell for long. The Carrion is filled to the brim with devils. We've even seen a Nephilim. Something's come here, Calimay. Something very powerful. Another Archdevil perhaps. Or maybe something even older. Something even worse. I've seen the soldiers who've allied themselves with demons, and I'm willing to bet you want to know who's made the deal with the devil."

Calimay stood up from her throne and walked down to him, stopping on the second step so that she was still a half foot taller than Galen.

"You think you can tell me who?"

Galen cocked his head to one side. "Are they coming upstream along the Lethe?"

"Yes."

"I know a way to get to the City of Blood and Stone. If you give me leave, I'll let you know all I find out. Up to and including whether Lucreas really is the one issuing the demon call."

If we make it out of this, I'm going to make Galen explain what the Hell is going on here.

Calimay smiled. "What good would that do me?"

"Maybe none. Maybe a lot. As I recall, you and Lucreas were lovers, once upon a time. If it is indeed he who is cavorting with them, perhaps a meeting could be arranged. Maybe, in exchange for help against Maab, he might spare you."

"These are just empty promises until fulfilled. And these promises are not likely to ever be anything but empty, because even if you somehow travel to the banks of Erebus and survive spying on the City of Blood and Stone, it still might not do me a damn bit of good to know if it was Lucreas who cast in his lot with Ahriman."

Galen nodded.

Calimay sighed. "Very well. Let me sweeten my side of the kitty. I have no real interest in having your boy. I just want his blood mixed with one of my priestesses so I have the line. If nothing else, that will give me leverage with Lucreas—even if Lucreas is not to return for many years. I have the clay of an earth mother. I can bring fertility upon one of my daughters."

Galen shook his head. "He's a virgin. This will confuse him. He should have time to learn of love."

"Our deal hinges on this. If not, you lose your boy, and Maab gets him." Calimay turned around and ascended back to her throne. She straightened out her lavender robe as she sat. "And neither of us wants that, do we?"

Galen looked back and met Arturus' eyes.

"Don't be a fool, Calimay," Galen said, turning back towards her.

Arturus swallowed.

"I will accept no less." Calimay said. "Lucreas be damned. He's either coming or he's not. I want your boy's seed, and I'm going to have it. Whether your broke dick son goes back to you or stays with Maab is your choice."

Shit.

"I'm sorry, son," Galen said, and then turned back to Calimay. "He chooses which of your daughters, then. And you must promise me you'll return him unbroken."

Calimay smiled. "He can choose which daughter. I'll advise her to try and keep her libido in check. Accidents happen, though."

The right side of Galen's top lip curled into a sneer. "Yes they do."

"I could be more persuasive, Galen, if I wanted. My daughters have been known to be obedient when I let them know how *very* important it is that they listen."

The priestesses began chuckling.

Galen nodded. "I consent."

Consent to what? What is he—

The lustful grin on Calimay's face hardened Arturus' heart.

"Deal then?" the Queen asked.

"Deal."

26

Katie shared a hut with Erica, but Martin hadn't seen Erica in over three days. A charcoal bird had been drawn on the door curtain. The drawing was amazingly well done, all things considered. In the old world, Erica had been an artist.

The girls had named the bird, and Martin greeted it as he pushed through the door curtain. "Hey, Reginald."

Katie lay unconscious within, her long brown, curly hair spread out all about her. She was unnaturally cool, as if the cold of the stone had somehow seeped into her body. She was breathing, he noticed with relief. Martin watched the rise and fall of her chest.

She'd lost a lot of weight. At first they'd joked about how sexy it made her, but he feared for her now. Clumps of fat still clung to her thighs and stomach, but her face looked gaunt. Dark circles spread out under her eyes, and her wrists were thinner than he remembered them being.

He knelt down beside her. "Katie?" he whispered.

She didn't stir.

He touched her shoulder and moved her a bit. "Katie, come on princess, wake up."

Her eyes opened for a second, then closed again.

"Come on!"

He shook her a bit more roughly.

This time her eyes stayed open.

"I brought you food, baby."

Without getting up, or even looking at him, she shook her head.

"You might as well eat it," Martin said. "The hunters have caught about half a dozen guys trying to steal from other people's tents. Everyone knows about my pot, Katie. They're going to get to my food unless you eat it."

She shook her head again. "I can't, Martin. I know how hard it was for you to save that food. I know it's everything you worked for. I don't want to."

I saved it so I could get a woman like you, Katie!

"Katie, we've just got a couple more days to go. It's bad out there, in the wilds. Our villagers have been going out there, spending the nights. They're not coming back. They're just sitting there, lying in the halls like ole Bense. They're getting the stilling. You will too, if you don't eat."

"Martin, I can't do this to you."

"The feast day is almost here. You've got to hold on. This is just a little. There's plenty left."

He pulled the devilwheat out of his hoodie's pocket with his weak hand. The limb had almost recovered all of its strength. He'd just been out hunting with Graham, and the hand hadn't let him down.

Katie turned towards him, looking at the food. He could tell how badly she wanted it.

"Take it, Katie. There's plenty left in the pot."

But there wasn't plenty left. Maybe one or two handfuls was all that remained of his savings. She pinched some of the devilwheat between her fingers and put it them in her mouth. Then she took another pinch, and another. Then she snatched it all out of his hands and began to gobble it down.

"Slowly," he warned her, "or it will hurt your stomach."

She didn't listen. After she'd eaten, she fell back asleep immediately.

Martin hung his head, touching her hand. She remained comatose.

"No harm," he told her. "I saved that food so I could get a girl like you. Be silly for me not to spend it." His voice cracked a bit at the end.

Don't you become a miser, Martin. Don't you do it.

He stood up and exited the tent. Michael Baker was there. Martin started.

"Martin Warwick," the First Citizen said. "I'm sure you

heard about some of the changes at our last vote."

"Of course," Martin answered. "I'm so happy that we've done the feast day. I can't tell you how great an idea I—"

"There's another thing we voted on," Michael interrupted, "and I just discussed it with Graham."

"What's that, First Citizen?"

"We're not happy with how he's been handling the temporary Lead Hunter position. He hasn't stopped the thieves from raiding tents. He hasn't stopped the villagers from murdering each other in the wilds or from leaving the village. He hasn't been killing any dyitzu. You're healed up now, aren't you?"

"Yes, sir."

"Good. You're promoted to temporary Lead Hunter. Hold on to it, and you'll get all of the things that come with it."

Martin froze.

Michael smiled. "Sorry, didn't mean to shock you."

Martin felt his blood pressure rising.

How the hell am I supposed to do this?

"I'm going to tell the rest of the hunters now," Michael said. "Do me some good, getting out of the Fore."

"Thank you, First Citizen," Martin managed.

He turned around suddenly and entered back into the tent.

"Katie! Katie! Guess what?"

She did not stir.

Martin felt keenly the weight of his new position.

My first priority is to protect the people of Harpsborough.

There were people just like Katie, in the village and all around the surrounding wilds. People who weren't going to make it until feast day. Now, suddenly, all those people were Martin's people. Each of them had someone who cared for them as much as Martin cared for Katie. Rarely had Martin ever felt such a singularity of purpose.

Aaron, I'm going to make you proud.

The soldiers had left Kelly in the audience chamber with Calimay.

"Well," Johnny said as they entered their new room, "it ain't a dungeon."

And a dungeon it was not, Arturus noticed—but only when

compared to their previous accommodations.

The room was brighter, but still dim. It was only about eight feet tall, and the floor was a ten foot by ten foot square. Two sets of bunk beds, made out of woodstone, were on either side of the room. Sheets had been laid across the wood, but there were no mattresses or pillows.

"We'll be a bed short when Avery comes back. Two, if we get Kelly." Aaron noted. "Galen, you and Turi want to share a bed?"

Galen shook his head. "I'll take the floor. Not much of a difference."

Arturus' father shut the door, which was made of wood and belted together by strips of iron, behind them. It closed with a thud.

"Are we good?" Johnny asked. "Can we trust this bitch to keep her bargain?"

Galen shrugged. "I'll be able to speak with her again tonight, and then I can give you a better idea of her intentions. Still, I bet you she'll stand by her word. She's obviously been pulled back into contact with Maab, and I don't think she likes it. That might be why she's let that Infidel Friend into her court. She may want to use us and Harpsborough to keep her people's autonomy."

"Speaking of which," Johnny began, "how on earth did she get an Infidel Friend to stay with her? You don't think she's fucking that asshole, do you?"

Aaron sat down on a bunk and shrugged. "She's evil, he's evil."

"By that count," Galen said, "we're evil, too, for being willing to deal with her. But one thing's sure, we all have some common enemies."

"Who's Lucreas?" Arturus asked. "And why is Calimay so interested in him? What's the City of Blood and Stone?"

Galen smiled. "One at a time, boy. Lucreas Crassus has been in Hell for a long time, and he fought alongside Saint Wretch against the Infidel. Lucreas made a deal with Tu-El, an Archdevil, and learned its secrets. Some time ago, the Infidel's people collapsed a section of the Carrion on top of Tu-El, but no one managed to kill Lucreas.

"Lucreas is the one who taught Gilgamesh how to affect hounds. Who taught La'Ferve to fight. Before Maab became

Queen of the Carrion, he raised Maab's predecessor to a level of power almost as great as Maab has now. Calimay was one of his lovers.

"There is a city, ancient and wicked, that he and Tu-El had some hand in building. Like Londinium, it is run by devils, but has men who live there as well. It is my guess that this new tribe with the upside down crosses is in some way connected to that city. Perhaps the Minotaur that rules there has become ambitious and wants to rule the Carrion. Or perhaps Lucreas has returned to the city, and he's the one causing the spread. That's what I need to find out."

"Does it even matter, though?" Aaron asked. "A Minotaur or Lucreas, it's all the same to us."

"Perhaps," Galen said. "But perhaps not. A Minotaur might be content with the Carrion. Then Harpsborough only need face Maab and her people as they flee. Lucreas, well, he'd never stop at conquering just the Carrion."

Johnny used the woodstone ladder built into one of the beds to climb up to its top bunk. He took off his shirt and used it as a pillow.

"Comfortable?" Aaron asked.

"It ain't a feather mattress," Johnny answered, "but 'twill serve, 'twill serve."

Arturus heard footsteps coming down the hall.

"Galen—" Arturus began, but his father cut him off.

"There will be time to answer more of your questions, but Calimay's people are coming for you now, son. You'll need to impregnate one of her daughters. Calimay has three, I believe."

Arturus suddenly felt his heart in his throat. "Which should I pick?"

"The nicest one," Galen said.

"How am I supposed to tell that?"

"Your best guess, son. Your best guess. Don't let them get on top. Do anything you can to assert some control over the situation. Make sure you don't look like a victim. Try to finish as quickly as possible. This is your first time, so that shouldn't be a problem."

The footsteps halted outside their door.

"Try to keep your wits about you," Galen said. "Don't let yourself feel violated. Enjoy it if you can."

"Enjoy it?" Arturus heard his own voice crack.

The door opened.

"If you can," Galen said.

Two Carrion soldiers flanked a lavender robed priestess.

Arturus nodded to his father and left.

27

Aaron watched Galen's facial expression as the door closed behind Turi. If there was any change in the warrior's feelings, Aaron couldn't detect it.

Surely, he must care about this.

"Well, Galen" Johnny said, "I bet I know what you're thinking right about now."

"Oh?"

"You're thinking, 'Thank God I didn't have a daughter.'"

Galen smiled.

"He'll be fine," Aaron said. "Turi is a tough kid. It ain't going to fuck him up."

Galen's smile disappeared. "It might. Surely you heard us arguing in the cell."

Aaron shared a glance with Johnny, whose head was peeking out over the top of his bunk.

"We did," Aaron admitted. "But it stopped. We thought, you know, that you'd handled it."

Galen moved across the room and sat on the bunk beneath Johnny Huang. Taking a cue from the hunter, Galen took off his shirt and used it as a pillow.

"They gonna give us our stuff back?" Johnny asked.

"They will," Galen said.

"What about Kelly? Are they going to make her one of theirs?"

Galen shook his head. "I doubt they'd dress her up in lavender. She's just as much a prisoner as us. Out of some feeling of respect, they might give her a nicer room. The Carrion tribes used to work like that, before Maab became so powerful she could dominate them all. There wasn't a single leader, and a priestess from another group was an honored guest. It looks like Calimay may in some way honor that ancient formality."

"Galen," Aaron said, "I want to say thank you, now, just in case we don't survive any longer. Without you, we'd have been dead a dozen times. This whole expedition—"

"Is a failure anyway," Galen finished.

Johnny was snoring already.

"Going to be hard as hell to sleep through him snoring," Aaron joked.

"I don't envy you that," Galen said.

Aaron heard more footsteps outside of their room.

But why were the Carrion men returning?

The hell?

The footsteps stopped outside of their door. When it opened, there was another priestess who was also flanked by two soldiers. Galen stood up and put his shirt back on. "See you in the morning."

They grabbed Galen and walked him out of the room.

Johnny sat up when the door slammed shut. "What happened?" he asked groggily.

"They took Galen."

"Why?"

"He promised himself to Calimay, remember?"

"Well, you got to admit it. That whole family has a way with women."

Aaron did his best to laugh.

Martin had gathered all of his hunters next to the wall by ole Bense. They sat in a half circle around him.

It was just an hour before the official morning, but that didn't mean what it used to. In the old days, the first few hours would be filled with the sounds of gatherers readying themselves for their journeys into the wilds. Today Martin expected a slow trickle at best.

Michael Baker had already taken his first look at his city. The First Citizen didn't look very happy, but he managed to give Martin a smile. That support made Martin feel bolder.

I won't let you down, sir.

"I ain't feeling comfortable with that man there," Marcus said of Bense.

"Me neither," Huxley agreed. "Martin, we know you like to talk to him, but he puts the creeps on me."

The hunters, all forty of them, were a chorus of disgusted grunts.

"Does he?" Martin asked. "'Cause y'all are pussies?"

There was a bit of laughter, but Martin could tell he hadn't earned anybody's trust yet. There were a few snorts mixed in as well.

"It's sick, Martin," Marcus responded. "The way you talk to him like he's still living is sick."

"Stilling bothers you, doesn't it?" Martin said loudly. "Turns the stomach."

Martin saw a few villagers poking their heads out of their hovels.

Good! A few of you folks still have some life left in ya.

"The way you talk to him, does," Marcus said.

"It ain't right, what happened to ole Bense." Martin pointed at his stilled friend. "It ain't right. He was one of us. He used to wander the halls. Marcus, I thought that'd make you feel a bit of comfort, ya know? Knowing that if you were ever to stop moving, you'd still have my ass to talk to."

This time the laughter was more genuine.

Martin forged ahead even louder, feeling heartened by his men's responses. "It ain't right. It just ain't right." He paced from one edge of his hunters' semicircle to the other. "And there are people, our people, out there in the wilds right now. We've seen 'em while on patrol. They're just lyin' there. Waiting. Just like ole Bense, but not quite. Not quite. Marcus, you've got a friend out there, almost still, don't you?"

Marcus nodded. "Jane."

"That's why you're here, waiting for the subsidy. I bet you intend to feed Jane with it."

Marcus blanched. "I . . . sir. It won't hurt my hunting. I swear. Don't order me not to."

Martin walked up to Marcus. "Stand up, hunter."

Marcus did so and looked Martin in the eye.

Martin didn't back down. "I would never order you not to help a villager in need. Never. You got that?"

"Yeah."

"Can I get a 'sir' on that, hunter?"

"Yes, sir!"

People had started to come out of their tents and hovels. One of those people was Katie. Martin felt a flash of warmth as he saw her.

Good to see you up, babe.

"Sit down, hunter." Martin ordered.

Marcus sat back down immediately as if Aaron himself had given the order.

"The tough thing about all those starving people like Jane is that they're just a couple of days short of a free meal. Just a couple of days. And the Fore's finally done it, they've agreed to help us out with the stores. Our friends will lie out there, the stilling in their bones, while the rest of us feast. That's what 'puts the creeps' in me. That's what 'ain't right.' Can I get a 'yes, sir' from you hunters?"

"Yes, sir."

"We don't want our people starving do we?"

"No, sir," the hunters replied in unison, a determined look on many of their faces.

"We don't want them sitting alone out in the wilds, waiting for a corpse to come by and rip out their eyes."

"No, sir!"

"We don't want to eat no feast, knowing that our own people are dying out there in the wilds while we can take care of them."

"No, sir!"

"We're going to do something about this shit, aren't we?"

"Yes, sir!"

"Aren't we!" Martin shouted at the top of his lungs.

"Yes, sir!" The echoes of the soldiers shouting reverberated off of the walls of the Harpsborough chamber.

Martin looked up and saw Michael and Mancini on one of the Fore's third story balconies, looking down on him. More villagers were standing and watching his gathering than Martin had guessed were left in Harpsborough. He even spotted Constance, though the sight of the dissident sent a cold shiver up Martin's spine.

"Aren't we?"

"Yes, sir!"

"Can I get a 'sir, yes, sir' on that?"

"Sir, yes, sir!"

Martin's hunters were with him, he could feel that in his bones.

Martin paced back across his semicircle. "Huxley, Tucker, follow the lad John over there and bring out our subsidy."

The hunters stood and walked into the Fore. Then they came back out carrying two boxes Martin knew were filled with devil wheat, dried dyitzu meat, and some pickled sinfruit. Huxley and Tucker set the boxes down next to Martin.

"Now this ain't no order," Martin said, "but I'm going to give up some of my subsidy and take it out into the wilds to feed Jane and the people like Jane. How much each of you give, or if you give it all, is up to you."

"Why don't we just give 'em one of these boxes?" Marcus suggested.

"Anyone opposed?" Martin asked.

He could tell some were, but they didn't dare say so with the entire village watching.

"Good," Martin said, nodding and pacing.

The village erupted into an applause. Martin felt hot blood rushing through his veins. His hairs were standing up on the back of his neck. For the first time in his life, he knew he was doing the right thing.

"Alright, I'm leading a crew down to the Hungerleaf Grove. Rick said he didn't mind if we picked through it while he was gone." That was a lie, but Martin figured Rick wouldn't be too angry with him when he found out about it. "Then we're going to break up into units and find all the starving people in the wilds. We're going to feed them and keep them from the stilling. Now we don't need to give 'em much. Just enough so they can make it to the feast."

Graham stood up.

Oh shit.

"Isn't feeding who's left in the village important, too?" Graham asked. "And if you're out running through the halls feeding those people, who will be catching the dyitzu? Who's going to be patrolling the outskirts, making sure to thin out the corpses that might kill the villagers?"

There was a sudden pause. Everyone was looking at Martin.

Martin's brain froze. He didn't know what to say. To buy time he paced back and forth again, looking at the faces of his hunters, and then at the faces of his people.

They don't like him. They want me to win.

His eyes fell on Constance.

Except for that guy. He just wants the Fore to fall. He's probably my worst enemy.

Martin walked back to Graham, but looked past him and addressed the hunters and the villagers. "You're right, Graham," he said loudly. "You're absolutely right. We're a little short handed. Constance!" Martin walked through the hunters towards the man. "You've got a crew who runs with you, right?"

Gotta keep my enemies close.

Constance seemed a little shocked at being addressed by a Harpsborough authority figure, but his blond-haired head nodded.

"This is a tough time," Martin said. "I know it's been tough. You've done a great job looking out for you and your own, even when it looked like no help was coming from the Fore. Will you help me now? Will you and your men help me pick through the Hungerleaf Grove? Will you help me save those people who need us?"

The entire village focused on Constance.

"It's about damn time we did something." Constance said. "You're damn straight I'll help you."

He ain't my enemy. Seeing starving people just hurts him in a different way, is all.

Martin offered his hand. Constance shook it firmly. Martin heard the knuckles of his hand crack, but the hand had recovered well enough that it let him grip back.

"Good, you and your men are with me. Huxley, Marcus, Pete, you too. Graham, I want you to supervise the normal hunting."

There was round of staggered "yes, sirs." Even Graham gave a halfhearted one.

Martin turned and addressed his hunters, but really he was addressing the entire village. "It's been rough. No one's denying that. But when we get back tonight, we're going to sit down and brainstorm a new way to do this hunting thing. Hell's changed, and we're going to change with it. It ain't like when Aaron was here, having to fight the Fore every step of the way. We're on the same side now. They're going to hear us when we ask for some changes. And we're going to hear them when they ask us to protect the people. Any questions?"

No one had any.

"Good! Move out!"

"Sir, yes, sir!" the hunters responded.

Martin moved towards Constance, who was talking to some of his people. Huxley, Marcus and Pete fell in step behind him. He saw Katie in the crowd and gave her a wink. She blew him a kiss back. He looked up towards the Fore.

Michael was grinning.

28

Ellen awoke from her slumber.

The Kingsriver slowed as it widened. As usual, the ceiling of this river soared high above them, coming together into irregular formations of small red bricks. The river split around a huge natural central pillar. Rick took them down the left fork.

"We're almost there," he said.

The walls around them were made of limestone blocks, each nearly five feet high. A small grate sat in one of the walls, blocking off a cavern. The entranceway was only about ten feet wide and five feet tall. Rick slowed the boat next to the grate, which was made of crossed iron bars.

Rick held onto one bar with one hand and rattled his paddle inside the grate with the other. "They'll be here in a second."

The water flowed slowly beneath them and ran down the long chamber. Molly stirred, scratching one breast and sitting up. Alice leaned over one side of the boat, rocking it slightly, and put her cupped hands into the water. She brought them up to her face before thinking better of it. She let the water flow out into the river, unscrewed the cap from her canteen and took a long drink from that instead. Ellen watched her screw the canteen's cap back on.

She must remember the corpses. Their dust must be polluting this river.

Rick rattled his paddle again. "Hello! Is anyone in there?"

No one answered. Rick looked worried.

"They may have moved on," Alice suggested.

Molly shrugged. "Or they could all be dead."

"It's not impossible," Rick said. "It could be all the corpsedust in the river. If they were using this as a water source, and anyone died, they'd be sure to rise. Town could have been overrun."

Alice looked worriedly about. "If that's what you think, then is it really such a good idea to be making all that noise?"

It was Rick's turn to shrug. "At least they wouldn't be able to get us."

Ellen watched the polluted water run for a while. Then she put her hand on the bar to help Rick hold the boat still.

Rick began banging the paddle against the iron, hard enough that Ellen was afraid it might break. The blows shook some of the red rust free from the iron. The red flecks drifted down into the river. After around ten hits or so, he stopped.

"Damn," Molly said.

Rick shrugged. "They've gone dark. I guess we'll go downstream a bit. Then we'll disembark and head on to Tucumcari."

"What if they're gone too?" Molly asked.

Rick looked suddenly unsure of himself. "I don't know, Molly. I guess we'll have to search the wilds until we . . ." Rick stopped talking and tilted his head to one side.

Ellen tried to listen for whatever Rick might have heard. For a second, she thought she was hearing hellsong again, but that wasn't it. This was something different.

Voices.

Ellen could hear them coming from the river beyond the grate.

Rick laughed, obviously relieved. "Little help?" he called.

One of the voices was higher pitched than the other. "I told you I heard something,"

"We're coming," said the deeper voice. "Just hold on, okay?"

"We're holding," Ellen shouted back.

Massan chuckled with relief.

Two men came around the bend beyond the grate and jogged up to them. They both wore the same kind of black boots, which seemed to have been torn apart and sewn back together with white stitching. Ellen was surprised to find that they were both male. She could have sworn that the higher voice was a girl's.

One rested his hands on the iron bars, leaning over the river to speak while the other disappeared from view. "Welcome to Macon's Bend." Ellen noticed that it was the leaning man that had the deeper voice. "Didn't know anyone still tried to come in the river way. Not since the dead took Cypress Lake, anyways."

"I told you I was hearing something, Sarge." the high pitched voice called out from behind the wall.

Rick put his paddle back by his side. "That lake almost killed us. Someone ought to put up a warning. We barely made it through."

"Glad you made it," Sarge responded. "We tried to clear it out once but ran into a stonewight. Bullets didn't do shit to the thing, so we just gave up. Give us a second here. I know for a fact that the downstream gate is rusted shut. I think we may still be able to force this one open." He turned to Ellen. "You look pale, miss. You alright?"

Ellen did her best to give him a smile. "I'm getting better. Hurt my ankle and," she said as she gave Molly a pointed look, "a zombie ate my toes."

Molly's jaw dropped as Alice laughed.

"But what's a stonewight?" Ellen asked. "How are they immune to bullets?"

"Magic," Sarge said.

Rick shook his head. "Hell works differently than the old world. Some of the items we have seem to have come from Earth. Our bullets, guns, clothes, stuff like that. Some devils aren't affected by that stuff. Other things are from Hell. Our bodies, the rocks around us, sinfruit and devilwheat."

Ellen frowned. "My body is not from Hell."

Sarge laughed. "You think so, girl? No scars? Eternal youth? Grow back any limb you like? That's not the body God gave you, sweetheart—"

"Give me some help, Sarge," the high pitched voice asked.

"One sec," Sarge told them.

Sarge moved away, disappearing behind the wall. Ellen felt her shoulders tighten involuntarily at the harsh squealing noises that came from whatever the Macon's Bend men were working on. It sounded like metal scraping on metal.

"I think it's jammed, Sarge."

"Of course it's jammed. Here, help me push."

The wrenching sound was so loud that it echoed up and down the river chamber. The grate began to rise and Ellen let go of it. Rick began paddling backwards to keep them still. Alice gasped as she saw how rusted the iron bars on the bottom half of the gate had become.

Rick nodded. "It's that corpsedust. Breaks even metals down eventually."

"It's safe to drink, mostly," Sarge called out over the squeaking of the rising gate. "Boil enough of the water off and drink it, then you'll get some righteous hallucinations, but as long as you don't do that you'll be just fine."

"That's been a problem here lately," the high pitched voice said. "People getting stoned that way. We've had a few guys do it so much they started to rot from the inside out."

"Highman Tucker outlawed the practice," Sarge said. "Some people weren't too happy about it. I'm just wondering how the hell they figured out they could do it to begin with."

The bottom of the grate rose out of the river. It got stuck after going up only a few feet. After a few more grunts from the men, it began to move again.

"Hold on," Sarge said.

"You can stop now," Rick told them. "That's high enough for us to make it."

The water fell like rain off of the raised grate and onto the back of Ellen's neck while Rick paddled them under it. With a squeal and a splash, the gate fell behind them. The two men from Macon's bend were both breathing hard. Sarge was bent over with his hands on his knees. They were standing next to a wheel which had an iron chain wrapped around its axle. Ellen figured that was what they'd used to open the gate.

"This way," Sarge said between breaths. "I'll show you where you can dock your boat."

The river's left wall opened up to the city of Macon's Bend. It reminded Ellen very much of a giant amphitheater except that there were rows of houses instead of seats. The river took them to the stage-like portion—a flat, cobblestone half circle where a few dozen people stood, lounging and talking. A series of four foot long woodstone docks jutted out into the river, each one buoyed by dyitzu bladders. Radiating back and up from the stage-like landing were semicircular rings of stone houses. People moved along walkways which were actually the roofs of the houses below. Each house had a stucco-like façade, but Ellen could see red Kingsriver bricks beneath where the stucco had worn away.

Half a dozen children were sitting together on the cobbled stage. They stood as the canoe approached and ran with them along the old woodstone docks. Ellen noticed that there were no other boats there at the moment.

"The one good thing about hell is," Rick said as he tied them up to a wooden pole on one of the small docks, "there aren't any barnacles."

He stood slowly, rocking the boat, and sat on the dock before pulling Massan up beside him. Together, they helped Molly and Alice off.

Ellen's toe stubs were hurting abominably. Rick and Massan's hands grabbed her under her arms, helping to lift her up onto the dock. Massan reached back in and picked up her paddle-turned-crutch out of the canoe. Ellen searched for exits to the chamber, finding two staircases which led up and out of the amphitheatre shaped village.

The children had stopped at the end of the dock. They were dressed similarly to the adults. Their shoes appeared to be the same black boots, only they had more of the white sewn seams in them. Their dress was ragged. A few of their shirts were made from dyitzu hide, but mostly they wore pieces of tattered old world clothing. Ellen was glad to see that their expressions were not bleak or empty. Hell hadn't broken them.

Behind the children, Sarge, his friend, and a third man that was taller than the other two by nearly half a foot, approached.

"Rick! How the hell are ya?" the tall man shouted.

Rick beamed. "They ain't got me yet, Jim."

Jim gave out a belly laugh.

"Out of the way, kids," Sarge said, dispersing the pack of them.

The rest of Macon's Bend was staring at them as well, but, as if dismissed with the children, went back to their own business.

"Can I help you walk?" the high pitched man asked Ellen.

"Please," she said.

He took her arm over his shoulder in much the same way that Alice had in their flight through the cypress forest. The dock swayed as they walked off of it. She was happy with how well her ankle appeared to be supporting her weight.

Jim was talking. "How are things back at that village of yours, what was it, Guitarville? Pianotown? Ukuleleport?"

Ellen laughed aloud.

Massan looked somewhat offended. "Harpsborough," he corrected.

"Same thing," Jim answered him with a wink. "You guys headed further downstream?"

"Probably not," Rick said. "We're planning to spend the night and then head out to Tucumcari. Put out word that we're looking to make contact with an Infidel Friend."

Ellen felt the man who supported her jerk at the mention of an infidel.

Sarge looked around as if to see if anyone other than his two companions had overheard them. "Best not to say that to too many people around here, friend. They don't exactly have a shining reputation."

"Nor do they at Harpsborough," Rick said softly.

"Well you're right," Jim said. "Heading downriver wouldn't do you any good. I don't think there are any Infidel Friend down there. They hate them even more than we do. The King of Kingsport has outstanding orders that they be shot on sight."

"Brave," Massan said, "but foolish."

"Follow me," Jim said. "I'll get you an empty house for the night."

"Thank you." Rick's voice was sincere. "You need anything for barter?"

"Wouldn't hear of it. Didn't expect to see you, even though I see Galen once a year or so. How's he doing?"

"He's dead." Rick's voice was flat.

Ellen stared at Rick.

How could he say that? They could be alive!

But maybe it was best they started thinking realistically. Maybe it was best that she gave up hope.

"And your boy?" Jim asked.

Don't say it. Please don't say it.

Rick nodded. "I'm afraid so."

Ellen felt her legs go weak. The man she was leaning on grunted from her added weight. She managed to regain her faculties before they both toppled over.

"I'm sorry to hear that," Jim's voice sounded distant for some reason.

The people in front of her were walking up the stairs now. Ellen's bad ankle throbbed as she lifted it to the first step. She and the man who supported her pushed up together. The voices of Rick and Jim were getting more distant.

"What about Kim?" Rick was asking.

"Lost her two years ago."

"Sorry. We probably shouldn't be asking these kinds of questions."

"No shit," Jim said. "I hate this place. Sometimes I can't wait to die."

Each step seemed to hurt more than the last.

"Are you okay?" The high pitched voice invaded her thoughts.

"Yeah," she answered.

"I do have some news for you," Jim was saying.

"What's that?" Rick's voice seemed strained.

"Had some longleaf traders in from Tucumcari. Said there was an entire crew of Infidel Friend there."

"That's lucky."

"Maybe," Jim went on. "It's El Cid's group, Rick."

Ellen kept moving up the stairs. She tried to continue, but after a moment her helper stopped. She looked up from the stairs to see what was stopping them. It was Rick. The man wasn't moving.

"You can still go downstream," Jim said. "Or you could pass Tucumcari by. You don't have to deal with her."

Rick's face became the stone block that Galen's had been. "Doesn't matter. One's the same as another. We'll head to Tucumcari in the morning."

They moved along a row stucco houses until they came to an empty one. The interior was comfortably dim and seemed somewhat cooler than the rest of Macon's Bend. Rick said a few more things to Jim and Sarge, but Ellen wasn't paying attention. Massan had her pack, and handed it to her as she sat down. She was careful to keep her hurt leg extended.

Alice knelt down beside her with her own pack. "I'm going to put your foot up on this, okay? Rick wants it elevated."

Ellen nodded. Her foot felt like a useless lead weight. It tingled with pain as she lifted it. The ankle didn't hurt nearly as badly after she set it down on Alice's pack.

"You're a trooper," Alice said, putting one hand on her shoulder. "I'd be crying like a baby."

Ellen looked down. Her cotton shirt had been ripped in several places, probably by the branches of the cypress. Her jeans, particularly near her feet, were caked with mud and blood and they had a hole where the corpse had bitten through to her calf. The bandages on her feet were dirty as well. The blood had soaked them through and then dried, changing the cloth to a dark brown color which reminded her of the rust on the iron grate.

Ellen leaned back against the brick interior. She felt sleep taking her, but hung on to consciousness as Rick and Massan started talking.

"Who's El Cid?" the trader asked.

"Before you were damned, the people who built Harpsborough escaped from the Carrion. There were a lot of them. Nearly a thousand. Galen and I helped them repair the barriers which the ancients had used to separate the Carrion from us. While that was happening, there were some disagreements between the escaped people. They agreed to settle down in different places. Charlie, Harpsborough's old leader, and Michael Baker went to Harpsborough. Father Klein and maybe seven hundred of the others went to Hellespont. Hellespont had it rougher, and their people, well . . ."

"Go on," Massan said.

"They managed to capture an Infidel Friend. Their leader hung him in a public square. Then the other Infidel Friend came. They said that the First Citizen of Hellespont had captured their man by betraying his trust. They gave the village three days to bring their leader to justice. When the city did not, a team of five or so Infidel Friend came in and did it for them."

Molly shifted uncomfortably. "You said the village had seven hundred people."

"When they left the Carrion, yeah. They got smaller as time went on. Still, there must have been at least three hundred left when the Infidel Friend came. Father Klein fled Hellespont when the threat was made. He and some hunters returned there. Hellespont's First Citizen had been hung in the square, right where they'd hung the Infidel Friend. There were maybe fifty or so corpses around the town. The rest we never saw."

"And El Cid?" Massan's voice was subdued.

"It was her team that did it."

Martin's men fanned out about him and Constance as they entered the Hungerleaf Grove. The hunters did so gracefully, moving to open areas with soft steps. Constance's men clumped together in a few awkward huddles.

Martin gave out a low whistle. The grove had been picked dry.

"I'll be damned," Martin said.

"Ain't shit here," Huxley reported over the soft running of the Kingsriver.

"Hux," Martin told him, "you ain't just whistlin' Dixie."

The long spindly, grey scaled branches were almost completely bare. It was like looking at an old world forest in the midst of winter. Martin looked about at the chamber beyond. There wasn't going to be any help here. What his hunters had opted to give up out of their stipend was going to have to be enough.

Martin turned to the two men, one of his and one of Constance's, who were carrying the provisions. "Alright everybody, listen up. We're going to divvy up the food here and break into pairs. I want all your weapons safetied. I don't want none of that Duncan bullshit pretend safetying either. I mean honest to God, 'my weapon won't shoot nobody 'cause Martin will have my hand if I do,' kind of safetying. You got my meaning?"

There was a chorus of "yes, sirs."

I'm starting to like this 'sir' bullshit.

"Good, 'cause we're about to be crisscrossing all over each other in these halls. I know some of you are going to want to eat some of the shares you got. I understand. We're all hungry. It's not like the old days where the Lead Hunter is a Citizen. My starving ass is just like your starving asses, and it shits once every three days the same as yours. But we are well fed enough to be able to move. That means we are better off than the people in the wilds. Now, it ain't fair that we gotta feed them. After all, we all worked for the food that's kept us walking. But this ain't about fair. This is about right. It ain't right for us to be eating when they're dyin'. I want us circling the halls around Harpsborough. I want every starving man you find fed and dragged to town. Any questions?"

Huxley raised his hand. "What if somebody's faking?"

"Faking?" Martin asked.

"Yeah. They all saw us in the village. They know what our plan is. They might go out into the wilds and lay down, knowing we are going to give them food."

What kind of paranoid bullshit is this man spewing?

"Ain't nobody faking. You got that? Nobody. If you think they are, you feed 'em, you drag their ass to town, and you tell me about it later. Anybody else?"

They were silent.

"Good! Then let's do this shit. Every person we feed is a life we save. Don't be slacking on this one. You may not get a chance to do something this important again."

Constance helped divide the supplies. Martin started to wonder how many of these pairs were going to cheat and start eating the food.

I just gotta trust 'em, is all. Like Klein says, I gotta have faith.

Aaron stood as the footsteps returned.

Johnny Huang sat up from his bunk, hitting his head on the stone ceiling. "Shit."

"Quiet, Johnny."

Who will they be taking this time?

The footsteps seemed slower than before. Someone was dragging their feet, perhaps.

The door opened and light poured in from the hallway. Two of Calimay's darkly dressed guards stood, Avery suspended between the pair of them. Avery's pants were stained through with blood, starting from the crotch, and running down the inside of both legs.

They tossed him to the floor.

Avery groaned in pain but did not move. The door closed.

Johnny hopped down from his bunk, hand on his forehead.

Aaron knelt beside Avery. He felt for the lock of Alice's hair at his belt. It was gone.

How long has it been missing? Where did I lose it?

He and Johnny turned Avery over. The man groaned. Aaron felt horribly lost. Of all the hunters he'd brought to the Carrion, these two were the last ones left. Of all the promises he made to the people of Harpsborough about their safety, he'd broken all but two.

"What happened?" Aaron asked.

"That bitch, the priestess," Avery answered. "I'm going to kill her."

"What did she do?"

Avery grabbed Aaron by the collar of his shirt. "I'm telling you. Don't leave me alone with that bitch. I'll kill her. You understand me?"

Aaron nodded. "Hell heals all wounds, Avery."

Avery's nostrils flared. He nodded solemnly. "Hell heals all wounds. All wounds."

Aaron and Johnny helped move the man to the bed below Johnny's. Avery curled up, his eyes wide open.

Aaron returned to his bunk and lay down. He did his best to sleep, but his mind was a swirling mess of worries.

Alice has probably found someone else by now. Someone who loves her and keeps her fed.

In that way, it was probably fitting that he'd lost her hair. She'd given it to him so he could think of her on his journey. Only this had turned out to be a one way journey. Galen kept saying that they were going to get back home, but Aaron knew better. The wilds of the Carrion were a different beast than those around Harpsborough.

But if I'm going to die, Alice, I want it to be while I'm trying to make it home to you.

He could only hope that she was still alone, then. How would it feel if he were to return to find her with another man? Aaron couldn't even figure out what to hope for. He couldn't stand the idea of her being alone, pining for him, never to return. But he couldn't bear the thought of making it home to her only to find out that she'd found someone else either.

Someone was whispering something. For a moment, he thought it was coming through the walls, but it wasn't. It was coming from Avery's bunk.

"All wounds. Hell heals all wounds. All of them. All the wounds. Hell heals them all. It's going to get better. All of them."

 — 29 —

Calimay rolled over. This bed was the most comfortable bed she'd ever slept in. There was another bed in an Embassy Suites hotel in Atlanta, Georgia, room 416, which she counted as being second best. She'd lost her virginity in that one, long ago in another world, before Maab had taught her what men really were. Before she'd known that Yahweh had tricked her. In those days when she thought innocence and purity were things worth a damn.

Sleeping with Galen reminded her of those simpler days. She reached out and touched him. His eyes opened. A few of the candles were still lit, and in that light she could see that he wasn't groggy at all. She could have sworn he was sleeping, but perhaps not.

He had the chest, shoulders, and arms of a body builder. She pulled down the sheet so she could see his magnificently muscled abdomen. He was like one of those Greek statues. It had been so long since she'd been able to have him. So long since she'd been able to live out her darkest fantasies.

She spent so much of her time being in complete control. There wasn't a moment while she led her people, now starving, separated from Maab and under the most intense pressure the Carrion had ever been able to give them, where she could show any vulnerabilities. With her mates, even her favorite and most guarded ones, she couldn't give in to her desires because they might speak to others about her weakness. Only with Galen was she free to allow her own domination.

Oh, sure. It was only pretend. She could break him on a whim, after all. But the feeling was so liberating that . . .

I think I want more. Can he give it?

It was such an odd thing to worry about. In any other situation she could demand more, and if the fellow failed to provide it, she'd just send for another. But catering to this man's dominance meant that she had to be careful about how she asked.

In the end, Maab is right. The male ego is why humans can't survive Hell.

She shoved the thought from her mind. Next to him she felt safe. Protected. As if nothing in the world, nothing in Hell, nothing in the whole universe, could hurt her. She tugged at his arm and curled up into his armpit. She closed her eyes, breathed deeply and felt the security that only this man's steely body could provide.

It was a sin, she knew, to feel this submission. In the old world, humankind had long prospered under matriarchy before Ahriman had come. She was not ignorant of how Ahriman had tricked women into submitting to men. How he had helped write the Bible to keep women enslaved. How in hunter gatherer cultures men accounted for almost none of the calorie production for their people. How men were too emotionally weak to rule without causing atrocities like war and genocide.

Nevertheless, she basked in the feeling. It was the same feeling she'd had all those years ago when her first string high school varsity running back had taken her virginity; and as it was also a feeling that she knew she was not likely to feel again, ever, she was not willing to let it go.

She snuggled closer to him, moving her face only inches away from his and looking into his eyes. His oh-so-intelligent eyes.

There were things a girl said in situations like this. She tried to remember what she had talked about with the boy who'd lain with her in the old world bed.

Ah, I remember.

"What are you thinking about?" she asked Galen.

Galen smiled. "The safety of my son, milady."

"Can I tell you a secret?" she whispered.

"I live for the soft words that ride on your breath, milady."

"I threatened my daughters with torture, if they broke him."

It was a lie, but not much of one. She had made it very

clear to her three daughters that this man's boy was to be left unbroken—though she hadn't gone so far as to threaten them with torture.

"You are as kind as you are beautiful."

"Stop that," she said, pouting. "I'll not have you speak to me like some Shakespearean lover. Then I know you're lying."

"You want the truth then?" Galen's voice was dangerous.

Calimay didn't want this moment to end, but she couldn't keep herself from answering his challenge. "Yes."

"I've missed you."

The compliment caught her off guard. She felt tears welling up behind her eyes. There was an uncomfortable warmth spreading through her body.

Oh please, Ahuramazda, don't curse me to love this man who knows nothing of your ways.

But maybe having his love was possible. She could subject him to an interrogation. A Little Lady might not be enough to cover it, but certainly one of her daughters could perform a conversion on the man. This one wouldn't dare lose his manhood, not Galen. Then he could be taught how a man ought to act. He might understand how fighting the demons head on, like a male would want to, was what made Hell so dangerous. That it was this strategy, driven by the male machismo, which had torn apart the world above. Surely, if he knew those things, he would start acting appropriately. He could be a mate for her. Her prime mate. Maybe even a life mate. Maab had outlawed those, but hell, that was why she had broken away from Maab wasn't it?

But I would not love the man I'd broken.

She sighed.

Galen nuzzled her, pushing her head gently to one side and then whispered into her ear. "Calimay, my dearest love. Why do you sigh so deeply?"

The admission of his love sent shivers of electricity through her body. The feelings inside her became so hideously strong that she was afraid she would cry. She didn't dare let herself do that. No priestess of Ahuramazda could do such a thing. It wasn't safe. If any one of her servants saw her crying, they'd have to be killed lest they spread the word of her weakness. Only a front of absolute strength could keep her people safe.

She breathed again, more easily, content now that she had decided not to cry. She felt something run down her cheek. Its warm substance touched her lips, and then tongue. It tasted like salt.

Her body wasn't listening.

She couldn't stop it, so she cried. She cried for a long time.

"I'm sorry," Calimay said after she had regained her composure.

He wrapped her up in his corded arms. "There's nothing to be sorry about, milove. Nothing at all."

"You don't understand. Everything's falling apart. There are so many devils that we can hardly get to our food caches. The walls are coming down around my ears. Most of my people have stopped caring enough to work hard. Maab would shuffle them around to other tribes to keep them engaged, but I have no other tribe to send them to. Things are getting worse and they only have me to blame. I'm in constant fear that my daughters are going to murder me and give my head as a gift to Maab in order to realign with her. I've even invited an Infidel Friend to live under my roof, Galen. Galen, I'm so lost."

Galen wiped the last of her tears away. "There is a solution, you know."

What would a man know?

"I didn't mean to break down on you," she said. "Everything will be alright. It's just difficult right now."

"No," Galen said. "Calimay, everything will not be alright. Your home's walls are crumbling. You haven't adapted to the higher devil population. And worst of all, you're trying to use the system which Maab uses to rule several hundred tribes when you have but one."

Is he right? Ahuramazda forgive me. Why am I listening to a man?

"I'm doing the best that can be done."

"Things have changed, Calimay. The maxims under which you act must change too."

She felt anger rising in her heart where only love had been previously. "Don't pretend to know the answers. You have never experienced ruling a people, Galen."

Galen laughed. "But the words I just said were your words.

You told them to the old High Priestess. Don't you remember? Right before Charlie's rebellion and the exodus."

So long ago.

"I remember what that Calimay would have said," Galen continued. "She would have told you that your slaves have nothing to work for. That they need rewards for working hard."

I used to think those things.

She shook her head. "Their survival is reward enough. It's foolish to think a man would work for anything harder than he would for his own life."

"What does a slave have to live for?"

"His life. A *serf* is not so bad off that he wishes a worse Hell than his current one."

"I don't think that serf is that smart," Galen said. "Do you? Or more importantly, did you before? It seems to me like this is a patriarchal idea, this punishment and slavery. Just like you'd expect out of an old military. I'd imagine that it was ideas like that which caused you to leave Maab."

"They were, Galen. But Maab was right about a great many things. I can't give them rewards they care about without giving them autonomy. There is no margin for error in Hell. What's to keep them from hurting us with their freedom?"

"The same thing you expect to be their reward. Their own survival. Only when you give them actual rewards, they might really want to survive."

Calimay sat up, letting the sheets fall away from her chest. New tears fell on her bared breasts. "My priestesses will never accept it. Any autonomy given to the serfs takes away from their power."

Galen stayed where he was, relaxed. "They'll be sure that the serfs will become dissident. They'll be sure that no leader could be strong enough to keep control over such undisciplined males. They'll think not even Maab could be that powerful. Imagine how afraid of you they'll be when it works. When all the serfs love you. When the soldiers and serfs adore you for your love and spite your underlings for resisting the changes."

It might work. It's the kind of thing I used to think of. Maybe Maab's style is too masculine still.

"I'll think about it," she said, and laid back down into his arms.

These arms which were about to leave her. But why? Why was Galen so interested in what happened in the Carrion? Why did he not simply want to flee to Harpsborough? And how had he gotten the angel's get out of the hands of the Infidel?

What kind of man am I sleeping next to?

"You're afraid," she said aloud. "You're afraid of what's happening in the City of Blood and Stone."

"Of course."

"It's not Lucreas, is it? It's something deeper. Something more horrific. Does it have to do with your son? Why did the Infidel want him anyway? And how the hell did you steal the boy away from the Infidel?"

"Calimay, there are things a man tells a woman, in bed, that he should not say aloud. Things that you can't tell another soul. Not Maab. Not the Infidel Friend. Not anyone."

"Tell me! What is the boy for?"

"I fear the Infidel is going to use him to find his mother. Or to get something from his mother."

Galen turned away, covering himself with one of her silken blankets. The slight breeze this produced helped dry the tears on her chest.

She pulled the blanket back off of him, rolled him over on his stomach and began to massage his shoulders. "That's possible, but I have another idea, as well."

"Oh?"

"I've got Malkravyan in my court, Galen, so I've heard the histories as the Infidel Friend tell it. But they don't say everything. They pile secrets on secrets, and I think even they can't untangle it all. But I've got help. You know I used to sleep with Lucreas, too, and he's very old. Very, very old. He knows the history from the demons' side.

"They tell a very different story. In some ways both tales are the same. The devils couldn't conquer the Infidel's empire until Saint Wretch came along. Saint Wretch became the focus of all the Archdevils the Infidel hadn't managed to kill yet, and they became a force powerful enough to topple the empire.

"But what the Infidel Friend won't say is that St. Wretch was once one of their citizens. That half of his army was made up of the Infidel's own men." Calimay stopped talking for a moment while she worked on a knot in Galen's shoulder. She leaned over and used her elbow to massage the tight spot when her fingers began to tire. "There's something else the Infidel Friend and Lucreas disagree on. Malkravyan says that the Infidel wounded Saint Wretch's pet Archdevil, and that this somehow threatened Saint Wretch's invulnerability. The demons claim something else. They say the Infidel found a substance that could actually hurt Saint Wretch. And not just Saint Wretch, but any devil, anywhere. Icanitzu, dark dyitzu, Archdevils . . . a Fury, you name it. They say he made a sword out of it. They say he left it in Sheol."

Galen interrupted her massage, turning to one side. He looked up at her. "I'm not sure how that has anything to do with Turi."

"Hear me out."

"Speak on, milove."

"So let's say this is true. If the Infidel left something in Sheol, and he hasn't gone back to get it, that means he can't get to Sheol again, for whatever reason."

Galen nodded. "Well, that reason is the Erebus. Or more importantly, the Furies which guard the Erebus."

"Right! And if that's the case, it would almost have to be that sword, because without it, he wouldn't be able to fight his way across anymore. His only other alternative way into Sheol would be to die, and that's too risky. Now you know that the Furies will attack anything that tries to cross the River of Darkness."

"That's right," Galen said.

Calimay smiled. "But they might not attack an angel. What if that's why the Infidel wants your boy? What if it's because the angel's get can cross the Erebus?

"Turi's half human, Calimay. Even if an angel could cross that river, Turi couldn't. For instance, a Fury won't attack a normal corpse, but as soon as Minotaur takes control of it, that Fury's coming. Sometimes they'll go miles into Gehenna just to kill the Minotaur that dared send their undead that way. And a magic sword? Surely you don't believe that's true. Devils have immunities to classes of material. There's not going to be one class that can hurt every devil."

"Think of it, Galen! Think of it. With a weapon like that, we could kill the Archdevil who rules Londinium. We could retake the city. Think what it would do to Maab's priestesses? They've been told that Mithras is the one who will conquer Londinium. Think what would happen if we took it? They'd flock to us in droves!"

Galen sat up and kissed her. "I don't think he can cross the River of Darkness, Calimay."

"Maybe not, but when you're scouting, you're going to see if he can."

His eyes narrowed. He had a dreadfully stubborn look on his face. "I can't protect my son from a Fury. I won't send him there."

"That wasn't a request. You do this, or you'll never make it home."

He met her gaze.

Who are you, Galen? Where did you come from? How did you steal my heart?

She leaned forward and kissed him lightly on the lips. "If you don't want to send your son into Sheol, that's fine. I understand. I won't force you to do that. I just need to know if he attracts the Furies. If he does, then run from the river. If he doesn't, just let me know. I'll have his seed soon. I'll send his child in to get it if I have to.

Galen nodded his agreement.

"Sing me that song, Galen. The one about the marriage."

"Another time."

"Why not?"

"I don't like the way it ends, Calimay."

"You never sang more than the first verse."

He nodded.

Tears were coming down her cheeks again. This time she didn't even bother to try and stop them.

"You really love your boy, don't you?"

"More than I ever imagined I could love anyone."

"Stay with me!" she begged. She knew that it was an impossibility, that such a romance could never work, but she didn't care. "Stay. Don't go back to Harpsborough. Be my lover. I'll love only you. I'll help you raise Turi. We'll keep him safe from Hell. Safe from Maab. Safe from the Infidel. Safe from Lucreas."

Oh, Ahuramazda. Malkravyan has seen Turi. He'll summon

the Infidel.

Cold fear took her breath away. "Malkravyan. You'll have to leave."

"I will. And so long as Malkravyan thinks I'm not coming back, then I can come back, at least for a short time."

"I love you. Promise me you'll return."

"I love you, too. I've missed you very much. I promise you. I promise you that after I've gone to the City of Blood and Stone, after I've looked across the River of Darkness and onto the Shores of Sheol, after we see if Arturus can cross the Erebus, that I'll come back to you. No devil, no Fury, no Infidel Friend will stop me. I swear it."

Her hands shook as she took his face in her hands. She could not help but be her dominant self. She leaned forward and kissed him as tenderly as if she were kissing a young and helpless boy. She pushed him back on his back and put her lips by his ear. "I can't tell you how much I love you. I can't describe it. I know you'll—"

Her door opened. Light poured into her bedroom. One of her Little Ladies had come.

"Queen Calimay," her slight voice said.

"Why are you here?" Calimay snapped.

"You told me to keep you updated on the angel's get."

Oh Mithras. I did.

"Did the boy remain unbroken? And which of my daughters did he choose?"

"He's unbroken, my Queen. And . . ."

"Which daughter? Little Lady, you had better answer my question."

"He didn't exactly choose one, my Queen."

Calimay glared at Galen. Hadn't the man given proper instructions to his son?

"That wasn't an option, he had to—"

"I mean, he did choose one, it's just that—"

"Well spit it out girl, did he choose one or didn't he?"

"All of them."

"What?" Calimay sat up again.

"He slept with all of them."

Calimay leveled a second glare at Galen. The warrior's brow furrowed as he pondered this. Then he smiled and gave out a soft grunt.

30

The hellscape changed dramatically on their way to Tucumcari. The walls and ceilings, previously made of various hues of hellstone, were now a grey substance more akin to hardened pottery than rock. Ellen could see in many places where these had shattered. She wondered if this substance had somehow been retooled, perhaps ground down and mixed with water, for use as the stucco on the outside of the houses in Macon's Bend.

In many places there were solid rectangular blocks of granite between the sheets of grey pottery stone, evenly spaced and set at the corners as if they were some kind of frame. The ceiling often sagged inwards around those blocks, as if it were possible that the substance was melting ever so slowly.

Ellen was happy with her progress. At times she would use the paddle as a crutch to give her ankle a rest. Usually, however, she was able to simply use it as a walking stick. Her missing toes threw off her balance much worse than she had supposed they would, but the paddle's constant support kept her from falling.

After what she guessed to be around eight hours of travel, she began to hear the sounds of people echoing in from distant corridors and rooms. Sometimes she could hear them talking. Other times she could hear them chipping away at the walls. She checked her pistol to make sure its safety was on. It was.

Here and there she saw where the pottery rock had been quarried, sometimes hundreds of square feet of it, exposing a bedrock of granite below.

A few men, perhaps Tucumcari hunters, would greet them

with a wave. They weren't nearly as talkative as the Harpsborough people, and their skin seemed to be tinged with grey. At first Ellen thought that they must simply have been dirty, but as they passed each new person, she started to second guess that explanation.

"Why are they all so grey?" Ellen asked Rick as they traveled.

"It's the clay," Rick said, pointing to the pottery stone. "They grind it down and mix it with water. It forms a paste they consume."

"It's safe to eat?" Alice didn't seem convinced.

Rick shrugged. "Safe, yes. And it does soothe one's hunger. Still, it doesn't give you much energy. A good way to get the stilling, if you ask me."

"Then why do they eat it?" Ellen asked.

"Lady," Massan said. "I've been lost up this way before, and I ate it. I was so hungry, I'd have eaten hellstone if my teeth had been hard enough."

Ellen shrugged.

It was only a few more minutes before they entered Tucumcari's chamber. It was bright, so bright that it almost hurt her eyes. The people here all wore light clothes, dirty whites and soft greys, all sewn out of similar sheets of burlap. Many wore the same black sewn together boots as she'd seen in Macon's Bend. The houses were made of clay bricks, which Ellen figured were almost certainly mined out of the quarries she'd seen earlier. They seemed to be in much better repair than those of either Macon's Bend or Harpsborough.

Ellen thought she could identify other strangers like herself, people who did not live here, moving through the town. Their skin was less grey, for one, and many weren't wearing burlap. Children were playing tag in the street. The sight of them almost made her cry.

There was a shop to her left. There was even a charcoal lettered canvas sign above it that read "guns." A set of woodstone steps led up to it.

"Is it always this nice, here?" Molly asked.

Rick frowned. "No. The devils moved out, remember? Harpsborough would also be thriving and bustling like this if the Fore hadn't weighed them down. That, and they know how to do some masonry work here, which helps the look of the place."

A boy, his skin so grey he hardly looked human, emerged from under the woodstone steps where he had been taking refuge from the intense light of the chamber. He rushed up to them. Ellen guessed he was probably around ten years old.

"What happened to your foot, miss?" He asked Ellen.

"Zombie ate it," Molly supplied for her.

Ellen laughed.

"That sounds very painful, miss," the boy said. "I can help you out. I know the whole town. Just tell me what you want, and I'll take you there. All I ask for is a bullet, so I can help feed my starving mother."

For some reason Ellen didn't find the boy's story very believable.

Rick pulled out a clip from his pocket and tossed it to the boy.

The boy's eyes widened and his face broke into a grin. "Thank you, sir! I'll take you wherever you need to go, sir."

"El Cid," Rick told him.

The boy's grin died on his face. Slowly he nodded. Without another word he turned and led them through the maze of brick houses. Ellen could have sworn that the closer they got to their destination, the quieter it became.

The house they were brought to looked like an oversized igloo, except with clay bricks instead of blocks of ice. There was an ironbound woodstone door set into the front of the structure.

Ellen turned to thank the boy, but he wasn't there. The sound of his quick footsteps caught her attention, and then she saw him, running away. Rick stepped up to the door. Ellen could feel her stomach tightening.

He knocked.

Kyle had heard them walking, day after day. Their sounds echoed into his room. He had called out to them, but they had not answered. Perhaps they could not hear him. Perhaps they had thought he was a devil.

Perhaps he had imagined them.

Their footsteps invaded his dreams, keeping him from sleeping deeply and threatening him with madness. They were human footsteps, he was sure of it. Thousands of human footsteps. And they passed through hell, day after day, not caring to stop and help him.

Kyle had envisioned for himself a glorious end. He had counted on the dyitzu coming in to find him. They would throw their fire. It would splash beside him, the liquid fire splattering across his skin. He would scream through the pain. He would take them down, one by one, until his M-24 gave out that final click that let him know he was out of bullets.

The dyitzu would descend upon him. They would think to get close to him, so that they could torture him. Then he would strike one with his knife. The rest would kill him then with their long claws ripping through his muscles.

But they never came.

The footsteps kept them away.

Or maybe it had only been a day. Maybe he really was mad.

Today he was determined to find the walkers. He strapped his M-24 to his back and began to crawl.

His legs dragged behind him. They were worse than useless, their weight holding him back, and their exposed nerves clouding his vision with pain. At times the agony threatened to knock him unconscious, but if there was one thing worse than the pain, it was the endless monotonous drum of those footsteps.

He dragged himself down a series of steps, turning sideways to keep his knees from catching on the edges of the stairs. His rifle bumped against each of those steps, but the noise summoned no devils.

They were there, in the room beyond, a single file line of walking humans. The room was large, maybe three hundred yards in length, and as much as fifty yards across in places. He could see them only as silhouettes outlined by the yellow light of a distant cubbyhole. Maybe they were one of the Carrion tribes. Perhaps they had decided to move. Kyle drug himself into the room. The even rock of the floor made it difficult for him to find handholds, but the sight of fellow human beings made him bold. Who cared if they were Carrion people? Who cared if they would make him a slave?

He could not see their faces even this close, so bright was the light beyond them compared to the dark of the room. Their step was uneven, lurching. They seemed as soulless as any men Kyle had ever imagined. He gritted his teeth and crawled on.

Let them take my soul, so long as I live.

Their long shadows were projected across the floor, and Kyle was close enough now that the dark projections of their heads covered his hands as they passed.

"Please," Kyle begged. "Please help me."

They did not seem to notice him at all. Kyle dragged himself even farther forward, intending to touch one of them, intending to make one of them listen—then stopped.

He could smell them. They were rotting.

Corpses.

A few of the dead turned their heads as they walked. Kyle could not make out their eyes against the light, but surely they must have seen him. The smell got worse. It became so bad that Kyle had to work to keep from retching. Bile rose into the back of his throat. His eyes began to sting.

He heard the sound of a feathered wing flapping.

A harpy landed beside him. He could see the right side of its body in the light. Her skin was as grey as a corpse's. Her eyes black, like a dyitzu's. Huge brown wings stood out from her withered shoulders. The skin around her mouth was wrinkled like an old woman's, and her hair was white, long and stringy. It was missing in places, as if she had some sort of mange. Her teats were almost human, ancient and wrinkled, hanging like used up udders well below her ribcage. They wobbled with the harpy's odd gait as she walked towards him.

Her legs were more like a bird's than a person's, though Kyle could see the definition of what looked like human thigh muscles as they disappeared into the mess of brown feathers that cloaked the thing's backward jointed knees.

The harpy's mouth opened. The teeth he could see were old, blackened and rotten. Many were broken and a few were missing. She let out a screech that was halfway between a woman's scream and a hawk's distant call. The rank smell of her breath overpowered that of the corpses. His eyes watered, and he vomited.

Kyle shook his head to clear it. He continued heaving, but nothing was coming up. He reached for the M-24 on his back and brought it to bear. The harpy's breasts stopped wobbling as she paused to take stock of the weapon. Kyle's bullet hit her in the face.

They harpy's neck jerked backwards, and then she fell to the ground, wings spread out on either side of her. She was twitching.

The corpses continued marching.

The harpy began to rise. Kyle could see where his bullet had hit her. It appeared to have shattered her cheekbone just below her right eye. Kyle worked his bolt, chambering another round. Between dry heaves, he fired again. Just as before, the head snapped back and the harpy toppled. And just as before, she began to rise.

God, if you can hear me, I could use you.

He fired again.

The harpy continued twitching. He heard more wings, coming from behind. He looked back to see another harpy rushing at him. Kyle swung his rifle around.

With one set of talons, the harpy reached out and grasped the barrel of the gun.

Kyle drew his knife and buried it in the claw.

The harpy screamed, but didn't let go. It put all of its weight on the rifle, pushing it to the floor and rolling Kyle over. Then it lifted its other leg. Kyle saw it hovering over his head.

It descended.

31

Arturus smiled as he entered the meeting room Galen had secured for them. Everyone who had survived was here. Aaron, Avery, Johnny, and even the priestess. The room had a single table and it was lit by a pair of slow burning woodstone torches. The smoke made Arturus cough as he approached, but it didn't seem to be bothering anyone else. Spread out on the table was a series of paper maps. They appeared to have been colored in by a graphite pencil. The paper sheets didn't seem to match each other. Some had notebook lines, others did not. Some had even been torn.

"Why is she here?" Avery asked, his emotionless eyes set on the priestess.

"Because she's coming back to Harpsborough with us," Galen answered.

Avery didn't blink. "I'll kill her, Galen."

"You'll do no such thing," Aaron told him. "That's an order."

Kelly, for her part, ignored the man. She was staring at the odd arrangements of maps. There were gaps between some of them.

"Now listen closely," Galen said. "We're going to make it home. If you recall, I made a few deals with Calimay. Turi has been nice enough to fulfill the first of those obligations. We've got two left."

Aaron nodded. "You've got to show them the rustrock, and then scout out the City of . . ."

"Blood and Stone," Arturus finished for him.

Galen grunted. "That's right. And I intend to do both of those in the same trip. This is where we are now." Galen pointed to a place in the center of the mess of maps. Then he traced his finger a few inches to one side, over a spot on the table where there was no map, and then to another sheet. "And this is where the gold mines are at the edge of the Deadlands."

Arturus did his best to follow the markings on the map, but he had no idea what they meant.

"The rustrock mines are right there. We'll escort some of Calimay's surveyors to the place. That part is going to be dangerous."

Avery snorted and crossed his arms. "You're telling me. We're almost out of bullets."

"We're in luck there," Galen said. "Calimay's agreed to furnish us with guns, ammunition and some backpacks. We'll be on our own for food. Now, I'll have to fix some things up around here as well hunt, so you won't be seeing much of me in the next few days. That's probably for the best, though, since it will give you guys a little more time to heal."

Avery turned red, his fists clenching at his sides.

"Can it, hunter," Aaron ordered him. "We are this close to making it home. You keep your damn shit in order. You got me?"

Still flushed with anger, Avery nodded.

Galen waited for Avery to calm down a little before continuing. "From there, we're going to head south, or what you remember from Harpsborough as the direction 'downriver.' That will take us to an aqueduct. It's not on the map, but it's right here."

Arturus nodded as he looked down. "That's not too far from the mines."

"Well," Galen said, "it happens that it's not. You should know, however, that these maps are many things, but they're not drawn to scale."

Kelly laughed. Avery looked at her angrily, as if the woman had no right to any amusement, but another sharp look from Aaron kept him quiet.

Galen looked at them all, perhaps making sure he had their attention. "Now the aqueduct is sealed, so this part won't be very dangerous. We'll run up the aqueduct, probably without seeing any devils, all the way to here." His finger ran up the maps until it left them, stopping at the edge of the table. "Then

I, and maybe one of you, will leave the aqueduct and scout. After we find out what we need to, then we'll return here, to Calimay's."

Aaron reached over and touched Galen's arm. "What is it we're looking for, old friend?"

"When I first saw the amount of devils in the Carrion, it was clear to me that some greater demon had called them here. After a while I guessed the Archdevil in Londinium was the one who sent out that call, but as we got closer to that area, I realized that the dyitzu got thinner there, not thicker. My guess is that they're actually thickest around the City of Blood and Stone. We'll figure out if that's true when we get there. Assuming that is the case, we'll check and see if they are also the tribe that's using the upside down cross as their symbol. Then, most importantly, we are going to capture one of their men and find out if their leader is a human named Lucreas.

"But I have something else to say. Something more important. It's no secret now that . . ." Galen paused, looking towards Arturus. "Well, that they think Turi is the child of an angel. The Infidel wanted him for that reason. Maab wants him for that reason. But the fact that he's the child of an angel means that he can do something. Can call something. Can affect something. I don't know what that thing is, but I know whatever it may be, they want it bad."

"The Infidel Friend," Aaron said, "won't he go and report where Arturus is?"

"Yes, very possibly. That's why we cannot tell Malkravyan that we're coming back to Calimay's. When we leave, he'll go and report that to the Infidel. If he doesn't know we're coming back here, he'll report our last known location as the City of Blood and Stone. If we can, we'll trick them into thinking that we died there."

He's lying. He doesn't expect to fool Malkravyan. We may get the other hunters back to Harpsborough, but Galen and I will have to keep running.

"How do we get home?" Aaron asked.

"We'll travel along the Carrion, here." Galen ran a finger along one map. "Calimay has a guide which can take us through this offshoot of the Lethe. Without the guide, I doubt we'd make it, but with him, we've got a decent chance. We'll stop when we run into these veins of pyrite. That's about where the barriers end. Then we can cross the Kingsriver and head upstream till we hit Kingsport. After that, Macon's Bend, and then Harpsborough."

Johnny started to grin. "I think we're going to make it."

"The new guns will help," Avery said.

"And if the Infidel thinks we all died, we should be safe." Aaron didn't seem too sure of himself on that count.

Avery crossed his arms. "This isn't going to be easy."

"I don't care," Arturus said. "I don't care if I have to capture that upside down cross soldier myself. I don't care if the Infidel finds me. Or if Maab shows up. I'll do anything to get back home. To see Rick."

To see Alice.

"Good," said Galen. "Then what we need and what we want are the same. Our path is clear."

Aaron nodded, his hand dropping to his belt as if it were looking for something. "Clear," he repeated.

The door opened. Behind it was one of the most beautiful male faces Ellen had ever seen. He had short cropped blond hair over piercing blue eyes. She felt stunned. His cheekbones were broad and high. Ellen would bet money that he was of German descent.

"Who is it, Aiden?" a feminine voice called from within.

The man focused on each of them, his eyes paying particular attention to their weapons. After a moment, he stepped back and motioned them into the room. From this angle, Ellen noticed that the beautiful man had a sword strapped to his back. The sword's crosspiece had a golden eagle etched into it.

Why use a sword when you have guns?

Rick led them in. Ellen stood next to him because it made her feel safer.

Infidel Friend were sprawled about the house.

There were five of them. Two sat together, one male and one female, on a small brick bench built into the wall on the left. Ellen guessed the two were a couple from how close they were to each other. A third sat at a table on Ellen's right. His skin was so black that it shone. He had a rifle disassembled in front of him that he was cleaning. The fourth, who was the pretty male, moved next to the fifth.

The fifth Infidel Friend stood up from behind a desk and moved around it towards the center of the room to greet them.

"Hi," she said. "I'm Cid."

El Cid was perhaps five feet tall. She wore some black cargo pants and a black tank top. Ellen could see the black straps of her sports-bra coming up over her otherwise nearly bare shoulders. Like the rest of the infidels, she was armed to the teeth. A short double-barreled shotgun was strapped to one leg and a rifle, which looked like the kind Ellen remembered American soldiers carrying, was slung across her back. There was no sway to her hips as she approached them.

The woman's arms were incredibly slender, but as El Cid drew near, Ellen could see how muscled they were. El Cid's hair, pulled back into a ponytail, was jet black, but her eyes were extremely light—a green that was almost blue. Her eyes bothered Ellen for some reason.

There was a look that all the Harpsborough girls seemed to share. It wasn't purely a look of wide eyed innocence—except for on Kylie—but it gave Ellen the impression that those women could be trusted. She remembered it from the old world, too. She had seen it on female athletes. On soccer or volleyball players from her old high school. In the athletes faces the innocent trust had been mixed with self-confidence. Sometimes Ellen had seen it on the deeply religious. A sheer credulity that made it almost impossible for anyone to wish them harm.

Whatever that look was, El Cid had the opposite of it. She was anything but innocent. Anything but pure. Anything but credulous. Her gaze was sharp, narrow and discerning. One would not want to deceive her, not out of any moral sensibility, but because one could be sure that this woman would not be fooled. It was the same look, Ellen realized, that was on the other Infidel Friend about her. The same look that Cris had worn. But for some reason, while Ellen found it to be very attractive on men, it disturbed her deeply to see it on the two women in this room.

Ellen had never been so afraid of anyone so diminutive in her life.

This woman and her team wiped out a village. She's a killer.

A murderer.

Those green eyes wandered up and down Ellen, and then did the same to her fellows. Eventually they settled on Molly.

El Cid is Turi's only hope.

Rick stepped forward. "We've come to find you because one of your kind, Cris, is in severe danger."

El Cid's eyes did not leave Molly.

"Actually," Molly said, "that's not true. Cris is just fine, and I have a message to deliver from him."

32

Rick's head snapped over to Molly. Alice's jaw dropped.

Massan stepped back. "You bitch."

El Cid shifted, smiled, and crossed her arms. "If you are so ready to dupe your friends, how can we be sure that what you say is really Cris' message?"

"Because I love him," Molly blurted out. "I'm sorry, Rick. But he said this message was so important to give. I had to lie to you. You wouldn't have taken me otherwise."

Ellen could only see the back of Rick's head, but if his voice was any indication, he was very upset. "I guess we'll never know."

El Cid leaned back upon her desk, placing her hands on its edges. This time she directed her question to Rick. "Where are you from?"

"Harpsborough," he answered.

Then she turned back to Molly. "Did Cris give you a story, so that we would know it was him?"

"Yes, but I've forgotten most of it."

The pretty one moved to sit on the desk next to El Cid.

The black skinned infidel put down the piece of his rifle he was cleaning. "Well, go on and tell it to us . . . what was your name?"

"Molly."

"Go ahead and tell us what you remember of the story, Molly."

"It was about a swallow, I think. It made a nest in a court house. It watched the judge give many fair judgments. Then a snake came and ate her eggs. The swallow was very sad and felt like it was very unfair that she would not receive any justice in a house of law."

El Cid's face was unreadable. "That's a good story, Molly. It is from the book of Gehennic Law. But there is a book of Gehennic Law located near Harpsborough, is their not, Q?"

The black skinned Infidel Friend nodded. "There is. And a traitor out in that direction as well. One who was once an Infidel Friend but now is not. How are we to know you haven't been sent by the traitor?"

"I don't know!" Molly said loudly. "I don't know. That story was the only one he told me. But the message was about the traitor you mentioned."

El Cid leaned forward, but her hands stayed on the desk. "Go on."

"Cris said that he'd gathered news on the traitor. Said that he had returned, or was returning, to the city on the edge of the River of Darkness. Said they were trying to get someone back from the other side. Someone who'd been exiled to Sheol."

El Cid's tiny chin rose. One of her thin fingers tapped that chin.

Q reassembled his rifle in a flurry of motion. "Can't be true. Nothing can cross Erebus. Furies would get them."

El Cid shook her head. "The Infidel did."

The male of the couple spoke up. "You mean to get Lilith?"

"Yes," El Cid answered.

"But I thought he committed suicide to get to the lower level?"

"That's the myth in Gehennic Law," El Cid answered, "but it's just a story. Surely you don't believe that. No, the Infidel found a way across Erebus, all those years ago. And if he did it, then it's possible that someone else could, too, provided that anyone remembered the method. Or if someone rediscovered it."

"The traitor was one of us," Q said. "It's possible he learned how to make the crossing from one of the old survivors. Maybe from Endymion, or Huginn or Muninn."

The female of the couple spoke, "I think Cris was telling Molly about the City of Blood and Stone. That's the only one I know of on the edge of Erebus. No purely human city could survive there, surely. If the traitor had the resources of that city at his disposal . . ."

El Cid stood up from her desk. "Molly, I want you to think very carefully. Where was it Cris said he was going?"

"He said he was going to the River of Darkness. He was going to scout it out. He wanted some . . . he called it redundancy. And to get word to the Infidel."

El Cid nodded. "Jessica, Eagan, send three messengers to Endymion. Apprise them of the situation. Make sure the message is in cipher." She turned to Rick. "These are your people?"

"Yes."

"Do you know where Cris entered the Carrion?"

"Yes."

"Then you will escort us there. Is that understood and acceptable?"

"Of course," Rick told her. "We're at your service."

"Yes you are," El Cid said. "We move out in one hour."

Ellen glared at Molly.

No wonder everyone thinks she's a bitch.

Rick touched her shoulder. "Don't be angry, Ellen."

"But she betrayed us," Ellen answered, a bit louder than she'd meant to.

Eagan and Jessica walked out of the door. The remaining Infidel Friend were up and moving, packing their things and preparing to leave.

Rick leaned forward and whispered into her ear. "Molly thought it was what she had to do. Maybe the lie wasn't the right idea, Ellen, but she did have to come here."

Ellen remembered Cris as he walked through the Golden Door. "Cris said something else, too," she said aloud.

The movement in the room stopped. Everyone was staring at her.

"Before he left," Ellen clarified. "The Harpsborough villagers had exiled him, and they forced him to go through this Golden Door. He called it a golden net."

El Cid smiled up at her. "What's your name, girl?"

"Ellen."

"I think I like you, Ellen."

Kyle awoke to the sound of whistling. It was a human's whistle, flippant, and it carried a tune he'd heard before but couldn't quite place. He opened his eyes.

I'm alive.

He found himself lying on the floor in a small room, well lit for the Carrion, but darker than the ones that typically surrounded Harpsborough. The floor felt freezing against his exposed legs. Someone had cut away his bandages and applied a cream colored salve.

A corpse knelt over him. This one was particularly well preserved, and the smell somewhat more palatable. The odor was more like an ancient, dusty bookcase than it was like rotting flesh. The skin on its face was also remarkable. Pale, certainly. Dead, definitely, and marked with a forest of soft blue veins which gave the thing's visage the look of marble. It appeared also to be devoid of any of the pestilential sores and blisters that usually marked the physiognomy of the undead. Its eyes were inhuman, completely black, like a dyitzu's.

Standing above them both was the whistler. Whatever the whistler was, it at least seemed human, and was wearing a hooded black robe. White hands, delicate and slender like a piano player's, pulled back the hood.

He was alive.

"Healed enough, do you think?" the robed figure asked.

His voice was musical. Soft, like a singer's.

The corpse's head swiveled so that its black eyes might regard Kyle's legs.

"Yes. He will stand," the corpse said.

Kyle struggled, trying desperately to pull himself up into a sitting position. His limbs were slow to respond.

Am I drugged?

"Good," the robed figure said. "Then let's get to work."

He rolled up his sleeves, revealing long, slim white arms. They were almost feminine.

The corpse stood and left the room. Kyle had never seen a dead man move so normally.

The robed figure knelt beside him. He produced a handful of white powder from his robe. Kyle watched the slender hand wave over him, and like a snow of saw dust, the powder drifted down upon him.

Kyle's skin tingled at the touch of the substance. "What are you doing to me?"

His words were slow and slurred.

The man's pale face broke into a smile. His teeth were perfect and bright white, even in the dim room. "Maab doesn't like God, did you know that?"

Kyle tried to shake his head.

"But in Him, I find . . . inspiration. What is your name?"

"Kyle."

"A good name for a wight, if ever I've heard one."

Kyle's tongue felt thick in his mouth. "What's a wight?" The words, like before, were malformed. Still, they were clear enough that Kyle thought this man must have understood them.

"Oh, it's an old word. Think nothing of it. When English was still young, wight meant creature, or person. Think of it as if I had said 'it is a fine name for a chap.'"

Kyle nodded. "What's your name?"

"Nephysis. Have you ever heard about Ezekiel, Kyle?"

Kyle didn't have enough energy to keep his head up, so he let it rest against the stone. He shook it, feeling the hair on the back of his head being pushed up into his skull from the rock below. "No."

"You haven't?" the voice sounded surprised, or perhaps it was mocking surprise. "Not a religious man then?"

"I am," Kyle managed.

One of those slender hands went back into the robe and came out with some red powder. It too rained down upon him.

"You are?" the voice asked. "Then certainly you have heard of the prophet Ezekiel. Or if you haven't, you've heard his song. Have you heard his song?"

"No." Kyle's voice sounded disembodied. It was dry and foreign, and he felt as if someone else had been speaking.

"Of course you've heard it!" the smooth voice said. "You probably just don't know it's Ezekiel's song. Here, let me help remind you." The slender hand brought out more red powder, letting it fill the air. Kyle could not help but breathe some of it in.

The whistle returned, followed by some humming. The tune was certainly familiar. Kyle could have sworn he'd heard it before.

"No? Don't recognize it?" the voice asked. "Then maybe the

words will bring it back to you."

The slender hand touched Kyle's injured leg at the ankle. He was surprised that there was no pain. The touch was firm, but in place of mind-stopping agony, all he could feel was a gentle tingling.

The rhythm of a thumb and forefinger snapping came to him. It was slow, as even as a metronome. Kyle could not move his legs, but he felt like dancing. Like dancing to the song of an all black, female choir.

An even voice, pure as a bell, fell upon him. *"Ezekiel cried, 'Dem dry bones!' Ezekiel cried, 'Dem dry bones!'"*

More dust descended upon him. He felt the hand moving higher up his leg. Still, no pain, only tingling. The music of the man's voice filled him with passion. He could feel himself grinning.

"Ezekiel cried, 'Dem dry bones!'"

The song sounded so familiar. He knew he'd heard it before. He just *knew* he had. The slender hand removed a silver dagger from the black robe. The dagger was held high, poised over him. It was distracting, so Kyle put it out of his mind.

The song was so familiar. If he could just remember what the next words were. It was a children's song, yes, but like so many things he'd experienced while young, it had held a deeper meaning than he'd known at the time.

"Oh, hear the word of the Lord."

The music was in him now. Kyle felt himself moving to it. His body didn't, because it was so far away, but *he* was. Kyle could see that body in the distance—miles and miles behind him.

"The foot bone connected to the leg bone."

That was the song! Now Kyle remembered it. He'd been taught it in elementary school once, except they'd taken out foot and leg bone and replaced them with the real names for bones. The names weren't the important part, though, Kyle knew that. The important part of this song wasn't something they'd been trying to teach him in elementary school. They were trying to teach him about anatomy. They'd taught him the other thing, too, but that was an accident.

"The leg bone connected to the knee bone."

The silver dagger sliced downward, swooping like a dove,

touching a distant stomach. It gently slid through the abdomen, separating it. As before with the hand on his leg, there was no pain, just a pleasant tingling. The noise of the body's gushing blood complimented the music.

"The knee bone connected to the thigh bone."

The song was about Ezekiel, a prophet. And he was supposed to have done something, or foreseen something. That was what was important about the song. *That* was what he was listening for.

"The thigh bone connected to the back bone."

The slender hands pushed into the stomach. They came out with intestines. Slowly, the knife moved into the wound in the belly. The arm, white and covered with red blood, began sawing.

"The back bone connected to the neck bone."

The song welled up within in him, nearing some sort of crescendo. He knew there was a lesson in the words, if only he could just remember them. He knew the climax would bring him an epiphany. An epiphany that would give meaning to his life. Something that he should have always remembered. Something that, if he had just known it before, would have been the one little extra piece of information he needed to turn the tide of the mediocrity of his life towards a new direction of greatness. It would have made him strong enough to thrive in the face of his tribulations. It would have emboldened him. But it wasn't too late. The lesson would save him now, as soon as he heard it.

"The neck bone connected to the head bone."

It was almost there. He was so close. Just a couple more lines. The hands continued pulling guts up and out of that distant body. They were landing in a heap nearby.

"Oh, hear the word of the Lord!"

The music raised his spirits. He knew what the words would be. The very next line held his salvation. He knew the lesson was coming! Things would be different now. The voice grew in volume and shouted out his epiphany.

"Dem bones, dem bones gonna walk aroun'!"

Of course! Those bones were going to walk around. They were! Ezekiel had foreseen it. The dead bodies would rise and take up arms against their enemies. Kyle's body was alive with the music. It was so many miles away, but the music was loud enough now that even that distant pile of flesh and bones could hear it.

"Dem bones, dem bones gonna walk aroun'!"

His body sat up. He was surprised by its strength. It was as if the wounds on his legs had healed. There was no pain anymore. None at all.

"Dem bones, dem bones gonna walk aroun'!"

He stood on solid legs, blood dripping out of the wound in his belly. The cut tingled as the wet, liquid parts of himself dribbled away. He felt lighter. He felt complete.

"Oh, hear the word of the Lord."

But his body was dead.

The pain came back in a rush. He was still standing, but the wound in his stomach made him want to double over. Only he couldn't. All he could do was suffer. The nerves of his body unified themselves, shouting out to him their agony, but he couldn't respond. His legs, flayed as they were, were lightning rods of misery, shooting their torment up into his consciousness.

"This way," the robed figure said.

Kyle followed, his legs obedient to the man's commands. He moved smoothly, not like a normal corpse, but with even, balanced steps. His master led him out of the room and down a long hallway. There he saw the line of corpses. The stone faced one was waiting for him.

"This is your brother Buen," Nephysis said. "You will follow him."

Kyle did as he was told.

"Ezekiel cried, 'Dem dry bones!'"

From Neostoicism: Philosophia

If you love an earthen vessel, say it is an earthen vessel which you love; for when it has been broken, you will not be disturbed. If you are kissing your child or wife, say that it is a human being whom you are kissing, for when the wife or child dies, you will not be disturbed.
—*Epictetus*

Human misery finds measure in the currency of bad ideas.
—*Endymion*

Part VI
The City of Blood and Stone

From Gehennic Law: The Peer and the Slave

When Elohim had finished making the Earth he placed upon it two people, Adam and Lilith, who he fashioned out of clay and breathed life into. He made them equal in strength and character and set them amidst the garden of Eden.

It came to pass that Adam stumbled upon Lilith and desired to know her.

"Lay down for me," he ordered.

But Lilith refused saying, "We are equal in all things. It is not right that you order me about. If you want to sleep with me, it must be as peers, not as a master and a slave."

Angry, Adam ran to Elohim and told him of Lilith's refusal to submit to him. Elohim was angry, and came to Lilith ordering she submit to Adam.

"Why?" she asked. "Why should I be Adam's property?"

Elohim replied, "Because not being so makes him unhappy."

"But being a slave makes me unhappy."

And Elohim sayeth, "I do not care."

But even so, Lilith would not submit and Elohim exiled her from Eden. Elohim then made another companion for Adam out of his own rib, one that was weaker in character and in strength, and he named this girl Eve.

It is said that after Adam and Eve were exiled from Eden, that one of their children met Lilith and mated with her. Thus Lilith's blood was mixed in with all of humanity's.

Know then that there is a time in every little girl's life when she must make a decision as to which woman, Lilith or Eve, she has descended from.

"You cannot go that way, Carlisle," the voice of Mephistopheles washed over and through him.

Carlisle looked to Simeon, expecting him to countermand the devil. Simeon's bearded face, however, was a mystery.

"But why?" Carlisle asked. "I can feel Benson. He's so close."

"This part of Hell is closed to us," Mephistopheles answered. "It is ruled by the followers of the Infidel. They have created creatures so powerful in this realm that even I dare not face them without preparation."

Carlisle stopped, letting the blood flow down the back of his leg for a moment. As always, it began to fill up his boot. "How could men create something that could strike at you?"

"It is will that affects this Hell," Mephistopheles answered, "and I have the will of nearly a thousand men. But the Infidel, when he was here, caught a devil called Legion. Legion would swallow the souls of humans and use their will to bolster its own. We think the Infidel broke it down, or perhaps some of his men took Legion over from the inside. They used Legion's secret to bind many thousands of their souls together, and they use that focused will to make this portion of Sheol stable. Worse, they learned to divide Legion into separate entities in order to spread their control. Inside that realm they have many cities, and the men who live there do so without any fear of devils."

Carlisle winced. No man should be beyond God's punishment.

"But we can go around them, can't we?" Carlisle asked. "We can push into an emotion where they are not touching. Then come back and attack them from behind."

The normally tepid voice of Mephistopheles burned hot inside him. "These men of the Infidel know much, Carlisle. Their realm cannot be breached by such methods."

Simeon's deep voice rumbled past him. Somehow, the words from that man seemed more real than the ones spoken by others in this Hell. "The men of the Infidel are very smart. Some of the devils trying to destroy them asked for my aid, for I walked Gehenna when the Infidel was in Gehenna, and I came here to Sheol when the Infidel came to Sheol.

"Knowing how ingenious the infidels could be at avoiding their deserved fate, I called for help from other fallen humans.

One was a mathematician by trade, and as we began to map the outsides of the Infidel's realm, he came up with a theory. He likened emotions to a fourth dimension in this place. To escape from an attacker here, you must realize, you can either run up or down, left or right, forward or back, or you can become happier or sadder. He guessed that the infidels had learned a way to map these emotions, and that they could produce them at will. Even so, we thought that there could be no defensive shape to their realm without some nook or cranny that we could find our way into."

The blood spilled out over Carlisle's boot. "What did you find?"

"That there was truly no entrance. The infidels had built a four dimensional shape called a glome."

Carlisle tried to imagine that. "But how?"

Mephistopheles' anger was steadily growing.

Simeon, however, remained unaffected. "Through no geometry we'd seen before. But we made one, and mapped the infidels' defenses, finding that they had indeed discovered this emotional dimension in Sheol. To face them is to face their Legions."

The blood pooled around Carlisle's feet. "Perhaps I could help. I could go in and be your spy. I could find a way to disrupt them."

"Perhaps," answered Mephistopheles. "But I would not take you away from your task. You seek the angel's get. This is more important than a handful of stalwarts who are putting off their rightful punishment for a few millennia. Come with me, I'll show you the way around. When you find Benson, you must climb the ladder of his soul. That will take you to Gehenna. That will take you to the boy born of an angel."

Mephistopheles' anger reached a boil. "I feel him, master. The boy is drawing near."

Simeon nodded.

Mephistopheles paused for a moment, consulting with whatever powers of observation he had. "Master, I think he's coming here."

33

Arturus continued his exploration of Calimay's complex after a hard morning spent helping Galen repair the plumbing. While they had worked, Galen had confirmed his suspicions that the complex itself had been built by the ancients, and that the walls concealing it had been added later by Calimay's people.

Arturus found that there were eight levels of the black marble corridors which made up the heart of Calimay's complex. Each was divided into four sections by two perpendicular hallways, and each of those four sections was then further divided into a smaller arrangement of chambers. The glass ceilings of these rooms shone down different colors on different floors, either because of a change in the hue of the glass or in the water itself—Arturus didn't know which.

His favorite had been the purple ceiling. The bottom level, which he was exploring now, had red illumination. As in the above rooms, the water caused the light to undulate with its movement. In the previous halls, Arturus had found the effect beautiful. Here it was somewhat unsettling, making the black marble look like it was covered in blood.

At least there are no devils.

Despite the odd lighting, he felt safer here than he had on the previous levels. He'd noticed Calista, Calimay's youngest daughter, had taken to following him around the complex while he explored. At first Arturus had figured that the young woman had been sent to keep an eye on him. It was Johnny who pointed out that she looked a bit love sick . . . only this girl wasn't like Ellen. He could say no to Ellen. Hell, he could say yes to Ellen and expect to come out of the experience in one piece.

He passed two of Calimay's soldiers as he traveled down the corridor. They were speaking in whispers but stopped as he approached. Their eyes focused on him.

Arturus nodded and smiled warmly at them. This always took Calimay's guards by surprise. Awkwardly, one of the soldiers waved. Arturus returned the gesture before passing them by.

The Carrion born continued their whispers as Arturus approached the end of the hallway. There was a single chamber beyond that was about ten feet wide and perhaps twenty feet tall. The red glass ceiling stopped at the room's entrance. This chamber had a vaulted ceiling made of solid ruby. The light from the red water filtered in through the semitransparent ruby, giving everything here a dim glow. The brighter light from behind cast Arturus' shadow in front of himself. Arturus watched his silhouette oscillate across the room with the waves of the water above. For a moment, he stood still, simply watching his shadow dance.

At the far end of the chamber was a half-carved statue. It was of the top half of a man, hands raised above his head, palms touching each other as if the statue were diving upwards. Arturus got the impression that the man was emerging from the rock.

My tattoo.

Arturus touched his shoulder with his hand as he walked forward. His shadow traversed the stone floor and fell upon the statue.

Whomever had carved this was possessed with a great passion for his work. While it lacked the practiced classical touch of the statues in the levels above, the roughness of the piece seemed to better express the artist's fervor. This was a work of zeal if Arturus had ever seen one. The rough marks of the chisel, along with the wavy red illumination, caused the stone figure to appear to be in motion.

Another shadow crossed the floor. Arturus shook his head.

Calista. She's found me.

Arturus turned to face her, trying to think of what he could say to stop her advances.

Maybe she can—

Malkravyan stood in the entrance of the room. Arturus caught his breath.

The Infidel Friend leaned up against the entrance's walls. "That's a statue of Mithras." The man's features were hidden, standing as he was against the light, and Arturus could not see his lips move as he spoke. "Like Maab, Calimay teaches that he is emerging from the stone. Someday he'll be freed, she says, and then he shall lead her people out of Hell and into a place of eternal reward."

Arturus' hand dropped, as if on its own accord, to his hip—but he had no weapon. Arturus looked about for a way to escape, but there was only one exit to the chamber, and Malkravyan was standing in it.

You can't let him think you're weak.

Arturus cleared his throat. "You don't believe that, do you?"

The Infidel Friend's head shook back and forth.

"What do infidels believe in?"

No response. Perhaps Malkravyan would kill him now, but it seemed more likely that the Infidel Friend would want him alive. Surely Malkravyan couldn't kidnap him and drag him back into the Carrion with all of Calimay's guards around.

He might know secret paths in and out of the complex.

Arturus advanced towards the man. Malkravyan made no move at all, either to capture him or to get out of his way.

Arturus stopped two paces in front the Infidel Friend, standing before him defiantly. "What gods do you pray to?"

At this distance, Arturus could make out the man's expression against the red light, but only just barely.

Malkravyan' lips curled into a smile. "The question of gods changes nothing."

"It changes good and evil. How can one be good if one doesn't know what good is? Why would one wish to be good if not to serve some deity? It is no wonder men call you evil."

"Sure of this, are you?"

"I am."

"A religious man might do good to secure paradise, or he might do good to please his gods. If it is paradise which he seeks, then his morality springs from his own self-interest. If self-interest is the motivation to do good, then surely we can just skip a step and say that I do good because it gives me pleasure and causes others to treat me better. And if, for the religious man, he does good out of love for some external thing, like his God, then surely I can just skip a step and say that it is Man that I love, so that I might do good for him."

The logic behind the statement struck Arturus as familiar, but it seemed incomplete somehow. "But then there is no reason to do good but your own whim. No objective reason for you to try and make everything better."

"If there were some ultimate purpose for my being, some guiding seemingly objective destiny for my behavior, why should I follow it? Would you have me believe, you son of an angel, that you would do an evil thing if a god asked you to?"

"Of course I wouldn't."

Malkravyan raised his chin. "Then why not skip a step and do right no matter what the gods say? If they are just, then they will reward you. If they are not, then you would not have wished to follow them anyway."

Galen might say the same thing.

"But what if the wages of good deeds are damnation, and the reward for vile actions is absolution?"

"Then I would make very sure, boy, very sure that you know that to be the case before you act. Were a man to say such a thing to me, my first guess would be that he is of an unscrupulous sort, a slave of ideas which fool good men into doing bad things. Do you believe we live in such a place where good is rewarded with evil?"

Arturus shook his head. The red light gleamed off of Malkravyan's shoulders. The hilt of the man's blade was almost invisible against the glare.

"The Infidel will never have me," Arturus told the man. "You can chase me through all of Hell. You can kill everyone I know. I will never be his, even if it means I am to die."

Malkravyan closed the small gap between them, his shadowed face now completely visible, only inches away, staring down at Arturus. "When the Infidel comes to you, it will not be as a kidnapper or as a murderer. He will come to you with an argument and an offer. I cannot tell you when he will find you, but it will be when he needs you. What he asks of you, you will not be able to deny him. You have no idea what kind of man *he* is."

Arturus felt anger burning in his chest. "I choose!" Arturus shouted at him. "No one chooses for me. I choose my purpose. I choose what I want. I choose my destiny. I do. Not him. Not the Infidel. Not my father or my mother. Not even . . ." Arturus stopped suddenly, realizing just what he was about to say.

"Not even God?" Malkravyan whispered.

Arturus stepped back.

The Infidel Friend turned about on his heel. Arturus watched the man leave through the haze of blood colored light.

Not even God?

Arturus looked behind him. The form of Mithras seemed to move in the dim, wavy light. It was as if the soul of the statue was engaged in some titanic struggle against the rock he was emerging from—a struggle that soul was inexorably winning.

But then, which God?

The Citizens had been very wise feeding the villagers shares of dried hungerleaf while they were cooking the stew, Martin decided. Even with the edge taken off of their hunger, the Harpsborough people seemed to be struggling to control themselves. On an empty stomach, they probably would have charged up to Kylie's Kiln where the giant cauldron bubbled, overturned the stew, and then eaten it right there off of the stones.

As it was, they were sitting and kneeling, staring at the pot with dead eyes. No one spoke. The only noises were the crackles of the fire which was heating the stew and the growls of empty stomachs.

Patrick Foodsmith was stirring the pot with a giant woodstone stick. He tasted a bit of the stew, holding up the stirring stick and eating the thickened devilwheat off of one end. As Patrick did so, Martin heard the woman next to him groan.

They're so hungry. How did we ever let it get this bad?

Patrick, having sampled his creation, added in some dried houndsblood.

But they're about to be in for a treat.

John's sandaled feet slapped their way from the Fore towards Patrick. He was carrying a box which was filled with chopped dyitzu meat. One of Martin's hunting parties had chanced upon three dyitzu on the Kingsriver. It was the most meat that had been caught since Aaron was the Lead Hunter. The men who'd shot the dyitzu had been camped along the river overnight. Since leaving men on the Kingsriver twenty four hours a day was Martin's idea, he felt rather proud of the kills.

None of the villagers were allowed past Kylie's Kiln, which meant John was able to bring the dyitzu meat to Patrick without being molested. Martin sighed and started his own trek towards the cauldron. He had his hunters there in force, lined up in front of the villagers. Supposedly they were there to enjoy the feast, but they were really there to keep order.

The sooner we get these people fed, the better. We should have cooked all this in the Fore.

Martin slowed down as he picked his way through the villagers.

Suddenly they came alive. A woman rushed up and hugged him. "Thank you so much for bringing Tyler in from the wilds! Thank you, thank you!"

He was surrounded by them as they congratulating him, shaking his hands and singing his praises. "Good job with the dyitzu. We knew you'd turn things around."

"You brought me back, Martin. If you had left me out there, I'd have caught the stilling."

Martin felt his spirit soar.

This is how they used to treat Aaron. This is how they treated Mike.

Their hands clung to him as he pushed his way towards the Kiln. Their warmth surrounded him. Martin had never felt so loved before, even in the old world. He looked around for Katie, but he could not find the girl. For some reason Martin really wanted her to see this moment.

You did good, Martin. You did good.

Finally the hands let him go. Martin passed by two of his hunters to get behind the giant black cauldron. He was surprised to see Kylie there.

"They like you," Kylie told him.

Martin could not suppress his grin.

Kylie leaned forward and kissed him on the cheek. "An excellent job, Lead Hunter. Well done."

The kiss started a fire on the side of his face. The fire spread to his neck and then rushed down his back. There was no doubt about it, Kylie was the best Citizen in Harpsborough.

Mancini came out through the Fore's door curtain and started giving orders to Martin's hunters. "Go ahead and get the bowls ready. We want to have a bunch filled before we start handing them out. This won't be much of a feast if a riot breaks out."

But that didn't seem like a danger now. The people were standing, milling around and talking. A few were even still shouting thanks towards Martin.

Martin moved back in front of Kylie's Kiln. Gemma, a cute little girl who Aaron had dated many moons ago, was signaling to him.

"Can I help you, princess?" Martin asked her.

"Oh, you've already done that," Gemma said. "Your men brought Laurie in from the wilds." Gemma looked him up and down. "You're looking svelte, Martin. Have you been losing weight?"

Martin looked down at his belly. Come to think of it, it was looking a bit smaller. Times had been tough.

"Guess so!"

She smiled and gave him a playful shove. "Don't deny it. We all know you're just trying to look good for the ladies."

The flush that Kylie had started with her kiss threatened to burn him whole. Gemma was a gorgeous woman. The kind of woman that Aaron would date. Martin had never guessed that he would have had a chance with her. He looked out into the crowd of Harpsborough villagers. He saw Katie.

She looked sad and alone.

Katie always liked me. Gemma wouldn't have given half a dyitzu ass about me before I became Lead Hunter.

Martin reached out his hand, beckoning to her. Suddenly the frown was gone from Katie's tired face. She made her way through the sitting villagers, tripping a little as she walked. She was anything but pretty now, Martin realized. The weight she had lost from the hunger had robbed her of some of her best assets while leaving her thighs and belly almost untouched. Dark circles rounded her eyes. Her hair was unkempt. Martin didn't care.

He took her hand and kissed her for a long moment.

A flush colored her face. Her eyes, watering from the smoke given off from Kylie's Kiln, seemed to sparkle.

"Well," Gemma said curtly. "Like I was saying, thank you. I'll leave you two to it."

Martin knew he wasn't missing anything. His father had warned him never to marry a pretty woman, and Martin now knew why. Katie would stick with him through thick and thin. Gemma would drop him if ever he lost his title as Lead Hunter.

The smell of the devilwheat stew suddenly filled the air. Martin felt his own stomach rumbling in anticipation. He looked towards the cauldron.

Patrick was ladling the stew into wooden bowls. Mancini was directing, trying to make sure that everyone got fed fairly.

You gonna eat last, Martin. That's part of being a leader.

"Run and get in line," Martin told Katie. "I'll have to catch up to you."

Katie, enlivened by the kiss, smiled at him. She made her way into the mass of villagers who were even now pushing against Martin's line of hunters.

Citizen Kylie came up behind him and put her hand on his shoulder. "You're a good man, Martin. I always knew you were, but I'm really impressed with you. I didn't know you'd make such a good leader."

Martin's stomach rumbled even louder as the first of the bowls were handed out to the villagers.

Hang on just a little longer.

"Kylie," he told her, trying to keep his mind off of the food. "I really don't think I did anything special."

And he hadn't. Everything that he'd needed to do had been so clear cut.

"Well I think it was special," Kylie told him, eyes wide with sincerity. "And the way you treated Katie just now . . . you're a rare man, Martin. A rare man."

Mancini, who must have figured that enough villagers were eating to make him safe from a riot, cleared his throat and began giving a speech. Martin had to give it to the wily Citizen, this was the perfect time to take credit. There was plenty of goodwill to be spread around, and Mancini seemed dead set in making sure that he and the Fore got their fair share of it.

As if they weren't the cause of all this trouble to begin with.

Martin, seeing that the line was letting up around the cauldron, headed towards it. Saliva filled his mouth. He had to swallow to keep himself from drooling.

There were only two people in front of him. Their bowls were filled far too slowly for Martin's taste. He saw Huxley come running out of the Fore.

Don't you dare run towards me. I've gotta eat.

Martin held up his bowl. Patrick gave him a smile and took it. He scraped his giant ladle against the side of the cauldron and brought up a large helping. Martin could see a dyitzu bone sticking out from it.

This is going to be so good.

He looked back to Huxley. The hunter was only a few feet away.

Damn.

Martin accepted the full bowl from Patrick.

"Sir!" Huxley was nearly out of breath. "The corpse eater is awake. He's talking clearly, too."

Martin frowned. He remembered someone saying that Rick had brought them one, and that they were keeping the man in the Fore, but he'd never seen the fellow. "I guess someone's gonna have to interrogate the guy."

He took a bite of the stew. The flavor of the houndsblood and dyitzu meat exploded in his mouth. The devilwheat warmed his throat as he swallowed. He let out a contented sigh.

"Sir?" Huxley was saying.

"What?"

"You're the Lead Hunter."

Oh shit! I have to interrogate him.

"Right, right." Martin took another bite and chewed quickly. "Come with me," he said around his food. "I want your opinion on what he says."

"Of course, sir."

Martin, bowl in hand, marched up to the Fore.

34

Calimay's slaves, Arturus noticed, were indistinguishable from Maab's. They were just as bony, just as malnourished, and if anything, they were more broken. Even their clothes were the same. Ripped and threadbare robes were draped over equally worn grey shirts and pants. Nearly a hundred and fifty of them, all that remained of Calimay's "serfs," were seated in an internal hellstone quarry deep inside Calimay's complex. They were surrounded by tons of broken up rock.

Avery had refused to leave his bunk, but the rest of them were here. Galen, Aaron, Johnny Huang, and even Kelly.

So few of us left.

Near the exit of the chamber was the lavender robed priestess, Tamara, and a couple of her Carrion soldiers. Calista was there as well, standing right next to Arturus.

"So this is what we have to work with?" Johnny asked.

"I'll be honest with you, Galen," Aaron said, "I'm not sure if we can do all this. Calista was saying this is normally three days' work."

Galen shrugged and then hefted a giant burlap sack he'd brought over one shoulder. "It needs to be done." He walked over to the pile of gravel which filled the chamber.

Arturus couldn't guess how far back that pile of broken up rock was.

"So you'll be working us today?" one of the slaves asked. "Will you, lamb?"

His tone was challenging. Arturus remembered what these kind of men were called. They were Kruks. Maab had implied that they bullied and sodomized their peers. At the slave's mention of the word lamb, a few others laughed. Most looked anxiously at Tamara and her soldiers.

Galen turned to Tamara. "You can leave us now."

She frowned. "Better get results, Galen. You won't be Calimay's little princess for very long if you can't fulfill your promises."

She had made the response, Arturus knew, because she would rather die than let the slaves see a man order her around. In so doing, she had managed to connect Galen to Calimay's authority, which probably was the last thing Galen wanted right now.

"We had better get results," Arturus' father answered. "If we don't reinforce the camouflaged walls you built so poorly, they will fall in."

Tamara set her jaw, turned about, and then left.

Arturus saw Calista getting closer to him. He tried to avoid looking at her. Kelly snorted, perhaps noticing his plight. The slaves began to look at Calista as well.

"You'd better go too, sweetheart," Galen told her.

"I am Calimay's daughter, Galen. You will not speak to me like that."

"Milady, if you get hurt down here, your mother will make sure I'm unfit to be anyone's princess." Galen turned to Arturus. "Him too."

Calista was suddenly pouting. "But I'll stay out of the way, I promise."

When did they get so familiar?

"You can rejoin us shortly, but for now I need to speak with them in a setting where they fear no punishment."

She nodded, then turned to Arturus and gave him a smile. "See you at lunch."

Arturus was amazed how much the little girl was able to get her robe to move as she walked away. He looked back to his friends and noticed that Kelly was staring at him.

"So you're going to try and be our overseer today?" one slave asked.

"Calimay thinks you can work us harder," another said.

Galen pulled stacks of shovels and picks out of his burlap sack. "I'm not here to work you. I'm here to tell you a story." He placed the tools next to a series of waist high stacks of wicker baskets. "Of course, I did make a deal with Calimay. If you were to somehow clear this room of all the rubble, and dump it into the gaps between the outer walls, the rest of your day would be free."

"Friend, I know you mean well," a tall skinny slave said, "but that is too much rock to move in a day."

"Of course," Galen said. "Even if you all were to work as hard as you could, you'd fail. But you're not here to work today, are you?"

The slaves mumbled amongst themselves.

Galen wandered up to the wall of gravel. "You're not even here to make fun of lambs."

"Baa," Johnny said, causing some laughter.

"You're here to listen to a story."

One slave snorted. A few others were still staring off into nothingness. Some, Arturus noticed, seemed confused. Perhaps they feared Galen was going to trick them into some sort of punishment.

"Oh don't worry," Galen assured them. "I know that you're afraid that this will be some kind of *verboten* story. That it might somehow be a subversive tale designed to weaken Calimay's reign. Oh, no. It certainly isn't *that* kind of story. It's a story about a would be princess, named Gala, who wanted to marry a prince . . ."

The slaves were at least listening to Galen as he paced before them, though Arturus couldn't guess as to what they were thinking.

". . . named Calimon."

That got them. A few sat up straight. Others looked nervously towards the exits, but not for long. As Galen walked back to Arturus and the hunters, he took their undivided attention with him.

Galen spun around on the ball of his foot, facing the crowd and gesturing with his arms at the rock. "Now Prince Calimon ruled the Castle of Nid, which sat on the hill of Nod before the plains of Ned. And Gala, his greatest love, was a farmer on those plains. Because she was just a peasant, the soldiers of the Prince feared her. They thought that if Gala were to get the Prince's ear, then the Prince might start doing things for the lowly farmers. He might start making their lives easier. He might even stop working them so hard—and we all know *that* cannot be allowed."

There was some mirthless laughter.

"So the Prince's most annoying soldier . . . named Tamarand . . ." Galen paused for their laughter. A smile spread across his face. "Whispered into the ear of the Prince, 'surely you don't want to marry such a baseborn woman?' The Prince replied, 'Of course I do! Haven't you seen her tits?'" more laughter. "And that *ass*?" Johnny was laughing too.

Galen put a hand to his chin, and for a moment stroked his well trimmed beard. "But Tamarand would not relent. 'Let us at least make sure she is worthy, my Prince.' And the Prince Calimon was a bit of a fool, so he agreed. Tamarand then came to the family of Gala and told them that the marriage was on, but that Gala had to complete a few simple tasks.

"The first task was to spin forty bales of wool into yarn in a single night. The family was horribly distraught, but they had no choice but to agree. Fortunately, word of the ridiculous task got around town, and that night, when Gala got ready to attempt the Herculean task of spinning the yarn, her village showed up to help. Sure enough, by daybreak, all the wool had been spun into yarn.

"Unfortunately, Tamarand had left spies behind. In the morning, the Prince received the report that his beloved Gala had somehow accomplished the impossible task. He was overjoyed. But Tamarand at the same time received word that the villagers had helped. So Tamarand came up with another task, a task so impossible that no one could accomplish it, and then he sent his soldiers to the town and arrested all the villagers so that they could not help Gala.

"This time he took Gala to a mountain. 'This is your last task,' he said, 'and if you move this mountain to the far side of the plains of Ned, you will be allowed to marry prince Calimon.'

"And Gala cried because there was no way that she could move a mountain. And her tears fell to the ground where she saw three ants watching her weep."

Galen sat down on the rubble, mimicking the pose of a weeping princess. "'Oh, ants!' Gala exclaimed. 'I was to marry the Prince, but to do so I have to move that mountain over there. I cannot do it.' The ants took pity on her plight. 'If we help you, will you speak with the Prince on our behalf? We ants are not well treated, you know.' 'Of course, of course. If I ever marry the Prince I will make sure all the ants in the kingdom are well fed. But can you really move a mountain?'

"Well, the lead ant thought about this. 'We can,' he answered, 'but it is a lot of work, and I cannot make my entire family do it if they do not wish to.' So he turned to the first ant, named John. And he asked John if he would help. John agreed, and he moved to the base of the mountain. And then the ant leader came up to another of his friends . . ." Galen walked up to one of the slaves and knelt beside him. "And he asked that ant what his name was. And the ant said . . ."

The slave Galen was kneeling next to looked at him in confusion.

Galen cleared his throat. "What was the ant's name?" Galen asked the slave.

"Porter."

"Porter, a good name for an ant who moves mountains. And the Princess asked Porter if he would help her, and Porter said . . ."

The slave was still confused.

"And Porter said?" Galen pressed.

"Yes?" the slave tried.

Galen stood up suddenly, his hands raised in the air. "And Porter said yes!" The serfs laughed again. "And he moved to stand next to the mountain." Galen helped the slave to his feet and pushed him towards the rubble. "Go on. Go and stand next to the mountain."

The rest of the slaves continued laughing as the man walked across the room.

"And then the leader came to another ant, and he asked that ant what his name was." Galen stopped before another slave. "And that ant's name was?"

"Chuck."

"And the ant leader asked Chuck to help, and Chuck said?"

"He said yes."

"And Chuck moved to stand next to Porter." Galen's voice was building in volume.

Chuck stood up and walked over to the rubble.

Galen moved to the Kruk. "And the leader asked a third ant, whose name was?"

"Sebastian."

"And did Sebastian agree to help?"

"He did."

Sebastian moved into the line. Galen walked over to the shovels and picks he had dropped earlier. He took a wicker basket and placed it next to the rubble. Using a pick, he pulled down some of the stones into the basket. "And the ants made a line next to the mountain. The first ant picked up a single pebble and then passed it to the next." Galen picked up the wicker basket and passed it to Porter. "Who passed it on to the next." Porter passed it to Chuck. "And the next." Chuck passed it to Sebastian. "And some of the ants gathered by the foot of the mountain to gather the pebbles." Galen pointed to a series of about ten of them. The men moved to stand next to the wicker baskets. "And the rest went to the line, stretching themselves evenly between where the mountain was, and where the mountain would go."

As one, the remaining slaves stood.

Martin took a deep breath as he approached Staunten's heavy wooden door. Behind that door was the captured corpse eater. Ben was the hunter on duty.

"He was calling for help," Ben said. "First time he's been able to string whole sentences together. We've had him unbound and ungagged since he calmed down a couple of days ago. I should warn you, sir. He is speaking, but you're not going to like the shit he's saying."

"Here, take this," Martin ordered, handing the hunter his half empty food bowl. "Only come in if we call you."

You've got to appear strong. You can't let him see any weakness. He's not going to want to talk. Try to say what Aaron would say.

He nodded to Huxley, who took out a key. Huxley worked the lock before tugging at the door. It swung open smoothly on hinges greased with dyitzu fat. The smell of rot poured out into the hall. The room's windows had been covered in black sheets. Light came pouring in from behind Martin, stopping mere inches from where the corpse eater lay. A rip had been made in one of the sheets, allowing another finger of light to crawl over the man's body. That finger showed grey tinged skin and a massive pus filled sore that rose from his exposed leg.

The corpse eater covered his eyes with his forearm.

Martin entered the room, his boots clopping upon the stone floor. Huxley followed, closing the door behind him, leaving the finger of light as the only source of illumination left. After a moment, Martin's vision began to adjust.

The corpse eater was pushing himself up into a sitting position. "Are you . . . are you real?"

The question took Martin by surprise.

Huxley leaned over his shoulder and whispered into Martin's ear. "The corpsedust has had him hallucinating. He might not know that there's none left in his body."

"I'm real, brother," Martin told the man.

The corpse flew to his feet and rushed him.

Martin raised his hands to defend himself, but he was too late. The corpse eater grabbed him tightly. The heat from man seemed unnatural. Martin tried to wrestle himself free but stopped when he realized the corpse eater was sobbing. Tears started to seep into his right shirtsleeve. Martin could hear the distant sound of the villagers laughing from the feast outside. The noise seemed out of place in this room.

Klein says that corpsedust is worse than heroin. Who knows what terrors this man's mind has imagined for him?

"Easy, brother," Martin found himself saying. "Easy."

The corpse eater let go slowly and stood back. Even in the dim light, Martin could see that his clothes were threadbare. The corpse eater did his best to straighten his shirt. His hands shook terribly.

Martin seized the man's shoulders and met his eyes. "You have a name, brother?"

"Caval."

"I'm Martin, and you may have met Huxley."

Caval shuddered as he looked at Huxley. "He's a face from my nightmares."

Martin snorted, letting go of the man's shoulders and looking towards the door. "This nightmare is on your side, Caval. He's been here to watch you, to feed you, and I assume to give you the sinfruit juice you've needed to clear your system."

Caval nodded. "Why am I shaking still?"

"Klein says it's withdrawal," Huxley answered. "Like from an old world drug. We thought about giving you small amounts of corpsedust—"

"Yes!" Caval was suddenly very animated. "You could give me a little. Just a little. Just enough to take away the pain."

Martin grabbed his shoulders again. "No."

"You don't understand." Caval's face was contorted. "I don't want it. I don't. I'll stop. We just need to give me a little. A little!"

Martin shook his head. He walked away from Caval and sat in the one chair Staunten had left in the room. "They say there ain't no reason to be good anymore, Caval. There's no God to write down your sins and hold them against you. That's already been done. What I can tell you is that the corpsedust has hurt you. Your body is covered in the sores it gave you."

Caval looked as stubborn as any man Martin had ever seen.

"I have information you want," Caval said. "I won't say a word until you ease this pain!"

Martin leapt back up from his seat. "And it wants to go on hurting you," Martin boomed, his sudden motion causing Caval to fall back. Martin advanced towards him. "Who needs devils to poison your soul when you can do it all on your own?"

Caval collapsed. "I'm sorry," the corpse eater was literally blubbering. "I didn't mean to hurt your people. It was the corpsedust. It drove me insane. It made us do things we would have never done. It led us astray. It whispered words into our minds . . . but there's more. The dust, it did one man's bidding. We didn't notice it at first. It was hard, through all the hallucinations. We'd sit in the chapel and partake of it together. But the hallucinations, the visions—they led us toward truth. Powell had taught us that it was leading us back to Heaven. And at first it seemed true. The highs were so high. I saw angels. Real angels! They sang to us. I cannot explain to you the bliss. But the dust took us back down too. I wasn't the only one who noticed. There was one among us who never started to rot. The visions we experienced, we learned that he was giving them to us. He was the real leader. I think he is the one who hooked Powell."

Martin leaned forward. Caval fell even further back, the

spear of light coming from the tear in the sheet illuminating his unkempt hair and his unshaven, blister covered face.

"What was his name? What was the name of the man who never rotted?"

"Buen. His eyes were wrong. They were all black, like a dyitzu's eyes. And his skin was wrong too. It looked like stone. Like marble. He never spoke, except once to tell us that the name of the God that ruled us corpsemen was Nephysis."

"And you're sure Buen is the leader, not this Powell?"

"I am. He had us do things, too. They could have been hallucinations, but I remember him making us knock down a wall. We worked at it for weeks.

"And there's more. You'll say this is a hallucination, I know you will, but you've got to believe me. One of us got angry with him. He demanded that Buen answer, or he'd shoot him. Then he did shoot him. Nothing happened. Buen's got some magic. The bullet didn't even bounce off of him. It just touched him and fell to the ground."

Sounds like almost Icanitzu, except for the marble skin. He must have been tripping.

"Can I ask what you are going to do with me?" Caval asked. "Will I be punished for

being a corpseman?"

"No one here blames an addict," Martin said. "Don't worry. We're going to take care of you, okay? You just have to tell us what you know so we can help the rest of your people. As long as you cooperate, you're going to be just fine."

"It was all Buen. He's the seer. He's the one who ordered us to kill your people. He communicated that to us through visions. He's the one who had us eat them after they'd come back as corpses."

How could anyone want to eat a corpse?

Martin thought this, but the image of his own people, staring into nothingness as they sat starving to death in the wilds, gave him a sudden stab of empathy. A man can get very hungry, Martin knew.

"Look," Martin said, "Hell's a tough place. We just need to stop the bad things from happening. We can rescue your friends, if they're still alive. Can you show us where to find your people?"

"Of course, of course. You just have to take me to the big river. The big one with the red bricks."

Martin began pacing across Staunten's quarters. "We call that the Kingsriver."

"I'll show you."

"Not just yet," Martin said. "I've got to get some scouts ready, and today isn't the day for it. I'm going to take you to Klein. Eating the flesh of corpses is a sin, and you're going to want to confess to him. You a Christian man?"

The corpse eater broke back down into tears. "I tried to be."

"You and me both, Caval. You and me both. Wait right here, I'll get Klein." Martin turned to the door. "Ben, come on in please."

Ben opened the door, Martin's food bowl in his right hand. Martin took it and gave it to Caval. Caval descended upon it like a vulture, and Martin couldn't blame him.

Martin and Huxley walked out of the room, down the hall, and through the door curtain which led back to the feast. Martin headed straight towards Kylie.

"Hey!" Huxley called after him, pointing to a group of people sitting on the church steps. "I thought we were getting Klein? He's over there."

"Are you shitting me?" Martin shouted. "I just gave that man my food. Klein can wait."

35

Ellen was happy with how well her ankle was holding up. They had to wrap it tightly again in the morning so her ankle would have enough support, but she could walk on it well enough to keep up with the infidels.

El Cid and her crew seemed almost lackadaisical at times, moving through the wilds of Hell without showing any sign of fear. At other times, and for no reason that Ellen could detect, they would become highly alert, almost paranoid. Then they would keep their rifles raised to the level of their eyes and move with short quick steps that kept those rifles level. They'd enter rooms in bursts, their guns waving in front of them. Two would always remain behind, watching the rear exits, but which two always changed. It took Ellen a while to realize where she had seen this kind of movement before. In movies, SWAT teams had acted the same way. Then, as quickly as they'd started, the Infidel Friends would go back to walking like they didn't have a care in Hell.

"It's right through here," Q said, pointing at a low corridor. "A great view of the swamps."

El Cid nodded and entered. She had no trouble going through the tunnel, but everyone else, including Ellen, had to duck. They emerged into a natural cavern that had a large opening at one end. Wind blew in through it, tousling the strands of hair which had escaped from El Cid's pony tail. That wind gave Ellen chills as it dried out the sweat in her clothes. It took her a moment to notice how high up they were.

El Cid walked to the edge of the cavern and peered down below. The rest of her team spread out around her. Alice whistled when she looked, and Molly quickly stepped back. Ellen walked up to the edge herself.

Whoa.

She was looking into the chamber which held the Cypress forest. The mist clung to the swamp in places, but for the most part the chamber was clear. She could see for miles. At first Ellen thought the forest was now empty, but as she continued to stare, she began to pick the corpses out. A few were moving, slogging their way through the root filled water. Others were still, standing beneath trees. Ellen shuddered when she remembered how their hands had held her limbs. The bite one had taken out of her calf began to hurt.

"Rick," El Cid asked, "how full was it when you boated through?"

Rick shrugged. "Thousands. Tens of thousands."

"Too many. We have to destroy them."

"I don't know that his estimate is likely to be accurate." Jessica's blonde hair shook with her head. "Besides, do we have time?"

El Cid shifted her weight from one hip to the other. "This is Cris' mission. We're a redundancy."

"A damned important one," Jessica said. "At least five teams should be sent for something like this. Maybe we should just pass them by."

Using her boot, El Cid kicked a stone over the lip of the cliff. It tumbled downward, bouncing off of the chamber's wall before splashing into the water. The Cypress forest was suddenly alive with moving corpses. Some rose, bloated to the point of bursting, up out of the water. Others, unseen amongst the trees, began walking towards where the rock fell. A few more, who had been still for so long that the trees had grown up around them, struggled against their bonds.

Rick inhaled deeply.

Eagan put his arm around Jessica.

"Damn," Jessica said. "There could be that many."

Ellen watched El Cid's expression carefully. The woman was thinking hard about this problem.

"You may still be right, Jessica," El Cid said. "Q, lead everyone to a good place to set up a base camp. We'll see if we can't build a crusher for these dead."

"What's a crusher?" Ellen asked.

"Roach motel," Eagan said. "Except for corpses."

Q took one last look down the cliff, his hand absently rubbing his shaved head. Then he turned and walked out of the chamber. "This way, people."

El Cid did not move as the group started leaving. Ellen lagged behind, studying her. The woman was so small, so slight, that Ellen had difficulty understanding why the other infidels listened to her. The woman's green eyes were on the massing corpses below. Did she hate them? Had a corpse stolen away someone that she loved? El Cid's face was an emotionless mask, but it was possible that it hid great sorrow. Maybe she'd understand about Turi?

The breeze which had given her such a chill earlier continued, now carrying the putrid smell of the waterlogged dead.

I have to ask her.

El Cid turned around and moved towards the exit. Instinctively, Ellen reached out and caught her arm.

Ellen's wrist was suddenly in burning agony. The force of El Cid's now spinning figure was somehow twisting her arm in a way which it could not turn. Ellen dropped to her knees, forced downward by the pain. El Cid's ponytail kept spinning even after she stopped, slapping across the infidel's face before falling down across her shoulder.

Ellen looked up at the woman from her knees. One of El Cid's hands had an iron grip on Ellen's fingers, keeping her wrist bent at an uncomfortable angle. El Cid's left arm and shoulder were cocked back, her tiny hand balled up into a tight fist.

I'm helpless. She could kill me without a thought, and there'd be nothing I could do about it. Turi would understand.

"There's a boy I love," Ellen was surprised by the strength in her voice.

El Cid's expression softened.

Ellen swallowed. "He went into the Carrion to try and rescue a friend. He had five days to get back. Five days. He didn't come back."

El Cid's fist unclenched and fell to her side. Her other hand let go of Ellen's wrist.

Ellen began to massage the pain out of it. "So they built a wall. He can never come back now. Do you understand? We buried him alive in the Carrion."

Ellen didn't want to cry in front of such a woman. The Infidel Friend would surely judge her for it, so Ellen fought her tears as hard as she could. "I didn't want to. I would go to the wall we built each night. I would place my hand upon it and try to feel him out there. He might be dead. Maybe that'd be for the best. But he could be out there now. Wounded, hurting, bleeding to death in some corner of Hell. I don't know why he had to go. Men can be so stupid. He wanted to impress his father. He wanted to save his friend. He shouldn't have gone. He was just a boy."

El Cid's head cocked to one side, and she crossed her arms as she listened.

"They say you infidels are godless. And maybe you are. Maybe you don't have to do things like the rest of us. But on Earth, whenever I wanted something, whenever a loved one was dying in a hospital, or whenever I was dying inside, I'd pray. Even if what I prayed for didn't come, I knew it was for the best. I knew that somehow things were going to get better. I knew that at the worst, they were only trials God sent to make us stronger."

El Cid reached down and put a hand on her shoulder.

Ellen didn't shrink from the touch. "But there's no one to pray to here. There's the Devil, but he'd take away my love. And there's no fate. If Turi dies, it won't make the world get better. It won't be for a reason. He'll just die because he died. A pointless, horrid death. And I can't stop it. There's no one I can speak to too make it right. No judge. No fairness. And no one to pray to. No one except you."

El Cid knelt down in front of her. "No child, you must not pray to me."

Ellen clasped her hands together. "I pray to you, El Cid, I beg you. You are the only thing that can make this right. You are the only person with enough power to help. Turi is my age. Just a few inches taller than me. He has brown hair and grows peach fuzz as stubble. I love him. You'll be going into the Carrion soon, to find Cris and the City of Blood and whatever else—but I want you to look for him. I want you to save him. If he's alive I want you to bring him back to me."

Ellen felt El Cid's arms wrap around her. Ellen's hands, still clasped in prayer, were pushed tightly into her body. She sniffed quickly to keep her nose from running and shut her eyes against her tears.

El Cid's soft voice whispered into her ear. "I will be in that Carrion soon, as you say. If I find him, if he is alive and I find him, this Turi of yours, I will save him. No devil, no group of people, no wall, no river, no cliff—nothing in Hell will stop me."

Ellen let her hands separate and then grabbed on to the Infidel Friend, clinging to the woman with all her strength. "You promise?"

"I promise."

Ellen squeezed her eyes shut even harder. Turi had made her promise to stay alive once. She had agreed just to appease him, but he had kept hounding her about it. Ellen opened her eyes and pulled back. She looked at El Cid. "Say it all the way."

Ellen felt El Cid's small hand pressing against the back of her head. She let her head get pushed down onto the woman's shoulder.

"I promise you," El Cid said, smoothing out Ellen's hair. "I promise you, if I can find Turi, I'll save him. I'll save him and bring him back to you."

Calimay stared into her silver framed mirror. The reflection showed her own face and the priestess Tamara, who stood behind Calimay while attentively running a golden brush through her masses of black curls. Calimay watched her own head's small jerks as it was pulled back by Tamara's ministrations. Instinctively steadying her head, Calimay let herself get lost in her own green eyes.

This antechamber was her favorite. It contained a marble bath which Calimay would fill with hot water. Each morning she would lie in that water and pretend that she was Maab. Someday, perhaps when she'd made the deal with Lucreas Crassus and after Maab had been weakened by their rising tide, there would be a shift in power. Maab's priestesses would change allegiances, giving their tribute to Calimay in order to gain protection from the armies of the City of Blood and Stone. Then someday it would be her, not Maab, who ran the great ritual. Who would break the bullman and perform the sacrifices. And when she did strike the deal with Lucreas, then she would have access to whatever Archdevil he prayed to. They would be able to change her body. She could have assets even greater than Maab's.

And then Galen would submit to her. She imagined him walking through the halls at her elbow. In public he would be perfectly in her thrall. In the bedroom she would let him play his masculine role, but he would know it was just an act. Their love would no longer be a tribute to Ahriman.

She began to hum unconsciously as she imagined the muscular warrior lying over her and between her legs. Her hand would rest on the small of his muscular back. She would . . . Calimay stopped humming.

What the Hell is that?

She raised one arm, and Tamara stopped brushing. The tune she'd been humming kept on going without her. It was distant, almost imperceptible, but it was there.

Hellsong? Here? Impossible.

She had heard hellsong before, in the silver mines south of the Deadlands. Then it had been higher pitched. As before, the tune seemed to conform to her own thoughts.

Rose, Rose, Rose, Rose,
Will I ever see thee wed?

Calimay stood suddenly, bumping her table, disturbing various beauty accoutrements and causing the mirror to rock on its tripod stand. That was Galen's song, the one he had refused to sing. Was it any wonder she desired to hear that?

I will marry at thy will, sire.
At thy will, sire. At thy will, sire.

"Do you hear that?" Calimay asked.

Tamara shook her head.

The music got louder, though barely so, as Calimay walked out of her antechamber and into her main room. She wrapped herself up in one of her purple robes. Now the music was less malleable to her desires. She could only hear that one song, no matter how hard she tried to listen to another, but she could play any verse that she wished in her mind. After a few attempts, she was able to make the music continuously sing the first line over and over again. Even so, it seemed like all the other lines were being sung simultaneously.

Rose, Rose, Rose, Rose,

Rose, Rose, Rose, Rose,

She walked out through her throne room, Tamara at her heel. The music became louder, lower, and more distinctive. It wasn't just hellsong. There really was music. All the lines of the song really were being sung simultaneously, and the harmony was breathtaking.

The hell?

The voices grew clearer. "Rose, Rose, Rose, Rose, will I ever see thee wed?"

She ran along the black marble halls. The music got louder in one of the spiral staircases. She followed the music down and came out at one of the mining levels. She could hear the individual voices now. They were singing the song in rounds. "I will marry at thy will, sire. At thy will, sire. At thy will, sire."

The music caused her heart to leap in her throat. This had to be Galen's doing. He was having this song sung for her. Her footsteps quickened. Tamara was tripping over her own robe, trying to keep up. Calimay rounded a corner and saw them.

Her men, stripped to the waist, were standing in a line all along the corridor. They sang as they worked, moving back and forth between each other, passing wicker baskets filled with gravel down along the line. Galen stood among them. Calimay's breath caught in her throat.

He was also bare-chested and covered in sweat. Her own daughter, Calista, was standing up on her toes and holding a ladle with one outstretched arm, pouring water over Galen's head. He flashed Calista a grateful smile and kept working. His broad shoulders tensed as he reached to one side and grabbed a wicker basket full of stones. Quickly and easily, he passed it on to another worker. Galen's baritone was deep, and looking at him caused warmth to spread throughout her body. Calimay swore that she could feel the vibrations of his singing voice in her loins.

"Excuse me, my Queen," a breathless male voice called from behind her.

Calimay stepped aside. One of her serfs jogged by, carrying an armful of wicker baskets. He was followed by another, and another. Calimay watched them hurry by. She looked back to the line of workers. She had never seen them work so hard or look so happy. Some were even laughing as they sang. The man closest to her was so off key it was almost comical, but somehow it fit into the harmony of the song.

"I will marry at thy will, sire. At thy will, sire. At thy will, sire."

Suddenly Calimay understood Galen. Galen knew that life could be like this. He knew that human beings could work together to fight the devils. He knew that this was the goal. This was why he fought so hard. This was why he was so strong. He just needed a chance to show other people the way.

"I don't agree with this," Tamara was saying. "They're making too much noise. They'll draw the devils. They're happy. You know that makes them unruly. You should have never let Galen lead them."

Tamara's a fool.

Calimay saw Calista moving along the line. She was pouring water over the serfs' heads. And they were grateful! They actually looked at her and smiled. They seemed to trust her, not fear her. It was as if a decade of Maab's conditioning had been erased in a day. Calista stopped before the young boy, the angel's get, who stood in the line between one of her serfs and the short Asian man Galen had brought with him. She poured the water on the boy's head more slowly than the rest.

"How many times are you going to give him water?" A serf shouted.

Calista and the other serfs laughed.

"If he wants, till he drowns," Calista said. "I'm carrying his child, after all."

There were more smiles and more laughs.

Another of Galen's basket carriers came running down the hall.

"Ahriman has infected your serfs!" Tamara's harsh voice reported. "You let that man control them and look what has happened. This damage will be irreparable. Let me stop this, my Queen. I know you like that Galen man, but let me torture him for his crimes. The rustrock is not worth it."

"Rose, Rose, Rose Rose, will I ever see thee wed?" her serfs sang.

"Quiet, Tamara," Calimay said. "This was my idea. I sent

Galen to do this. This is our new way."

"My Queen!" Tamara's eyes were wide. "This is the work of the God of Lies."

"Hush, hush," Calimay ordered, her eyes resting on Galen's body. "You're making it hard for me to hear the music."

"I will marry at thy will, sire," Calista's high voice sang. "At thy will, sire. At thy will, sire."

36

As Graham opened the hatch to Mancini's still, he looked across Harpsborough. He could see the steeples of Father Klein's Church over the top floor of the Fore. Taking a deep breath, he lowered himself into the hole. Graham had been in the still a couple of times before while buying bloodwater, but this was the first time he'd come by invitation. It was also the first time he'd come when Mancini hadn't been firing the still. The chill took him by surprise.

With the hatch closed behind him, precious little light managed to filter into the stairway. By touch alone, he followed the steps down into the still.

The stairs wound around and around until he made it to the bottom. The room below was lit by a single one of Copperfield's torches, held up by a sconce in the wall. Mancini sat on a wooden crate nearby a small table. He poured a glass of bloodwater, the liquid gleaming in the firelight.

"I'm here," Graham told Mancini.

The man's beady eyes turned towards him. "Congratulations on your new appointment. Have a seat." Mancini gestured to another wooden crate before pouring a second glass of bloodwater.

Graham felt a twinge of wounded pride at Mancini's words.

Don't let that weigh on you, Graham. Jealousy will poison you for sure.

Graham's mouth salivated as he watched the flowing bloodwater. It was a shame that Mancini had perfected his finest brew just before a famine. Mancini crossed the room with a few steps and pulled the box closer to the table. It grated on the stone floor. Graham sat down. He noticed his hands shaking. Quickly, he placed them beneath the table.

"It's the best I could hope for, Citizen," Graham said.

"Was it?"

"It was. I failed at being Lead Hunter. Getting the Enforcer position was more than I deserved."

Mancini leaned forward. "The hell it was."

Graham was surprised by the man's sudden vinegar. "You all made a good decision. I wasn't doing my duties—"

"The Fore made a terrible mistake when they demoted you. Did you know that had I not made the Enforcer position, they were going to have you return to being just a normal hunter? I made that position, Graham, and I specifically asked for you to fill it. Specifically."

"But we weren't capturing any dyitzu."

Mancini shook his head before taking a sip of his own bloodwater. "Of course you weren't. The villagers were still in the wilds, they were taking your kills."

"But Martin's split them into smaller units. He's covering more area. And he's gotten the Fore's permission to send groups out at night to watch the Kingsriver. I'd never have done any of that."

Mancini nodded. "That's true. But Martin was your man, wasn't he? Why didn't he suggest those things to you?"

Graham leaned back. "Maybe you're right. But the Molly thing—"

"Could have happened to anybody. The way I see it, you rid us of a problem that we'd been struggling with for years."

Graham's testicles ached just thinking of the woman, but maybe Mancini had a point. Martin hadn't been actively hunting while Graham was Lead Hunter, and he was the most experienced. Help from a lieutenant of that caliber, well, it would have done him more good than Huxley had. At the moment, Martin was benefiting from all that Graham had done, and he was using his own ideas, too.

"What's done is done," Graham said.

"It is," Mancini said. "And that's a sad thing. Harpsborough's coming apart at the seams. If it wasn't for my idea of a feast day, Constance might have started a civil war already. The last thing we need are extra leadership changes, never mind changes going in the wrong direction."

Maybe he's right.

Mancini swirled the bloodwater around in his glass. "And I for one," he said, breaking for a moment to take another sip of his drink, "Would have enjoyed your company in the Fore."

Graham set his jaw.

I was that close. That close. They took it away from me.

"That's one of Michael's failings," Mancini said, looking at his wine while he thought aloud. "Sometimes he's not the best judge of character. Hopefully that failing won't be enough to undo us."

Graham drank more of the bloodwater. The fire in the back of his throat caught him by surprise. He suppressed a cough. "Is there nothing that can be done?"

"Nothing now," Mancini answered. "What's done is done, as you said. But keep your eyes open. Do this Enforcer job as best you can. If there's a way this can be righted, you have to believe me Graham, I'll right it. You deserve better than this. Anyone can see it."

I knew it. I knew I was good enough.

"Anyone, that is," Mancini said with a sad smile, "but Michael."

Massan was already snoring when Ellen came back from the river. She usually felt pretty guilty when she shit in a river, but since this river was just going to flow into the Cypress swamp, she figured it probably didn't matter.

Her ankle was feeling pretty sore. Rick knelt beside her and began to unwrap it. As the strips of cloth came off, she could see that the swelling had come up a bit. Still, it was in good shape when compared to how it looked a few days ago.

All of the Infidel Friend had left the camp room except for El Cid, who was inspecting its walls. Ellen watched her as she did so. The small girl climbed up in certain places.

"What are you doing?" Alice asked El Cid in a friendly voice.

El Cid grunted as she pulled at a rectangular brick of sandstone near the base of one wall. "It's a good idea to check out the room you sleep in. We do it whenever there is time to. It's not so bad in this section of the labyrinth, but in others there can be hidden openings. Occasionally they even have devils waiting in them."

The Infidel Friend continued her search as they watched.

"Can I help?" Alice asked.

El Cid studied her for a moment. "Sure, come here. See if you can tap at some of these stones that are too tall for me to reach."

Alice stood up and walked across the room. Ellen closed her eyes and eavesdropped.

"How do you think all those undead got there?" Alice asked.

"Who knows? Sometimes they just group together in a herd, following the topography of the Labyrinth. Could be caused by a call, though. When the greater demons call the lesser ones in, they create little highly populated pockets in Hell. The undead tend to avoid dyitzu. You don't notice it much, normally, because the dyitzu are evenly dispersed. But when they're not, you get this effect which we call a dead ring. That's where you get a circle of undead surrounding a pocket of devils."

"So it's a dead ring, you think?" Alice asked.

El Cid shrugged. "Could be. They're not really in a ring shape though. Feels more like a straight line. Still, if the call were very, very large, the outside of the ring might look like a line."

They continued searching the walls in silence for a few moments."

"It must feel good to order those men around," Alice said conspiratorially.

"Why so?" El Cid answered.

"Well, you know."

"Do I?" El Cid's voice seemed almost disinterested.

"You're a girl, like me. Men don't like taking orders from women."

El Cid grunted, perhaps as she was reaching for a rock. "Ah, I see. You think it is ironic because from your perspective, there is a change in gender roles."

"I guess." Alice's voice wavered.

"We are not people of God, however, so we did not notice when He told you that women should be quiet or subservient. To us, it would be a little appalling to discover that a girl was getting some sort of rush from ordering her fellows around."

Ellen struggled to keep from giggling. Infidels, it seemed,

didn't engage in small talk.

"There are women in power in Harpsborough," Alice said, seeming defensive.

El Cid grunted again. "So what you're saying is that all broad reaching generalizations are wrong?"

"Huh?"

"Little joke. Here, can you try that stone there, the one with the chipped corner?"

"Sure."

Suddenly everyone was quiet. Ellen opened her eyes to see that Rick was still by her. He and El Cid both had their heads cocked to one side. Each of them were slowly moving their heads back and forth.

All the infidels listen that way. Rick does, too.

And if Rick did it, he'd learned it from Galen.

The infidels say there's a traitor. Someone who used to be one of their own.

Ellen heard footsteps coming from one corridor. Molly and Q entered the room. Alice had drawn her pistol and it was pointing straight towards Molly. El Cid put her hand on the gun and guided its barrel down.

"She's not bad, sir," Q reported to El Cid. He pointed to Molly. "She kept up nicely, and she has a good sense of direction."

Molly nodded, giving no response to the compliment she'd received. "We might have found a place for the crusher, Cid."

She's estranged herself from us. The infidels are going to make her one of them.

"Good," El Cid answered. "We'll check it out in the morning. If it doesn't look like it will take too long, we'll be able to clear that lake."

37

The serfs sat at the long woodstone tables Galen had set up in the fountain room, their faces illuminated by the ceiling's wavy blue light. Because Calimay had no extra chairs to spare, Galen had everyone sitting on the lips of the fountains. This meant that the tables were set up in two lines on either side the carpet, and that each table only had serfs sitting on one side. The workers' faces were still red from exertion. The salty smell of sweat filled the air, though it did nothing to calm Arturus' furiously hungry stomach. Many were dipping their cupped hands into the fountain's water and were splashing it on themselves to help cool down.

There was a buzz of conversation in the room. The serfs were laughing and smiling. Arturus could hardly believe that these were the same people he'd seen this morning.

They stopped talking immediately as Galen entered the room.

"My furious ants!" Galen cried.

The serfs' laughter echoed throughout the room. They seemed so carefree, here, out of the mines, in the relative open and with no priestesses around them.

Galen took no pains to hide his pleasure at their response. Actually, knowing Galen, the man had probably taken pains to make sure his face had a grateful expression on it. "I promised you that you would only work until the room was clear. We have cleared the room, and I have kept my promise. But I have more to give you. I have been allowed to leave Calimay's compound these last few days in order to gather weapons and ammunition for the Harpsborough hunters. In so doing, I have killed many dyitzu. While you've been working, they've been cooking."

Many of the serfs stood up at their tables. Their shouts were so loud Arturus feared they might travel through the stone walls and into the wilds. Johnny Huang and Kelly entered, each carrying plates of steaming meat. Arturus' mouth watered as the sweaty odor of the serfs was overpowered by the smell of cooked dyitzu. He felt his stomach tumbling.

Galen pointed to two of the serfs. "You and you, help them pass out the meat."

How different these men seemed from the ones that had screamed so madly at Maab's ritual. Avery limped into the chamber, taking his seat at one of the tables. Aaron entered shortly thereafter, giving Arturus a smile. Johnny Huang, Kelly, and the two helpers Galen had picked continued divvying up the meat amongst the hundred and fifty or so serfs. With a show of willpower, the serfs did not immediately devour their food. Each one looked at Galen for permission.

Johnny smiled at Arturus as he placed a still sizzling plate of shaved meat in front of him. Arturus leaned forward, closed his eyes, and let the steam condense on his face. The smell was intoxicating.

When all of the food had been spread out, Galen nodded. "Gentlemen," he said, "dig in."

Arturus did not need to be told twice. The meat had been prepared simply, lacking any of the spices, salts, or sauces that Rick might have added to it, but this was the first hot food Arturus had eaten since he'd entered the Carrion. Arturus felt a groan escape from his mouth as he devoured his first piece. He picked up a second, this one too large to eat all at once. The hot meat was burning his fingers a little, but he didn't care. He ripped off a smaller bite with his teeth. The juices rushed into his mouth as he chewed. He paused after a quick swallow and took a deep breath. He looked up suddenly as he noticed everyone had stopped eating. They were all looking towards the curtain at the end of the red carpet.

The golden priestess and bull curtain was waving back and forth. Calista had entered the room. They watched in silence, a hundred and fifty odd heads swiveling as she walked across the room. She sat down next to Turi. No one spoke.

She gave him a peck on the cheek.

Suddenly everyone was laughing and eating again. Arturus smiled. Her hand wormed its way into his.

I can't really say no to her, can I?

Still hungry, he returned to his food, eating one handed.

"Is it going to be this way from now on?" Arturus overheard a serf asking.

"I don't know," Galen's voice answered. "I've spoken with Calimay about having you all trained for soldier duty as well. About giving you all a life worth living. I think the results of today were very promising. We shall see what she has in mind."

A shadow came across the table, blotting out the blue light from the ceiling. Arturus looked up to see Kelly.

Kelly was smiling, a sickeningly sweet smile, and it was aimed at Calista. "Would you like some dyitzu?"

Calista nodded, not taking her eyes away from Arturus.

Kelly passed over a plate, her eyes boring holes into the oblivious princess.

Arturus wanted to give her an apologetic look, but Kelly's eyes didn't leave Calista for a second.

"I hope you enjoy it," Kelly said. She turned quickly, her all black robe swirling around her.

She'd been able to repair it, Arturus noticed. He watched it cling to her figure as she walked away. Arturus could not help but remember how her body looked when Calimay's soldiers had stripped her.

He turned back to Calista to see that the girl's deep blue eyes were still focused entirely on him.

I have got to talk to Galen about this.

Galen stood up, walking between the tables. "I have one more gift for you all."

The talking and eating stopped.

Galen walked out of the room.

"Should we follow him?" A serf asked.

Arturus shrugged his shoulders. He thought about standing up, but then he felt a strange vibration coming from the stone lip of the fountain on which he sat. There was a low pitched noise as well. Arturus stood up and looked all around, trying to figure out what the sound could be and where it was coming from.

The fountain's marble soldiers and the swirling stone women on their shoulders started shaking violently. Then the noise stopped, and everything became still.

Arturus looked around the room.

Suddenly water was everywhere, filling the air. A mist of droplets descended around him. Galen had turned on the fountains.

Martin entered to find Michael alone in the parlor room, sitting in his favorite chair. For once, there was no chess game set up. The room was brighter as well, and more blankets than usual lay around the base of the light orbs which served to illuminate the room.

"I've been talking to Klein," the First Citizen said. "He's given me the same reports you have on the corpseman. You did a good job interrogating him."

"Caval wasn't very hostile," Martin said.

"No, he seemed pretty nice for a leper." Michael stood up and walked across the plush dyitzu skin carpets. He stopped by the liquor cabinet. "You want some of Davel's new brew?"

Martin nodded.

Martin was surprised by how red the bloodwater looked. He'd known that Mancini provided a different product to the Fore than he did to the villagers, but he hadn't tasted it yet.

Michael poured the bloodwater into two crystal glasses. He swirled one absently while he handed the other over to Martin. Martin took the glass with both hands. The idea of drinking out of one of the Citizen glasses made him feel nervous.

"Have a seat." Michael motioned towards the couch directly across from his favorite chair.

That's where Mancini usually sits.

Martin moved slowly across the floor, careful to keep his glass from spilling. He sat down. The softness of the couch surprised him, and he nearly spilled his drink when he sank further in than he'd expected. The couch's frame was made of stone, but it had been extremely well padded with skins and pillows.

"I've been impressed with you, Martin," Michael said.

"Thank you, sir."

"To tell you the truth, right after we'd chopped off your

hand, I never imagined that you would have been the right man for this job. I underestimated you. You're a fine Lead Hunter."

Martin took a sip of the blood water. The burn in his throat surprised him. He tried to keep from coughing, but couldn't. A bit of the bloodwater spilled over the lip of the glass. He caught the liquid with his finger and then sucked it up into his mouth. "I'm not half . . ." he sounded a little hoarse from the burn of the bloodwater. He coughed again. "I'm not half as good as Aaron was," he continued, his voice a little more steady this time. "I hope I don't let you down."

Martin leaned forward in his chair and rubbed the back of his neck with one hand. "No one expects you to measure up to Aaron. But you've done well. Far better than Graham. You're the right man for this job. Now you know that all promotions to Citizen have been frozen because of the famine, right?"

Martin nodded, taking another sip of the bloodwater. He was prepared for its sharpness this time.

"Well, there's a vote tonight. I wanted you to know that one of my motions will be your induction."

"Thank you, sir."

Michael pursed his lips for a second. "I wanted you to know that even if the motion fails, that your Citizenhood is guaranteed. It's just a matter of time. You will be the very next Citizen inducted."

If the devils ever come back, I'll be in good shape.

Martin nodded.

I'll be able to feed Katie!

Martin smiled.

"The other thing we're going to vote for has to do with the corpseman."

"And that is?"

Michael leaned back, swirling the bloodwater again in his glass. He took a sip. "He thinks he can lead a group of hunters back to where the corpse eaters live."

Martin sat forward, feeling the cushion beneath him shifting from his weight. "I don't know if that's a good idea."

"They've killed a few of our people, Martin. People you are sworn to protect. There are some caches out there they've taken over as well. Right now we really can't afford to be losing food. We've lost so much with Julian's stash. And the dyitzu are gone. There's not much of a choice left to us."

Martin set his glass aside on an end table. "Then we should be able to talk with them. Let them know it was ours first. We can make a treaty."

Michael nodded. "That's my suggestion. But I should warn you, Mancini wants war. A lot of the other Citizens do too. I'm going to make our case to them. They're worried that the only thing negotiation would do is warn them that we're coming. I'm going to say that the risk is worth it for the chance of avoiding an all out confrontation."

"But you're the First Citizen! Order us to try and work with them."

"I won't make it an order," Michael told him, "but with the way things have been going, I have a lot more influence on the vote than I used to. These days, when I and Mancini disagree, things go my way."

"Will it this time?"

"I don't know. I have to admit that even I have my doubts on how much negotiating you can do with men who've got the rot. Their mind rots too, you know. Not just their bodies."

Martin stood up. "I understand, sir. I will do whatever you order. But I beg you this, when you make your speech to the Citizens, let them know that the acting Lead Hunter recommends against going to war."

Michael smiled. "I shall, hunter. I shall. And you should know that the words of Martin carry more weight amongst the Citizens these days than they ever have before. You're dismissed."

With a nod so deep it was almost a bow, Martin headed towards the stairs.

If Aaron were here, would he want to go to war?

The thought haunted Martin as he walked down the Fore's steps, following him like a black cloud as he walked through the waiting room. He pushed through the Fore's door curtain, entering the Harpsborough chamber.

Martin had to admit that he had no idea what Aaron would have done.

 — 38 —

Dakota and Tamara knelt around the hole to their exit passage, eyes lowered. Four other Carrion born were interspersed between Galen, Aaron, Johnny Huang and Kelly. Arturus was surprised by how comfortable those soldiers seemed standing amidst his own crew.

And why shouldn't they? We're all on the same side.

Aaron was fiddling idly with his new shotgun. The weapon didn't seem to suit him.

Avery entered the dark room. His limp was barely noticeable, but Arturus was worried about his ability to run over long distances. Like the rest of their group, he'd been given a pack, canteen, shotgun and pistol. He sat down next to Arturus.

"What are we waiting for?" Avery whispered.

"The mists to drop," Arturus answered softly. "They've got a guy down in the tunnel now with a light. When the mists come in from the Lethe, they pour down into the secret tunnel. That way a dyitzu won't see us as we come out."

Avery nodded. He gave a long and hate-filled look to Kelly. "I can't believe we gave her a weapon," he muttered.

Arturus sighed. "I guess we need every gun we can get."

Avery snorted and crossed his arms. "I guess."

Galen walked over and knelt between them. "You guys clean your shotguns and pistols? Calimay lets them get pretty dirty."

Arturus and Avery both nodded.

"Wish they'd given us more shells, though." Avery said.

"I had gathered a lot more than this, but they confiscated it," Galen said. "I guess they want to make sure we don't make a break for home after we show them to the mines." Galen nodded towards Dakota. "They're sending him with us, all the way up the aqueduct, to make sure we behave."

"We could kill him," Avery suggested.

Arturus bit his lip and looked about to see if anyone had overheard that last statement. It appeared that no one had.

Galen frowned, scratching his beard. "No need. Calimay's been good to us. Let's not ruin her newfound taste for hospitality."

Light started coming up through the hole. Arturus leaned forward.

A Carrion soldier's head poked out. "Mist is starting to drop. I'll give it another few minutes to make sure it's good and thick."

Tamara nodded, and the soldier disappeared back down into the secret passage.

Arturus met his father's gaze.

"Are you ready for this, son?" Galen asked.

Am I?

The Carrion had no doubt left deep scars in his soul. Was he ready to face it all again? Was it a sign of how much this Hell was getting to him that he was afraid to leave Calimay's complex? The woman had, after all, ordered he be raped just so she could possess the angel portion of his bloodline.

"Would it matter if I wasn't?" Arturus asked.

Galen smiled. "No."

"Then I guess I'm ready."

Arturus heard footsteps coming towards the room from Calimay's complex. Kelly's face broke into a sneer. Arturus turned to see Calista. Her eyes were for him alone. Her dark curls bounced as she hurried to his side. She held his hands in hers, almost like Maab had once done, and kissed him softly on the lips. Her tongue slipped playfully into his mouth.

She drew back. "I brought you this," her throaty voice reminded him of the noises she'd made during their lovemaking.

She produced a thin marble dowel that had a curly strand of black hair snaking around it. "It's my hair. Aaron told me that his lover had done as much for him."

Arturus gave Aaron a pointed glance. The Lead Hunter shrugged as if apologizing.

Arturus accepted her gift and put it in the pack Calimay

had provided him.

Calista grabbed both of his shoulders. "I want you to know I'll keep our baby safe." One of her hands left his shoulder, dropping to her belly. "Promise me you'll return."

"I will."

Calista turned to Galen. "You'll keep him safe?" Suddenly she seemed very sad.

Galen nodded.

Calista kissed him again, fiercely, and then fled. He looked towards Kelly. The priestess, her eyes dark burning coals of spite, were fixed on the passage where Calista had just left.

Oh, hell. I'm going to be a father.

At first the thought seemed innocuous, but as he continued to think about it, the idea grew like a cancer in his mind. Everything that Galen had ever done for him, had ever taught him, hit him all at once.

That's what I have to give to that child.

What a cruel thing, to make him a father. To make him give so much without him even consenting to the coupling. Since his seed was taken against his will, did that mean he was justified in denying any responsibility for his child? And what of his responsibilities to Hell? What did the Infidel want from him? What did Maab want from him? What could he possibly do to make a difference in a place so filled with devils?

"Father," Arturus said. "I'm not ready."

The Carrion soldier's head came out of the hole again. "The mist is nice and thick. It's safe to go."

Arturus was suddenly reminded of the words Rick would say during one of his childhood games.

Ready or not, here I come.

 — 39 —

Martin leaned back against the Fore's wall next to ole Bense. Then, with a sigh of exhaustion, the acting Lead Hunter let his knees bend so that his back slid down the wall. His hoodie bunched up as he did so, and he felt the cool stone touching his back. Eventually, his rump met with the cold, hard floor, and he straightened out his hoodie. He'd been out hunting on the Kingsriver for several hours, and this was the first time he'd gotten to sit down since he'd made his report to the First Citizen about Caval, the corpseman. Absently, he put his hand into his hoodie's front pocket and scratched his belly.

"You know, Bense," Martin told the still man, "sometimes I'm thinking you've got the right idea here. Just chill out. Let other people worry. Nothing bothers you, does it?"

Benson's bloodshot eyes kept their fixed, unblinking stare.

"Famine? Nah. Who gives a damn, right? You don't even fucking eat. Tribe of corpse eaters? Don't bother you none. They ain't going to eat you. The Fore wants to go to war? How are they going to draft you, Bense? Shit." Martin spat. "You got the easy life alright. I'm tellin' you. I'm jealous."

Martin chewed on his lip. Some villagers were leaving, probably heading towards the river room. Martin watched them go and then took a look at Benson. The still man's wan face seemed skinnier than usual.

"You losin' weight, Bense? Hell of a diet. You just sit here, don't eat a thing, and watch all the fine ladies go by. I envy you. Look man, I know you ain't much for talking these days, but I got some questions for ya."

Martin stopped talking as a pair of villagers walked by. They were two of Constance's goons. They each wore blue t-shirts.

That was becoming the Constance gang's de facto uniform. Martin had never liked gangs. There had been a pretend one in his high school where he grew up. They had delusions of being Bloods. Of course, it was sort of hard to think of them as hardened criminals when they all went home to their mothers after school.

Still, the idea of Constance's gang bothered Martin.

Maybe it's because the Fore's got me on their side, now. I wonder if I would have supported them before I was put in this Lead Hunter position.

The two men were pretty damn well armed. Each had a belt of ammo around his waist. They carried 700 Remingtons, the same as Martin's hunters. When they were out of earshot, Martin leaned over and whispered into Benson's ear. "I can't figure out what I'm supposed to be doing. I told Mike I didn't want to go to war. But maybe, maybe I'm just . . ."

Martin stopped talking as he saw Katie. The girl was looking much healthier now, after the feast. The dark circles were gone from under her eyes, and Martin didn't know if it was just his imagination or the cut of her blue tank top, but it looked like she'd packed a little weight back into her bosom. She had a white sarong wrapped around her waist, too, which added to her curvaceousness.

"Hey!" Martin said.

"I thought you might need someone to talk to," Katie's smile covered her face.

"How'd you know?"

Katie walked past him and then sat down. She scratched the back of her head, causing the extra skin under her arms to jiggle. "You're talking to Benson. That always means you need to talk."

"Oh yeah? I guess it does."

"And frankly, I need to talk to you, too."

She did look a little worried.

"What's on your mind?" Martin asked.

"Erica says the Fore's considering going to war. Says they are going to vote on it."

Martin straightened his legs from where he sat, feeling a bit of a pull in his hamstrings. "Yeah, princess. That's true."

"If they vote for war, they aren't going to send you, are

they?"

My God, this girl really cares for me.

The idea of someone actually loving him seemed a foreign one. It was an idea he'd left behind long ago. Hell, he hadn't even found someone to love him in the old world—except for his dog.

"I'd send myself," Martin told her.

"Don't go. Send Graham. No one would care if he dies."

Martin laughed, but he noticed that Katie wasn't making a joke. She was dead serious.

"I'm afraid, princess," Martin admitted to her. "I don't know what's right. I keep trying to think about what Aaron would do. Aaron wouldn't want to hurt a fly. He wouldn't even let Mancini kill ole Bense." Martin pointed a thumb at his friend.

"Then don't go!" Katie said. "Don't let the Fore send you."

Martin shoved his hands into the front pocket of his hoodie. "But Aaron wouldn't be afraid, either. Corpse eaters are unpredictable. They've killed some of our people. I don't know if we can afford to let them alone. Maybe I want peace because I'm a coward?"

Katie leaned over and kissed him softly on the cheek. "You're the bravest man I know."

Martin snorted. "I hope not, princess. I can feel my balls rising even just thinking about going after them corpse eaters. I wish Aaron was here."

"Look at me, Martin."

Martin stared into her dark brown eyes.

She put a hand on his arm. "It doesn't matter what Aaron would do. He might have wanted war, or peace. Either way, it doesn't mean a thing. You're Lead Hunter, Martin. The people in Harpsborough are asking themselves what you'll do now, not what Aaron would have done. You decide what you want."

Martin looked back over to Benson for a moment. "Well I fucking want peace."

"Is that what you told the Fore you wanted?" Katie asked him.

Martin nodded.

"I love you, Martin."

Martin turned towards her in surprise. "Really?"

She smiled.

He grabbed her arm. "I love you, too!"

She stood up and then bent down, kissing him on the forehead. "You better."

Martin watched her walk away, her white sarong swishing back and forth with the motion of her hips.

"Did you hear that, Bense?" Martin asked his still friend. "She said she loved me."

Martin jabbed a friendly elbow into Benson's arm. The still man slumped over from the force. Horrified, Martin reached over and grabbed him. He looked about to make sure no one was looking. Thankfully, no one was.

The passage that Q led them to was a square one, about ten feet wide and ten feet tall. The floor was sloped at an odd angle which Q had described as being about ten degrees. To Ellen it seemed a lot steeper than that. Traveling here was made even more treacherous by the fact that a small amount of water, perhaps only an inch deep, flowed down it. The sound of the trickling water filled her ears.

Ellen stood at the base of the corridor where it bottomed out into the Cypress swamp. She looked out into the trees, searching for any sign of the corpses. She didn't see any.

"Ellen, dear," Rick called to her. "Stay away from the entrance. There could be corpses."

Ellen nodded and started coming back. Aiden gave her a hand, and pulled her past him. She felt a twinge in her ankle from the way it had to keep her moving up the corridor, but the pain wasn't bad.

"Since we don't have much time," Q was saying, "and since there are so God damned many of them, I figured the river would be a good way to clear out the crushed corpses. We can cut away this part of the ceiling, here." He pointed over Ellen's head. "Put a large rock there. We can raise it with a waterwheel. We'd have the lure behind a grate here." He motioned to where there was a jut in the otherwise mostly straight corridor. "Only tough part would be the gear switch. After the rock was pulled up all the way, the waterwheel would have to switch to the lure. Maybe fifteen minutes later or so we could rig it so that the rock would fall, crush the corpses, and then the process would repeat."

"Crush 'em and Flush 'em," Eagan said.

That's just like the battery in Rick's house.

Massan was staring at Rick hard.

Alice was too. "Is there an Infidel Friend named Galen?"

Ellen caught her breath.

El Cid looked at her. "Not that I know of." She looked about to her comrades. They all shrugged their shoulders. "Why do you ask?"

"I think he built a machine very much like the one you're talking about now."

El Cid gave her own shrug. "We make no secret of the way we fight devils. I don't know every Infidel Friend in Hell, however, so you never know. But Infidel Friend are disliked in your town, are they not?"

"You'd know," Alice said. "You killed half of my people."

El Cid turned away from Q and advanced on Alice. The poor blonde girl did her best to hold her ground.

"I lived for fifty-two years on earth," El Cid said, "and I've spent over forty more in the labyrinth. In all that time, I have not regretted any of the lives I have taken."

"Then you're a monster," Alice said.

"No I'm not, but the people I killed were."

Alice raised her chin. "Would you regret it if you killed me?"

Ellen held her breath.

"Ladies," Q broke in, "you'll have to finish measuring your cocks later, we've got company."

El Cid, who could not possibly be a woman at the age of fifty-two, seemed reluctant to take her eyes off of Alice. Finally she did so, turning her head quickly, her pony tail swinging back around her head.

Ellen looked too.

Five corpses were wandering together through the Cypress knees. One of them met her gaze. Ellen was suddenly reminded of the corpse eater.

"Q, Aiden, lead them off," El Cid ordered. "Kill them quietly. No need to make this place any busier than it has to be. We'll have to set up a temporary lure near here anyway to cover the noise we'll make building the crusher. Keep your eyes out for a good place to set one up. Everyone else, let's clear out. Back to camp people."

Alice turned away and began to walk back up the tunnel, but El Cid reached out and grabbed her wrist. With what appeared to be no effort, the little Infidel Friend jerked Alice back around to face her.

"Yes," El Cid said, staring into Alice's eyes.

"Yes what?"

"Yes. I'd regret it."

Katie felt tears of pride in her eyes for Martin.

The Citizens were meeting, and none of the villagers dared go anywhere near the church. Even so, they were too curious to remain inside. The people of Harpsborough were all out of their huts, hovels, and tents, grouped together in a huge semicircle that rounded the Fore. Only Martin was brave enough to stay near the meeting. He was alone on the church steps, standing like a statue, looking up to the closed double doors.

"They've been in there for so long . . ." Erica whispered.

Katie nodded, keeping her gaze on her man. "It's a very serious question. A lot of lives are on the line."

Martin's life. If it's war, he'll be the one running it. If it's peace, he'll be the one making the deal.

Erica gave a short laugh. "Our lives. Not theirs."

Martin's life.

She should have never let him kiss her, or take her, or hold her hand. It was best not to be close to men like that. She'd never seen herself as the kind of girl who'd date the Lead Hunter. That was for pretty skinny little things like Alice. But now Alice was gone, maybe never to return. Aaron was dead.

Katie felt lightheaded. She gnawed at her lip. Her bottom lip had a scab on it. She pressed into it with her teeth, feeling the pain.

"Stop that!" Erica ordered her. "You'll chew through it again."

I don't know if I can handle this. I need to break it off with him.

That had to be the right answer. She should just find someone who wasn't going to be sent out to die every time the Fore wanted its dirty work done. Martin would find another girl. Another girl like Gemma. Women were all over him these days, now that he was the Lead Hunter.

But Erica, he had saved Erica when he took the hunters out to feed the people. And he had pleaded so hard to Michael in order to avoid this war. Because he was so gentle. Martin may have been the gentlest man she'd ever met.

Katie had to move back and forth to try and keep her legs from shaking.

The people around her caught their breaths, and Katie could hear the distant squeal of the church doors opening. The Citizen's began pouring out, but they stopped when they saw Martin there on Father Klein's steps. They spread out around him. Michael Baker pushed his way through and then walked down towards Martin.

Oh please. Don't send him out there to die.

Moving wasn't helping her now, her knees were shaking so badly she couldn't walk. She felt an arm circle around her shoulders. It was Erica's. Katie chewed her lip. She tasted blood, but didn't care. She clasped her hands together and held them up over her heart.

Michael was next to Martin now, looking at him, saying nothing.

Please. Please. Please.

"Oh, no," Erica said.

For a moment, the two just stood there.

From this distance, Katie was barely able to make out when Michael began speaking. Then Michael stopped.

Martin's head hung in defeat. Like a corpse, her lover turned back towards the villagers.

War.

40

Dakota stood nervously at the left side of the exit, looking down the mining tunnel where Galen, Tamara, and the rest of the Carrion soldiers had gone. Arturus guessed that being alone and away from the rest of his people was bothering Dakota. For a man who braved the Carrion on a daily basis, he wasn't handling the stress well.

"I'm telling you," he said to Aaron, "we've been through these mines before. There's only silver. No rustrock."

Aaron, who was standing to Dakota's right, shrugged his shoulders. He gave up watching and sat down with Arturus, Johnny, Kelly, and Avery.

"If Galen says there's rustrock down there," Johnny broke in, "then there's rustrock down there."

Dakota turned back and sneered at him. "Keep your nose-busted-ugly-ass out of my conversation, you dirty little chink."

Kelly sucked air in through her teeth.

Arturus wasn't sure why, but what Dakota said had crossed some sort of line.

Johnny's eyes narrowed, and his hand came up reflexively to his still healing nose. "Well, boy, you've got a pretty mouth." The hunter mimed playing a banjo on his shotgun, complete with a little song.

Arturus didn't get the joke, but Avery laughed. Aaron was smiling too, but he put a hand over his mouth, hiding his amusement.

Dakota was fuming. "You won't be laughing when you wake up with your throat cut. Better sleep next to one of your little friends, yellow fucker."

Johnny stood up and advanced on Dakota. "You wanna fuck with me? I guarantee you you'll regret it. You'd better not sleep alone, either. I'll put whip cream in your hand and tickle your fucking *face*."

Aaron lost his composure, giving out a surprised laugh.

Dakota got within inches of Johnny and stared down at the small hunter.

"Dakota," Kelly said, her voice high and sharp.

The Carrion man stopped.

Kelly stood up, her black robes swishing around her. "Johnny Huang's a good soldier and a brave man. You know you're going with us to the City of Blood and Stone. His gun's going to protect you, and he won't shoot you in the back. Stand down."

Dakota snorted his mucus and then spat some of it on the wall beside him. Arturus watched the snot creep down the natural, uneven rock. Then the Carrion man turned on his heel and walked back to the exit, continuing his vigil.

Avery stood up gingerly. Arturus had worried that the walk would open some of the stitching they'd had to do on his privates. So far he seemed to be holding up pretty well. The hunter stretched his legs. Aaron stood up as well, pulled Avery aside, and started whispering to him.

Arturus tried to listen in, but Kelly sat down next to him. He felt suddenly uncomfortable, noticing the sharp natural rocks digging into his back.

"So Calista gave you a lock of hair, huh?" Kelly's voice was quiet enough to where Arturus doubted the others could hear her.

"Yeah."

"And you kept it?"

Arturus looked at her. She seemed nonchalant, as if she didn't really care what he'd done with Calista's gift.

"Yeah. I figured I should keep it. I mean, we are coming back. She wouldn't be too happy to find out that I didn't have it."

Kelly nodded. "You could throw it away. Pretend that you lost it."

Arturus frowned. "Why would I do that?"

"You wouldn't have so much to carry." Kelly's face was

suddenly taut.

"Are your ribs okay?" Arturus asked her.

"They're fine," she said harshly.

She stood up and stalked across the room, moving to stand near Aaron and Avery.

"I know you're talking about me," Dakota said.

"You'd better start whispering too, soldier," Kelly shot back. "We're deep in, but dyitzu hordes can still come . . ."

Arturus heard footsteps. Kelly must have noticed them as well, because she had stopped talking. The sounds were coming from the exit to the mine.

Torchlight illuminated the dark, jagged stones down that passage. It grew closer.

Tamara entered. "The rest are right behind me. He's right. Under that silver vein is a ton of rustrock. More than we could ever need."

Johnny gave Dakota a smile and a wink. "Told ya."

Dakota spat again.

Galen and the rest of the soldiers came up, bearing a second lit torch.

Tamara looked at her Carrion men. "Report this place to Calimay. She'll have you lead miners back here. Dakota, you're with me. We're accompanying them to the City of Blood and Stone. We have to make sure Galen completes his special task."

Special task? What's she talking about? Maybe she just means the scouting?

But Galen's narrowed eyes told Arturus a different story.

What aren't they telling me?

Ellen and Alice were preparing to bathe while Aiden checked the exit.

"Bear with me a second," the gorgeous infidel said. "I'm going to check down these hallways. Don't drop your guard, yet. I'll be coming back through, so keep your safeties on."

Ellen nodded.

The infidels didn't seem to care about who bathed with whom, so long as it was accomplished in an orderly manner. El Cid had ordered them into pairs for safety, so Ellen had become Alice's bathing partner.

Alice seemed distracted. Actually, she looked downright

distraught.

"Are you okay?" Ellen asked.

"Huh?" Alice turned towards her. "Yeah. I'm fine."

"Okay."

"It's just, I thought I knew Molly, you know?"

Alice wasn't looking at the exit to the room at all. Ellen couldn't blame her. Except for the corpses, they hadn't seen any devilsign at all.

"I know you guys used to be best friends," Ellen said. "And when you were talking with her on the way back to camp, she seemed upset."

"She lied, Ellen." Alice bent down and began to untie her sneakers. She stopped and stared into the river, both sets of her laces untied. "She told us we were coming here to save someone, not to complete some Infidel Friend mission."

"She did lie about that," Ellen said. "Rick was pretty angry, too. But it's not like she lied to hurt us."

Alice rolled her eyes. "But she always does stuff like this. One time she told me that Aaron was stealing from the Fore. Then she gave me dyitzu meat someone had traded her to convince me it was true. It wasn't. Who the hell does that?"

"I don't know." Ellen said.

"I mean, really?" Alice shook her head, unknotting the blue cord that kept her hair tied back. "And you know she still says she loves Cris? After one day? Really? Talk to a guy for one hour and you're in love? Molly falls in love twice a minute. You've seen how she looks at Aiden."

Yeah. You'd have to be blind not to look at that guy.

"And then she accuses me of not treating Aaron right." Alice held her hands up in exasperation. "She sleeps around on him until he has to break up with her. Then she lies to me about him when he and I are together, does everything she can to keep us apart, and then tells me *I* treated him badly."

Ellen didn't know what to say.

"Aiden," Aiden reported.

Funny. The Infidel Friend announce themselves the same way Rick taught me to.

Aiden entered the room. "All clear, ladies. Feel free to bathe. Be thorough, but don't waste time."

He turned his back to them and faced towards the exit.

"Don't turn around," Alice warned him.

With his back still to them, he nodded.

To hear El Cid tell it, they needed to get all of the corpsedust off their clothes and weapons to make sure they didn't rot. Looking at her dirty and torn jeans, Ellen couldn't help but feel that the effort was coming a little late. Ellen made sure to look away from Alice, stripped, and dropped into the river. Its current was stronger than she'd expected. The chill felt good on her body.

Ellen saw Alice out of the corner of her eye as the girl left the river. She had a svelte figure, like a model.

No wonder Turi was so smitten with her.

Ellen put her clothes into the river, trying to get out some of the dirt. It helped a little.

That's probably as good as it's going to get.

She got out, splashing water all over the stones as she did so. Alice was gone already. Her clothes couldn't have had time to dry.

Maybe Aiden made her uncomfortable. Or maybe she's still upset from Molly saying whatever it was she said about Aaron.

Ellen began to wring out her wet clothes.

"If you run your hands over your body, you'll dry faster," Aiden suggested.

Ellen felt a flush coming to her cheeks. "You just keep watching for corpses, Mister."

He shrugged. Ellen watched him suspiciously, but he gave no sign of wanting to peek. She tried out his suggestion. It worked surprisingly well.

She heard what sounded like a hiccup coming from the corridor that led back to camp. At first she feared it was an enemy, but then she saw Alice's wet footsteps leading out into the wilds.

She heard the noise again.

Ellen put on her bra, panties and her shirt, even though her shirt was still wet, before trying to struggle into her jeans. The struggle wasn't an easy one while her pants were still damp, and it was particularly hard to get her wounded ankle through, but she managed. She limped out into the corridor to see Alice.

Alice was crying. She'd managed to get her shirt and blue skirt on, at least. Her hair was a disheveled mess. Ellen could see where she'd cut off a strand to give to Aaron. She was fiddling with the shorter hair there.

Ellen caught her up in a hug. "You miss Aaron, I know."

"I treated him so badly."

"He loved you. He knew you loved him."

Alice's tears added to the dampness of her shirt. "I threw things in his face. I demanded that he make me a Citizen when I knew he couldn't. Then I said he didn't love me because of it. I knew he loved me. I just . . . I don't know what I was thinking."

"He forgave you. I know he did. I was there when you and Chelsea saw them all off."

"But why should he have?" Alice was asking. "There is no reason for me to act like that. I just wanted to hurt him. I was frustrated at something else, and I hurt him for it. That's what a child would do. And look at me. I'm crying like a baby."

Ellen held her tighter. "We're women, Alice. It's okay. Sometimes we just need to cry. Sometimes we just need to be irrational."

What she said calmed Alice considerably, but in a flash of terrible insight, Ellen knew how that statement would sound to a woman like El Cid. Hearing her own words from that point of view made her feel sick inside.

Acting like a child.

If El Cid could have read her thoughts then, the Infidel Friend would have been overcome with disgust.

Someone had lied to her, Ellen realized. Society had gone and tricked her, deep within her soul where such deceptions could do the most damage. Somehow they had planted a seed inside her that was short circuiting her ability to be a human being. Somehow they had forced a crutch into her hands that she hadn't wanted or needed.

They taught me it was okay to act like a child because I was a woman. As if only men could behave like adults.

Ellen's jaw clenched. She felt her breath coming faster.

Alice drew back. It was as if she had somehow sensed Ellen's change in mood. "Are you okay?"

Ellen nodded. "Yeah. I just thought of how much I hate the things that hurt us."

The distant sound of gunshots echoed through the wilds of

Hell. Arturus watched his father whisper with Tamara and Aaron. Tamara motioned towards Kelly and Dakota. The pair followed her out of the room.

Tamara only trusts Carrion people. She should have taken Johnny.

Aaron walked over to him. He knelt down, holding his shotgun at the ready. "We think it's probably one of Calimay's people," he whispered. "Probably ran into trouble on the way back."

It made sense. The Carrion was crawling with packs of dyitzu, and without Galen's uncanny senses to guide them, they could well have run into trouble.

There were a few more gunshots, closer this time.

Or they could have just gotten unlucky.

Long, high pitched howls echoed through the chamber.

"Hounds," Johnny said.

There was more shooting, and it seemed even closer.

"Jesus," Aaron said a little louder than Arturus was comfortable with, "that's from our people."

Kelly and Dakota burst back into the room. Dakota's eyes were wide with fear.

"Minotaur!" Kelly shouted.

Oh no.

Galen was already running for a corridor. "After me."

They ran through a natural chamber and then into one that had been worked over by Hell's architect. It had low ceilings and was lit only by cubbyholes. Arturus was starting to get a good intuitive feeling for these kinds of rooms. He guessed correctly which exit Galen took them through. They were heading back to the mines.

Avery collapsed without warning, his face a mask of pain. Johnny dragged him back up to his feet.

His injury.

They ran through two more chambers before Galen suddenly stopped, cocking his head to one side. Dakota ran right up next to him, shifting quickly back and forth from one foot to the other. Galen put a finger up in front of his lips and then placed his free hand on Dakota's shoulder. Dakota took the hint and remained still.

They were in a huge room, maybe three hundred yards

long. To their right, at the end of the chamber, a river flowed. Arturus was looking behind them, half expecting the Minotaur to come barreling into the chamber, but Galen didn't seem concerned about that.

"What is he doing?" Galen whispered to himself.

Arturus' father closed his eyes and crouched.

I don't hear anything. Just that river.

Galen's eyes snapped open. "This way." He darted off to the left.

Arturus was about to follow when he heard Kelly's gasp. She was looking back towards the river. The Minotaur was right there, coming out from a passageway on the far side of the water. Its skin was dark and ruddy. One of its horns had been broken off. A pair of hounds sprang up beside him, one on either side. A pack of dyitzu began to enter as well. The Minotaur spotted them, snorted, and charged right at the river. Arturus could hear its heavy hoofed footsteps clopping over the rush of the water. The thing leapt mightily, soaring across the river. It landed with a tremendous thud, skidding to a stop in a kneeling position.

Its hounds landed on either side of it. The dyitzu were tossing fire and leaping into the river, swimming towards the other side.

"Turi!" Johnny shouted.

Arturus realized he was the last one in the room. He ran after the hunter. Galen was indeed leading them towards the mines, and Arturus was able to use that information to guess the next several passages they took. But then he got one wrong.

Galen wasn't leading them to the rustrock mine. And of course he wasn't. How would Calimay get the rustrock if a Minotaur was hunting there?

Galen led them into a different mine which had been dug into architect worked stone and then down a series of short tunnels. They entered a large chamber lit by a ruby vein. In it was a large overshot waterwheel, perhaps sixty feet tall. Galen had taught Arturus about such structures. They had been used back in the old world to clear water out of mines.

That means this mine was once flooded.

"Quickly," Galen ordered, jamming a pole between the spokes of the waterwheel. "Climb the wheel. Get off at the ledge."

Arturus spotted the ledge about midway up the wheel. There appeared to be a passage leading away from it. Arturus could not shake the idea that his father had somehow known about the layout of the mine before he'd taken them in. Maybe he'd scouted the place when Calimay had allowed him to hunt the wilds. Maybe he'd known about it from before Arturus had even been born.

The sound of a hound howling in a nearby corridor raised the hair on the back of Arturus' neck. He leapt upon the waterwheel. It moved a little beneath his weight, but then it jammed on the pole Galen had used. It was an easy thing to climb since it had woodstone braces every few feet. Arturus was the fastest climber, so he made it to the ledge first. There was indeed a passage there. Johnny was coming up next. Arturus gave him a hand. Then came Kelly and Dakota. Avery struggled up after them, grimacing as his pack caught for a moment on one of the waterwheel's struts. As Arturus helped him onto the ledge, he noticed that blood had stained the crotch and the right leg of Avery's pants. Aaron joined them moments later.

Tamara's still back there, somewhere. Or dead.

Galen was still down in the chamber. He'd kept watch on the entrance, his MP5 leveled, until Aaron was safely on the ledge. Galen removed the woodstone rod from the wheel and practically flew up the wall. He pushed them all back into the corridor behind the ledge. Hound howls and dyitzu hisses echoed in from the room they'd just left. Galen dropped to his belly and crawled back into the chamber.

He returned to them after just a moment, coming back up to his feet. "Follow me."

"Are we safe?" Dakota asked.

Galen shook his head. "I'm afraid not."

41

"That Minotaur was smart," Galen explained as he led them up a mine shaft. "There's a crystal labyrinth near where we were running, he thought we were headed there. He split away to make sure he could cut us off."

Arturus wondered how long the woodstone ladder rungs had been left in the rock. If the mine had been dug by the ancients, then it was entirely possible that some of them had gotten corpsedust on them and had rotted through. Every twenty or so rungs, he'd find one missing, which didn't make him any more confident in their ability to hold his weight.

"How we doing?" Avery called up.

"Another hundred rungs or so," Galen answered.

I hope Avery's doing okay.

Arturus tried to look down, but all he could see below him was Dakota's worried face.

"There were humans with the Minotaur," Dakota said. "Had upside down crosses. They got Tamara."

"Shame," Johnny said. "Could have happened to a nicer girl."

Avery snickered.

Avery can't be that bad off if he's laughing.

"Wait?" Galen stopped climbing. "Killed or captured?"

"Captured."

"Damn," Galen said, continuing upwards.

"What are we going to do about the hounds?" Aaron asked.

Galen grunted, which made Arturus feel slightly jealous.

"We've got to kill them," Galen said. "If we enter the

aqueduct while the Minotaur still has hounds, he'll follow us in. We've got to take them out."

"Will this help?" Dakota asked, hooking one arm through a rung and holding up a small canister.

Galen stopped again, and Arturus leaned to one side so that Galen could look past him.

"Is that pepper spray?" Galen asked.

Dakota smiled. "Yeah. Before I defected with Calimay, I was one Gilgamesh's men."

Galen led them off of the ladder and onto a ledge. The light was a little better in the tunnel. Most of it was coming from the ceiling, causing their shadows to pool around their feet.

"That wasn't a hundred rungs," Avery said as he crawled off of the ladder.

"You complainin'?" Johnny joked, sitting next to Dakota.

Dakota moved to stand behind Galen.

Kelly settled down next to Arturus. Her warmth seeped in through his shirt. He felt comfortable next to her. Her face was flushed from the climb, and her cruel lips were curled into a smile. Arturus could not help but wonder how she would feel when compared to Calimay's daughters. Then he looked at the bloodstain in the crotch of Avery's pants.

Bad idea.

Galen pulled them in close. "Johnny, run down this passage about a kilometer. There's going to be some openings on the left-hand side. If I'm right, you're going to see the Minotaur through one of them. He'll be about a hundred feet below you. Let me know if he has his two hounds with him. Don't tarry there long, or they'll smell you. Make sure you find Tamara as well. The rest of you, stay here. I'm going farther up, make sure I can still get us out of this place."

Johnny nodded and moved quickly down the corridor. Galen got back on the ladder. Dust fell from the rungs as he climbed, drifting down beside them.

Arturus felt something touching his hand. He looked down. It was Kelly's hand. His heart beat faster as he held it.

Really bad idea.

"Hidalgo," Martin called. "You in there?"

The dwelling had a single artificial wall made out of stacked woodstone planks that had been placed across the entrance of a cave. It had a shuttered window that was protected with iron bars. A sinfruit vine, devoid of any fruit, crawled down next to the door where it was coiled, almost like a rope, as a sort of welcome mat. Along the top of the wall, where the woodstone met with the hellstone shaped by Hell's architect, a series of dyitzu and hound skulls were hung. There were a few human skulls too, which Martin hoped were from corpses.

"I be," Hidalgo answered from within.

The response struck Martin as almost philosophical. "Harpsborough needs you."

The door opened. The smell of rank dyitzu hit Martin full in the face. The man's dreadlocks jingled. Martin realized that the smell was coming from the man's pants.

"Hidalgo, why in Hell are you dressed like that?"

Hidalgo gave him a broad smile which Martin would have considered happy-go-lucky if it weren't for the fact that Hidalgo had filed his teeth into points.

"Hidalgo, he be getting very hungry," Hidalgo said. "Before, when I hunting, I be wishing that the dyitzu not be noticing me. Now, me, I be so hungry I hope dyitzu attacks. You say Harpsborough, it be needing me?"

Martin nodded. The smell of Hidalgo's pants almost made him swoon. "Did you put corpsedust on your pants?"

Hidalgo nodded his head, causing his beads to rattle. "Yes." He gave his grin again. "But Martin, he not be saying why he be here."

"You know of the corpse eaters? Of their village?"

"I be knowing."

"We need someone to scout for us, make sure we don't get ambushed. Someone who's familiar with the far downstream Kingsriver."

"I be familiar."

Martin nodded. "Then we really do need you, friend."

Hidalgo's eyes narrowed, and his face became more serious. "Martin, you be calling me friend. Harpsborough, it be calling me friend too. But I, I've been noticing some . . . what you call them . . . 'inconsistencies?'" Hidalgo flashed his filed teeth with a smile. "Once, Hidalgo, he be hunting along the Kingsriver. Once, Hidalgo, he be picking the sinfruit by Tulic's fountain.

Then Harpsborough hunters, they be coming, they be telling Hidalgo he don't own things. Hidalgo, he a nice man, so he don't kill them for it. But then the hunters, they be coming back and their saying Hidalgo their friend. Maybe Harpsborough, they don't know what a friend is. When we came from the Carrion, the people, they knew why I kept these scars in my arm. Now, people, they be saying that it be sin. Hidalgo, he don't hurt people. But people, they be hurting Hidalgo. Then they be calling him friend."

Martin gritted his teeth. "I, uh. I don't know what to tell you. None of that was me, but if the Fore tells me to kick ya, then I'd probably do it. Maybe we could pay you?"

Hidalgo's eyes went wide. "Martin, he'd bribe me? What person you be thinking Hidalgo be?"

Martin set down his pack and took out a jar of Mancini's bloodwater. "Well, I was kind of hoping you were a drunk."

Hidalgo laughed long and hard. Then, wheezing a bit, he spoke, "Martin, you be my friend. Hidalgo, he not be leading Harpsborough people. He be leading Martin. If Martin, you have the hunters with you at the time, I be . . . uh . . . 'A okay.' When Martin makes a deal, he knows what friend is, yeah? Bon, Martin, I lead you and your men. First, we have the drink, yes?"

Martin pinched his own nose with one hand and held up the other. "I'll come in, I really will, and I want you to realize I've never said this to a man before, but you've got to take your pants off first."

Hidalgo opened his eyes in mock surprise before letting out a laugh loud enough to make sure that every devil within miles knew where he was.

— 42 —

Johnny came running back down the corridor.

"What'd ya see?" Aaron asked.

"That Unitaur is down there, alright."

"Unitaur?" Avery asked.

"Fucker's got just one horn."

Arturus laughed, noticing Avery was chuckling along with him.

"Anyway," Johnny went on, "I only saw one of the hounds. Tamara isn't there either, nor are the people. But he's there with a fuck ton of dyitzu."

Dakota stood up. "We've got to find Tamara."

"Look," Avery told him. "I realize you've got a hard on for the bitch, but sometimes you just have to let people go."

Dakota wheeled around on him. "You don't understand. I don't give a damn if we rescue her or not. I'd be just as happy if we shot her."

"Oh shit, he's right," Johnny said.

Dakota looked at the small hunter in surprise.

"What do you mean?" Aaron asked.

Johnny slid down the wall into a sitting position, one hand on his forehead. "Tamara knows how to get into Calimay's. It's not like she was captured by dyitzu. Humans can torture her, can interrogate her. If she gives away Calimay's location, we won't have a place to regroup."

Dakota sneered at them. "And you won't have a guide to get you down the Lethe either. You won't ever get home."

"Oh God," Johnny said, his eyes wide with horror. He

pointed at Dakota. "No wonder you want to kill her so badly. If you don't, you'll be stuck with us."

It seemed to Arturus that Dakota was about to laugh, but the Carrion man managed to only give a slight smile.

Galen was coming down the rungs.

"Just one hound," Aaron reported. "Tamara and the humans are gone, too. Dakota's worried that she'll give away the location of Calimay's place."

Galen dropped on to the ledge. "Not good. But you did see the Minotaur?"

Johnny nodded.

Galen shook his head. "There's no way we can get to Tamara."

"We have to," Dakota said. "I won't let my people die."

"I understand you, soldier, but we're no match for a Minotaur even on its own, never mind one armed with a pack of dyitzu. It's just not safe to go traipsing around the Carrion. That one's angry, too. I think it was the one in the battle with La'Ferve. It's looking for human blood, and it probably can't tell we're not on the same team as Maab."

Dakota stepped forward. "Galen, without our guide—"

"I don't care. Our best chance is still the aqueduct. We'll make it to the City of Blood and Stone long before those soldiers do. That aqueduct is a straight shot. We'll find the entrance to the city and set up a sniper. When they come, she dies. Agreed?"

Dakota nodded.

"Good. Now the fact that only one of the hounds is with him is bad, but I do have a way out of here. With the hounds split up, we won't be able to kill them together without giving them a trail. We're going to have to get fancy."

"Sounds good to me," Aaron said. "What do you have in mind?"

"We'll walk straight past the aqueduct until we reach a river. Then we'll double back. We'll burst Dakota's pepper spray near there. Normally a hound's sense of smell is sensitive enough to notice a double back, but that pepper spray should keep them out of operation for a while. By then our trail might be cold enough that they won't notice. Even if they do, that will hopefully have given us enough time to get a good lead."

"Sounds good to me," Aaron said. "You good, Dakota?"

"I'm good."

Martin moved quickly across Harpsborough. It was early, so early that Michael wasn't even up on the balcony. Martin meant to get into the church before anyone could stop and talk to him about the war.

As he was passing the Fore, its door blanket opened. Chelsea walked out. She seemed wide awake. Her hair was brushed back. Martin always liked that style better. There was a time when she wore it in a ponytail, like Alice did, but it didn't suit her. Martin thought of her red hair as a sort of mane. It may not have really looked like one, but Chelsea could be one fierce woman.

"You're up early, princess," Martin told her.

She gave him a fake smile. "I was waiting for you to get back into town." She stopped and sniffed the air. "What's that smell?"

Martin rolled his eyes. "Hidalgo. He's got these pants . . . well, you'll see. He'll be in town in a minute."

"For your meeting." It was a statement, not a question.

"Yes."

"I'm going with you," Chelsea said, folding her arms beneath her breasts.

Martin felt confused. "To the meeting?"

"To the meeting and to the war."

Martin wasn't surprised that the Fore had picked a Citizen to supervise things, and he was happy it was Chelsea they chose, but he was a bit surprised that they would send a woman to do such a thing. "The Fore sent you?"

Chelsea smiled and shook her head. "They didn't want to send anyone. But they didn't say no when I decided to go. Of course, I told them, as I'll tell you now, that I'm just here to observe . . . and maybe shoot a little . . . but not to give orders."

Martin took a deep breath.

She's right, I smell like Hidalgo's pants.

"I'm happy to have you," Martin told her.

Chelsea started walking towards the church, and Martin hurried to catch up.

"Good, because you don't have any choice in the matter,"

Chelsea said. "Temp Lead Hunter or no, you're still a villager, so technically I outrank you. Also, I can't let you die."

Martin felt off balance. "Thank you."

"No, I'm serious. If you die out there, Graham will go back to being Lead Hunter. Only difference between this time and the last time he was Lead Hunter is that this time he'll be in Mancini's pocket."

Martin stopped dead in his tracks.

Politics. Don't worry. Chelsea's a good girl. You win this war. She'll take care of the politics.

Galen had brought them to the river before walking them backward, retracing their steps. He stopped everyone at a black wall made of whetstone. It was marked with a symbol cut into its side—a triangle within a trapezoid cut by two horizontal lines. Below the symbol was a series of letters. Arturus moved closer so that he could read them.

VENIA CCCIↃↃMMCIV

"That's Infidel sign," Kelly warned. "Galen, where the hell are you taking us?"

"It is indeed Infidel sign," Galen said, "but this is also a symbol from an earlier time. The ancients used to rule this place, before the devils swallowed it and made it their own. This is something they built."

"What is it?" Aaron asked.

"An aqueduct's service tunnel. It will take us where we want to go. Wait here. I'll open it."

Galen trotted off, leaving them alone by the whetstone. Arturus thought he heard a click, but he couldn't be sure. Galen returned after a few more moments.

"Help me," he ordered.

Galen got next to the whetstone wall and began pushing. Aaron and Dakota joined him. Slowly, the wall moved to the right, sliding open. When they had it wide enough to slip through, Galen motioned them in. Dakota was the last to enter. He cast a worried glance behind him as he crossed over the threshold.

"Let's close it up," Galen ordered.

Aaron and Dakota helped him in closing the wall, though Galen stopped them when it was about six inches from being shut.

"Toss out that pepper spray," Galen ordered.

Dakota did so, tossing it out onto the stones outside.

Galen raised his shotgun. "Get ready to close it."

Dakota and Aaron braced themselves. Galen fired, and the pepper spray can exploded. Aaron and Dakota were quick to shut the door, but Arturus felt his eyes stinging nonetheless. After a moment, he started to cough.

The place they had entered was pitch black.

"Ancients didn't need to see?" Johnny whispered harshly.

"Will we be safe?" Aaron asked.

"I don't know," Galen said. "Sometimes, when the settling occurs, these passages get exposed. Devils can get in them."

"They'll win, if we have no light," Johnny said.

"I'll lead us a few hundred yards in, just in case the hounds recover quickly. Then we'll get some sleep."

43

Julian looked across the room by the flickering light of their single stolen candle. There was a new face, a sixth when there had been but five. New faces were dangerous things. A new face could report their prayer services to a priestess. And if Selena were to hear this, well, Julian knew he couldn't withstand another conversion session. His soul would simply break.

But new faces were necessary if God was going to be brought into the hearts of the men of the Carrion. Throughout the day, Julian and the others would speak to the serfs. They would gauge their answers. They would listen to what the men said—and to what they didn't say—and then guess which ones might be amenable to Christ.

John, the man who had found Julian, had brought the guest.

"What's your name?" Julian asked the new man.

"George."

"And will you break bread with us, George?"

The question was strictly metaphorical here. In place of bread, they had some devilwheat that they mixed in a cup and drank from. It was the best they could manage under the circumstances.

"I want to," George said. "I really do. But Maab's right on this one. The God I worshiped on Earth, whoever He was, is not in Hell. This is the domain of Ahriman. Look how powerful Maab and her people have become. We've all heard how terrible the Christians do."

John spoke up. "Brother Julian is from one of those cities."

"How many men are in it?" George asked.

"Five hundred."

George shook his head. "But Maab has over a thousand in her complex alone, and those are just soldiers. She has over ten thousand slaves. That's not even counting how many men she could call to her side from the other priestesses. Your village is but an afterthought."

"It's true," Julian answered. "But Harpsborough is pretty close to one of the minor priestess' complexes."

"I'm sorry, but if you want me to pray with you, you're going to have to show me something solid. You've heard those Little Ladies talk about the Bible. Everything I've learned from speaking to others is that they're right. Unless you can show me how they're wrong, unless you can show me how your God is in Hell . . ."

The candlelight flickered for a few moments.

"I don't know that God is in Hell," Julian said. "I don't. But I can tell you that if you were to find God here, I know where you'd look. I didn't notice it when I was in Harpsborough until I left, but there was a feeling, almost like a spirit, that bound us all together. They have their problems, that's true. People hurt each other. There are fights. Occasionally there are even murders. But compared to this place . . ." Julian paused. "If you're gonna find God in Hell, then it's in community. You'll feel it in your connection with the other people that you love. Maybe that's what they meant when they said God was love. I don't know.

"But what I can tell you is that there is this bond that the people in Harpsborough share. And I can tell you that bond is here, in this very room, between those of us who have gathered together to pray in His name. You asked me, George, you asked me how many soldiers Harpsborough had. And I told you. Let me ask a question. How many slaves does Maab have?"

"At least ten thousand."

"And do you know how many slaves Harpsborough has?"

George shook his head.

"Zero." Julian handed him their communal bowl. "The blood of Christ. The bread of Heaven."

George drank from the cup.

Galen's torch sprang to life. The firelight danced,

illuminating their surroundings.

They were in a single cylindrical tube whose ceiling was about twenty feet high. As for how far back it went, and how far forward, Arturus could not tell. After a moment, he realized the tunnel was sloped slightly downwards.

In the center of the tunnel ran the aqueduct itself. It was a large trough, about twelve feet tall. Along the base of the aqueduct was a series of stone cubbies which a man could lie down in. Arturus wanted to climb up those cubbies and get to the lip of the aqueduct. Then he could look down in it and see if there was any water. The cubbies and the aqueduct split the cylinder in two, and Arturus would not be able to see the other side without making that climb. There was a walkway that ran alongside the aqueduct, flattened into the otherwise curved stone. It was about four feet wide.

That's where we'll walk.

Galen led them forward, his bubble of torchlight beckoning Arturus onward. Avery had a severe limp, and the blood had made it all the way down his pant leg.

I hope he didn't rip a stitch.

The stones forming the aqueduct and the chamber itself were different than Arturus was used to. Their shape was entirely uniform, and they had been mortared together. Undoubtedly, they had been treated with rustrock. As incredible as it seemed, Arturus figured this place must have been built by humans.

As Arturus' eyes adjusted to the flickering light, he was able to see a good ways down the long and seemingly endless tunnel. The cubbies were built about four feet high and were located every thirty feet or so. A small ladder, apparently made out of metal, was placed beside each set of them.

We must have traveled a few hundred yards by now.

Avery was breathing hard, but he hadn't complained at all.

Over the walkway was a long pipe, perhaps made out of whetstone. Arturus found it hard to believe that the pipe was made by humans. You couldn't just chop up whetstone like it were hellstone. Hell's architect must have had something to do with its creation . . . but that seemed counter intuitive. Why would the architect make anything of the sort? Maybe the ancients had found some way to work whetstone.

Arturus watched his father duck into one of the cubbies.

Avery breathed a sigh of relief. Arturus settled down on the other side of the cubby wall from his father. The rest followed suit. Predictably, Kelly lay down next to him. For some reason, Arturus felt more comfortable with her there by his side.

"We'll sleep for a few hours," Galen said. "We should start moving then, just in case the Minotaur sees through our little trick."

"You mean Unitaur." Johnny said.

Galen laughed. "Yeah. That's what I meant."

"Who could have built all this?" Arturus asked. "It must have taken thousands of people."

"It did take thousands to build aqueducts like this one. Hundreds of thousands." Galen answered. "The ancients were very numerous and very skilled."

Johnny nodded. "And this whole thing carried water?"

"Millions and millions of gallons," Galen said.

Johnny put his hand up on his chin. "Those ancients, they must have been very thirsty."

Arturus smiled.

"Quiet down, now" Aaron whispered. "We should get to sleep."

"Lights out," Galen warned.

The torchlight was extinguished and all became dark. Arturus put his pack behind him and laid upon it. It felt rather comfortable. He felt Kelly laying down next to him, touching him. He felt her lips on his neck, then his cheek, and then he was kissing her.

44

"Guns at the ready," Galen warned. "I'm about to light the torch."

"I thought you said it was safe?" The whisper sounded like it was Johnny's voice.

"Should be," Galen answered. "Like I said, the settling can sometimes open the aqueduct to the outside of Hell. It can get very dangerous in here. Only one direction to run."

Arturus heard the strike of stone on stone. There was a sudden flash from the sparks from a firerock brick. Then another strike and another flash. Then a third strike and the torch caught fire. The bubble of light seemed puny compared to the seemingly infinite tunnel. Small metal bridges crossed over the aqueduct itself in places. Each one grew dimmer as they receded into the distance.

I wonder how many bridges there are.

Avery was slow to get to his feet. The blood on his pants had dried. There was a small patch near his groin that was fresh, though.

"I need to check your wound," Galen told him.

Avery shook his head. "I'm fine."

"You're bleeding. You're not fine."

"I will not strip down for you." The anger in Avery's voice surprised Arturus.

Avery looked at Kelly. He wanted to kill her, Arturus knew. He wasn't even trying to hide it.

Aaron looked at the ceiling for a moment before walking over to Avery. "Galen needs to inspect your wounds, hunter.

You will allow him to do so."

Avery crossed his arms. "I told you, I'm fine."

"That wasn't a request, hunter. That was an order."

Avery's nostrils flared. "Fine. Take that little bitch away."

Galen turned towards Arturus. "Take her up ahead, stay put for a while. We'll be there shortly."

Arturus nodded. "This way," he told Kelly.

He led her a hundred feet or so down the aqueduct. At this distance, the light wasn't much to see by. Arturus settled down into a cubby. Kelly sat next to him, stealing a kiss. Her hands started to wander across his body.

"Not now," Arturus said. "Not unless you want Avery to kill me."

"Who cares what he thinks?" Kelly asked. "He's a God damned rapist."

He is. But he'd never rape a Harpsborough girl.

"He doesn't count you as human," Arturus told her.

Arturus heard the rustle of her robe as she shrugged.

They waited there, holding hands in the darkness. After a few minutes, the torchlight started creeping towards them. Arturus freed his hand from Kelly's and he stood up.

As the group approached, Arturus could tell that Avery was waddling.

"Everything okay?" Arturus asked.

The torch in Galen's hand wavered as he nodded. "Wound reopened a little, but the stitches are holding. We're ready to go. It's good to have a scout go first. Less noise. That way we can hear our enemies before they hear us."

Arturus nodded. That seemed wise.

"You ready to scout, Turi?" Galen asked.

"Me?"

"You're our tunnel rat, remember?"

"Oh yeah," Arturus said. "I'd forgotten about that."

"Up the wall," Galen ordered. "I want you on the lip of the aqueduct. That way you'll be able to hear anything in it. There's also a sister service corridor, just like this one, on the far side."

"Yes, sir."

Arturus used one of the cubbies to help himself up. With a jump, he was able to grab the lip of the aqueduct and pull himself up on it. At that height, the ceiling was too close for him to stand comfortably. He knelt instead, uncertain of his balance. His pack shifted, almost knocking him over. He cinched it tighter around his midsection.

In the distance, he heard a hound's call. He hoped it wasn't from inside the tunnel.

"I'm going to check the other service walkway before we start," Arturus said.

He heard Galen's grunt come up from below.

The dim light from the torch wasn't much to go by, but he could see the dark grey form of the empty aqueduct below him. He lowered himself into it. The stone was slick, not because it was damp, but because it was well polished.

It's whetstone too.

Like the pipe above, Arturus wondered if it was even possible that humans could have constructed such a thing. Maybe it was. Hell's architect made many wonders, but somehow creating a system of deliberate water distribution didn't seem to be in its character.

"Be quick, son," Galen's whisper carried into the aqueduct. "You heard that hound's call. We may not be alone in here."

Arturus climbed up the far side, the tread of his boots slipping on the smooth whetstone.

The other service tunnel looked the same as the one his friends were in, though it was only illuminated from the unsteady torchlight reflecting off of the cylindrical ceiling. Arturus spent a moment searching the place carefully while his eyes adjusted. It seemed safe.

What people could have built all this? How long ago? How could a people so powerful have fallen?

Arturus returned to the right lip of the aqueduct and looked down at his father and the hunters. "Ready."

Galen extinguished the torch.

"Keep pace with us, just stay a few hundred yards ahead." Galen said.

"How can I know where you are?" Arturus asked. "It's pitch black."

Galen didn't respond, but Arturus knew the answer anyway. He listened as the sound of the moving Harpsborough hunters filled the chamber. Slowly, careful not to fall from where he was perched, Arturus moved ahead. At times he started to get too much of a lead and was forced to slow his pace. Avery must have been slowing them down.

My father is wise. This aqueduct cuts in a straight line right through the labyrinth. Even running, there's no way they'll get Tamara to the City of Blood and Stone before us.

He thought about this some more.

If only they'd built an aqueduct that led to Harpsborough.

Martin opened one of the church doors for Chelsea, letting her in before closing it behind them both. The heavy thud of the woodstone running into the granite doorway sounded strangely comforting. Martin knelt for a moment in the aisle, crossing himself—up, down, left, right. He could never remember whether left or right was supposed to come first.

Doesn't really matter now, does it?

Graham, Constance and Huxley were waiting for him before the pulpit where Father Klein gave his sermons. He and Chelsea strode side by side down the long walkway, his boots clopping purposefully against the stones. Their echoes made him feel important. Chelsea's footsteps were as soft as a rabbit's.

Or as a lion's. She's got her hair down today.

When he approached the trio, the church door opened again. He looked back over his shoulder to see Hidalgo. The man had dressed more appropriately. He almost looked like a villager might, wearing a sleeveless black vest to carry his ammo. Hidalgo had worn no undershirt, but his pants were respectable. His dreadlocks had been pulled back and tied neatly, though their beads still rattled as he walked. Hidalgo's long arms swung wildly as he hurried to catch up. Martin could not help but smile.

Thank God he brought nicer pants.

"I be," Hidalgo reported, catching up with him and bowing towards Chelsea.

"Yes you do," Chelsea said, giving the man a hug.

Martin was surprised by their show of familiarity.

They joined Graham, Huxley, and Constance.

"Why's he here?" Graham asked.

Hidalgo poked Martin in the side. "Me, I be thinking he not coming to kill the rotten people."

"He's not," Martin answered.

"Then him, why he be here?"

Chelsea laughed.

"He'll be defending Harpsborough with his collectors in case of a counterattack."

Hidalgo's beads rattled loudly as he nodded his head. "Yes. Graham, he be having a very important job."

Graham snorted.

"It is important," Martin turned towards Graham. "Katie will be back here. I love her, and Graham, I must tell you I feel safer with her in your hands—and that's no joke."

Graham nodded solemnly.

How come everyone in Mancini's pocket looks so depressed all the time?

"Constance, I asked you to come because I've been speaking with Michael. He says it's okay for me to deputize you and your men. You all did such a good job when we were saving people from hunger that I knew I could count on you."

Constance grimaced. "You know my people follow me because they're not happy with the way things are around here."

"I know it. They don't like the way the Fore has been acting. But things are changing. You won't say no now that the Fore's giving in to your demands, will you?"

Constance pulled a loose thread out from his blue t-shirt. "We don't much like the new taxation law." He flicked the thread aside.

"No shit," Chelsea said, crossing her arms and nodding her head in agreement.

"I don't like it either," Martin jumped in, "but we got the feast thing in. And you know I'm doing my best to make it like it was when Aaron was in charge. That's the way you want it, right?"

"At least that's acceptable," Constance said. "I'll have to talk to them, but I bet I can rally a few."

Martin nodded. "Tell them they'll get a Fore sponsored meal and some ammo. If they really want to hurt the Fore, they can accept the Citizen's meat and bullets."

Constance smiled. "I'm with you, Martin."

"Good," Martin said. "Huxley and I will have our men ready to go in two days. We'll leave in the morning. Caval and Hidalgo will lead us to their village. We'll assess the layout and kill them. Chelsea will be going along with us as an advisor. Any questions?"

Constance shrugged. "Not really. I'll get to gathering my people."

No one else had any questions either, for which Martin was thankful.

He stayed behind as the others left, bending down to pick up the blue piece of thread Constance had tossed aside. Best to keep God's house clean, just in case.

Hidalgo stayed behind too. He was watching Chelsea, Martin could tell.

"Chelsea, she be a fine lady. Even if she not be having the thick thighs."

"She is indeed," Martin answered. "She's single, you know. How long have you liked her?"

Hidalgo gave a soft laugh, and his hair rattled. "Me, I be loving her since I was hellborn."

"Have you asked her out? Tried to kiss her?"

"No."

Martin balled the thread up and put it in his hoodie's pocket. "Well, why the hell not?"

"Me, I be . . . what is it that you people be calling it? Chicken shit?"

Martin burst out laughing. The echoes of his own laughter had made him feel a little sacrilegious. "Yeah, Hidalgo. That's what we call it."

Galen stopped them periodically so that he could exit the aqueduct through a service door and look around. He did this twice before letting everyone sleep again. Time here was immeasurable. Arturus wasn't sure if they were marching full days and sleeping eight hours a night, or if they were sleeping in short shifts and only moving about for a few hours at a time.

In the beginning, he suffered some vertigo while climbing around in the dark, but his sense of touch and hearing helped steady him. He felt almost as comfortable moving now as he would have in the light. There was a nagging fear he harbored in the back of his mind, however, that he would come to a point where the aqueduct was broken and that he might fall. Thus far the ancient's architecture had been in remarkably good condition. It seemed almost as if they had tricked the stones into thinking they had been laid that way, so that they fixed the aqueduct as they healed instead of destroying it.

With the vertigo gone, all he had to worry about was the cramping of his legs. Moving in a crouch for miles at a time was no easy task. He wondered how much longer he could go on doing this.

The only changes in the structure of the aqueduct itself were the metal bridges which spanned it every so often. Arturus had taken to counting them. He'd lost count twice already, but his best guess was that they had passed by over eleven hundred so far. As his hearing became better attuned to the echoes of this place, he began to fear that they were not alone. Behind him, he noticed the sound of his friends and sometimes, when he let them get too close, he could even hear their labored breathing—but every so often he heard noises which didn't seem to be coming from behind him.

At first he thought the extra noise was just an echo, but as he moved on, mile after mile, he began to identify sounds which couldn't be so easily explained. Maybe it was the scrape of a dyitzu claw or the skid of the hoof of a Minotaur. Maybe it was just the stones, creaking under the mighty weight that Hell placed upon them.

He began to worry that they were being followed by pursuers who were not in the tunnel. Maybe their enemies were on the other side of the wall to his left. Maybe they were just over his head, a few feet beyond the stone ceiling.

Arturus froze. He'd heard something.

That was close.

He tilted his head. The hunters were unusually silent. Either they had heard it as well, or he had wandered too far ahead while he was trying to listen.

Silence.

Dead silence.

As his breathing slowed, he was able to hear the pounding of his blood in his ears. It thudded slowly with his heart.

Do I hear someone else breathing?

Or maybe that was just him. He tried to concentrate on the noise that his own breath made. He listened to it carefully, inhaling and exhaling. He couldn't be sure, but it sounded like there was someone else nearby.

He held his breath.

The noise kept going, and now he could hear it clearly. It was coming from the service tunnel. It was something breathing. Or several somethings.

As slowly and as carefully as he could, Arturus backed up a few feet along the aqueduct.

He climbed down into the service walkway, knelt next to a cubbyhole, and tried again to listen. It took a moment before he could identify the sound again.

They've got to be on the sister walkway.

The breathing never stopped.

Maybe it's wind?

But it wasn't. There was a definite pattern, and there was more than one thing breathing out there.

Something touched his arm. Arturus started and reached for his gun.

I'm going to die.

But the touch wasn't hurting him. He felt hands moving along his body, as if trying to identify him. The hands were rough and calloused.

"Shh," came the softest of whispers.

"Move back?" Arturus asked softly.

"Yes," Galen said.

Together they moved a few hundred feet back down the tunnel.

Galen stopped him. "What? How many? How far?"

"Not sure, I think they're on the sister walkway."

Galen left his side for a moment. Arturus heard his father's whispers, as soft as the breath of their enemies, as he spoke to the rest of the group. Galen's touch returned to him and gently guided him back to the others.

Now that they were all silent, the sound of their enemies became audible even at this distance. Their breathing was an almost steady hum.

They've gotten louder.

"We should go back," Aaron whispered into their huddle. "We can exit further down there."

"Last entrance is about three hours back," Galen's soft

voice responded.

"That far?"

"Of the last two I checked, one was jammed and the other was too hairy."

"You want us just to keep on marching down there?" Aaron whispered back. "With whatever that is out there waiting for us?"

"We may not have much of a choice," Galen answered. "Stay here."

45

Martin was shocked when he and Hidalgo entered Harpsborough. Everyone was there. People were standing in a large group amidst their hovels. The brightly dressed Citizens were out in force on the streets. Others were standing on the Fore's roof and balconies. Michael Baker himself was on one of those third floor balconies, Mancini at his side.

Harpsborough felt warmer even though neither Kylie's Kiln nor Mancini's still were lit. The crowd began to cheer. It took Martin a second to realize that they were cheering for him.

Why are they cheering for me?

"Harpsborough, it be wishing us well," Hidalgo said.

Of course they were cheering for him. They'd cheered for Michael when he came back, a giant spider leg slung over his shoulder. They'd cheered when Aaron had left, with promises of rescuing Julian and bringing back his devilwheat. The whole city of Harpsborough was on his side. They wanted him to succeed.

Martin had never dreamed of being the focus of all this attention. Or, he hadn't since he had spent two months practicing bass guitar in the old world's Winston Mill apartment 111D. He remembered how it felt to be a member of that Harpsborough crowd. How it felt to be looking up to the people who were going to be fighting on his behalf. He remembered how jealous he was of Aaron when Alice had seen him off.

It'll be like that now. Except I'm the one that everyone is looking at.

Beyond the crowd, standing by the Fore's door curtain, were forty of his hunters. Standing in a clump to one side were

Constance and his supporters. They were easy to spot in their blue t-shirts. Somehow Constance had managed to convince his entire crew to go.

To join his men, Martin had to pass through the crowd. The villagers gathered around him, reaching out and touching him. Their hands almost felt painful. Some were shouting encouraging things at him. Others were asking him to protect someone.

"Make sure Ben comes back alive," a woman shouted. "He's supposed to cook me dinner."

"You'll get that dinner, miss!" Martin spoke loudly so he could be heard over the crowd.

Oh, Jesus. I really do have to make sure that he's safe.

The burden of being a leader hit Martin all at once. These people were asking for him to be in control of things that were uncontrollable. Not only was he supposed to kill all the corpsemen, he was supposed to do it without anyone being killed.

But what can I do? I can't tell them I can't protect them.

So he did what Aaron had done. He promised he would keep them safe. No one held it against Aaron that he hadn't been able to.

Of course, that's probably because Aaron's dead.

Martin looked back to make sure Hidalgo was still with him. He was. It was almost a shame that he hadn't worn his hunting pants since they might have kept the crowd at bay. From this angle Martin saw that Hidalgo's quiver didn't carry his normal woodstone arrows. This time the quiver carried silver colored shafts.

Arrows for killing men, maybe. Or maybe he's suspicious, and thinks silver will work better against the undead.

Finally the hands gave way and he was free, standing next to his men. Chelsea was the closest to him. She hugged him.

"Looks like Constance has his whole crew," Martin said to her.

She pulled back from his hug and stood next to him, looking to the clump of blue at the edge of the hunters in their black hoodies. "Yeah," her voice was soft, but its higher pitch made her easier to hear over the crowd. "Same thing happens with sheep. After more than half of them change direction, the whole flock follows."

Martin laughed. He looked around for Katie, but he couldn't figure out where she was. Maybe he'd see her when he made it to his men. He moved over to join his hunters. They were happy to see him, and many of them shook his hand. Some gave him hugs or patted him on the back.

"We're ready," one man said.

"Gonna kill those damn corpse eaters," said another.

"Twice if we have to," Constance added.

A few people laughed at his joke.

"I'm happy you were able to get all your men," Martin said. "I know how much they don't like the Fore."

"They didn't come to follow the Fore, Martin. They came to follow you."

Martin smiled.

Katie wasn't on this side either.

I must have missed her.

He searched again through the crowd.

She's not here.

He turned to Chelsea. "Have you seen Katie?"

"I think she's still in her house."

"Stay here," Martin ordered anyone who could hear him. "I'll be right back. Make sure that you've got all your supplies in order, that you've got bullets in your guns, and that you're ready to fight."

As he made his way back towards the crowd, Martin saw Ole Bense sitting alone against his Fore wall.

I wish you could see me now, Bense. Who'd have guessed that I'd end up as Lead Hunter?

He was able to break through the crowd more quickly this time.

Erica was near the hovel. She stood between him and the door curtain. "You shouldn't . . ."

"Shouldn't what?"

Erica didn't say anything. She just looked down.

The noise and the people were getting to be a bit too much for Martin, so he passed Erica and walked briskly up to Katie's hovel.

"Hey, Reg," he greeted the bird drawing. "You in there, Katie?"

No answer. But he thought he heard a noise. He pushed his way through, letting the door tapestry close behind him. The tight confines of Katie's hovel were a welcome reprieve from the attention of all those villagers.

Katie was lying face down in the pack she used as a pillow. She was shaking.

"Are you alright?" he asked.

"I don't want to see you," she said into her pack.

He could tell from her voice that she was crying.

He sat down beside her. "I'm going away. Katie, I'm going to war. I need to say goodbye to you."

"Just go. I don't want to talk to you."

She rolled to one side, turning her back to him.

Martin put a hand on her hair covered shoulder. "Why? Katie? Don't you care about me? Don't you want to say goodbye? What if I die?"

She sat up and turned towards him. Tears were running down her face. Her eyes were bright red. "Don't go."

"I have to. Katie, that's my job."

"Make someone else do it."

Martin shook his head. "I don't want to go, but this isn't one of those things I can avoid."

"You can't go."

"I have to. I need your support. Just tell me you love me. Why won't you just say goodbye?"

"Because you're going to die, Martin!" she shouted. "You're going to die. They never should have made you Lead Hunter. You're a good man, but that's all you are. Everybody knows you're a bad fighter. Everyone knows it. You never killed many dyitzu. You weren't picked to go on the expeditions. You're not qualified for this. You're going to get killed, and you're going to get a lot of other people killed too."

Martin was stunned. He tried to stand up but lost his balance for a moment.

She doesn't believe in me.

This kind of betrayal was something that Martin had never experienced before. He wasn't sure if there was a worse kind.

It was dead quiet.

Outside, all of the talking had stopped. They'd heard her. The entire village had heard her say he wasn't a good fighter.

How could she do this to me?

Martin made it to his feet this time. He stumbled out of the tent.

Everyone was there. Staring at him. The hunters, the villagers, the Citizens, Constance's men. Caval. Everyone.

I need to say something.

But Martin didn't have the first clue about what to say. Kylie believed in Michael. Alice believed in Aaron. But Katie, Katie didn't think he was worth a damn. How could he have been so foolish? Of course it had seemed like a dream when everyone had been singing his praises. Of course he was shocked to find out that they'd put him in charge. Men like him weren't supposed to be in charge. He had only gotten the position because Michael had retired, Aaron had died, and Graham had gotten unlucky. Any one of them was a better hunter than he was.

If you can't think of anything to say. Try the truth.

"She's right," Martin said. "I'm not a good fighter, so the rest of you are going to have to take extra care in protecting Chelsea."

Suddenly everyone was laughing. Martin felt the back of his neck heat up. The embarrassment cut him to the quick.

Wait, they're not laughing at me.

He was very confused. They may not have all been laughing at him, but they *were* all laughing. Martin thought back on what he had just said, trying to figure out why they were laughing.

Do they think I'm joking? They think I'm joking!

They were being fooled by an illusion. The Lead Hunter was supposed to be a good hunter, so they all believed he was. It didn't matter that he wasn't. Katie may have given that illusion a huge blow, but she hadn't done enough damage to dispel it. Sure, if he fucked up in the battle, that illusion might fade away faster than it might have otherwise, but if he didn't fuck up, no one would be the wiser.

Was it like this for Aaron and Michael, too? Were they really just people, the same as he, put into positions where people counted on them? Where people's illusion of their abilities inspired them, drove them on? Did it even matter if he was a fake?

Oh shit, I need to keep talking.

"These people, these corpsemen, they've murdered some of us. They killed our villagers in cold blood. We can't let them kill any more of us. Now, I'm not sure why Katie is on the corpse eaters' side . . ." He had to stop talking while the village laughed. "Hell," Martin adlibbed, "maybe she's spent even more time with Ole Bense than I have." More laughter. "But we've got to act justly. We have to deliver vengeance to them." Martin paused, unsure on how he was going to end this. "We know from Caval that they worship death. Well that's fine. I feel happy for them. After all, we didn't ever get a chance to meet our God. They should count themselves lucky. Their God is coming for them."

The cheering erupted again. Chelsea was smiling. The faces around Constance were no longer worried. Even Caval seemed confident.

Really? That's all it takes?

Of course that was all it took. His speech wasn't very good on its own, it was just that everyone else had a dog in this fight, too. The men were risking their lives. The villagers were going to lose people that they knew. Hell, if Martin lost, then they could very well get killed by the corpse eater counter attack. They wanted the speech to be moving. They wanted to be moved. They wanted Martin to win.

"Alright soldiers!" Martin screamed at the top of his lungs over the supportive shouts of the crowd. "Move out!" The people of Harpsborough erupted into cheers again.

The villagers parted, and his hunters started making their way to the exit. Hidalgo stepped up beside him to his left. Chelsea came up to his right. With them flanking him, Martin prepared to follow his army out into the wilds—but paused. He looked over at Katie's home. The door tapestry was folded in a way that hid the picture of the bird from view.

"It's okay, Martin." Chelsea told him. "She'll love you when you get back."

She'll love me if I get back.

Martin started walking, following the path the villagers had cleared for him. Somehow having Hidalgo and Chelsea around made him feel safer, more important. As if he was actually a leader.

Well, here goes nothin'.

"Come here, son." Galen's voice was so loud it caused Arturus to jump. "I want to show you something."

"Father! There are dyitzu close!" Arturus whispered frantically.

"This way," Galen's voice beckoned, as calm as ever.

Arturus followed his father's footsteps through the pitch black tunnel. Galen was scuffing his boot every three or four paces, presumably so Arturus could keep pace with him.

"Climb here," Galen ordered.

Arturus did as he was asked, climbing up over the cubby, and then onto the aqueduct. He heard Galen come up beside him.

"Now to the other side."

Arturus slid down into the aqueduct. Then he worked his way over to the lip on the far side. There was a metallic thud, and the chamber was suddenly lit up with a shower of sparks. Galen had struck a firestone rock against one of the whetstone pipes. The shower of sparks set his torch alight.

Quiet hisses of dyitzu filled the chamber. Weak hisses. Desperate hisses.

Arturus looked down over the lip and into the tunnel's sister walkway. The ground was littered with fallen dyitzu. Their bodies were skinny, skinnier than Arturus had thought possible. Their muscles were terribly atrophied. Their skin seemed paper thin, and was paler than Arturus had ever seen on a dyitzu. Their all black eyes were sunken into their sockets. Their ribcages stood out in intense relief in the flickering torchlight. Their heads seemed overly large, but in reality, Arturus knew, it was their bodies that were too small.

"Are they . . . starving?" Arturus asked.

Galen grunted. "They are."

"But I thought you said dyitzu didn't need to eat?"

"They don't, but they do need a tiny bit of water. It is rare to see them like this. They must have entered the aqueduct when a settling cracked it open. When the stones healed them in, they had no way to escape. If we were to keep this torch lit, I bet we would see places where they tried to force themselves out. Perhaps by clawing into the stone or throwing fireballs. Or perhaps all those have healed up, too."

"How long have they been here?" Arturus asked.

"At least for a hundred years. Perhaps more. It takes a long time for a dyitzu to starve. Perhaps as many as a thousand."

Galen dropped down from the aqueduct, his torch sputtering loudly in protest as he fell. He landed amongst the dyitzu and drew his dagger. "Help me, son." He bent down and slit the throat of a dyitzu.

Arturus drew his razor and jumped down beside his father. He began cutting their throats. He could see the dyitzu struggling to tilt their heads towards him. Some of them would breathe heavier as he approached.

They're just dyitzu. It doesn't matter.

His razor was sharp, but even so, he was surprised by how easily it sliced through their throats. Barely any blood came out. What little did was a thick, oozing substance. Some of the dyitzu were still strong enough to move their arms a little, though they weren't able to claw at him.

They'd kill you, if they could.

Arturus knew he had to kill them. If there was another quake, and Galen was right about the aqueduct being opened, then a breach in the wrong place might allow a Minotaur to come in and help them. They would have a chance to rise and kill people again. What he was doing now could very well save human lives. It didn't matter that the dyitzu were helpless.

Tears were collecting in his eyes.

Don't you dare cry, not for dyitzu.

His hands were shaking. He looked over to his father who was moving with the bubble of torchlight. Galen had no qualms about this at all. The warrior efficiently slit their throats, one after another. No hesitation.

I can be like that.

But his hands would not stop shaking. His next cut wasn't perfect. The dyitzu tried to cry out, but all it could manage was a low guttural whimper. Arturus' vision was now as shaky as his hands. He forced himself to try and finish the cut. He missed again. The whimper continued. Finally, on his third cut, he got the vocal cords. Even so, the dyitzu was still moving, twitching weakly.

Arturus sobbed. The tears he'd kept bottled up came

pouring out of his eyes. His razor fell from his unsteady hands, clattering against the stone.

The torchlight grew brighter. He felt its heat coming from above. Arturus looked up and saw his father.

"Didn't I ever tell you the story of the Scorpion and the Turtle?" Galen asked. "How the turtle takes the scorpion across the river, thinking it won't dare sting him lest they both drown. But the scorpion stings him anyway. When the turtle asked him why, the scorpion replied that it was his nature."

Arturus shook his head, more tears falling from his eyes. "This isn't right, Father. They can't resist. They can't even beg. All they can do is die."

"These dyitzu are killers, Turi. They're nothing more. It's their nature."

He could barely see his father through his tears and the brightness of the torchlight. "That's an Infidel Friend story!" Arturus shouted. "The story of evil men! Of course they'd not take mercy on a devil. They wouldn't even take mercy on a human."

Galen tossed the torch aside. It skittered across the stones before coming to rest. Galen's eyes were tempests of anger. "Stand up boy."

"I won't do this."

Galen reached down and grabbed him by the collar, dragged him to his feet, and then threw him towards the aqueduct.

"I said stand up!" Galen's voice echoed down the tunnel.

Arturus barely kept his balance. "I won't do this."

"Pick up your razor!" Galen yelled.

"No!"

"Pick it up!"

Arturus had never seen his father like this. His heart beat in his chest. Galen was advancing towards him. Arturus had never feared the man before. He had never been so keenly aware that Galen could tear him limb from limb. He had never imagined that Galen might be capable of doing such a thing, but now, looking at his father, Arturus really believed that the man would hurt him.

Arturus reached down and picked up his razor.

"Kill them, son."

Arturus looked at the dyitzu at his feet. It was there, helpless. Its face was so devoid of flesh that Arturus could hardly believe that the thing was alive. But it was alive, and Arturus could see the terror on its nearly human face. This one's stub wings were folded under its body, but he could see the muscles contracting there, as if they were the only things the dyitzu could move.

"Kill them."

The tears formed in his eyes again. His hands were shaking. "Please, father. Don't make me do this."

"Now."

Arturus knelt. He tried to control his sobs. More than any time before, he needed to be strong for his father, but he couldn't. The sobs were too powerful. The tears were dripping off of his chin and onto the dyitzu beneath him. Snot was pouring down from his nose. His crying shook him so badly that his razor's cut wasn't fatal. He tried again, and again.

"Please," Arturus begged.

But Galen would not relent. Arturus moved to the next. He was no longer able to keep his sobs silent. They echoed down the tunnel, just like his father's anger had. He killed another, and another . . . and another. Each one seemed more difficult than the last. Arturus had never done anything he'd felt was truly evil in his entire life, until today. He had never wanted so much to ignore his father's orders.

But Arturus would not disobey.

He killed them. Every last one of them. And as they died, so too did the child inside him.

— 46 —

"Should start any minute now," Q said.

The cool water of the inch deep stream flowed up and over the back heel of Ellen's tennis shoes, bringing a feeling of relief to her sore ankle. Alice was crouched the farthest forward as if she was the scout. El Cid said nothing about this, apparently content with Alice's ability to perform that duty.

Eagan and Jessica were the only two missing from the group. They were off setting up the lure, which El Cid had warned them would sound very much like a human screaming. Ellen did her best to brace herself for the impending noise.

They were only a hundred or so feet up the river from where the Cypress swamp room was, so Ellen feared that the corpses might find them again. She looked towards Rick for support. He gave her a smile, his face unworried.

A long, tortured scream echoed up through the chamber. Ellen started, her hand reaching for her pistol.

No one else was reacting.

That's the lure?

El Cid held up her hand. "We'll be working right next to the swamp, so let's give the lure a few minutes to pull them in. Even so, I should let you Harpsborough folk know that we will almost certainly have to stop working at some point to kill some corpses."

Q smiled, hefting his pick over one shoulder.

The long call never stopped, but it rhythmically became louder and then softer. After a minute or so, Ellen was able to convince herself that the cry wasn't human.

"I think I hear something," Alice said over the lure's call. "Something else."

El Cid nodded towards Q. The black man moved quickly, passing Alice by. Ellen would have been afraid to travel so quickly down the treacherous slope, but Q was as surefooted as she had ever seen. He stopped near the entrance. He waved them down with one hand and put another finger over his lips. As quietly as she could, Ellen walked down the river. Her ankle stung with each step.

They grouped around the entrance. Ellen tried to get close enough to see, but most of her view was blocked by their bodies. She found herself right behind Massan. His smell didn't bother her like it used to. The aroma seemed pleasantly familiar.

"Harpies," Q said, pointing across the Cypress swamp. "Good ear, Alice."

Alice nodded.

The harpies were calling each other. They sounded like angry birds—or angry women. Or maybe both.

"You think Jessica and Eagan see them?" Aiden asked.

Ellen pushed her way past Massan to the front and looked along Q's pointed finger. She saw them, five of them, flying near the ceiling of the tremendous chamber. They were almost obscured by the mists.

El Cid shrugged. "Well, if they don't, they'll sure as hell notice when the harpies break the lure."

"We're pretty far north for harpies," Q said.

"Or east," El Cid suggested. "They could have come from the Carrion."

Q grunted.

Their flight almost seemed graceful. As the flying devils came closer, Ellen began to see that they had human torsos. For some reason she felt bile rising in the back of her mouth.

Her eyes followed along the chamber towards where the harpies were flying. A large group of corpses had gathered there, maybe a quarter of a mile away.

That's where the lure is.

"There's five of them," Q said. "You think Eagan and Jessica are going to try and kill them on their own?"

El Cid shrugged.

Three of the harpies began to descend, lowering themselves down to the swamp in lazy spirals. The two remaining reared backwards, beating their wings and clawing at the air with their legs, hovering in place. Ellen strained to see what their faces looked like, but they were still too far away for her to discern any fine details. Their skin was more grey than human flesh was. Their feathers were a dark brown, but that was all that she could determine. She noticed that her eyes felt like they were burning.

"That's odd," Rick remarked. "Why would they leave two behind?"

El Cid gave him an approving look. "It is odd."

"I swear I can smell them." Q remarked.

"You can," El Cid said. "We're downwind."

Ellen's nose was running a little.

The first of the harpies had landed amidst the corpses. Its body was as tall as the undead it moved amongst, but its wings made it seem larger. It stalked its way through the swamp. Two others landed behind it. The trio disappeared from view.

Ellen waited. The long whine of the lure continued.

"They're coming back," Q warned.

The three did reappear. They moved clear of the wandering corpses, spread their wings, and took off amidst little bursts of water. They rejoined the pair of hovering harpies, and then all five began to fly back through the chamber.

"They didn't kill the lure." Aiden seemed surprised.

"Maybe Eagan and Jess caged it?" Q asked.

El Cid shook her head. "No, they were going to keep it raised on the cave wall. The harpies could have easily flown up and stopped it. They're scouting."

"But for whom?" Aiden's beautiful blue eyes narrowed as he gazed across the chamber. Ellen felt her heart fluttering.

"A wight." Aiden said.

El Cid nodded. "Time to go. This isn't a fight we want to pick right now. Follow me."

She led them back up the river, her steps as sure as Q's had been. Ellen's ankle gave out, and she fell to one knee. Rick and Aiden helped her to her feet.

Ellen put weight back down on it. It supported her. "I'm good," she told them.

Eagan and Jessica appeared further up the river.

"Did you see that?" Jessica asked.

"Harpies," El Cid answered. "From a wight, probably."

Jessica shook her head, her eyes wide. "No. We saw a houndrider."

El Cid's head jerked back, her pony tail bouncing with the quickness of the motion. "A Piper?"

Jessica and Eagan nodded their heads simultaneously.

"Move it!" El Cid ordered.

"What's a Piper?" Molly began to scramble up the river.

Aiden turned back for a second, his blue eyes flashing. "It's one of us."

"An Infidel Friend?" Molly asked.

"No, not an Infidel Friend," Aiden answered. "One of us. A human. A necromancer."

"Here we are," Galen said, extinguishing his torch. "Help me open this door."

Arturus remembered when the darkness used to bother him. When he'd first entered the Carrion, he'd seen devils in every shadow. Now it was bright rooms that he wished to avoid. It was he, Arturus, who hid in the shadows, and the devils that needed light. He was the heartless killer. They were the victims.

He heard the scrape of metal on stone as someone brought Galen's crow bar to bear on the stone. Then there was the sound of stone grating on stone. Light, bright light, poured into the tunnel. Sounds came in too, as if there were thousands of people working the stone of the chambers beyond. Arturus moved forward, letting the light pour over him, waiting for his eyes to adjust.

"Oh," Johnny said. "Oh God. Oh fucking God."

Arturus' eyes were having trouble focusing. It looked as if the chamber beyond were miles deep.

Shit. It is miles deep.

"Close it," Galen said. "Very slowly. Leave it just a crack open."

Arturus added his weight to Aaron and Johnny's, pushing the door.

"That's good," Galen said.

A crack, in this case, was large enough for one of them to put their heads through. Arturus did just that. He could feel the others crowding in around him.

"What do you see?" Dakota asked.

There were human workers in the chamber. Thousands. Maybe hundreds of thousands. It looked as if they were carving their way miles down through the stone. They lined the walls, like the hordes of silverleg spiders had, moving on forests of woodstone scaffolding. Perhaps they were trying to expand that way too, or maybe they were just fighting the natural tendency of the rock to heal. Lines of them formed up in the base of the chamber, each person looking no larger than a single grain of threshed devilwheat. That many people would be able to move tons of rock in seconds, Arturus imagined.

Standing amongst them, acting as overseers, were dyitzu. Here and there about the chamber, Icanitzu and harpies flew. Some of the harpies had human riders. There were hounds on the ground who also had men mounted on their backs.

"Oh shit," Johnny's voice came from above him. "How could there be so many people?"

Arturus looked up. Dakota was standing to his right, carrying Johnny on his shoulders.

When did those two become friends?

"Keep your head down, Turi," Johnny said.

"Tu-El," Galen said, his fingers slowly stroking his beard. "That's what they're digging for."

"That's the Archdevil you said was tied to Lucreas?" Aaron asked.

"Yes."

"And you said the Infidel collapsed an entire section of Hell on top of Tu-El."

"Yes."

"And was it this section?" Aaron's voice was full of trepidation.

"Yes."

"And if they find him?"

"There was a time, Aaron, when the ancients almost had Hell whipped. They had conquered entire regions of it with their armies. They had teased from the stones themselves the very secrets of the Architect. They had warped chambers into giant growing fields of wheat and fruit. They had herds of hounds they raised for slaughter. The Infidel and Tu-El fought at that time, when humankind was at its peak. Now, very little would be in Tu-El's way. Maybe the Infidel and his people can stop him. Maybe they can't."

"Assuming they can't?" Aaron asked.

"We die."

For a few moments no one said anything. Arturus watched the slaves work away at the stone.

"Well," Johnny said, "it's a good thing they haven't found Tu-El yet."

"How can you be sure?" Dakota asked.

"Because if they had found him, they wouldn't still be digging."

Dakota snorted. "Good point, little man. Good point."

"Wait," Johnny said, shifting on Dakota's back. "What are they doing over there? To your left Turi. Along that wall."

Arturus looked out across the masses of people to see what Johnny was talking about. "I think those are bridges . . ."

"Get back, Johnny," Galen's voice was dead even. "Turi, drop further down."

Arturus knelt lower, looking at the bridges. They jutted out from the wall, and though several were low enough that they could have had supporting pillars, none did. Arturus could see the whetstone beams reaching up and over like a skeleton to help support the stones that would be placed upon them. For the bridges to stay up, Arturus imagined that they must have similar whetstone support structures inside the wall they were emerging from. None of them were completed, most stopping after going only a few hundred feet into the cavern.

Maybe they don't have pillars because they're going to dig the ground out from under them.

The bridges were thickest next to the walls they sprung from, but they narrowed, their bases shrinking, the further out they went.

Galen's body armor dug into Arturus' back as the man put his head out through the door.

"Do you see the beams, dad?" Arturus asked.

"Made of whetstone. Not stronger than clearsteel cabling, but almost as good."

Arturus frowned. "Easier to make?"

"Easier to salvage."

Arturus watched a work crew laying a stone. There was a row of bridges, ten of them, and each of them were at exactly the same level of completion. After that crew finished, they were brought to the next bridge. They performed the exact same task.

That makes no sense. Why wouldn't they just lay more stones on their bridge?

As Arturus watched, he began to realize that all of the work crews were working in this way, each group performing the same single task over and over again on different bridges.

And stranger yet, none of the bridges had been finished. After they'd been built to be about one hundred and fifty yards long, construction on them ceased.

What in the Hell are those bridges supposed to be for?

"Enough," Galen ordered. "Head out, son. We're closing the door. We'll have to exit farther down."

The door closed, leaving Arturus in the comfort of darkness once again.

Aiden stood guard by the door while the other infidels gathered their packs and equipment.

"What's the plan, Cid?" Q asked while rolling up his bedroll.

"This isn't a fight we want," El Cid answered. "There's no way we can face their main force. Even if they don't have control over any of the corpses, which is unlikely, they can at least retreat into the Cypress swamp. As for us, we're too quick for them to bring their main force to bear. The plan is to kill as many harpies as possible, make the Piper realize we're in a stalemate. As soon as we can verify we're not being hunted, then we're going to hoof it to Harpsborough."

Jessica had Aiden's pack ready to go, so she handed it to the warrior. Jessica held her M-16 at the ready, taking up watch for a brief moment while Aiden put on the pack. As soon as Aiden was ready again, Jessica dropped her guard, moving back towards the center of the room to prepare her own equipment.

"Did you see how they took turns?" Rick asked Ellen.

Ellen nodded. "Why aren't the Harpsborough hunters like this?"

Rick shrugged. "Probably because they weren't trained by the Infidel."

Ellen saw that Molly was still fixated on Aiden.

She probably can't help but want to be with him.

Ellen's eyes started to burn.

"I can smell them," Aiden warned.

"Let's go," El Cid ordered. "Move out."

Q led them out of their camp's chamber, bringing them into the wilds at a brisk pace. Ellen saw a sinfruit vine down one corridor. Its fruit were ripe and heavy.

Shame there's no time to pick them.

"Piper has got to have a wight in order to be controlling all those corpses," Eagan suggested while Q led them up a stone staircase.

"It'd have to be an old one," Q shot back.

"Why?" Ellen asked.

"The older a wight is, the more undead it can control," El Cid answered. "Each person it kills rises as a corpse that does it's bidding, to a point."

"Could just as easily be a Minotaur," Jessica suggested. "The Piper was riding a hound after all."

"Could be both," El Cid suggested.

Rick nodded.

The burning sensation in Ellen's eyes was getting worse.

"They're close," Aiden warned. "I can hear four or five, I think."

Ellen could hear their calls. They were strangely human at times. At other times, they sounded like hawks.

"Break up," El Cid said. "We don't want to lose any of our Harpsborough friends. I'll take them to safety. Kill as many harpies as you can. Aiden, stay with me."

"We saw a male with the Piper," Eagan reported. "Six winger. Be careful."

Q whistled.

Q, Eagan, and Jessica split away. Aiden knelt on the ground while El Cid waved the group onwards. Ellen was too curious to leave, however, so she lingered in the exit hallway. Molly did as well.

El Cid held Aiden's face in her hands. She leaned down and kissed him on the forehead. "Fuck 'em up, baby."

Aiden smiled, drawing the sword that was sheathed behind his pack. The blade was long and thin, made out of what seemed like a blue tinted glass. It reminded Ellen of the chess pieces that Arturus had made, with a blue glittering liquid elegantly swirling amidst the rest of the transparent substance. The hilt of the thing was golden, an eagle etched into the crosspiece. Aiden stood still, like a statue, his sword held at the ready in his right hand.

El Cid left him as the harpies began pouring into the room. As she passed between Ellen and Molly, she reached out and hooked them by the shoulders. "This way, ladies."

Aiden came alive, his sword moving in a blur, and the harpies' screams of pain and terror filled the corridors. Ellen wanted to stay, but El Cid was pulling her away.

47

Hidalgo and Caval leapt into the dried out riverbed Martin and his hunters were taking refuge in.

"I thought you said the corpsemen wouldn't see you!" Martin shouted as a bullet skipped over his head.

Across the chamber, the corpsemen were pouring in, taking cover behind a copse of dead hungerleaf trees.

"Corpse eaters, them not be seeing me!" Hidalgo shouted. "Them be seeing Caval."

There were maybe three hundred dried up trees out there, and it seemed like there was a corpse eater behind each one of them.

"God damn it!" Constance shouted. "Sir, they've got us outnumbered. Shall we withdraw?"

Run away, he means. Then they'll know Katie is right. They'll know I'm no fighter.

Martin felt how badly his hands were shaking. Blood dripped onto his arm. He looked above him, but then realized it was coming from his own nose.

Hell of a time for a nose bleed.

His enemies were men who didn't fear death. Why should they? They were half dead already. He'd seen them as they took cover amongst the trees. They'd half shambled, half run, to their positions. Somehow, the fact that they were alive and still rotting made them worse than normal corpses.

And they could think. That made them much, much worse.

We've got to run.

Another bullet skipped by.

It's not safe to.

He looked over at his soldiers. They were all looking towards him. None of them were peeking over the ridge.

But we have to run.

Chelsea reached over and grabbed his arm. "Are you okay? You almost look like one of them."

"Katie was right," Martin said. "We have to run."

More bullets.

"I thought there was only supposed to be twenty of them?" one of Constance's blue shirted men shouted.

"That's what Caval told us!" Martin screamed back, looking over to the former corpseman.

Caval was hunkered down, shoulders hunched, his face a mask of terror.

He was hallucinating half the damn time anyway.

Chelsea's hand squeezed him tightly, bringing his attention back to her.

She smiled. "I believe in you."

Martin was reminded of an old show tune, one that his grandfather had loved.

It wouldn't be make believe, if you believed in me.

More bullets skipped by. Martin looked to his soldiers to see which of them had been foolish enough to put their heads over the edge of the riverbed. None of them had.

Well, what the hell are they shooting at then?

He remembered how jumpy Caval had been. These corpse eaters weren't men who were fearless. They were men who had the rot.

What the hell was I thinking?

Martin peeked his head over the river bank. They were still there, hiding behind the trees. In the time that Martin's men hadn't shown their faces, the corpsemen could have probably walked over to their river and slaughtered them all.

I have got to get better at this.

Martin ducked back down. "Guys, take off your hoodies. Wave them over the edge!"

"What?" Constance shouted.

Martin took off his hoodie and waved it over his head. "Do this!"

A hail of bullets sang through the air.

"They're all tripping," Martin explained. "they'll shoot at

anything."

One bullet ricocheted along the stones, bouncing right by his head.

Jesus.

His soldiers complied.

After another hail of bullets, Martin dared to take a second look over the stone bank. They were still coming, but they seemed to be running out of ammunition.

"Fire!" Martin ordered.

His soldiers stood as one, weapons in their hands. The enemy was coming fast. Their run was stilted, as if their legs had already been stiffened by death. The rifle shots started to mow them down. The shotgun booms of Constance's men were less effective.

"Hold your shotgun fire until they're close!" Martin yelled.

Maybe fifty of them had started the charge. They were getting closer.

Forty feet.

Thirty feet.

"Shotguns!" Martin yelled.

Twenty feet.

Ten.

The blasts went off. A few corpsemen came toppling down into the riverbed. Martin thought that surely the one next to him was completely dead, but slowly, it started to stand. It was shaking, probably hurt from the fall. Martin realized he hadn't fired a shot yet. He pointed his rifle at the creature and pulled the trigger. It dropped.

Martin was seeing bright spots on the edge of his vision.

I'm not breathing.

For a brief second, he thought he was dead, but then he took in a breath. More blood was coming out from his nose.

"There's plenty more still up there," Constance shouted.

Chelsea was right, he was in bad shape. Without his hoodie, and with blood pouring out of his nose, he probably looked even more like the enemy.

They're on hallucinogens.

"Keep waving those hoodies!" Martin yelled. "Hidalgo, Huxley, Ben, you're with me. Constance, you're in charge here."

Huxley ran up next to him as they followed the riverbed out

of the chamber. "Where we headed?"

Martin let the blood drip down his face. He could taste it on his lips. "Downriver, Hux. Downriver."

Galen's firerock slammed against the whetstone pipe sending out a bell-like sound and creating a rain of sparks. His torch sprang back to life. The aqueduct bent to the right, but Galen had stopped them where another service corridor continued forward.

"What's this?" Johnny asked.

Galen walked up to the bend and looked at some letters etched into the wall. The branching service corridor was only about eight feet tall, and the bulk of it was filled with a single pipe. They would have to walk single file if they were to go that way.

"It's for overflow," Galen said. "It shunted the excess water into the Erebus. The aqueduct itself leads right into the city. We probably don't want to go there. I didn't mean to take us out so close to the River of Darkness, but there are no other good exits."

Johnny frowned. "Well why didn't they just use water from the Erebus?"

"Because the Erebus isn't that kind of river," Galen answered.

With his torch still lit, Galen took them down the service corridor. The construction here seemed older than in the aqueduct proper. Small, grey stone bricks were fitted together, almost haphazardly. The builders of this corridor had used those small stone bricks which reminded Arturus of skulls.

Wait a minute.

Arturus stopped everyone and turned to look at one of the skull stones.

"Galen!" Arturus said. "Look."

The torchlight stopped. Galen moved towards him, shuffling past Johnny to get the torch up to where Arturus stood.

"I'd always thought these looked like skulls," Arturus said. "But now they actually do. See? The ancients actually carved in shallow eye sockets."

Galen took in a deep breath. "We're closer than we thought."

"To what?" Johnny asked.

"To the Erebus. On the far side of the River of Darkness is Sheol. Reality in Sheol is different. The rooms change pending on what you think they are. Men must gather round each other and try to imagine the same reality into the hell they're in. These stones were indeed carved to look like skulls, but not with hammer and chisel and rustrock, but with the minds of thousands of workers who saw the same illusion as you."

Arturus stepped back from the skull stone, running into the pipe behind him. He suddenly felt claustrophobic.

"Does that put us in any danger?" Aaron asked.

"A little," Galen said. "Reality is very resilient, still. But what it really means is that you should listen carefully to Hellsong. As always, you can hear in it what you wish to . . . but when this close to Sheol, you can make others hear your music as well."

Johnny smiled. "Good. I hope you guys like 'Fat Bottomed Girls.'"

Dakota snickered.

Galen is lying. There is great danger here. We could believe ourselves to death, if we got in the wrong mindset.

But then he realized that, because they all believed Galen, in a way he was telling the truth. If they truly believed they couldn't hurt themselves with thoughts, then that would become their reality. What did you call it when a man lies, but the lie is self-fulfilling? What kind of dishonesty is that?

It reminded him of Father Klein and his sermons. In some way, even the parts of Hell not subjected to Sheol's subjectivity could be affected by self-fulfilling thoughts. Maybe that's what Klein understood about Faith. Maybe he was lying to Harpsborough in the same way that Galen was lying about this place.

But what if the lies in either place became harmful? How could one ever know the truth, if you had given up reason to gain Faith? The ideas troubled him as they made their way down the long corridor.

He was almost surprised when Galen stopped them. There was a service ladder that led up to a hatchway at the top of the eight foot corridor. Galen climbed up it and worked on the hatch. It had a wheel descending from it which Galen turned three times. Then he readied his MP5 in one hand and pushed up with the other. The hatch opened, and Galen stuck his head through it.

"Okay," he said. "It's clear. Stay behind, fellows. Turi and I are going to scout out the entrance to the City of Blood and Stone. We'll be back for you after we find it and some ambush spots."

Dakota shook his head. "I'm going with you."

Galen shrugged. "So be it."

The burning in Ellen's eyes got better as El Cid led them forward. The Infidel Friend's pace was quick, but not a run. It reminded her very much of the pace that Rick had set for them through the Cypress swamp. Ellen could feel her ankle swelling, but she felt no pain at all.

The wilds of Hell were filled with sounds. The repeated three shot bursts of the Infidel Friend weapons mixed with the wailing of the harpies and the occasional shouts between Eagan, Jessica and Q. Every once in a while, Ellen would see one of the other Infidel Friend through a long corridor or on the other side of a large room. Always they were moving, their assault rifles held at the ready.

Suddenly the burning got worse.

El Cid stopped.

There was a ruffling of feathers. Molly and Alice looked behind them, but Ellen followed El Cid's lead. El Cid seemed to think the sound was coming from the tunnels ahead, or at least that was where she was focused. The chamber they were in was fairly large, almost fifty feet wide. The stones here were almost four feet tall and were made of a blue colored hellstone. There were three exits to the room. Two behind and one ahead.

The harpy came through the exit ahead. It was radically different from the others.

Its face and long slender torso were masculine. It had to bend down and pull its wings back in order to enter the chamber. It was probably eight feet tall with brown patchy hair on its head. Its arms were long and spindly. Its manhood was a gross, swollen thing, emerging out of a nest of feathers and dangling between its backward jointed legs.

This one had more wings than the others. Two large ones

sprouted up from its shoulders, the same as with the female harpies, but four more wings, slightly smaller, came out from its back—one set from about midway down its torso and another from the level of its hips.

Its eyes lacked any iris and were all black. When its lips curled back into a rictus grin, Ellen could see its yellow and brown broken teeth.

"Stay back," El Cid warned as she advanced toward the thing.

El Cid seemed so small before the tremendous male harpy. It spread its wings out wide, making it seem even larger.

"I'm with you," Rick warned the Infidel Friend.

El Cid nodded and began angling towards the left side of the room. Rick moved to the right.

El Cid raised her M-16 and began firing quick three shot bursts. The male harpy screamed, its voice deeper and more birdlike than the others. It folded its top wings over and in front of itself, using them as a shield. The bullet impacts caused small eruptions of feathers and blood. The harpy started advancing towards El Cid.

Rick opened fire from behind, his shotgun booming. Ellen could tell from the pattern of blood spurting out of the thing's back that Rick was firing slugs. The harpy wheeled around, folding its middle wings behind its back and keeping its top wings forward. It rushed towards Rick, but El Cid was faster.

She tossed her assault rifle aside and sprinted at the beast. She leapt up, wrapping her legs around its long torso between its bottom and middle sets of wings.

Molly shouted suddenly.

Ellen turned to see a female harpy emerge from the passageway behind her. She tried to spin away from it, but her ankle gave out and she dropped to the ground.

The harpy advanced, its grey, wrinkled breasts wobbling as it approached. Molly, still shouting, let loose a round of buckshot. The shotgun blast caused the harpy to drop back a step, then it pushed its wings and arms forward, and with a powerful backward thrust, launched itself towards Molly.

Molly fired another shot, hitting it full in the face. She ducked and spun away, staying clear of the thing's reaching arms, but still getting knocked to the ground by an outstretched wing. The harpy reached out to claw at Ellen. Its nails were long, dark and yellow. They grew out from the entire top half of its fingers, sloping down into a single point.

Massan rushed forward, hitting it in the face with his pack. Molly fired up at it from where she lay on the ground, knocking it off balance. Another attack from Massan sent it sprawling to the floor.

Ellen struggled up to her feet, looking back towards Rick and El Cid. Rick was dancing away from the swaying beast, trying to stay out of range. His shotgun had been knocked across the room, and he was using his rifle as a club. El Cid was still on its back, her legs wrapped around its torso. She was grabbing on to the middle wing on its right side. With her right hand, she gripped some of its feathers. She thrust her left hand through the wing, pushing her arm in until it was shoulder deep. Then she retracted her elbow, forcing the wing back into her armpit and freeing her other hand. The male harpy turned for a second, trying to claw at her. El Cid fended off the attack with her now free right hand. Rick took the opportunity to hit the thing in the face with the butt of his rifle. When the male harpy turned back to him, Rick retreated towards his shotgun.

As the male harpy moved forward, El Cid let go of the creature's torso with her left leg, and swung it over so that her legs enveloped the middle wing at its base. She now had her entire body wrapping up that wing, almost in a fetal position. She straightened her body. The wing straightened with her. She began to arch the wing backward. The male harpy leaned its head back, screaming in pain at the ceiling. Ellen could see El Cid shaking with the effort. With a tremendous pop, the wing snapped at its middle joint.

Another blast from Molly brought Ellen's attention away from El Cid. The female harpy had risen. Massan was sprawled across the floor. The creature took Molly's shotgun blast to its chest without care. Blood spurted out of its torso from the buckshot as it reached down with its claws towards Massan. Alice's pistol rang out. The bullet hit the harpy directly in the eye. It also screamed with pain, covering its face with a wing. Massan stood quickly and continued to beat at it. Molly let another blast go.

El Cid was still climbing on the harpy. The thing was ignoring Rick's blows now, and was reaching back to try and hurt the Infidel Friend. She released the broken wing and wrapped up the shoulder of the reaching harpy with her left arm. She let go with her legs, her weight pulling the harpy downward, doubling it over at the waist. For a brief moment, her feet touched the ground, then El Cid leapt up, her left arm still trapping the harpy's shoulder. With her right, she encircled the harpy's neck as well. It stood up tall, bringing El Cid up with it. Rick dove at its legs, driving them together. The male Harpy toppled over backwards.

El Cid landed, mounted on top of the thing, her left leg intertwined with its broken wing. She beat at the male harpy's face with her fists, hitting it with quick snapping punches, bouncing the harpy's head into the stone.

It let out its loudest call yet, a shout of deep fury which shook Ellen's insides. Then it opened its mouth wider still and let loose a sudden exhalation of air. The putrid stench was so vile that Ellen almost vomited from across the room. She could see flecks of green phlegm spewing up into El Cid's face as the male harpy breathed. Ellen could barely keep her eyes open. El Cid was visibly affected. She covered her eyes with one of her forearms. Then El Cid let loose her own scream, a high pitched vitriolic call.

For a brief second, the male Harpy seemed surprised by the Infidel Friend's ability to resist its rotten breath. Then it took El Cid's vomit full in the face. El Cid wretched again, covering the thing's eyes completely with her bile. The harpy gurgled, choking on the fluid, and covered its eyes with its hands. With a renewed fury, El Cid pounded at the thing with a rain of alternating elbows. Blood began to spew up from the harpy's face as her relentless assault continued.

The battle with the female harpy was heading her way. Ellen moved quickly to the side, trying to stay clear of the thing's batting wings. Once again it had managed to force Massan to the floor. Alice emptied her pistol's clip into the things knee. The female harpy attempted to advance, but wobbled awkwardly. Its wounded knee failed to support its weight and it dropped to the ground. Molly fired another shell while Alice changed clips.

Rick had mounted the harpy now too, his own eyes half-closed against the noxious vapors. His knee was placed firmly on the thing's testicles, and his right leg was straightened and out to one side. He had his knife in one hand, and was driving it down into the thing's abdomen. Whatever flesh the male harpy possessed was tougher than a human's because it took Rick several strikes before he got the knife in hilt deep. Then he began to saw the male harpy's belly open.

"Ellen," Rick shouted, "get my shotgun, load it with buckshot."

The female harpy was moving as best it could on one leg and one arm. Its wings and free arm still struggled to fend off Massan's attacks. At some point he had discarded his pack in favor of using his rifle as a club. Massan stepped in closer to the thing, rifle raised high. The harpy responded, using its wings to propel itself at him in a desperate lunge. It got its weight beneath Massan and flapped its wings again, throwing him across the room. Massan impacted headfirst into a stone wall. He collapsed to the ground, blood pouring across one shoulder from a wound on the back of his head. Trying to stand, Massan pushed himself up the wall. His balance failed him, and he crumpled sideways to the ground. He tried again, but his legs would not hold him up.

Ellen moved around the battle and rushed as fast as her wounded ankle would allow towards Rick's shotgun. She picked it up and looked behind her.

The male harpy was bucking wildly. Rick and El Cid were keeping it down, but the motion was causing El Cid to have trouble getting at it with her elbows. Ellen rushed over to Rick's pack and opened his ammo pouch. With shaking hands, she loaded the shotgun full of twelve gauge shells.

Molly had stepped forward, brandishing her shotgun over her head to take Rick's place. The harpy's claw ripped open her abdomen. Blood spilled out. Molly shoved her shotgun into its chest and fired. It fell back and Alice released a clip into the female harpy's remaining leg. It fell on its stomach. Molly, paying no heed to her wound, emptied round after round of buckshot into the thing. One of the ricocheting balls of buckshot hit Ellen in the arm. She saw the blood welling out of the wound, soaking into her white cotton shirt.

"Now!" Rick shouted at her, holding up one hand.

She was about to toss him the weapon, but the male harpy bucked and Rick had to grab both of its legs to keep it from escaping.

Ellen rushed over, dancing by one of its flapping wings, and shoved the shotgun into wound Rick had made.

"Clear!" Rick shouted.

El Cid stopped mid elbow strike and wrapped up the male harpy's right arm and neck. Then she pulled her body off to one side, like a wrestler pinning her oversized opponent.

Ellen held down the trigger and cocked the shotgun again and again, filling the male harpy's body with buckshot. It tried to scream once more, but this time only blood fountained up from its mouth. Finally, the shotgun was out of shells. Ellen fell back. The male harpy had stopped moving.

The female harpy also appeared dead. Everyone looked to El Cid as she stood.

She was covered in feathers. Her own vomit had drenched her hair and was dripping down her ripped clothing. Her ponytail had been completely undone, and some of her hair had been ripped out in the struggle. An errant blow had bloodied her lip and was causing some swelling on the left side of her face. Tears and snot, not from sorrow or pain, but from the vapors of the harpy's breath, poured down her face. Her fists and elbows were covered with harpy blood. Her chest rose and fell with her quickened breath.

Ellen had never seen anyone more powerful than this girl, at least, not since she'd seen Cris.

"I," El Cid said, "need a fucking bath."

48

Martin, Hidalgo, Huxley, and Ben crept into the room. There the dead copse of Hungerleaf trees was, just like Martin had hoped it would be. More gunshots were being fired, and it sounded like they were coming from his men in the riverbed.

"Good navigating, sir!" Huxley whispered. "We're right behind 'em!"

"You be careful," Hidalgo said.

With their hoodies off, Martin hoped they would look enough like their enemies to pass as one of them. He walked amongst the trees, his pistol drawn. He saw the back of one of the corpsemen. This man had no shirt on at all. His skin was mottled with dead patches. They almost seemed like stripes along the man's back. The most revolting parts of the skin appeared where dead flesh met live flesh. There pus filled sores and infected skin bubbled up into oozing masses. The smell was pretty bad. Martin shot him in the back of the head.

He looked around to see if any of the other corpsemen had noticed. They had not. They didn't even look. If anything, Martin's shot encouraged a few more to fire towards the river.

Thank God these people are stoned out of their minds.

Martin waved Hidalgo, Huxley and Ben in.

Martin moved amongst the trees, finding another victim. This one had chunks of his leg missing. His khaki pants were ripped where his skin had been torn away. Like the previous man, he was shirtless, and his body's flesh was also engaged in the same struggle between life and undeath. Martin shot him too.

He heard a shout, and when he looked back, he saw Ben being accosted by the striped corpseman he'd shot earlier.

What? I killed him. I know I did. I shot him in the back of the . . .

Ben fell to the ground, his throat pumping out blood from where the corpse eater had bit him. Hidalgo's silver colored arrows whistled through the air, one after another, burying themselves into both Ben and the corpseman. Hidalgo approached, silent as death, moving up to the bodies he'd just shot. Ben started to rise as a corpse, his body twitching. Before this new undead thing could stand, Hidalgo put his foot on it. He grabbed one of his arrows in the dead man's chest, and ripped it, along with some blood and a few chunks of an organ, out. Ben's body stopped twitching. Hidalgo nocked the bloody arrow, looking about for another target.

The hell do you make your arrows out of?

"Stay behind me," Martin ordered. "Kill everyone I kill. Pretty much everybody here is going to have to die twice."

They moved through the trees together, with Martin killing the corpse eaters, and Hidalgo and Huxley killing the corpses that rose. Martin had brought five clips, but he had the feeling he was going to run out of bullets.

The corpsemen began wailing. They could tell that something was wrong, but they didn't seem to know exactly what.

One of them, who looked mostly alive except for a few sores on his face, shouted out. "Who's in charge?"

"I am," Martin answered, then gunned the man down.

The amount of gunfire coming from the corpse eaters had decreased dramatically.

Have we killed that many of them?

He saw a corpseman to his left. The man had tossed his gun aside.

No. More of them are running out of bullets.

"Put your hoodie back on," Martin ordered Huxley as he moved towards the right side of the copse of trees.

"What?"

"You heard me, Hux." Then Martin, having hid behind a stump, shouted out as loud as he could. "Alright, Constance, they're almost out of bullets. Charge!"

Shouting in unison, the Harpsborough Hunters, along with a dozen or so blue shirted compatriots, emerged from the riverbed. The corpsemen, many out of bullets, dropped their rifles and ran, moving out from their cover. Shotgun and rifle blasts began to tear them down.

"Don't forget!" Martin cried over the havoc, "kill every enemy twice!"

Galen closed the hatch after Dakota exited. Arturus could hear Aaron turning the wheel that sealed it from within the corridor below.

We won't be able to get back in unless he lets us.

This area was covered in a darkness every bit as deep as what they'd experienced in the service corridor, but unlike the aqueduct, the darkness was pierced by intermittent flashes of intense blue light. They were coming from a passage to Arturus' left. Mist clung to the ground of that tunnel, almost waste high.

"It's like lightning," Dakota whispered.

For a moment the corridor lit up, and in that moment, Arturus could see Dakota's awed face.

"That's the Erebus, isn't it?" Dakota asked.

There was another series of blue bursts.

"Isn't it?" Dakota asked again.

"Yes." Galen's answer was strangely reluctant. "Follow me."

"No." Dakota answered.

Arturus stopped, surprised by his reply.

The sudden flashes of light were disorienting.

Galen was facing Dakota as if the man were an enemy. "There is no reason to do this, Dakota."

No reason to do what?

"You and I both got the same orders from Calimay," Dakota insisted. "If you try and go back now, she won't let you go home. And you know you need a guide to get down the Lethe offshoot."

In another flash of light, Arturus saw that Galen's hand was on his pistol. "You don't have to make it back, Dakota."

"If I don't make it back, you don't get a guide. You think she'll help you if you come back with all your people alive, but with both me and Tamara dead?"

"Yes."

"Bullshit. Send Turi, Galen."

"No," Galen's voice was no longer calm or collected. "I will not send my son to where the Furies can catch him. I know they'll see him. They're so sensitive they'll even kill devil controlled corpses. My son is at least half human."

"That might not matter. Send him across the Erebus. If the Furies come, he can run. Can't you see! Galen, that's why the Infidel wants him. That's why Maab wants him. He can bring back the weapon from Sheol."

There was a sudden terrible crack. It sounded like bone running against stone. In the next moment of light, Arturus saw Dakota on the ground. Blood was coming from his head.

"Come with me, Turi," Galen ordered. "You don't have to go."

My destiny.

"Come!"

The light came and went again. Arturus saw his father standing over the unmoving Dakota.

"Turi!"

"I'm sorry, father," Arturus said, "but you're going to have to stay there."

Galen started to move forward, but stopped. "Come here, son! Don't go. You're too close already. No force can resist a Fury. Not me, not a Minotaur. Not even a Nephilim. I won't be able to protect you. Stay away from the Erebus. There's no way to know how close they'll be."

"I'm sorry."

"I can't protect you from a Fury." Galen's voice was desperate. "I spent fourteen years raising you. I will *not* lose you now."

"You brought me to the Carrion, father. If you hadn't been comfortable with me dying, you shouldn't have done that."

Another flash of blue.

Arturus headed towards the light.

Martin and his troops stalked through the halls beyond the dead hungerleaf trees. Caval and Hidalgo led them forward, unerringly, through the low circular tunnels. They reminded Martin of drain pipes, only they were slightly larger.

"This is it," Caval reported, pointing to an arched entryway.

Martin held up a hand to stop his hunters and moved

forward. Huxley and Hidalgo crept after him. The three of them paused under the arch.

The room beyond the entryway was perfectly circular and about fifty feet tall. The floor was made of grey cobblestones, smooth in the way that river rocks had been in the old world. Towards the center of that cobbled area, which was perhaps one hundred yards in diameter, was a small temple.

It was not a temple in the traditional sense, seeming almost Greek in construction. Like the room, it too was perfectly circular. It had an outer wall of sorts, made up of a series of pillars, and an inner wall made out of fitted marble bricks. There was a single entrance which Martin could not see through.

A few of the corpsemen were in the chamber. Some almost certainly had the stilling. Martin knew how they looked from Benson. They seemed to be far too thin to be alive. There was another pair still moving. One was lying down, fiddling with the cobblestones, stacking them on top of each other in the same way that a child might have, oddly oblivious to the second corpseman who was diligently eating his leg.

For a second, Martin thought that the cannibal might have been only a corpse, but the reality was far more sickening to him. The cannibal had pink flesh in places, like those he'd killed amongst the hungerleaf trees. Martin strode boldly into the room, the cobblestones grinding together under his feet. None of the corpsemen responded to him.

Slowly, Martin's men fanned out into the room behind him.

Martin stopped by the pair of corpses. He shot the cannibal first. If the other noticed, he did not show it. The corpseman lifted up a cobble that had fallen from his mound and added it back on. It fell again. Martin waited politely for the man to get it to stick before he shot him. Huxley fired a second shot, re-killing the cannibal. A few moments later, he re-killed the builder too.

Chelsea and Constance walked up next to Martin. The vibrations of their footsteps caused the rock mound to tumble. Martin sighed.

"This is unholy," Constance said.

Chelsea nodded, her blue eyes on the pair of dead men.

"Over here, sir!" A hunter named Marcus called.

Martin looked across the chamber to where he was pointing. A carrion barrier lay there, completely destroyed.

Caval walked up beside him.

"Is that the wall you were talking about? The one your men took down?" Martin asked Caval.

Caval nodded.

"God damn," Martin said. "We're going to have to rebuild that quickly. Though I don't suppose it's too dangerous if the Carrion's devils didn't come in and kill these guys. Any idea how long it's been down?"

Caval grimaced. "I'm sorry Martin. Time didn't really make sense to me then, when the corpsedust had me."

Martin turned to his men. "Search the rest of the chamber! Hidalgo, Huxley, Chelsea, you're with me. I want to see what's in that temple."

Martin's boots ground more cobblestones together as he crossed the distance. He could see into the temple now. There was a single circular bench inside that lined the temple's inside wall. Seated on it were some men which might have been corpses, or could have been corpsemen. Martin couldn't tell. He opened fire. Hidalgo, Huxley and Chelsea followed suit.

None of the corpsemen even bothered to move as the bullets tore through them. Black, half-congealed blood spewed forth from their bodies. Chelsea's shotgun left huge craters in its victims, allowing Martin to see the corpsemen's organs.

The ones whose eyes kept blinking, Martin realized, were the corpsemen. The others had been undead for some time. After another round of gunfire Martin was confident that their enemies had been destroyed, though a few were still twitching.

This is the worst job I've had in my life.

And that was saying a lot for Martin, because he'd once worked in waste management.

"This one here," Chelsea was saying. "I think he was the leader." She bent down by the body and looked at his arm. "Martin, do you see this?"

The body had an odd tattoo on its shoulder. It was of a man who appeared to be encased in rock from the waist down with his hands raised in the air—like he was praying, or diving upwards.

I've seen that before . . . but where?

"Martin, do you know who else has that tattoo?" Chelsea asked.

Not on Hidalgo, but I have seen it before.

"Father Klein does," Chelsea said. "He was trying to keep it secret. I was in the church late one night about a year ago. When he exited his sleeping chamber, he was changing his shirt. He tried to cover it, but I saw it. It was too weird a symbol to forget."

Klein? What could he have to do with the corpsemen? What does he have to hide? Mark my words, Father or no Father, he's going to be telling me.

"Martin, Chelsea, you should be looking at this one," Hidalgo said. "He be still alive, a little. And I think he be humming."

Martin moved closer as Chelsea knelt by the corpse.

"Oh, God," Chelsea said. "Look at his legs."

The man's pants were so tattered that they ended at his mid-thigh, revealing a pair of skinless legs. The exposed muscles were dark grey, almost black, and so smooth that they looked oddly metallic. Perhaps one of the corpsemen had been eating off of this one.

Martin leaned forward to examine it. The thing's skin was unusually pale. As Martin got closer, he noticed that the face was colored like marble, with light blue veins running under the skin in way that made them look like a pattern in stone. This corpse showed no signs of rot. The body's eyes were closed, and its head leaned back against the wall of the temple as if in peaceful repose. There was something about the man's face that bothered Martin. Something that was hauntingly familiar.

"His skin looks like marble." Martin said.

Huxley leaned in beside Martin, and picked something up out of its mutilated lap. It was a spent bullet.

Martin shook his head and went back to inspecting the corpse. Hidalgo had been right, this one was still alive, but barely. Its throat was vibrating a little. Martin looked again at the thing's face. He was sure he'd seen it before. Death had changed the man's features dramatically. The cheeks had sunken in, the complexion was different, but the man was . . .

Kyle.

"It's Kyle," Martin said.

Chelsea's lips parted. "Oh no! Please be okay, please be okay." She put her hands on Kyle's cheeks.

Kyle, or what was left of him, was still breathing.

"You be knowing this one?" Hidalgo asked.

Martin nodded. The fellow was still breathing, though with what had happened to his legs, Martin wasn't sure how. Chelsea stepped back, her hands covering her mouth, her eyes glistening.

Wait. He's not just breathing, he's Humming.

Martin tried to listen.

"Hmm . . . hmm hm hm. Hhm dum dum."

"You've got to be okay," Chelsea was saying. "Martin, we have to take him back to Harpsborough. We can feed him the sinfruit juice. He can tell us what happened to the expedition. Tell us if Aaron is okay."

Kyle's eyelids fluttered open. *"Ezekiel cried, 'Dem dry bones!'"*

Martin leapt back and Huxley let out a high pitched scream. The eyes were all black, like a dyitzu's.

That is not *Kyle.*

The body lunged forward, its head colliding with Huxley's. The scream was cut short. Huxley collapsed backward to the ground. A single line of blood began to trickle down from a cut along his brow. The blood spread out, forming tiny rivers which flowed across his face.

It went for Hidalgo next, its arms swinging like clubs. Hidalgo skipped back, tripping over a fallen body, and landing on the ground. The black eyed thing was on top of him. Hidalgo shouted in pain as it took a bite out of his shoulder. Red blood spurted up from the wound.

The creature reared back, spitting blood and chunks of Hidalgo's skin out of its mouth.

Martin fired two bullets into the back of its head. The bullets stopped, robbed of all force, and dropped to the ground where they bounced, tinkling along the marble floor alongside Martin's spent shell casings.

Martin had helped fight an Icanitzu once in the Bordonelles, and his bullets had been similarly ineffective.

The creature rammed its head downward, slamming it into Hidalgo.

Martin attacked the thing, clubbing at it with his rifle. The rifle stopped, just like the bullets, and Martin lost his balance, falling into his opponent.

Unlike his rifle, Martin's body was able to affect the thing. They staggered together over the fallen corpses littering the room.

It turned on him suddenly, arms flailing. Martin blocked one strike with his rifle, then another, and another. One slipped through, hitting Martin in the stomach hard enough to make him double over. He tried to stand back up straight, doing his best to ignore the pain. He could not. Martin tried to flee from the creature, but it managed to land another blow on the back of his head during his mad dash towards the temple's exit.

Martin fought to keep his balance, but the blow had blurred his vision so badly he couldn't get his bearings. He reached out but his hands grasped only air. He toppled down a few stairs and landed on the cobblestones. He struggled to his hands and knees, his world still spinning.

He looked behind him.

The flayed legged creature stood in the doorway of the temple. It walked out into the cobblestoned chamber and began to descend the stairs.

Martin's hunters and Constance's men opened fire. Bullets skipped off of the marble flagstones beneath its feet and buried themselves in the temple wall. Stone cracked from the barrage, sending out jets of dust. The Harpsborough men stopped firing.

Bullets rolled like marbles down the stairs.

The creature was unharmed. It descended another step.

Martin clutched at the loose cobbles and tried to stand. The world was still spinning too quickly for him to stay upright, but even through his shaky vision, he spotted his rifle ahead of him. He threw the cobblestone in his hand backwards and lunged for his gun.

His heart soared as his fingers clasped around his weapon. He used it to support his body's next attempt to stand. He succeeded.

His legs felt shaky beneath him, and his world was still spinning, but he was on his feet. The cobblestone he'd thrown was skittering across the ground to the right of the creature. Martin's men hadn't retreated, but Martin couldn't understand why. Their weapons were useless against this thing.

It's me. They're not running because I haven't been defeated.

This was all wrong. Martin wasn't supposed to be the hero, he knew that. Heroes were people like Aaron, or Galen, or Michael. Martin was just a hunter. He wasn't even a particularly good one. Even Katie, his girlfriend knew that. He was no fighter.

But they were all looking at him—and at the creature.

You took this job, Martin. Fuck Katie.

The creature was approaching. Martin walked towards his fate.

It swung again. Martin's rifle stopped the blow.

It started to circle him. Martin tried to keep up with it on his shaky legs. It struck out again and again, but both times Martin backed out of range. His footing was starting to feel a bit more secure. The world's spinning was slowly grinding to a halt. Martin kicked out at it, his foot hitting the thing's knee. He didn't do any damage, in fact, he only pushed himself away from the beast, but at least his foot wasn't affected by whatever magical immunity this thing had to bullets.

Even so, the creature's body seemed to be made of stone. It attacked him again, low and high, low and high. Martin picked off the attacks, one by one, retreating. He swung out with his rifle on instinct, but again there was no effect.

The creature moved forward. Martin tried to dart back, but his strike had left him off balance. He took a blow on the shoulder and fell tumbling to the ground, his rifle flying from his grasp. Again he struggled to his feet, his fingers clasping around the loose cobbles. It was almost on him. To buy time, he threw a stone. The stone bounced off of its forehead even as Martin found his footing. He didn't have time to make it to his gun, so he backpedaled away in the other direction.

His legs were still shaky, and his ankle turned on a loose stone. He dropped to one knee. The creature was coming fast. One image stuck out in Martin's brain. It was of the stone bouncing off the creature's head. It had *bounced*. The stones could hurt it.

Martin picked up two more stones and powered himself back up to his feet. Perhaps sensing his newfound confidence, the creature stopped. Martin felt the rush of blood in his ears.

His heart was pumping like it had never done before.

He breathed in, filling his lungs with air. *"STONE HIM!"* Martin's voice boomed.

He hurled one of the cobblestones at the creature, then the next. His men were complying. Stones, a few getting dangerously close to Martin, flew in from all directions. Martin backpedaled again. The creature tried to stay with him, but the cobblestones were coming in fast and thick. One strike jerked its head to the side. The rain of rock slowed it down.

Martin grabbed two more stones and flung them. One struck home, hitting the thing in the chest. The Harpsborough men, emboldened now, were getting closer. Their throws were getting more accurate. It was the creature's turn to lose its footing. Martin joined in, picking up cobbles and throwing them as fast as he could. Black blood, slick like oil, was coming out of the thing now. It crawled forward, but only for a moment. Even after it stopped, the stones kept coming.

After a while, a few hunters paused. Then a few more. Then all of them. Everyone was looking at Martin. He moved forward to inspect the creature. Its brains were leaking out of its nose.

"It's dead," Martin reported.

His men broke into cheers.

49

"You think it's coincidence?" Rick asked El Cid.

Q had brought them all to another room that looked down upon the cypress swamp. This one was even higher than the first, and the mists had almost cleared completely off of the lake.

El Cid let her binoculars fall away from her face. "This corpse trap was set years ago, perhaps even anticipating the call. The corpses have been gathering here for at least that long. I think it's safe to say that our clash with their harpies has caused them to adapt their schedule. And Q, you were right. Those aren't people on the backs of the harpies, they're wights."

Jessica was leaning over Molly, sewing the girl's abdomen together with a needle and some devilgut thread. Molly's face was red, and she was tearing up. Even so, she didn't cry out. Ellen felt a bit of jealousy, since unlike her, Molly didn't need anything to bite down on.

Massan wasn't in very good shape either. A bump the size of a golf ball rose up from the back of his head. His eyes were unfocused, and he kept asking where they were and what they were doing. Rick said he'd be okay in a few days.

Ellen walked passed them to stand next to El Cid and Rick.

The corpses were gathering, grouping together. After a group got large enough, a harpy would fly out, bearing a wight. Then the group would march in a single file line out of the chamber. Q had said they were heading west.

Rick frowned. "So you're sure it's a call that's caused the devils to leave here?"

El Cid nodded.

"We had thought it was a wave."

"I can see why you thought that. But like I've said before, the circumferences of very large circles can end up looking like lines."

A particularly large harpy took flight. Ellen couldn't tell from this distance, but it might have been larger than the one El Cid had fought.

Eagan whistled. "How many wings is that? Eight? Ten?"

"Twelve." El Cid took her binoculars off her neck and pulled their string around her ponytail. "Take a look."

Eagan accepted the binoculars and held them up to his own eyes. "That thing's going to be as hard as a Minotaur to kill. How old do you think it is?"

El Cid shrugged. "At least a thousand years, by my guess."

"Can I look?" Ellen asked.

"Sure, kid," Eagan answered. "Just be careful. Binoculars aren't easy to come by."

Ellen took them and put them up to her face. At first everything looked blurry, but then she was able to focus the lenses. Her field of vision shook radically with the trembling of her hands, and she had to struggle to keep them steady. She saw the long lines of corpses moving slowly across the Cypress swamp. The binoculars brought her close, scarily close, to them. She could see their facial features. One's nose had rotted away. Another had no arms. A third's skull had been cracked open and never grown back together.

"A Minotaur?" Rick was asking.

The one with no nose was stumbling through the cypress knees. Ellen wondered if corpses ever sprained their ankles.

"Maybe." El Cid's voice did not carry with it great conviction.

"An Archdevil?" Rick tried.

El Cid was silent.

"You think it's Tu-El, don't you. You think they've found him. You think he's returned to the City of Blood and Stone."

"Maybe," El Cid answered. "There's an Archdevil at Londinium too."

"Who the hell is Tu-El?" Massan asked.

No one answered him.

"Surely calls this big have happened before," Rick said. "To fight the Spanish Imperials, maybe. Or the 1860 Americans."

"Yes," El Cid answered. "At those times, great calls went out. You know your history well. But there is no empire for them to face. There is no great enemy. This is too . . . too human a time to attack."

A corpse toppled over into the swamp. Slowly, it managed to drag itself back up to its feet.

"Where are they going?" Ellen asked.

"West," Q answered.

This wasn't telling Ellen much. "What's west?"

"The Carrion."

Ellen took the binoculars away from her face and looked towards Rick. "But that's where we're going."

"Hold your fire!" Martin shouted as the corpsemen reinforcements entered the room. "There's too many."

And none of the new corpsemen had guns, for that matter.

Wait. Those are just corpses.

But there were a lot of them. At first Martin thought they were moving as a mob, but then he noticed that there was an unnatural order in their formation. It was more like a column. And they weren't heading towards his men.

Maybe they haven't seen us.

But the dead had seen them. Their heads were all turned towards Martin and his hunters, even as they walked the other way. That defied everything that Martin knew about corpses. They were unthinking attacking things, he'd thought. They'd never ignore a warm blooded human, he'd thought.

Martin and his hunters backed away, moving to the exit of the chamber. The corpses, now perhaps numbering over a thousand, stumbled past the temple.

They were heading to the Carrion.

"Move," Martin said, his victory suddenly stale. "Back to Harpsborough."

Chelsea grabbed his arm. "Martin."

"Yes, Citizen?"

"We've got some questions to ask Klein."

Martin nodded. "Yeah. Yeah we do."

The march of the dead continued unabated as the Hunters left the room. One thousand. Two thousand. Three. There was no end in sight.

Aaron was right. He was always right. The famine was the calm before the storm.

The doors to Father Klein's church burst open, slamming against the stone walls of the church. Father Klein himself was seated in a pew, head bowed, praying with three women.

Martin and Chelsea strode in. Father Klein slowly raised his head. For some reason his calm demeanor bothered Martin.

We'll see how long he keeps that up.

"I need to speak with Father Klein alone," Martin demanded.

"You're alive!" one woman exclaimed.

Another stood. "Is Ben okay?"

"I said get out!" Martin shouted.

The women hurried out. Chelsea watched them go and then closed the doors behind them.

Martin and Chelsea advanced on Father Klein. The Father stood up and moved to the pulpit. He picked up a cross and some hellstone rosary beads.

Martin sneered.

That won't protect you.

Chelsea and Martin walked to the front of the church, looking up at Klein who stood before the pulpit.

Chelsea stepped up onto the raised stage. She was a full head shorter than Klein, but her anger made her seem the fiercer of the two. Martin also mounted the stage.

"Let me see your left arm, Klein." Chelsea's voice was cold.

"No sister, I will not." Klein said. "This is my church, and I—"

"She said to show her your God damned arm!" Martin yelled, his blasphemy echoing out through the church.

Klein drew himself up. "This is a house of God. I will *not* have you—"

Chelsea's slap caught him full in the face.

Klein's hands clenched around the cross, crunching it together with the beads.

Chelsea raised her hand again. "Right now, Father, this isn't God's house. At this exact moment, it's my house. Chelsea's house. Are we clear?"

Father Klein stared at her, his calm façade broken, his nostrils flaring with his anger.

"Now, Father," Martin said, dropping a hand to his pistol. "I think you ought to show the lady your arm."

Father Klein unbuttoned his black shirt. He removed the white piece of cloth from around his collar. He was wearing a dirty wife beater underneath, but it didn't hide the scarification on his arm. There it was, just like Chelsea had said, a man half encased in rock with his arms pointed upwards.

"We've all got things we're not proud of," Klein said. "Before the exodus from the Carrion, we were evil. It's not right for you new people, who haven't walked those miles, to pass judgment on those of us who did. We all agreed, Charlie, Michael, everyone, that what happened back there was to be forgotten. It's not to be spoken of in this town. That's not God's law, that's not Klein's law, that's Michael's law."

What is he talking about?

"No offence, Father," Chelsea said. "But we're all in Hell. We already knew you weren't a priest worth a damn. We're here to find out what that tattoo means."

"Maab favored me, okay? She watched me . . . do things. Things that I'm not proud of. But they weren't our fault. You can't go blaming us for what we did to the children . . ."

Chelsea's face screwed up into a mask of horror. "The tattoo, Klein," she spat. "It's about the tattoo. The leader of the corpse eaters had it. What does it mean?"

The cross in Klein's hand, along with the beads, fell to the floor. The string holding the beads together snapped, and the little hellstone marbles scattered all over. A few rolled off of the stage and bounced across the stones.

When the last of the beads had stopped, Father Klein regained enough of his wits to speak. "What did you say?"

"The leader of the corpse eaters. He had that tattoo. What does it mean?"

Father Klein turned his back on Chelsea and Martin, looking up to the huge woodstone cross that adorned the back wall. "It means Maab's not content to stay in the Carrion, anymore."

"We defeated the corpse eaters easily, Father," Martin told him.

"Fool!" Klein shouted, turning around and facing him straight on. "Fool! Maab, if she calls in all her tribes, can field a tribal army of over ten thousand men. And it's worse than that. She has resources we can't begin to match. Her soldiers are tougher, strengthened by some dark ritual. She has a general, Gilgamesh, who makes hounds do his bidding. One of her lovers, Nephysis, can control corpses! Her priestesses can make wounds which Hell can't heal. That's why we ran. That's why when we revolted, we fled the Carrion and built up walls behind us. Because if Maab's coming, we can't stop her."

50

The subjective nature of Hell crackled with the power of Arturus' will. He had never felt so singular a purpose. The swirling mists surrounding him obeyed his whims, parting to create a straight path towards his destiny. He could almost feel the rock on his mind as he pushed at it with his ideas. The rocks glittered with energy where his thoughts touched them. The hellsong heeded his wishes, becoming a distant operatic voice.

The blue light was brighter and more constant the farther he walked.

His heart beat fiercely, a steady rhythm in his chest.

The tunnel ahead opened up into a chasm. There was a ledge, extending ten paces out into the emptiness.

He perceived the Erebus.

They were right to call it a river, but it was not made of water. Nor did it flow along the ground like water did. It was a darkness, or a dimness. A transparent taint that clung to the air of the chasm, hanging amidst the mists. Streaking through it were miles long streams of blue energy. Arturus had never seen lightning, but he'd heard it described. Perhaps this was something similar, a pulsing power that gave off an intense blue light. He had always been told that lightning was fleeting, however, this energy was not so. It hung in sheets, twisting up, around and into other strands. Each sheet wavered, following some rippling pattern that affected the tangled strings of this otherworldly web.

There were at least three sheets that hung along this chasm between himself and the far wall.

He walked up to the edge of the stone and took in the hellscape. The chasm in the dark natural rock extended as high above him as he could see, as if it went up infinitely. He realized with a sudden moment of clarity that it very well might. The sheets of lightning-like energy soared up into that space, filling it with their intensity, pushing their brilliant light out against the dimness of the River of Darkness.

He looked below. The sheets of light continued down there as well, as far down as he could see. They illuminated juts and twists in the natural rock that descended below him at a sheer angle. Arturus did not know how far down that chasm went, if indeed it ever ended. Nor did he know, if he chose to fall down into it and wait three hundred years before landing on another ledge so far below, what type of creatures he might find roaming those halls.

It was the same to his left and his right. The River Erebus was unending—but there was something about a quarter of a mile to his right.

Arturus gasped.

There was a bridge, only partially built, half spanning the distance between his Hell and the one beyond. Half spanning the distance between Gehenna and Sheol. This bridge was supported from the cliff below. Arturus could see the whetstone beams jutting out from the worked rock, reaching up like a skeleton to help support the stones that would be placed upon it. Moving like ants along it were corpses. They were carrying bricks, and no Fury was coming to bother them. As Arturus watched, two toppled uselessly over the edge, falling down through the sheets of preternatural energy, disappearing and reappearing as they descended through the waves of darkness.

A third put his rock down in its correct place.

In the distance, Arturus heard a howl. It was long and low. It was more resonant that even the call of a hound. The ripples of the sound sent shockwaves through the darkness and the sheets of blue oscillating energy.

A Fury. It has sensed me.

"Galen!" Arturus called.

Arturus' father came running. Galen stopped when he made it to the ledge. Slowly, he walked the ten paces to stand next to his son.

"Look," Arturus said, pointing to the bridge. "You said that corpses would be detected, at least if there were a Minotaur's will upon them."

Galen nodded. "But these corpses have no devil's will controlling them."

"But if they're undirected, how could they build a bridge?"

"If you raised a man from birth, and you had him do the same task from dawn till dusk for his entire life, and then you killed him—he just might complete that same task after death."

And that, Arturus realized, was how the bridge was being built. That was how the leaders of the City of Blood and Stone were going to cross the Erebus.

The howling was getting louder.

"We should leave, son," Galen said. "We don't have much time before the Fury gets here."

But it would have been enough time for someone to cross. Particularly if you were a cruel people, and willing to sacrifice many slaves to distract the Furies.

But what could they want from Sheol?

Arturus looked towards the rocks on the far side. It was difficult to see through the Erebus, but in places he was able to. The blue sheets of energy cut through the darkness so that right around them was an area of transparency. When the three different sheets of energy matched up, Arturus could see the far wall.

Sheol was more real than Arturus had expected. Perhaps he was projecting his own unconscious expectations on it, or perhaps, even as Sheol left an imprint of subjectivity on the closer edges of Gehenna, then so too might Gehenna leave an imprint of objectivity on the closer edges of Sheol.

The howling of the Fury was getting even louder. The river trembled, rippling with her approach. Arturus saw her, almost a mile away, a brilliant shining devil of white energy.

Then he saw something through the waves of Erebus. He saw a pocket of ruddy and orange light. It was as if that portion on the far shore was lit by a torch.

Standing in that bubble of light, in a cave on the other side of the river Erebus, Arturus saw three figures. The center one was the strongest, a broad man dressed in a black cloak. At this distance Arturus could not tell if the small silver pendant around his neck was indeed an upside down cross, but he guessed that it was. The man had a beard, like Galen's, but much darker. Even from across the river, the man seemed cruel.

To the man's right was a shadowy figure, a devil that appeared to be made out of the same stuff as the Erebus itself. It had two red eyes, glowing, seeking, staring.

On the man's left was another person, slightly shorter, and much more slender. He wore the clothes of a serf. There was a large puddle of blood at the man's feet, dripping down off of the edge of the cliff.

It seemed that the central figure, the one dressed all in black robes, was staring at him. Arturus could feel the man's malevolence traveling across the great river.

Arturus turned to point out the figures to his father, but Galen was already looking at them.

"Saint Wretch," Arturus said.

Galen nodded. Arturus remembered what Galen had said about Saint Wretch. Nothing of either Earth or of Hell could harm the man.

But I might be able to hurt him. My mother was of Heaven. If I have children, my seed might spread through all of Hell. Saint Wretch has to come now or he'll not know which men carry the blood of angels in their veins. He'll not know which men can hurt him.

"Dakota was wrong," Arturus said. "I'm not the one who can get the weapon. I *am* the weapon."

My existence forces Saint Wretch's hand. He has to try and return to Gehenna now. And when he does, the Infidel will come to me, like Malkravyan said, with an argument and an offer.

Arturus felt his father's arm circle around his shoulder.

"Now do you understand, son?" Galen asked. "Now do you know the fate the Infidel wishes for you?"

"Yes," Arturus said, his voice shaking. "Yes I do."

 — EPILOGUE —

My love makes this place real. In the room with the cool stream where the herrings swim, there is an arch with an orange keystone. Beyond that are silver floors and walls of golden daggers. And then there is the path of broken bones. Finally, the tent. And in the tent is my love, the maid with braids of auburn hair.

Benson sat by the cool stream where the herrings swam. He'd had a dream where his old friend Martin had been made a leader and that all the people of Harpsborough had cheered for him. Benson was afraid of dreams. Dreams made a man travel. He'd have to remember those dreams if he was to make it back to these rooms. Make it back to the woman he'd learned to love.

Together they'd imagined this place. They'd fought to keep it the same. Each day they went over their mantra together, assuring themselves that this place existed, this place with the cool river and fish.

The fish that he would catch.

Benson sighed, as content as a damned man could be, and waded out into the cool water. It was cooler than he remembered. That was the way he liked it. His love wanted it different. She wanted it slightly warmer. The fish were more his style too. She imagined them bigger.

Benson knew it was a bad sign when his reality won out too much over hers. It meant she was sad.

Don't feel sad, my love. We live in a pleasant tent. In a place where there is a cool stream where the herrings swim. And in that room there is an arch with an orange keystone. Beyond that, the silver floors and walls of golden daggers. And then the path of broken bones. Finally, the room with the tent. And in the tent is my love, the maid with braids of auburn hair.

But he understood her sadness. He'd felt it himself. The Hell here, on this second level, had emotions woven into its fabric. They had tried to stay in anger once, but they'd had no defense against it. They'd fought with each other tirelessly. No, melancholy was a much better emotion. It could even be sweet.

As sweet as it was, it was a constant reminder of all the people he'd lost. Of all the tortured souls who had not found such a sanctuary. Of all the things he should have done and never did. Of all the people he should have told that he loved. Of all the petty sins he'd never forgiven or been forgiven for.

That sadness could get very heavy.

He heard footsteps behind him.

My love!

Benson turned.

A man was standing on the shore, blood pouring out of a wound in his side. The man held something in his hand. It was a scalp. Hanging from the scalp were auburn braids.

"Hello, Benson," Carlisle said. "Good to see you again. Tell me, do you still dream of Harpsborough?"

Hellsong continues in Book III: March till Death

Hellsong Series

MARCH TILL DEATH

HELLSONG
BOOK III

Shaun McCoy

"This is McCoy at his best."
—Matt Michaelis, Author of Kids Summon

Does a damned man dare dream?

Driven ever farther from his home, Arturus must come to terms with the fact that, as a denizen of Hell, it simply may not make sense for him to feel things like hope or love.

In a place where all that ends is ill, hope is a lie.

In a place where all who breathe are selfish, love is a liability.

But Arturus can't help himself—his heart longs for his home and for the people he left so far behind. All men dream, didn't you know? Even the damned ones . . .

Especially the damned ones.

Look for *March Till Death* and continue exploring the Hellsong Universe!

Want to be notified when sequels are released?
Register as a Citizen at hellsongseries.com

Need to look up a term?
Check out the Gehennic Encyclopedia as a free
download on Kindle or view at our website:
hellsongseries.com/encyclopedia

Sisyphean
Publishing

Shaun McCoy lives in South Carolina. He is an
accomplished Pianist, Cage Fighter, Chess Player
and Writer. You can check out his fan page at
www.facebook.com/shaunomccoy